SEPTEMBER THOMAS

Walk on Water

The Elemental Gods Book One

Second edition

ISBN: 978-1-7342545-0-1

Editing by Fiona McLaren
Cover art by Natasha MacKenzie

This book was professionally typeset on Reedsy.
Find out more at reedsy.com

To Mom & Dad
For believing in me, no matter what

Introduction

In the beginning, there were only fey.

Wild people with wild magic roaming a wild Earth they called their own.

For a while, they were content. For a while, there was peace. But like all things, that came to an end. For there were those discontent with the status quo, those who thirsted for glory and power, and those who took it by force and sheer brutal will.

Of those who thirsted for greatness, rose four friends who became the four leaders of the four worldly regions. They called upon the Earth to gift them with her bounties, for there is no stronger magic than Earth itself. For years, they prayed and sweated and sacrificed and bled until at last Earth was satisfied with their offering and gifted them control over the four earthly elements.

And the fey hailed these four as Gods.

For some time, these Gods reigned supreme. They drank and danced and feasted, they ruled with mighty yet just fists; they hunted the traitors and killers and monsters, and they rewarded the heroes and survivors and supporters. But like all things, their reign came to an end. For their might, and the cruelty they couldn't contain, threatened the existence of all living things.

As one, the fey rose up against the Gods and called upon Earth to retake their powers. But the Earth could not, for a gift once given cannot be reclaimed. Instead, Earth urged the fey to set things right. If they bested the four Gods, Earth would correct the balance.

A long and great war followed; the longest and bloodiest of wars. The immense Gods crumbled and surrendered, drained from the fighting. They realized in a fight against millions, the millions would win. As promised, the Earth shackled their magic and stripped them of their vast immortality. For never again would the Gods be all-powerful.

Those loyal to the Gods revolted. Those followers, too, stripped away their magic, and created a religion devoted to their names. And so became the first humans.

But the Gods were now necessary to Earth, their untold powers too vast and mighty to be extinguished. And that, the fey understood. For the fey found balance in everything. They called upon Great Creatures the Gods dared deem as pets and loaned them the abilities of the Gods, commanding them to rebirth four new spirits with the four Earthly elements when the Earth was most in need.

And for a while, the cycle worked as it should. For a while, the Gods were reborn again and again, trained by those still loyal to their cause; those who still recorded the Old Stories, the Old Magics, the Old Days. But like all things, that too passed. When the last God breathed her last breath, magic faded, humanity advanced, and it appeared the Earth no longer required Godly saving.

Two thousand years followed, the mighty Gods vaporizing into mere myths.

Until one day -

When the pendulum completed its swing -

And those who once rose up to save the Earth -

Became its biggest threat.

1

Geoffrey

Snap. Nine.

Crack. Eleven.

Molars ground together, the gritty noise sharp in my head. The unforgiving silver edges of the casing of *The Word* ground into my fingers. The hardened, scarred flesh of my back separated, peeling back with each lash. The metallic scent of blood hung heavy in the air.

Crack. Twelve.

Snap. Thirteen.

Sweat poured from my face, my back, down my chest, mixing with blood and salting my wounds, pooling in the waistband of my cropped white pants. The wine-red stains darkened, proud evidence of my accomplishments. My shoulders had barely healed from my last Christening. I knew the pink and white scarred skin was now mottled again, ropey and red. The whip sunk into muscle, striking against my bone.

But I wouldn't cry out.

It wasn't the way of the Order.

Snap. Fourteen.

Snap. Fifteen.

An X sharply ingrained in my back. The pattern familiar and painful.

Two more to go. Two more. Sweat dripped into my eyes, the sweet and salty mixture stinging and biting, but I blinked it back, refusing to tear my gaze from the altar.

Sixteen. The bottom of my left foot caught fire.

Seventeen. My right foot soon followed.

Seventeen lashes. Each lash for one year of servitude to the Order. Each year as necessary as breathing.

For the Order was family. I, Geoffrey Marcuzzo, had been left at the gates to the Citadel at the tender age of three days, my mother seemingly unable to endure my existence a minute longer. Maybe she'd learned something during my time in her womb that I was destined for greatness. Maybe she'd planned to keep me up until the moment of my birth. Perhaps she'd looked at me in anticipation and love until the doctors had presented me to her, revealing the four dark symbols on my forehead that marked me as the next Hand of the Order.

Marks that hadn't been witnessed by human eyes for more than two thousand years.

Even now I could imagine the fright of their expressions as they looked upon my face—my sweet, baby face swaddled in a yellow blanket, before they turned to my mother, and watched her go pale with realization.

Maybe she'd even considered keeping me, raising me as her own.

Well, she'd certainly kept me long enough to give me a name and make sure she had the documents to prove it.

But she hadn't kept me.

Instead, she'd left me in the hands of the only ones who could properly prepare me for the future, for my path.

"On your feet, boy." Eris' voice knocked my thoughts back into the moment. His normally deep and milky voice was sour. Despite the unusualness of the circumstance, for many had believed the time of Gods and their Hands to be a thing of the past, Eris had taken up the reigns as my master, my mentor, dedicating his life to guiding me on my mission and showing me my potential. He'd administered my final lashes. My lips curled and my back bowed, the pain too much to stand. It was time to embrace who I was to become, if the Gods would have me.

Painfully, I forced my fingers to relax, the bone-white flesh of my knuckles fading as the tension eased and blood flowed through my hands once more. I pulled *The Word* to my chest, ignoring the stickiness of my blood against it. The metal box, gleaming and unremarkable in every way except for the title hammered into its surface with a careful, practiced hand, would protect it from any lasting damage. Stiffly, muscles groaning, I rolled to my feet, biting back a gasp as the raw flesh on the bottoms of my feet touched the cool, grey stones.

"Take your place at the altar."

Fighting back swells of pain, I took the loose white robes from Eris' extended hand and shrugged them on, slowly advancing on the dais as I did. Each step left a footprint-shaped smudge of blood on the ground. Grit and dirt worked into my wounds. As I approached, I moved *The Word* from my chest and held it over my head, ignoring the bite on my back and shoulders, muscles protesting.

The silver words etched into the cover of the book glittered bright in the sunlight streaming from a large window expertly carved in the wall and ceiling above the altar. It was a clear, cold day outside, nothing to obstruct the view of the Gods.

I rounded the dais and placed the holy copy of *The Word* in its rightful spot, surrounded by the four sacred tools: The Trident of Kaleal, Ash's Cursed Sword, the Chakram of Lyre, and Davarius' Sling.

Four powerful symbols of the four Elemental Gods.

Water. Fire. Air. Earth.

The soft scent of lavender and incense teased my nose as I breathed in deeply, squaring my shoulders and looking out over the Faithful for the first time. The pain of my ordeal faded into the recesses of my mind as the magnitude of this moment overcame me. The room was overflowing. Every acolyte of importance was required to be in attendance. If all went according to plan, they would soon witness history.

"Oh Great Ones, we gather before you today as humble servants, born to carry out your will." Eris' voice was clear and commanding. He raised his dark arms over his head and a soft clatter sounded as more than a thousand people rose from their benches. "You've gifted us with a disciple bearing Your holy mark. He is of age to take control as your Hand, as leader of the Order, Your Order. Your faithful servant everlasting. We implore you now to find him worthy of the honor."

Eris approached me now, rich brown eyes proud and steady as they found my bi-colored gaze. I tipped my head, and a hint of a smile touched his lips. His sinewy hands gripped my arms before lifting them to my forehead and wiping the sweat and blood from my Mark.

It was really four brands, a series of symbols etched across my forehead right under my hairline: a mountain peak, a cresting wave, a lick of flame and a gust of wind. Each black as ink and far more permanent than any tattoo. Nothing could remove them from my body or from visible sight. They shimmered through blood and sweat, glittered through hats and hoods. You could probably cut the flesh from my forehead and they would shimmer through the gore and bone.

A gift and a curse.

Yin and yang.

My breath was caged in my chest as I stood, waiting, hands folded before me in submission. The entire congregation remained still. Quiet. Nothing moved, no one made a sound, not a sneeze or a sigh. No one wanted to miss a moment of this wonderment. If the Gods deemed me truly worthy of my position, I would be the first official head of the Order, the first Hand of the Gods, in more than twenty centuries. Two-thousand years since the passing of the last Gods and their Hand.

A glory no human still breathing had borne witness to before.

It was the breeze that embraced me first. Barely noticeable from the onset it quickly strengthened, casually swiping at my hair and clothes. It blew warm, soft and comforting, wrapping tight around me. For a moment, it felt substantial enough to touch, firm as a person and just as tall. But when I reached for what might be its face, it vanished in a haze of dust motes.

I didn't have a moment to mourn its loss as the ground rumbled beneath my feet, rattling the walls of the chamber. The stones beneath me liquefied and I sank into quicksand. My stomach lurched. I struggled to not reach out and grab the altar like I knew it wanted me to, dared me to. It sucked me down to my knees before spitting me out. I landed hard on the newly solidified stones, knees grating.

As suddenly as it started, the rumbling stopped.

Leaving a deafening silence.

Before me, disciples and guards glanced around at the white stone walls, the grey-washed floors, unsure what to expect next. A sharp crack echoed around the room, bouncing off the vaulted ceilings and many windows. A crevice, jagged and deep as a canyon, carved its way down the center of the congregation, splintering the stairs to the altar, stopping mere inches from where I knelt, body shaking from equal parts excitement and fear. Clear liquid bubbled up from the center, icy water slowly filling the room, pooling around me. It stopped when it reached my knees, pausing as if considering.

I tried to lift a hand, to do what exactly I'm not sure, and a wave rose up, hovering high above my head for before toppling over, smashing me into the ground and sending my body rolling over the floor. I floundered, struggling to not breathe under the torrent of rushing water.

The burn of fear blistered my veins.

It was going to drown me.

Not yet, a soft voice whispered in my ear.

It was impossible to tell if it was male or female.

And the water was gone.

My nostrils cleared.

I could breathe again.

Blinking and choking on life, I scrubbed lingering beads of moisture from my face and looked up, only to find a towering beast of flames. Searing heat slammed into me, knocking me flat on my back. Orange and red and yellow flickered together dangerously as the being approached, footprints of fire left in each step, its horned head lowered with aggression. I struggled to keep my eyes open; the heat burned my skin and something hot pressed under my chin, forcing my head up into the white-hot center of the mass to somewhere its face might naturally fall.

And I saw.

A girl, tall and light and slender, gripped the legendary trident, a scream twisting her face as a wave of water towered behind her. Three others flanked her, spun tight in their unique, individual gifts. A boy with deeply tanned skin and long, dark hair fanning around his face crouched on a tornado, a twisting ball of currents clutched in one hand. Flames licked the heels of a second, smaller girl with short, fiery hair. Her face pulled back in an ugly, animalistic snarl as she raised an arm to fend off an attack I couldn't see, a blue inner-flame of fire bursting forth from her palm. Set farther back from the rest stood another, slighter boy with glowing, golden eyes. He stood stiffly, arms locked at his sides, palms horizontal to the ground as if he struggled with a massive weight. Behind him, a wall of rock rose into the skies, lava cascading down its many ridges and crevices.

I saw a clash of titans, a mash of people, human and magical, locked in eternal war.

The first girl yelled a command I couldn't hear, lips twisted in anger and anguish as she slammed the ancient trident to the ground. A long fissure split the earth and rattled the stars in the skies. An acrid, chemical taste coated my throat.

All went black. And then came the blast of a mushroom cloud, the impact shredding massive trees, blistering homes and buildings and vaporizing people where they stood, where they ran. The dark tower of dirt and chemical and haze rose high in the sky.

More clouds arrived. Many, many more clouds. A horizon of mushrooms, the air thick with the tang of blood and ash and death.

I saw disaster.

I saw the end of the world.

And I knew what I, Geoffrey Marcuzzo, must do.

It took a few minutes for the vision to clear. As my sight returned, I realized the tower of flames still stood before me, flames flickering and snapping. It regarded me silently, its black pits of eyes staring at me hauntingly, before nodding and turning back. Something blisteringly hot burned across my forehead and spots of black dotted the edges of my vision.

I heard the voice again, faint in my ears like a badly tuned radio.

They aren't the only ones faced with a challenge, dear Hand.
Question your reality.
Shield yourself behind your sanity.
Only the truth will set you free.

It was too much to absorb, too much to think.

But a few realizations became clear, bright beacons shining in the night.

The Gods were coming back.

They would destroy humanity.

They must be stopped at any cost.

That was my task.

And the Order was mine to command.

2

Zara

17 YEARS LATER

"If you make trouble, you walk the plank."

My foot hovered over the ramp and I swiveled to stare at the crusty captain tucking four Benjamin Franklins – four of *my* carefully haggled Benjamin Franklins – into one of his many shirt pockets. "Seriously? That still happens?"

Blue eyes twinkled beneath a thick knitted cap full of holes as he fluttered scarred fingers at me. "Nah, I'm messing with you, *American*. Get on board, we're departing soon." His accent felt thick in my ears, but I shrugged and climbed aboard the trawler into the crush of middle-aged men rushing to and fro across the deck.

I was completely out of my element.

And I couldn't be more excited about it.

"Over here, girl, away from the rush of things." A hand gripped my biceps and pulled me to the side of the ship. When I finally found my feet again, I peered into the face of a man in his fifties with big bushy grey brows and cherry-red lips. One of those brows quirked as I eagerly thrust out a hand to accept his handshake. "Now, surely

9

you've seen better blokes than me before."

"I'm not so sure about that." I hurried to accept his welcome before running a shaking hand over my long, silvery hair. "I'm Zara."

"Kristoffer," he replied and continued in English, just like the captain, "and what brings you aboard our fine specimen of a ship today?" He gestured grandly to the well-used industrial fishing boat with its peeling paint and rusted hinges.

I smiled. "I'm not entirely sure, actually."

"Nothin' wrong with that. I'll give ya the tour as they set off."

I hadn't even realized we were moving, but when I turned to the shoreline, sure enough we were no longer connected to the docks. I swallowed hard but didn't resist as Kristoffer tugged me under his wrinkled but surprisingly muscular arm.

"Come on," he said with a wide grin, "the wind can sure pick up around here, so let me show you the open decks first."

His tour was brief but enthusiastic. I found myself beaming at his shipmates despite their long, curious stares. As we walked, Kristoffer pointed out hooks and cages and nets and all sorts of things I couldn't remember the names of. White sails billowed in the morning air, and the foreign calls of the men drifted into the background the longer I listened. He was clearly showing off when he demonstrated how to tie a series of complicated knots in a matter of seconds. Afterward, he returned me back to the spot along the side of the boat and left me with a stern order to "find him if I needed anything at all."

Norway's shore wasn't visible any longer in the rosy dawn light. I leaned out over the rail. The sting of sea spray scalded my skin. The sharp chill of the boat's thin railings bit into my fingers, making me yearn for the warmth of the woolen gloves I'd left at the hotel. The water before me was vast, a dark grey behemoth stretching farther than the eye could see.

I wanted to dive in, clothes and all.

Too bad I knew without protection, the salt would chap my skin in minutes, and my blood would curdle in the bitter cold of the waves of the North Sea.

It was summer in the States. Typically, I spent that time at my New York boarding school where teachers were more invested in training future athletes than drilling students on calculus. Instead, I'd joined a group of twenty or so impressive swimmers in a competition tour overseas. We were taking a small break before hard-core Olympic training picked up once again. The Summer Olympics in Japan had wrapped up last year and many of us were antsy, awaiting the next challenge ahead of us.

I grinned as a wave tilted the ship. Seventeen years old and I already had a gold, three silvers, and one bronze medal under my belt.

This relatively *playful* competition was small beans in the grand scheme of things, but it was nice to have a breather for the first time in what felt like years of intense training.

A bell clanged in the distance. Dozens of feet encased in black rubber-soled shoes stomped quickly across the salt-torn planks as the fishermen raced to the back of the boat and the newest catch being reeled in. The thrashing of equipment stirred the sea, the bitter scent of brine grew heady once more. The fervor and energy in their voices revitalized my own flagging brain. I was exhausted from the early wake-up call and jet-lag. Our next meet wasn't until tomorrow, and we'd arrived early in Norway after a scheduling snafu.

My nails dug into the soft wood of the rail, and I winced as a splinter pierced a fingertip. I sucked on skin that tasted of salt to soothe the ache. Waves slapped against the side of the ship, sending it rocking from side to side. I realized the ocean seemed more aggravated than it had earlier. Might just have been a change of direction. Whatever it was, the occasional splash into my face invigorated me.

The second the wheels of the small jet had touched the runway late last night, my blood sang, calling for the sea. It's like I'd been a needle on a compass my entire life, spinning and spinning and spinning and for the first time I finally pointed due north. Turns out, due north had been the docks. The docks had turned into this shabby fishing boat crudely dubbed *Tispe*.

Not that I minded the slur much.

Bitches got shit done.

My long, gray scarf fluttered in the wind, drawing my thoughts back to the ocean. I'd grown up in Nebraska, about as far away from a large body of water like this as you could get. It reminded me of the text message from my mother burning a hole in my jacket pocket. We rarely saw each other now that I was out on the coast, and our relationship had grown strained. The more I competed, the less connected I felt to the people who had adopted me—maybe it was the lack of time spent together; or perhaps I was just growing up. The feeling was completely opposite to the sensations I had the more I flew over oceans and stayed in cities near them.

My blood churned with the waves.

My skin craved the salty water.

I longed to *live* in it, if such a thing were possible.

And here I was, Zara Ramone, on a boat in the middle of the North Sea.

Maybe this would finally fill the small void inside me I'd never truly understood.

A hand thumped between my shoulder blades, sending me reeling.

"How are you holding up?" Kristoffer said. This time he'd addressed me in his native tongue, probably a mistake, but my ability to follow foreign conversation wasn't anything new. I liked languages, always had. I picked them up almost immediately.

I smiled up at his grizzled face. He'd abandoned his hat somewhere else. "Pretty well; appreciating how beautiful the sea is," I replied in his language.

He tensed, looking past me and rested his forearms on the railing. "That she is. But she can be a turbulent beast, and a deadly one if you don't know what you're doing."

He pointed up at the large swells of thunderclouds cresting before us. They were angry: bold and black, bellies rumbling with thick thunder. The waves beneath the ship had turned choppy and dark, a sharp contrast to the blue glass that hypnotized me not all the long ago.

"Like that. Storms that come out of nowhere," he said.

At that, the wind picked up, fast and demanding, tearing at my clothes and hair. It felt wild and raw. A feeling rose sharp in my chest, something a lot like...*anticipation?*

I leaned a little over the side of the boat, staring hard at the frigid water, contemplating how much time it would take for even a seasoned swimmer to drown beneath those waves.

Then something moved.

Something big.

Something sliding under the boat in one long, smooth motion.

Was that a tentacle?

Kristoffer yanked my arm, pulling me toward the center of the boat as I started to get a good look at the beast. He flipped up some sort of door cut into the bowels of the ship and motioned toward it.

"Get down to the mess and stay there until someone comes to get you. Pull the door shut behind you. We can't have you going overboard." The merry twinkle had vanished from his face. He barely looked at me, his gaze flitting around the ship where he was clearly needed elsewhere.

"But there's something —"

"Get below deck."

He cut me off before I could tell him about the monster and spun away, yelling orders to his mates as they maneuvered ropes and traps in an effort to get the haul in before the storm hit full force.

My lime-green Converse slipped on the rungs slick with water and worn smooth over time. But something made me stop. It felt wrong, very wrong. No, I wasn't needed down there. I needed to get to the side of the ship. I *needed* to tell the captain about those tentacles.

The trapdoor banged shut behind me as I hauled myself back on deck. The wind roared now, the ship rocking dangerously side to side, sending lines and hooks flying. I tripped on a hank of rope, going down hard. But I clawed my way back up, trying to find my footing as the boat crested wave after ever-higher wave.

There it was. My heart almost stopped. A tentacle with suction cups the size of sedans hovered, suspended right below the surface of the water. I looked up in time to see the massive wave bearing down. My grip on the railing wasn't going to keep me on board.

There wasn't any time to react.

One minute I stood upright, feet firmly planted on the planks.

The next, I was airborne as the wave crashed into the vessel.

For one glorious moment, I flew, the wind whistling past my ears, hair torn from my hair tie, breezing past my face reaching for the heavens. Then I slammed into a concrete wall. Searing pain engulfed me as bones cracked and joints shattered, rendering me blind as I slipped beneath another wave. I was falling, falling faster than a cannonball into the dark depths of the sea. With one last ounce of effort, one last thought of survival, I flipped my eyelids up. But I couldn't see. My fingers clawed for something to hold onto. Which way was up? My lungs screamed, crying for me to release my breath.

I was going to die.

I'd spent my life in the water. Spent my teenage years craving the ocean.

And I was going to die in it.

The irony hit me almost as hard as I'd hit the water.

Breathe. The word echoed through my head, soft but stern. A single word spoken by something that sounded very large and very intimidating.

Breathe.

I'll die. I can't breathe underwater, I thought, knowing I was moments away from losing the battle with my lungs. Fireworks popped behind my eyelids.

Dark laughter rumbled. *Have you tried?*

I must be delirious. That actually sounded like a reasonable question.

The Gods must be ready to take me into the afterlife.

Why not?

What could it hurt?

Carbon dioxide rushed out of my mouth in one large burst.

My body felt weightless, motionless. My extremities nonexistent.

I was merely another organism in the vastness of the sea.

Why not?

I drew in a breath.

3

Zara

I almost choked on the air that flooded my body, sending life, glorious life, tearing through my veins. Yes, liquid was definitely filling my mouth but bubbles were coming out. I must, most definitely, be dying because that definitely didn't happen in real life.

Unbidden, my hands drifted up, cleanly parting the water. I touched my mouth, my jaw, my neck. When I'd hit the water, I'd felt my body break, the bones in my face shatter. But now it, and my arms and legs, were whole again. Free of pain. The tips of my fingers met thick ridges cut into my skin. The flaps of flesh were flexible, and I drew in another belly-fully of air, feeling the ridges lift away and expel a rush of water.

I had gills.

There was no way this was happening.

Yep. I had to be dead.

Dear, silly girl, what nonsense. You're finally alive *for the first time.*

The whispery voice was back, the same voice I'd heard moments after I'd belly flopped into the sea. The same voice that had caused chills to course through my body earlier now felt familiar, even friendly.

It felt like coming home.

That's because you are *home. I've searched for you for so long, Zara, and here you finally are.*

It could hear me. Damn.

Yes. We are connected in many ways.

Something large and long rolled by my left side. Ripples in the currents wrapped around my body, warming and cooling it all at once. For the first time, fear trickled across my skin. This was wrong. So wrong. I reached up, not sure where the surface was, but needing to get there no matter what. Something hard wrapped around my foot, holding me fast.

Spots danced before my eyes as I forced myself to calm down.

A panic attack might actually kill me this time.

Who are you and can I see you? I thought.

That quiet, deep rumble of laughter quaked in my chest again.

It wasn't mine.

Of course. I forgot how limited your sight would be so early.

Something blue and pink and gold dimly flickered below my feet. The light warmed, brightening like a fluorescent bulb. At first, it stung my eyes, and I blinked rapidly. What emerged from the darkness was something beautiful and enchanting and...broken. A fortress with large columns of rock and marble dove low and rose high. Within those walls, windows and doors and turrets spread out. This monstrosity was as large, no *larger than*, any of the German castles I'd toured last week. The history this place must have seen made my seventeen years seem very small.

Never-ending currents of water had worn away some of the features, but chipped surfaces and scorch marks among the wide array of sea creatures carved in the stones that made up the outside walls could still be made out. One of the front doors—they seemed too grandiose to be *only* doors, but I was at a loss at what else to call the two-story opening—was cracked in half, hanging by one massive hinge as if someone had crashed through it, desperate to get inside.

As if sensing my hesitation, the voice came again. *Go.*

And like every character in every horror movie I'd ever criticized, I did, too intrigued to stop.

I took a deep breath and pushed my hair behind my ears. The strands appeared more pale gold than silver in the eerie light. I sank lower and ducked under the splintered wood, working my way inside the castle, marveling at what used to be some sort of grand hall. Coral in all shades of the rainbow made up the columns holding the ceiling up. Heavy tapestries hung in silken strands that fluttered in the subtle currents. It was impossible to tell what scenes they used to depict. I ghosted to the floor, realizing only now it was composed of millions of glittering, crushed shells. It, too, was cracked down the middle and arranged in a deliberate pattern I couldn't quite work out. My high-tops touched down, and I was surprised to find the surface smooth, free of sand and grit. It shouldn't be possible here, underwater, but I could walk.

That's because you were always meant to be here. You've always belonged to the sea, the voice came again.

I glanced over my shoulder at the doors, but couldn't see anything indicating another person or... creature. Shrugging, I turned back to the room. Along the interior walls lay further evidence of destruction. From smashed pottery on broken pedestals to gouges scored deep into wooden tables, something horrible had happened here.

My gut twisted.

My clothing floated around me, periodically twisting tight around my body as I strode past long windows that now housed jagged edges of shattered glass. I wanted to get closer to the magnificent throne that towered high above the room, commanding complete attention. The chair was raised up and the back spanned high toward the ceiling, chunks of coral and shells spilling outward, encompassing the entire wall. In the shells, artistic shapes of sea creatures wove in between one another; most I recognized, like dolphins and starfish, and some I didn't. Like one particularly worm-like beast with a body of a snake but a face that twisted into something resembling a wolf, complete with two hairy front feet. Across from it slithered some sort of water-dragon with legs like a centipede.

When I got close enough, I touched the smooth grey stone of the seat itself. Where my fingers touched, a ripple of light passed *through* the rock, highlighting crevices and revealing hidden creatures carved inside. My body stiffened. The light rippled up the length of the back of the throne.

I gasped. The light was the exact color of my eyes—my aquamarine eyes that appeared a size too big for my angular face. When I got emotional, they'd turn stormy, like liquid lightning filled their depths, and that's what I saw now, the color brought to vivid life.

It's beautiful.

Yes it is.

How did it end up down here? I wondered, somehow forgetting I was conversing with an unknown entity that was, in all reality, probably my own delusional brain. Or death. I hadn't yet counted that option out. *When did this happen?*

Nearly two decades ago. The victim of a horrible onslaught.

The twisting in my gut clenched into a fist. *Who does this belong to?*

A pregnant pause followed.

It felt like I was missing an obvious answer.

You.

Yeah. Sure. Right. *Me.* A normal nobody when this castle clearly was built for a king or a queen.

Or a God.

Come again?

My left arm flung wide, spinning me 180 degrees as a long tentacle wrapped around my waist, drawing me back outside where It released me. Just as quickly as my heart jacked up its frenetic pace, it stopped. I floated face-to-face with a large, golden eye. Its iris, with flecks of amber floating in the black spot, loomed as big as a healthy, two-story house. I paddled backwards, both in awe and in self-preservation, taking in the expanse of the monster.

It regarded me solemnly and blinked. Thick, leathery, grey skin folded down over the bulb like a blind shuttering a window. And then it went back up, exposing Its intense scrutiny once more. Awestruck, I broke Its gaze and took in the rest of Its body. A bulbous forehead loomed high over that single eye and below us tentacles swirled like a mass of hungry snakes. The creature shifted, turning in the water, and within moments a second piercing eyeball appeared, staring at me as curiously as the first.

Yep. It was an octopus.

One. Big. Freaking. Octopus.

I tried to hide my shaking fingers, locking them behind my body. I floated there, suspended in the water, mind whirling with the possibilities. That large tentacle I'd seen on the side of the boat reached up between us and flicked at the water. The motion sent my hair swirling. It was almost tender.

Giant octopus, yes. It's voice sounded almost amused. *But I'm called many other things, too: Giver of the Sea, Mauara, Sea Mist, Destrado. But you may be most keenly acquainted with Kraken. I've grown fonder of that title as the years have passed by.*

The Kraken.

I was looking at THE Kraken.

A mythical Beast that only existed in legends.

A creature that, if I remembered my religious history classes right, was created to draw forth Its God and gift them with their magical prowess.

This wasn't possible.

It huffed, a wave of bubbles rising up. *If I'm not possible, then* you *certainly aren't possible either, seeing as you're the God of Water.* Yep, I was definitely picking up on a wry tone. Not that it mattered much because...

That's not possible, I scrambled for what little else I remembered from class, *the Gods of Water and Air were killed in twin terror attacks two decades ago.*

Well. It would actually be seventeen years ago now.

And I remembered something about Water's temple sinking into the dark depths of the ocean.

You'll come around, the Kraken said unhelpfully. *Besides, if you aren't who I say you are, then why is it you healed so quickly in the waters of your birth? Why do you have that symbol on your shoulder? The one you touch when you get scared or sad or angry, the one that brings you comfort when you least expect it; the one that if you were to touch it now would connect you with every living thing on this planet because of what you are. Because the Gods are the beginning and the end. And you... are a God.* Its large eyelids slid closed once more.

How did it...

How could it know about the birthmark on my left arm under the swell of my shoulder?

The birthmark about four shades darker than my normal skin in the exact shape of a cresting wave.

The wave I'd seen in history books, sprayed in graffiti, and immortalized at the museum; the wave I'd never really given much thought to until...

The pounding in my head reached a crescendo.

How did I not see it until now? I wondered.

The magnitude of this moment was about as large as the monster floating before me. The tentacle that had brushed my hair earlier moved around my body, exploring without touching. Barely holding myself together, my heart thundering from my chest, I made the first move and stroked It, shocking both of us. Tough flesh met my touch, like the hide of an elephant, but firm and incredibly warm. I hadn't expected It to be warm. My fingers brushed over deep grooves and thick scars. The Kraken was known for downing ships at sea. I imagined the battles It must have endured to get such massive injuries. Its flesh flexed. I imagined It arching Its back like a cat, utterly content.

You see, you feel it. We are connected, It said.

I couldn't deny that. I could feel the pull between our bodies, something otherworldly. Something dangerous and comforting and raw. In that moment, a vision flashed in my mind, flickering before me like a memory, worn with age. Flashes of light. Burning towers. An attack, a siege. The unmistakable scents of smoke and ash touched my nose. In the distance, a palace, one I now recognized, crumbled. Wait. No. It was sinking.

I shuddered, realizing I was seeing the attack, seeing what had happened to something this spectacular. I knew this place. I shouldn't. I'd barely been alive when the palace still existed. But I couldn't deny the pull, the memory, the *knowledge* that I was meant to see this, *know* this.

You were there? I asked.

I was.

Anger flared. *Why didn't you stop it! You're a Great Beast, aren't you? If you and I are connected like you say we are, if I'm truly a God, then why didn't you...*

I knew you were safe. The creature interrupted me with a rumble. *Your haven, your domain, your temple was already destroyed by the time I surfaced. It was better to let it crumble than give away our secret.*

I hugged myself tighter, the warmth of the Beast's hide vanishing as

I pulled away. Cold shivered down me—so very, very cold. Like I'd never be warm again.

What secret? I asked.

They believed you to be dead. The High Priestess wasn't aware, but I knew of her plans. The Kraken scoffed. *I knew of the measures those devoted to you would take to ensure your safety. She got you out. She sacrificed her people, herself, her child, to make sure you survived.*

More words I didn't want to hear. More words that should mean nothing that instead slammed into me like a hammer, pounding away at the truth.

It was better they think you dead, child, to give you a chance to grow into your powers later, It said. *If I'd surfaced, they would have known the lie. Where Great Beasts live, Gods are sure to follow.*

How did they know that child wasn't me? I asked.

While the Temples may be affiliated with the Order, they hardly follow the rules. They serve themselves first, the Order second. They all have members who swear fealties not to the Order but to the Gods themselves. And most importantly, they take measures to protect the Gods.

The High Priestess' child, you see, was tattooed with your elemental birthmark. All mortals look the same in the beginning. It's only a matter of playing it off. They swapped you for her and... you vanished. Even I barely felt the strands of our connection until very recently.

I dropped my head into my hands and I scrubbed my fingers over my face. Exhaustion muddied my thoughts. I wanted to lash out, I wanted to tuck myself away and hide, anything but face something that was edging closer to reality. I couldn't deny the Kraken sounded sincere. The longer I floated here, the more I became convinced I wasn't dreaming this whole mess. Surely, I would have woken by now, or I would have passed through the gates of the afterlife—something other than this.

And if that was true, then I most definitely was breathing under water.

I most definitely was standing outside a sunken castle.

And everything I knew was a lie.

As if to emphasize that, the Kraken said, *You* are *a God. You* are *the First of Four. The Elemental God of Water.*

The First of Four. That meant something, too. But I couldn't quite remember what...

Before I could even open my mouth to argue some more, a different voice, a distinctly *male* voice, interrupted us. "Are you two seriously still going at it? When you pulled me out of my slumber, I thought this all had to be some stupid joke. Now I *know* it's a stupid joke." I whirled, searching for the owner of that snotty voice, a voice that made me want to punch its owner in the face.

Finley...

4

Zara

inley? Someone had been here this entire time? Just listening? Who does that?

"...Gods above save us all. Let me guess what you were about to say next." The man pitched his voice an octave higher as I craned around on my toes, hands tight in fists. At least I didn't feel cold anymore. "The Gods died out more than two thousand years ago! It isn't possible they're back. They were last needed when The Great Plague wiped out two thirds of the world's population. That's not happening right now. Surely this is some sort of mistake."

Sort of. I had been thinking along those lines, but he didn't need to know that. My gaze flicked around the remains of the palace until I spotted a hint of movement from one of the tallest spires. A man raised a hand to the side of his forehead and tipped a sardonic half-salute.

The Kraken wrapped a tentacle around my feet, bracing me in an oddly comforting way. A suction cup pulsed gently against my leg.

You're early, Finn, the Kraken rumbled. *I said I wouldn't need you for at least another hour.*

The man pulled himself out of the broken window. I jerked. The lower half of his body was that of massive black horse. His six-pack formed a vee where it merged with the horse, and I quickly looked away. Four powerful-looking legs slowly propelled him through the water toward us.

"Centaur?" The word passed my lips as a question, but it wasn't. Wait. I could speak underwater?

Finn's very human nose wrinkled in distaste. "No. No I'm not. I'd never be as uncivilized as that horde. You're going to need to get your fey in order if you want to survive much longer." Before I could interrupt, he continued haughtily. Clearly, I'd touched a nerve. "A, I don't need a herd to prop up my delicate ego 24/7. B, like I want to go around starting murderous wars with everyone else around me, and C, I don't murder human newborns for fun."

Finn's bright, grass-green gaze burned hot on mine, his face close enough now that I could make out the cleft in his jaw and the midnight shade of his shaggy hair that brushed the tops of ears. His full lips quirked up on one side in a smirk, revealing a tiny, teasing dimple. I tugged on my ear and swallowed, resenting how his olive-colored skin drew tight over thickly-muscled arms and a chest that spoke more of a life spent working in hard labor over working out at the gym. His lower half, the half that was made of horse, was as dark as the hair on his head and just as shaggy with slimy strands of seaweed clinging to it.

I hated him on sight.

"Take a picture. It'll last longer," he said.

I bristled at the condescension dripping in his tone, but a tentacle tightened painfully around my leg in warning before I could fire off a response.

Enough. You're being rude, the Kraken said. *Either let me finish or go away.*

Finn quirked a brow and popped one of his cheeks with a finger, but shut up.

Good. Zara. Time to wake up and smell the magic. Literally. Now that we've finally connected, I can wake up the energy inside of you. That warm feeling in your veins? All me. That's my job since you're the First of Four to awaken. After this, it's up to you to find and wake up the remaining Gods. Have you read The Word? The Kraken referenced the religious book of the Order.

"It's been a few years, but I remember some," I admitted. Then I asked, "But what's that about finding the other Gods, again?"

Finn jumped in. "Kaleal's crutch, you don't even know the old stories?" He dramatically smacked his forehead. "Of course, the Gods would curse us with a complete and total rookie this time around. As if *last* time wasn't hard enough."

The Kraken's whole body shifted. *Enough.*

In that moment, I was one with the Beast, the slide of Its tentacles through the water like one of my own arms, the clutch of Finn's body between Its sucker cups strong and firm. Finn's expression darkened and he mouthed something vulgar before slipping away.

Last time? I wondered about that. He was maybe my age, if not younger. I eyed him quizzically when he leaned against a spire toppled on the ground. He caught the look as he batted away another tentacle. "That's right, I was around for the last war between man, Earth, and the Gods. Makes you think twice about dismissing me, huh?"

I made a show of extending a middle finger. But rather than piss him off, he laughed, a full-bodied, rolling sound.

You might not know much of your origin, but it's only a minor setback, one I was prepared to help coach you through. Before I go farther, the Kraken said, *that's why Finn is here. He will serve as your mentor and guide as you depart for your journey. He may even help protect you from danger.*

Sure, the Kraken probably wouldn't be able to haul Its massive, water-loving body after me whenever I left... here. But how exactly was a half-horse-man supposed to be much more help? I held my tongue.

Things you aren't going to understand will start happening soon and you have not been rehearsed in the Old Ways. The Gods act as a catalyst and now that you've awoken, things are going to start changing. Fast. Are you following me? the Kraken asked.

I wasn't. But I nodded.

You now need to find the other Gods. You are going to need their assistance. The Gods are only born when the world is in a detrimental state or on the precipice of making some catastrophic decision. As Gods, your job is to ensure that the Earth, and subsequently humanity, survives.

But as you can tell by now, it isn't only humans that call this world home. Mythical creatures of all kinds will start to emerge once again. They've been here this entire time, awake and functioning, but hiding behind human facades. Now that magic is stirring once more, they will come out of hiding. That will be both good and bad. It's up to you and your fellow Gods to determine who is friend and who is foe.

"And what are you to me again?" I was feeling a bit light-headed.

I am the one who calls forth you and your power. I am not a God, but I am an instrument. Your most important instrument. We four Great Beasts hold your magic safe while you slumber and unleash it in doses. First a small blast when you're activated, and then full strength when you pass your test, proving your worthiness. The tests are rarely troublesome, but you must only attempt them when you are sure you're ready.

Before I could ask how I'd possibly know when I was ready, the Kraken waved me on.

In addition to finding and awakening your fellow Gods, you will need to master your element. That's also what Finn is here for.

Finn was, at that very moment, waving his hand wildly above his head like an annoying know-it-all in school. The Kraken blinked in a manner that reminded me of my third-grade teacher when she finally reached her last straw and was barely holding on to sanity.

"Now," he said, "when you say that, you mean I'm not only here to help figure out where the next God is? I'm actually supposed to help her figure out how to draw on her power, too?"

Yes.

Finn threw his head back, sending his hair flying. He muttered something to himself, something I'm positive wasn't accolades about me.

I folded my arms over my chest. "Yes, speaking of *Finn*, why does it have to be him? Isn't there someone else in this vast world of *mythical beings* who wants to *actually* help me? That ass over there," I flicked my gaze at his hind parts deliberately and his jaw flexed in response, "couldn't want less to do with whatever is going on here."

The Kraken didn't stand a chance at beating Finn to the response, and with it, I saw a flash of *guilt* wash over his face. "Not that it's any of your business, but I do want to help. I wasn't expecting some nobody to be the next all-powerful commander of Water. I'm not a babysitter, I never wanted to be. And part two," he flashed two fingers before his face. *Boy did he like his lists,* "I don't have a choice in the matter even if I *didn't* want to help."

Because that clarified things.

"You're half horse. How exactly are you supposed to board a plane with me if" - when - "whatever *journey* we're about to go on takes me away from Europe?"

"Who said anything about this being my natural state? Did you hear nothing the Kraken said? I've been around hiding among all you humans. Looking just like you. Dressing just like you. *Entertaining* just like you."

I rolled my shoulders noncommittally.

"I couldn't resist trying out my form when the Kraken stopped by for tea."

Finn here is a kelpie. One of the last kelpies left alive, in fact. Despite that, he's relatively young, which is apparent in how he acts. The Kraken paused and a tentacle swayed between us. *However, I believe you'll find that he will be well-suited for this task. You will need fey and humans alike at your back if you hope to overcome the odds.*

A kelpie? My mind whirled as I struggled to identify the word. What was the myth again? Something Irish? Maybe Scottish? Something about a horse...

"You drown people!" The words exploded out of my mouth before I could stop them. Finn drew back, his brows drawing sharply together. I caught a glimpse of something that looked a lot like fear flash across his face before he covered it with a sneer.

"Don't you dare judge me. Like you've ever had to sacrifice anything in your puny life."

"Who says I haven't?"

"Please. You're not even adult in human years. Shut up now before—"

"I've lived my entire freaking life not knowing my heritage! My family. MY FATE! What would you call that? I call that loss."

The water boiled where it touched my skin but was too angry to do much about it. We were now nose-to-nose, eyes like daggers pinning each other in place. My chest heaved, barely sifting the oxygen from the water before being expelled once more. He wasn't much better off, with a snarl marring that too-beautiful face of his.

Enough. The Kraken's mental command was firm, brooking no argument. *You're tired. You have a lot to take in. It's time I returned you to the surface, Zara.*

I swallowed. Hard. Trying to shove past the lump that had formed there. A warm tentacle wrapped around my middle. The castle drifted farther and farther away as the Beast propelled us upward.

I was going to leave the Kraken? But I'd only just met... It. Did It have a gender? Were the Great Beasts something beyond male and female? My arms wrapped around me, clutching my body tight in a very different way than I had before. This time I was struggling to keep a wrap on my pain.

...Finn will accompany you topside.

Stars. In my musings I'd missed some of the Kraken's instructions. The subject of Its sentence was still staring me down, glaring like I'd killed his favorite pet. What would a creature like a kelpie keep as a pet? A piranha? An eel? Some sort of blood-sucking leech?

...make sure that's your top priority. I expect results soon.

And again.

I dragged my fingers through my hair. I'd stopped paying attention again. Like, really stopped paying attention. The ruined castle was long gone. Instead, gold-green rays of sunlight filtered through the water and moments later, my head broke the surface. I gasped. He, she, It had done more than that. We were back at the docks. The octopus' head, which now looked more purple than grey, had crested the water and no one was screaming in panic. I figured It must have cast some sort of magical cloak of invisibility.

A loud slurping sound came from my right. Finn hauled himself onto the dock. Shockingly, his horse-parts had transformed into a pair of regular, human legs. Legs now suspiciously clothed in a pair of dry track pants. Hell, his entire body was dry, his hair artfully sculpted but purposefully-messy spikes. It was the kind of look you'd expect to find on an anime character, but it somehow looked completely natural.

I, on the other hand, looked about as good as I always did after a long day of swim practice: wet, exhausted, and bedraggled. My hair tie was long gone, and my hair hung limply around my face, strands sticking to my cheeks and neck here and there.

I propped my arms on the dock and started to heave myself out of the water. Finn didn't offer me a hand up. Instead, amusement danced in his expression as he watched me struggle. The dock was situated much higher out of the water than I was used to from competitive swimming. Finally, I was able to kick my legs in such a way what I flopped onto the wooden boards. I snorted out a laugh and glanced back at Finn's perfection, waving a hand vaguely. "How do you look so..." I trailed off and motioned at myself instead, "And I look like..."

"A drowned cat?" he offered.

I bristled.

"Kidding. Maybe. It's called magic. One of these days you'll figure out what that means."

Fed up with his attitude, I turned away and gazed back out over the water. A wave of sadness drifting from the Kraken hit me in my core. In only a few short hours we'd bonded. It felt like a part of me, as vital as my liver or heart or blood. I rolled over to my stomach, ignoring the large wet splotch where I'd fallen, and dropped a hand into the sea. A pinkish tentacle reached up and brushed my skin.

"Why do I have to be the Goddess of Water?"

"You have to be kidding me! *God.* There aren't any Goddesses."

One guess who that was.

"Anyway, why do I have to be the *God* of Water? It doesn't seem fair that I have to leave my partner behind because I live on land instead of the ocean," I continued.

It won't be easy. None of this is. Unlike older generations, you've had zero preparation, no time to brace yourself for the possibility of assuming the role of eternal protector. It blinked one large, golden eye. *But I sense greatness in you, Zara. I sense the spirit necessary for success as the representative of water. You will do us proud.*

I gulped, a heavy weight settling on my shoulders.

Besides, we'll never really be separated. Now that we've connected, as long as water is nearby, we will be able to feel each other. That's important to remember, Zara. If I can't feel you, then I can't help you. That's a very dangerous situation. Make sure you have water with you at all times and learn to rely on Finn. He's your guardian. He wants what's best for you even if he has an odd way of showing it.

I tapped an index finger on the wet dock, the chilly air wrapping around my soaked body for the first time. Finn's stare was a heavy weight, his eyes practically boring holes in the back of my head.

My head bobbed once.

I'd try.

A hand dropped into my line of vision, palm open and fingers extended. "Come on," Finn said, "you're exhausted. I'd rather not carry you back to wherever you're staying."

I *was* tired, and I grabbed his hand. His palm felt rough with callouses, and he tugged me to my feet. Then he brushed off my shoulders like one of those annoying fashion designers on TV, as he cast a forlorn look over my hair and clothes.

"If anyone asks, tell them you fell in the sea."

"I *did* fall in the sea."

"I meant, like you tripped on a shoelace." He stopped walking and pointed at my shoes. They were definitely untied. "And fell off the docks in front of all your friends. How embarrassing for you."

My sigh was deep and heartfelt as I knelt. Rather than attempt the complexity that was the bow, I tucked the laces underneath the tongue. A thought crashed into me, and I paused. "What about the boat?"

"The boat?"

"The boat I was on. I went overboard. Aren't they going to wonder what happened to me?"

Finn shrugged. "The Kraken probably took care of it. You worry too much."

"I worry the right amount," I retorted. I got to my feet and started in the direction of the hotel. I remembered the way because of its proximity to a crumbling, gothic-era church and its bell tower that extended high over the other buildings. Thankfully, we didn't have far to walk.

"Hypothetically speaking, how would a Kraken *take care of this?*" I asked.

"I don't know." Finn said. He hooked his thumbs in his pockets and slung his shoulders back with his strut. "Wipe their memories? You're asking me how the magic of a Great Beast works. It's not like there's a user guide for this stuff."

My eye twitched.

Finn kept rambling even after I threw my entire weight into opening the hotel door, spilling us into the outrageously-average lobby with worn floors and dusty upholstered chairs. The desk clerk looked over, a white phone receiver tucked between her shoulder and ear. I didn't miss the way her gaze skipped past me and lingered on the man who looked like a celebrity who'd stepped off the cover of a magazine.

If I were her, I'd probably look at him too.

If only she knew what a jerk he was.

The kelpie was surprisingly quiet in the elevator ride up. His head bobbed to the tinkling music spilling from the dying speakers overhead.

"You *like* that stuff," I said, aghast.

"I don't *dislike* it, if that's what you're asking."

"It's elevator music."

"Fitting. Considering it's playing," he spread his hands, "in an elevator."

My head thunked as it hit the wall. The doors opened and Finn grabbed my hand, tugging me forward on legs that *really* didn't want to move anymore.

"Come now, no rest for the weary."

"That's exactly who *does* need rest."

"Look who's got jokes," Finn said.

"You're a joke."

"Here, give me that key card. You're barely hitting the box and... yep. That definitely wasn't the slot. I'll just—" He guided my hand so the plastic fitted into the card-reader and pushed the door open.

I think I mumbled something about needing to hit the gym because I'd missed an entire day of workouts. But I couldn't be sure, because the white comforter and sheets tucked around the edges of the twin beds inside the room looked incredibly inviting.

"Yeah, that's not going to happen," he said with small grin. It was utterly unlike his other flashy smiles, and I almost wondered where that other guy had gone. He pulled back the sheets and pushed me down to the pillow-top mattress.

"Why the hell not?" I asked.

"Somehow I imagined you to be more eloquent."

Rather than answer, I snuggled into the pillow that smelled of bleach. The heavy weight of the comforter dropped on top of me, and the warmth soothed my sore muscles and aching bones.

"You're about to pass out for a week. Whether you believe it or not, today was pretty hard on you. The last thing you need is even more adrenaline."

"Fine," I slurred out, sleep already dragging me under. "I'll kick your butt in the morning."

He smiled and I shut my eyes while trying to formulate a better response. Before I completely passed out, though, I could have sworn his hand brushed my cheek softly. "Whatever you say, Z."

5

Geoffrey

P *resent Day*

The Gods never announced themselves quietly.

One single thought passed through the space between my ears before searing heat blasted my skull. Another wave of nausea sent me sprawling over the porcelain bowl. What little was left in my stomach came right back up. I coughed wetly, bile dripping from my lips as I waited for the next round of crippling pain.

Three beats.

Four.

The tension knotting my shoulders eased. The lid clattered as I collapsed around the toilet, limbs trembling with the sudden release of adrenaline. Sweat stained the collar of my grey shirt, turning the fabric nearly black. The first icy whisper of magic I barely remembered blasted a warning that had driven me to my knees. Only luck would have it I was in my inner chambers at the time. The second rattle of millions of rocks banging inside my skull knocked me nearly to the ground, the vertigo wrecking me.

I swiped the back of my hand, cold as marble, across my mouth and coughed again, eyes squeezing shut against the harsh glare of the fluorescent lights. The third punch was the screaming of thousands of tortured souls. I'd barely made it to the bathroom.

But it isn't possible.

The reflective surface of the vanity mirror seemed far away from the ground.

I killed them. I wiped them out. I ensured they couldn't...

A toothbrush went flying as my forearm swiped across the quartz counter top.

Two of four had survived. But why emerge now? Had one of them been the First of Four to emerge, they would have risen up as a child. It was far too late for that now. What changed?

The soap dish shattered into hundreds of jagged pieces that crunched beneath my shins, digging dozens of tiny trails of blood across my skin. Fingers grasped the edge of the sink, knuckles paper-white.

After all this time, that must mean...

A face carved thin by starvation, and pale from lack of sunlight, stared back at me. Across my forehead four symbols blazed black as sin, edged with lightning white. Four symbols that hadn't seared with life for nearly seventeen years. Four symbols that, though they could never be hidden, I'd thought I'd extinguished forever.

Treachery.

A tendril of something curled through my chest, turned to sand in my throat.

A decoy.

My clenched fist opened, one finger lifting at a time. Breath hung in my chest, sticky as webs.

Could one have survived?

A single flickering flame burned in my palm.

Then a wisp of smoke.

Magic.
A curl of liquid.
A mottled pebble.
One awakened.
But which?

6

Zara

Water dripped behind me.

Or was it in front?

I couldn't see. *Was I blind?* No. Neck muscles strained as I attempted to turn my head, the soft fabric of a blindfold wrapped tight around the edges of my face. It was impossible to tell in this utter darkness where the steady ping, ping, ping of liquid on metal was coming from. But I did know it was sending tiny spears of pain shooting through my brain with each drop.

Weakly, I tested my mobility. My arms and legs were still attached, which was good. But when I tried to move them, they met the resistance of some sort of rope. The cords wrapped around my limbs, but not tightly enough that they cut off my circulation. Something wet coated my fingers.

Blood.

My gut twisted.

No.

I couldn't think that way. I needed to stay calm, rational.

It was probably water. Or sweat. Something inconsequential.

But that didn't stop the next thoughts: Where was I? Why was I tied up?

Was I kidnapped in my sleep?

I'd never felt those sturdy muscles in the back of my tongue work harder as they did now, struggling to spread thick, waxy saliva around the inside of my mouth. It tasted like fear and helplessness. I wanted to scream for help, but my voice remained lodged in my throat. My heart pounded, lungs expanded rapidly. The air smelled crisp, clean, and a little salty. It was not at all like the dank and dirty basement I envisioned myself in.

I rubbed my wrists against the binding again. A low moan caught in my throat as the elastic material tightened with my movement. I was completely, thoroughly trapped; incapable of sneaking away before…

Before what?

My heart kicked into a full-on gallop.

Was that a noise? The unmistakable wooden creak of a door? Yes. Definitely footsteps beating a fast tempo across the floor. The pattering of two feet—one person—came closer. I gulped, trying to think past my fear.

"You're here. And you're awake." The warm, masculine voice sounded surprised. Like he hadn't expected to find me here in this state of duress. "When I called you, I wasn't quite sure what to expect."

"Who are you?" I cut into his ramblings, having finally found my voice. I was growing increasingly aware that not only was I tied up, but I was in the company of a *complete* stranger. "Why did you bring me here?"

"I needed to talk to you." He made it sound like the most rational thing in the world. Something soft brushed over the bindings and I flinched. "But it didn't quite…"

"So you kidnapped me? Where are you from that it's OK to take someone in their sleep, tie them up, and then… what?" The grip of ice on my skin tightened. *What was going to happen to me?*

"Please take a deep breath. You're starting to hyperventilate. I'm trying to help you out here."

"I doubt that."

"Your magic is fighting you."

Hold up. "What?"

A match struck the side of a box, the sound as unmistakable as the soft fizz of resulting flame. It was quickly followed by the mellowing scent of eucalyptus. I forced myself to take deeper breaths. Seconds passed, maybe a minute. I blinked and realized the blindfold wasn't blocking light as effectively as it had before. I could make out the silhouette of a person slouched in a chair in front of me.

"I thought that might help. I find candles to be particularly soothing. Same with incense. I've never been sure why that is. Maybe it has to do with the air magic." He hummed low in his throat, and I wondered about the sanity of my maybe-captor. "Anyway. You asked who I am. I'm Geoffrey. And I have a great many questions for you."

The ties twisting around my hands tightened. "First let me go."

"I'm not really sure how to do that."

"Why?"

"It's your magic. Or what I assume is your magic, anyway, if water is your affiliation."

"How can you tell?"

"A few ways, I guess. I mean, it's blue for starters. There are also streaks of water running down your arms. It's a bit of a giveaway, really."

See, Zara. Water. Not blood.

"If you can see it, why can't you fix it?"

"I'm afraid I've had my share of your magic for an even shorter span than you. I'm not quite sure how to use it myself. You see, that's why I reached out to you. We need to talk." Geoffrey's chair creaked as he shifted. "You've already inadvertently answered my primary question. It was important for me to know which element you controlled because we are connected; the stronger you get, the stronger I get. You're also my main contact between the other Gods when we can't physically talk to one another."

My blood hummed, electrified. He knew who I was. Kind of. He definitely knew *what* I was, anyway. "I don't understand."

"I'm the head of the Order. Maybe that will help if you have a limited understanding of our organization. As the head of the Order, I'm your Hand. I'm supposed to help guide you and teach you."

I'd heard that title before. The person that served as a guide to the Gods. I blinked beneath the fabric-that-wasn't-fabric. More light was filtering through the folds now; the shadow that was his person was growing darker and the air around him lighter. I could now make out a man's blocky build. It was oddly reassuring.

"How are we talking like this?"

"I'm speaking to you through a mental connection only shared between the Gods and their Hand. It's like sharing a room between our minds, confidential and safe. I can't hurt you here and you can't hurt me."

My stomach clenched hard. "You want to hurt me?"

"Not necessarily. But depending on your intentions, that could change. And, considering your lack of control, I'm a little more concerned about you hurting me—accidentally or on purpose."

"And that's why can't I see?"

"That's my best guess," Geoffrey said. "I can see your magic spinning and swirling in and around you like a drunken butterfly: beautiful yet chaotic. Uncontrolled. I'm not really sure why your mental self is resisting this connection, to tell you the truth. But, if your knowledge is as limited as I believe it is, then it could be a simple lack of understanding."

I sucked on my tongue. The Kraken spoke mind-to-mind. It really wasn't all that crazy to think other beings could do the same thing. "Why, exactly, did you call me here to this... whatever this is?"

"We need to talk."

"You said that already."

"What's your name?" I asked.

"I want to know why I'm here first."

"Alright then," Geoffrey said. "There are questions I have about... everything. About your existence. About your desires. About how we're going to proceed..." He was rambling again, muttering to himself as he stood and started pacing across the room. Geoffrey's features were still blurry, but the more I concentrated, the more I could tell he was of average height for a man because he didn't tower over the muted television flickering on the table behind him. A television.

That was new.

Geoffrey held his arms behind his back, fingers laced together as he strode back and forth, head bowed to the floor as he muttered words too quiet for me to hear. Then he stopped, body angled toward me. "What do you intend to do?"

"I don't know what you're asking."

"With your powers. What are your intentions?" He'd sounded warm before, but Geoffrey's voice had chilled considerably.

"I... I don't know. I guess I still need to figure out what my powers are."

"What about the world?" he demanded. His pacing stopped. The blurry outline of a hand swiped over his smooth head. Listening to him was like listening to politicians debate policy: the words themselves made sense, but strung together and their meaning was a mystery.

"What about the world?" I threw back at him, unable to hold back my frustration. "I don't think I have the answers you're looking for."

He moved closer, his movements jerky. "What's your name?" he asked again.

"Zara." The word blurted out of me without thought, my fear returning in full force. I didn't understand what was going on.

"Zara. That's pretty." He sucked in a hard breath and resumed pacing, the loose fabric of his shirt flowed around him in waves. He passed in front of the television again, and his arm shot out, grabbing some sort of round device I couldn't see. "Your magic is pretty, too."

The saliva in my mouth evaporated. He'd said he couldn't hurt me here, right? I hadn't misunderstood.

"Zara, I'm conflicted right now."

"Why are you conflicted?" I asked the strange man in the most soothing voice I could muster.

"I don't quite know what to do with you."

I could almost see him now, if only he'd turn toward me, then I'd have a clearer picture.

"What does that mean?"

"I once made a very difficult decision. A decision I wish I hadn't had to make. A decision I still stand behind even though I regret it..." He paused by a large window that looked familiar, peering out into the blue depths of the sky. From my angle in the chair I couldn't see much of the landscape except for a blurry blob to the right. And something about it seemed...

I couldn't quite focus.

He whirled on me, hands slamming down on the wooden arms of the chair. Bi-colored eyes, one the color of smoke and the other bright as emerald, grew wide with eagerness and maybe a hint of insanity. I jerked backward, heart kicking into overdrive. "We need to meet. In person. There's much we need to discuss. Tell me where you are."

The haze had cleared.

I wished it hadn't.

I was staring into the face of someone who'd known pain, who'd

44

realized grief, who'd paid for the emotions with his very being. Scars the shapes of X's cut deeply into pockmarked checks, equally spaced on either side of his thin nose. My eyes darted between his. The madness I'd glimpsed earlier had receded; now I only saw hungry curiosity reflected back at me, an expression like he had found a prized possession he planned to hoard away.

Across his brow glimmered four symbols shaded black, edged with luminescent white. One of them was a replica of the wave branded across my arm. It must be true, if he had those brands. He must be the Hand of the Gods, the leader of the Order. Someone I should trust, but also someone my gut screamed at me to pull away from. If I could. My magic—I could now see in the blue strands that held my arms down—remained unrelenting.

A hand ghosted over my cheek. "Tell me where you are, Zara. I'll find you."

My insides quaked with a heady mixture of wariness and adrenaline. "I really don't think that's a good idea."

"Tell me where you are. I must know. That's the only way."

He talked too quickly, his eyes bright with frenzy. My own eyes darted to the window, to the tall bell tower I could see spearing the sky now that the haze had faded. I knew that tower. I'd woken to it and its incessant clanging before. The breath caught in my chest.

Catching my expression, Geoffrey turned to see what I was looking at.

My arms wrestled with my magic as he turned back, a touch of a smile gracing his lips. My mind screamed at me to wake up, wake up now. "Zara..."

I blinked.

And he was gone.

7

Zara

"Zara? Seriously, Zara. You need to wake up." Kazandra touched my arm, her short nails tapping a tempo to some song existing only in her head. "Come on. You're starting to scare me."

I rolled toward my best friend and roommate, groaning, but my vision remained blurry with sleep. In the background, the peppy voice of the anchor on the television droned on about the heightened nuclear threat level. My curiosity piqued. Norway was back in the red. Pretty standard for most nations these days. It was threat level black we had to worry about. Not that we'd be alive much longer to worry much about anything.

The room blurred again, and I blinked. This time, Kaz's rich, brown eyes were level with mine. She peered at me, lines etched deep around the corners of her mouth. "Oh, thank the Gods. You're awake. I was about to get Coach."

It was all a dream? But it felt real.

"What happened?" I mumbled.

"You weren't responding. I kept trying to wake you up, calling your name, shaking you, but you were out cold. It was scary." She wrapped her fingers around my arm again as if to reassure herself I was, indeed, awake and present before flitting off to the far side of the room. I pulled myself up onto my elbows as she her threw odds and ends into her duffel bag.

"What time is it?"

"Late. Really late. You'll only have, like, an hour to get ready." Which was huge considering my normal prep-time took at least twice that. I was going to miss warm-ups for sure.

"Damn."

"Yep."

How had I slept so late? I never slept through my alarm on my phone…

The waterlogged, broken, and now-useless device had fallen out of my pocket when I'd crashed into the water in a storm I was ninety-nine percent sure the Kraken had started. The phone I hadn't recovered or even thought about until now.

The Kraken. Stars, that part *hadn't* been a dream.

My fingers flew to my head, pushing hard on my temples. It was a sorry attempt at shutting down the ache brewing deep in the recesses of my head.

That's what I needed before a competition.

"Another migraine?" My eyes opened to slits again, and the soft dawn light filtered in.

I forced my fingers to stop digging into my face and tried to focus on my bunk mate instead. She was a classic Middle Eastern beauty with the rich heritage to prove it. I envied her full lips, flowing dark hair, and gorgeous olive skin. At the moment, her glossy locks were pulled back, and she'd already shrugged on a long-sleeve Under Armor shirt and yoga pants as she prepared to head out to warm-ups. Genuine concern tinged her tone, and I shook my head.

"No, sorry. I can feel a little bit of a headache," I fibbed. "I took something for it last night, and that must have knocked me out more than I thought. I meant to text you, but my phone died." Sort of. My lips twitched in a hint of a smile and she relaxed a touch.

"That's what roomies are for! Stars knows how many times you've pushed my ass out of bed during this tourney." Her accent flared with her excitement. Kaz rarely expressed negative emotion. She swore by some mantra about positivity making the world a better place.

"Speaking of yesterday," she slicked her tongue over her lips with a suggestive wink. "What did you get up to? Or down to, should I say?"

The banter pushed my headache back, thankfully. I shoved the covers off and rolled my legs out of bed, my toes clenching around the thin fibers of the carpet. "Nothing like that, Kaz. I wanted to get out and see some of the town for once. Clear my head."

She pursed her lips. She wasn't buying it. But she didn't say anything. Good woman. "If you say so." She turned the statement into a question. "Anyway, you should probably start getting ready." Kaz smoothed her hands down the front of her shirt and glanced at her iPhone when it beeped an incoming notification. "Most of us are heading over now. Want us to wait for you?"

"Nah. I'll meet you poolside."

Her head bobbed and she stooped to pick up her duffel before heading out the door. When the door clicked closed, automatically locking behind her, I let out a deep sigh, reluctant to fully peel myself off the mattress. I braced my elbows on my thighs, bones digging deep into the muscles, and scrunched my nose. Could yesterday have been a dream? A dream within a dream if that unhinged man had anything to do with anything?

If it were true and real, shouldn't I feel differently?

I flexed my fingers experimentally but didn't feel any of those wonderful and weird vibrations sparking from under my nails and skin. Sensations I'd felt when I'd brushed against the Kraken.

No. I needed to get ready. This was ridiculous. I shoved the thoughts away and attempted to focus on the upcoming competition. Despite how poorly I'd slept and the strain of yesterday, I felt fresher than expected. Thankfully, I hadn't taken my iPod on the boat with me, and I blasted some Cardi B while starting the long, practiced process of preparing for the races. In the shower, I tried to see if I could change the temperature of the water. When nothing happened, I was deeply glad no one could see the embarrassed blush painting my cheeks and chest red.

Maybe they had the wrong person after all. Maybe everything had been in my head.

Twenty minutes later, dressed in my typical baggy shirt, grey sweats and a jacket, I shrugged on my black duffel bag and its many ironed-on patches from my global expeditions, headed out the door... and almost collided with it when I jumped back in surprise. Someone I'd hoped to never see again leaned on the wall opposite the door, gazing steadily over a cup of what smelled like coffee at his lips.

He sported two legs instead of four.

Nope, definitely not a dream.

None of it.

"Stalking me now?" I turned to make sure the door was indeed shut, trying to hide the shaking of my hands. "Seems a bit unnecessary if you ask me."

"Stalking, observing, monitoring. It's all about the same right?" Finn said dryly, lifting one of his eyebrows. It was pierced, with silver balls above and below. He toyed with a silver loop hooked through his lower lip as he spoke. "And yes, I find it absolutely necessary, O wonderful, gorgeous, well-spoken God of mine. Who knows what mess you'll get mixed up in if I'm not here to keep an eye on you?"

I eyed him skeptically. From the black-shirt that molded to his abs to the tight, black jeans that brushed the tops of stylish, white, combat boots, it seemed more likely that even in human-form *he* would be the one more likely to get into trouble. He ruffled his shaggy, rock star hair in an attempt to move it out of his face, but it flopped right back.

"Uh huh. Well, today I've got a swim meet, then dinner with the girls, and then probably sleep. Doesn't that sound exciting?" I started to move past him, anxious to get going. "And thanks to you, I wasn't able to carbo-load yesterday or do any of my other routine stuff. Who knows how my races are going to go. Do me a favor and leave me alone for a while."

"Excuse me, but my fault? I seem to recall *you* wanted to hit the gym after your excursion at sea yesterday." He jogged, a wide array of zippers and metallic bracelets jangling together as he easily caught up with my quick march down the hallway. "You said nothing about food. I would have remembered that. I'm *all about* eating."

We stopped at the elevator where I punched the down arrow a little harder than necessary. I glared at the doors, wishing I had the ability to make them open faster. My fingers tapped a furious rhythm on my arm. I wasn't sure if I should tell him about my dream. It was only a dream, after all. But I didn't really trust him. Finn's fingers brushing my elbow drew me out of my head again, and I sealed my lips, deciding against telling him about my bout with Geoffrey. Although...

"You know, the Kraken said I'm supposed to find the other Gods. They'll help solve whatever global crisis is coming. Do you think the Order can help with that? They're supposed to—"

"It's more important to teach you to use your magic," Finn interrupted. I took an involuntary step back. Gone was his easy smile, instead replaced with a dark expression I couldn't interpret. His leg jiggled, and when he glanced over at me, he sighed.

"Listen. I don't... I don't trust the Order." His head tipped back at an angle and his arms folded across his chest. "I trusted my temple, *your* temple, before it fell. And I trust the Kraken. But the Order, let's just say the Order operates on its own level. As your guardian I want to get a feel for what's going on first. Until yesterday, no one even knew you were alive. We don't need to rush anything; let's take it a day at a time. We will find the other Gods. But I'd rather get through some of the basics first. OK?"

"Sure." I shrugged. I hadn't exactly gotten warm and fuzzy vibes from Geoffrey anyway. No one else I knew was part of the church or knew its leaders, so it was difficult for me to get another read on the situation. If it bothered Finn to reach out, I'd go with his instincts—for now.

The elevator dinged and Finn extended his hand, ushering me into the confined space first.

"Speaking of yesterday, I want to apologize."

It seemed that awkward conversation was going to accompany this equally awkward ride. Didn't he know the rules of elevators? Once those doors closed everyone politely ignored everyone else inside them from start to finish, then bum-rushed the doors when they opened at the right floor.

"You have nothing to apologize for," I said.

"I disagree," Finn said. He shifted his weight from one foot to the other, and for the first time, I became truly aware of his average height that still somehow towered over my five foot two. He wasn't heavily built, but judging by the ropes of tightly-corded muscles wrapping around his arms, he was incredibly strong. The tan tint of his skin was somehow darker in the daylight than it had been underwater. It contrasted sharply with my almost alabaster tone. "I wasn't quite myself and I came off more abrasive than I normally do."

The elevator doors opened, and I used my duffel bag as a buffer between us. I was already late to the meet and this conversation was making me later, but he *was* trying to be civil.

"Are you feeling better today?" I asked.

"Yes." He nodded at the desk clerk leering at us. "The Kraken yanked me out of a particularly long, deep nap rather rudely. And upon awakening, I was informed that I had a new charge to take care of: no ifs, ands, or buts about it."

"How long of a nap are we talking about here?"

"Oh, about seventeen years. Give or take a handful of months." He tossed his paper cup in a trash receptacle outside the doors. "A little longer than usual."

Time didn't make sense in this new-found world of mine. However, I really didn't have the time—*ha ha*—to think about it right now, so I decided against responding and marched faster down the worn, cobble-stoned street. Finn matched my speed. The building was about two blocks away. Despite saying he'd been unusually terse yesterday, Finn still seemed ill at ease with his fingers twisting around his many bracelets.

"What happened to your horse parts?" I asked.

"I could bring them back, if you're asking. But I warn you, I'll leave the explaining to you."

"Seriously, where did they go?"

"I willed them away. It's easier to look like a human right now."

"Are you a shape-shifter?"

"Of sorts," he said.

"You really do turn into an actual horse?"

"Head, tail, and all that comes in the middle."

"What's it like?" I pulled the zippered edges of my jacket tighter as a cool breeze blew down the street. It was my most favorite piece in my wardrobe; a warm, waterproof, red-white-and-blue spangled piece given to all American athletes when they made it to the Olympics. The rest of the uniform was back at the fancy boarding school my parents had enrolled me in when I was eleven with the rest of my non-travel clothing. But I rarely took this jacket off.

"So many questions, Z. I think we might actually be on our way to becoming friends."

A sarcastic response jumped to mind, but before I could snark it out, his finger pressed against my lips, stopping me in the middle of the street. "As much as I'm dying to know what's about to come out of your mouth, let me respond to your question. When I fully transform into my other state, other, more animalistic, impulses become sharper. I'm still cognizant of my being. I still think like a human, but it's like it takes a back-burner to needs. Things like food and water and running and... other things."

Wait. Were we talking about drowning people here? Or a normal innuendo? I felt a tinge of red flush over my cheeks, and his gaze swiped across the rosy hue. He shook his head, hair flying everywhere, in a manner I'd seen on horses at the racetrack on TV. The movement put me on his right side for the first time, and only now did I see the large tattoo on his neck.

"What's that?"

"What's what?"

"This." I reached a shaking hand out, the tips of my fingers drifting against the soft skin under the curve of his jaw and traced the black replica of my birthmark until it vanished beneath his collar. He flinched but didn't move away. "Why do you have it?"

"I swore an oath once." Now he stepped away, a hand nervously rubbing the flesh I'd traced. His gaze skittered over mine again.

Right.

"Do all fey have them?"

"No. They're very special and very sacred." His shoulders tensed, eyes unfocused as he scoured the lobby.

"You realize that I'm going to need more than that right?"

"Hold on a minute." He seemed to find what he was looking for and pushed me softly into an empty room. Or closet. Most definitely a closet full of brooms and mops and bitter-smelling cleaners. "This isn't exactly a conversation we should have in public," he explained.

"Start explaining."

"What's on my neck is a brand. Fey get branded when they swear oaths of fealty to one of the four Gods. To swear fealty is extremely significant in the magical community. It's also very powerful: like a double-edged sword and equally as deadly. On one hand, the God is required to protect you within reason, but you're also required to back them no matter what. This was a much bigger deal back tens of thousands of years ago when bloody wars were more common. Now, though, they're more..." he seemed to struggle with finding the right word, "symbolic."

I didn't interrupt, giving him time instead to gather his thoughts.

"Most fey already have natural allegiances. For example, I'm a kelpie, a creature of water. That means I'm already within the purview of the Water Temple. Pixies have wings and can fly. They naturally fit in with Air. So on and so forth. For most of us, that's enough when it comes to choosing sides.

"But things can get tricky when a fey chooses to change sides or swear fealty to a different God. That only happens when that God has done something significant to or for them. It indicates they believe in their abilities more than those of the God with which they are naturally aligned. And even with creatures of the same court, swearing an oath is a huge deal because it means you will always stand with them."

"Sounds dangerous," I said.

His expression darkened and he nodded. "There are some fey—and humans—that are required to swear an oath. Typically, those are the people who serve within the temples themselves. It's a requirement because the temples are... well, the temples are strange places."

Something about his words resonated, but I let him continue, keen to know more.

"They are both of the Order and not at the same time. They answer to the politics of the Hand and the Council, but their first and primary loyalty is to their individual Gods. It's super complicated to get into, but think of it like the relationship between states and the federal government: everyone answers to the same rules, but the states are much more concerned about their individual well-being than the well-being of everyone as a whole."

I thought of back home. That made sense. "If the brand magically appears on fey, how does that work for humans?"

"They get it tattooed on." He shrugged. "It's considered holy and equally binding. To break that vow is sacrilegious."

It was on the tip of my tongue to ask what made him decide to swear his oath, but something about the way he was staring at me told me to back off. I gave him a half-smile and fumbled for the door handle. "Thank you for explaining that," I murmured softly, trying to make out the dark mark against his skin. Somehow, I felt better knowing he had it.

"You should start getting ready," he said when we reemerged into the light of the hall. He forced a level of candor. "I'm interested to see if you're as good in the water as they say you are."

8

Zara

I was a muddled mess of thoughts as I pushed through the locker room doors, bee-lining for my assigned spot. My concentration for the meet was completely shot. Kaz had just come back from warm-ups and gave me a funny look as I scrolled through the combination to my lock, but I shrugged. Now wasn't the time to talk about personal issues. She would ask me whatever was on her mind afterward.

I dressed quickly, the routine helping reset my brain and refocus my energy. I tugged on my favorite yellow swim cap and orange goggles before taking a quick dip in the warm-up pool to loosen my muscles. It felt good. It felt really good. Energy hummed in my veins, the water recharging parts of me I hadn't known were tired.

I followed Kaz to join my teammates by the side of the pool and listened to the droning pep talk from our coaches. This was our second-to-last meet. After this was Denmark. Then I'd find myself back on a plane to New York and the brutal, mechanical training schedule that awaited. I enjoyed it—the competitive nature of my top-of-the-line school. We didn't waste time on traditional learning. Instead, world-class trainers worked us to the bone, honing our talents, eliminating our weakness, and turning us into future champions. There would be more gold medals in my future. But all that time training didn't leave much room for a social life, let alone opportunities to visit close family.

My heart lurched in my chest as I thought about the text message I'd ignored from my mother: *call me when you get a chance, honey. There's something we need to discuss.*

This was it. They were finally getting a divorce; I knew it in my gut. It wasn't particularly surprising. My mom and dad had been at odds for years. It traced all the way back to my childhood when Mom decided to fill me in on the fact that I was adopted. My father made it painfully clear he'd wanted to keep that particular detail a secret. It created a chasm that only expanded over time. That chasm only deepened when my dad made the decision to ship me off to school on the east coast without consulting my mom first.

Somehow, I was always stuck in the middle of their arguments.

Oh well. I didn't have a phone anyway. That particular conversation would have to wait.

I looked out over the crowd, not surprised when I found Finn's grass-green gaze on me. Or was it? He was glowering at someone over my shoulder, but when I turned to look, I only saw a gaggle of girls from the other team stretching their legs and gossiping. When he caught my attention again, his look lightened, and he shoved a handful of popcorn in his mouth. I could almost taste the buttery-goodness on my tongue. He lifted his other hand a bit and wiggled his fingers in a semblance of a wave. The man was impossible. I huffed and returned my focus to the coaches in time to put my hand in the middle and give our customary pre-game cheer.

Riley, with her ringing laughter and bold curves, was up first for the breast stroke. For a swimmer, those curves should hurt her odds, but somehow, she toughed through it. Only half my attention was on her setting up at the blocks when I heard snickering from the girls on the opposing team, sniping at her, gossiping about her weight.

"Hey! How about you worry more about choking on her wake when she smokes you?" I snapped. "Or better yet, try to actually get some nutrients from your next meal before you hawk it up again."

Four faces snapped to me, but my coach pulled me back before they could respond. "Zara, enough. We've talked about this." Admonishment washed over and past me. I couldn't keep my mouth shut in the heat of the moment. It was a major strike against me and one my coaches still hoped to break me of.

No luck thus far.

I caught the flash of fingers from behind Coach's back and shifted a bit, making an even cruder gesture right back. The girls sneered and tsked, then huddled up as the next race got underway.

Riley aced the breast stroke as expected.

A few more beeps of the starting buzzer before it was finally time for freestyle. I looked over at Finn in the stands again as he stuffed another handful of popcorn in his mouth. He must have gotten up for a refill given the speed I'd seen him packing it in earlier. Surprisingly, he seemed to be thoroughly enjoying the entire event. He caught me staring and winked, a huge grin spreading over his glistening lips.

I swung my arms a few times to loosen them up and mounted the block. Of the seven teams participating, the girl to my left was from the team that had picked on my teammate. Her features pinched when she looked in my direction. She was probably very pretty, but the nastiness turned her ugly. "Watch your back, slut," she muttered in French, not looking at me. It was probably something I wasn't even supposed to have heard, let alone interpreted.

"Glad to know you're cool with coming in second, since you plan on seeing my back and all," I fluidly replied in the same language.

Her lips curled. I would have tossed my hair over my shoulder impishly if I could have. No such luck with the swim cap and all.

"You know what they say about counting chickens."

"I'm not counting chickens. I already have the eggs."

The guy over the loudspeaker called us to take our marks before she could respond, and we both stepped into position. The moment I looked out across the water, the conversation drifted away along with everything else swarming my mind. This was what I lived for: moments like these, just me and the water. I gripped the front of the white platform, the slick rim of water reassuring under my touch. I'd already shut out all other sound, the lapping of water, the rustle of the crowd, the whooping of my teammates, waiting for the buzzer.

BEEP!

My arms swung over my head, meeting in a sharp point, and I hit the water in one smooth, practiced dive. Keeping my arms in front, I dolphin-kicked, staying underwater as long as I could. As I crested, I felt something burn on the outsides of both forearms. Before I broke the surface, I realized ridges of fins had sprouted from my skin, a long firm flap that would help me immensely, enabling me to push more water behind me faster. Why had these emerged now? Would anyone else see? Praying they wouldn't, I pushed forward. I felt the change, the ease of slicing through the water, the steady burn of energy. I flipped under the water, and my feet hit the opposite wall first, easily a half-second ahead of everyone else.

Three laps later I'd confirmed what I'd known from the beginning.

I owned this sport.

I owned the water.

I owned the competition.

My fingers tapped the wall one final time. When I gripped the gutter, I immediately turned to look at the scoreboard. Two seconds. I'd beaten the runner-up by two insane seconds.

I was used to winning, but this was ridiculous.

Thankfully, my fins had retracted as I'd made my final approach, and I hauled myself out of the water, only pausing to give an "I told you so" head bob to the French chick. She'd come in fourth.

Coach gaped as I joined the rest of the team. "You beat your time in the Olympics, Zara! Your gold medal event! Where the hell has that speed been? What did you eat last night?"

I shrugged and chewed on the inside of my cheek, not responding to the whoops and yells of support from my teammates. Kazandra was looking at me with equal parts admiration and reproach. Her interrogation tonight was *not* something I was looking forward to. I didn't have answers to give.

I slicked a hand over my cap and looked out over the crowd again. Finn's scowl stood out. I'd messed up. I shouldn't be drawing attention to myself like this. I knew it. He knew it. My fingers brushed at my temples as a budding headache formed there, and I nodded subtly. I'd be more careful the rest of the meet.

And I was.

I couldn't stop the fins from sliding out every time I was fully submerged, but I checked my strokes, fumbled with turns, and hesitated longer than I needed to before jumping from the blocks. I was still performing slightly better than I normally did, but the numbers weren't anywhere near as crazy as my first race.

We easily won first, and the girls were jubilant in the locker rooms after the final results were announced. Our strong performance combined with the impending knowledge of our last meet together filled the locker room with vibrant energy. After a quick powwow with the coaches, my teammates filtered out of the room. We were all going to meet up for dinner at some fancy restaurant to celebrate. I took a bit longer than usual to gather up my stuff, mostly because Kaz kept trying to pester me with questions, so it came as a bit of a surprise when one of the girls backtracked and stood in front of me as I tugged on my jacket.

"Might want to hurry it up, Zar. There's a boy outside the locker rooms to see you." Her eyes glittered with mischief. "And he's *hot as sin.*" She clicked her tongue with each of the words and tipped her head back in a luxurious motion, exposing her neck. "Maybe when you're done with him, you'll let the rest of us have a chance at those tight muscles." She whistled, then left Kaz and me alone.

"Seriously, what the heck has gotten into you?" Yep. She was furious. "You've been an open book this entire tour, and now all of a sudden you're staying out late, getting incredible times at meets, and hanging out with mysterious men. I thought I was your friend." Her tone pitched to levels that only dogs could hear.

Okay. Not pissed. Betrayed.

I got that.

I totally got that.

"Listen, I'm really sorry," I said. "Things got a little weird really fast. Like, really fast. I'm still trying to figure out what all of this means." Her expression softened as I shrank away from her, my back smacking hard into the lockers. "I met this guy yesterday and he's, well, he's another complication right now. And I forgot that we agreed to go on a date after the meet. I promise I'll come right home afterward and I'll tell you everything. Okay?" I extended a pinkie, and she looked at it like I'd pointed a gun at her. "Pinkie swear?"

"Whatever," she huffed, but she still hooked her pinkie around mine. I could have died from relief. She was my only friend in this world. I couldn't stand losing her. "You're adorable. Infuriating. But adorable all the same. I feel like we're back in fifth grade or something. And I want details. Juicy details. *All* the details."

She slung an arm over my shoulders as we exited the locker room. As promised, Finn leaned on his elbows against the opposite wall, staring straight down at the ground. Chunky black hair fell vertically across his face. Kaz's arm tensed around me as she took him in.

"The more juice on him, the better," she whispered, lips pressed to my ear. She then smacked a loud kiss on my cheek and ran to catch up with some other girls heading back to the hotel to change. I flashed a peace sign at her back before turning to Finn.

"I'm exhausted. Again. It seems to be a recurring problem whenever I see you," I deadpanned. "Maybe we shouldn't keep doing this."

"The break-up speech already? We haven't even gone out yet." He picked at his fingernails, and his mouth tipped up a bit as he traced his tongue over his top teeth. "Not that I'd ever want to date someone as prickly as you, anyway."

"Whatever. You'd be lucky to date someone like me."

"You're not my type," he fired back, not amused. "You have training to do. The sooner we get to it, the sooner you can go to bed."

"I just swam my butt off at a meet. I don't have any energy left." I was whining, but I seriously was not in the mood to head off with some stranger and practice powers that not only sounded made up, but I wasn't even fully sure I possessed. Granted, I had sprouted fins out of nowhere. Maybe there was some truth to it. Or maybe I was losing it.

He flipped up an index finger.

Oh goodie, more lists.

"One. That was your choice. You heard Lucy yesterday. You're a God. That's top priority right now. Two," a second finger flipped up, "You don't really have much choice in the matter. Every hour that passes that you don't have control over your abilities the more danger you're in. And the more danger you're in means the more danger I'm in. And I *really* don't like dealing with danger."

"Lucy?"

"Yeah. The Kraken. It's what I call It. Seems less intimidating that way."

"It's a she?"

"Did I say that? No. I like the name Lucy. I don't think the Great Beasts have genders."

"Oh."

He clicked his pierced tongue against his teeth and grabbed my elbow where I'd propped it away from my body, my hand braced on my hip. "We're burning daylight. Let's go."

Stupid kelpie didn't leave me much option to argue, and I settled for asking if we could at least get food first. He pulled a granola bar from his backpack and handed it over. I grudgingly took it, trying to pretend the dry oats were something more rewarding. Like tiramisu. After a few minutes of silence, Finn spoke again, breaking his solemn revere.

"You have a bit of an attitude problem."

"What of it?" I asked around a bite of granola.

"I would never have guessed."

"I can't help myself when someone presents a challenge, verbal or otherwise. I've always been like that. I drove my parents insane as a child. And still kind of do." Finn's grip on my arm relaxed. "It's also fun talking smack to people who dish it out, not expecting a response."

"You swam well today. Really well. You messed up with that first race, but Gods did you look glorious doing it." He met my gaze, the green of his eyes had deepened to pine. "Truly. You swim like you were born to do it. Which is good. Because you were. That will make training much easier."

I was oddly touched by the compliment. I didn't know why his words mattered more to me than those of my teammates, my friends, my coaches, even my parents. But they did. And I'd only just met him.

"I almost forgot something." He dropped my arm and rummaged in the front pocket of his jeans. He removed a slim plastic box and presented it to me.

"My phone! Where did you find it?!"

"The castle."

"Then it's wrecked." The heartbroken tone of my voice startled a bark of laughter from Finn.

"No, I fixed it. Magic, remember." He twiddled his fingers as if that explained everything. I grimaced and tugged it away from him. Sure enough, the lock screen turned on, illuminating a candid picture of me and Kaz laughing about something hilarious. He smiled at the picture and hurried me along. It was weird being around him, hanging out with him. It felt like some part of me had known him forever, like we were meant to find each other. It was confusing.

"Sharing is caring."

"Hmm?"

"I can see the cogs spinning in your head. What's going on up there?"

"Oh nothing." I chewed on my lip and used my forearm to push open one of the large front doors. It was significantly cooler outside than in. "Seriously, it's nothing to talk about." And definitely not something I planned on *ever* speaking to him about.

Finn followed, his hands folded into his pockets as he wove through groups of people clustered on the sidewalk. His hand clasped mine so we didn't get separated. "Whatever then. You'll tell me when you're ready. But moving on. We need to transform you from a baby God who doesn't even know what she's capable of into a fully-fledged, kick-ass warrior in a few weeks." He rocked the corded muscles in his neck back and forth. The black slashes of his brand flexed with the motion. "In case you weren't following me, that means time is of the essence."

"Weeks?" I cried. "No one said anything about weeks! I leave Norway in two days. I'm not sticking around to play 'magic' or whatever else you want me to do."

"Funny," he repeated in the same calm voice that one would use when addressing a wild child. "Actually, all of this was outlined to you yesterday. But that was probably one of those things you quietly phased out in your inner musings."

I did recall hearing the Kraken mention something about intense and rigorous training, but that had all seemed so completely unreal at the time. We hung a left at one of the corners. The buildings were becoming more sparse, the people less frequent. I wondered where we were going.

"You can't be serious."

"Serious as stir fry. Consider me your bestest, best friend for the next, oh," he tapped a finger to his jaw, light glittered off his lip ring, "rest of your life. Because, baby, we're sticking together like pollen on bees." Lovely. I really wasn't going to get rid of him. "I say 'rest of your life' because we literally have centuries of shit to work through, and you don't know jack. That means I'm going to spend the remainder of my days hanging out with a petulant child."

"You're a jerk."

"We've established that already. Stop stalling."

"You haven't given me anything to do!"

Something sharp and wicked crossed his face, and I immediately regretted my words. We'd stopped in some small grove of trees, and he gestured at a pond behind him I hadn't noticed due to the encroaching darkness.

"Pull the water toward you."

Nope. I didn't care for that sneer at all.

I snapped my hair up into a tight ponytail using the elastic, orange hair tie I always kept on my wrist, and rolled up the star-stitched sleeve of my jacket. I approached the water like I'd approach a dog frothing at the mouth. Though why anyone would go *toward* a dog like that was beyond me.

Okay.

No big deal.

I needed the water to come to me.

Stuff people did all the time. Nothing hard about that. I mean, I'd grown *fins* this afternoon. I could *breathe* underwater. Pulling a puddle toward me was nothing.

Right?

My fingers pressed lightly on my temples, pushing back at the early stages of a headache forming there, before I reached out toward the water, fingers splayed. Okay. Yesterday I'd felt something burn in my veins. That must be whatever it was I needed to tap into.

I clenched my teeth, enamel grinding, straining for *something*.

Nothing happened, and I shook my hand.

Burning sensation, feel free to start anytime now.

Anytime would be *great*.

Still nothing.

"Hey there," Finn's voice came from behind me, quiet and neutral. "You look like you're staring at the executioner's chair. It ain't like I'm asking you to do the impossible and walk on water. Dial down the intensity. You're asking something that has always belonged to you to do what you want it to. It's nature at her best. Let her in. *Listen.*"

He was right.

Maybe a new approach.

Maybe I was being too abrasive.

Behind me, Finn sprawled on his back, head propped on the cushion of his arms. His eyes were set on the stars overhead. Some teacher if he couldn't even *see* me do the very thing I was supposed to be doing. Also—no way in hell was I saying anything *out loud*. Just what I needed was him ribbing me for the rest of my life for talking to an inanimate object. Maybe mentally would work. Telepathy was a thing, right? Feeling insane, I shaped words in my head, asking the water to respond.

Nothing.

Ok. Not exactly *nothing*. The surface of the water rippled in the wind, but that certainly wasn't anything caused by me. I could feel Finn watching me now, his stubborn stare an itch between my shoulder blades. I shrugged off the pressure. I silently called for the water two or three more times, struggling to feel even a hint of magic, before stomping my foot in frustration.

I huffed and glanced over my shoulder. Finn raised his eyebrows, clearly unimpressed. He also gave no indication he was ready to spout out some additional magnificent wisdom that would solve all my problems. And *he* was under some insane illusion we could be friends. Friends didn't let friends flounder.

As if knowing exactly what was going through my mind, the kelpie pinched his finger and thumb together and dragged them across his lips dramatically. Jerk. Double jerk.

I'd show him.

Time for a new tactic.

I collapsed to the ground, my knees folding smoothly into criss-cross-applesauce, and I scooted toward the edge of the pool, aware my sweats would probably have grass stains on them later. I eyed the pond again. Moonlight glinted off its surface, creating a clear, dark mirror. It was nearly impossible to see past the surface, but something told me nothing in there was going to hurt me.

How did I know that?

I struggled to grasp that instinctual thought as I reached out a hand again and beckoned the water toward me.

Still nothing.

Patience had never been a strong suit of mine, and I struggled to keep my temper in check. Ok. I accepted the possibility I was the God of Water. Even a baby God knew how to connect with his or her element. I'd won Olympic medals. I was a straight B+ student. I could do this. I beckoned at the water again, scooting closer to the edge. My knees almost touched the pristine surface.

Nothing.

My mind whirled. I'd been swimming in the stuff for the better part of my life, but I was finding out we were still really only strangers. It knew human Zara. It didn't know God Zara. I sighed. Thank the stars Finn couldn't hear my convoluted thoughts right now. Here I was treating a thing like a person. This better work.

Cautiously, as if holding a flame near a pool of gasoline, I pressed my palm to the surface of the water, sucking in a sharp breath as the chill wrapped around my fingers, sucking at the grooves in my skin. It didn't feel like water. It felt like molten silver, thick and dense and eerily smooth.

Do we know you? The words formed in my head like calligraphy. Words that weren't mine.

I hesitated. Then responded similarly, writing: *Yes. But I want to know you better.*

The liquid quivered like jelly under my palm. *Hmmmm.* A tough read there. I sucked my lips into my mouth and thought for a moment. I pulled out my mental pen again, the writing fluid and beautiful as a dolphin swimming through the ocean. *I don't know what I'm doing. Will you help me?*

A tinkling of bells chimed in my head. Laughter. Light peals of fluid laughter. I jerked. My hand pulled back, but the liquid clutched at my fingers refusing to let go, drawing out of the surface like an arm. Ok that was freaky. I was about two seconds away from hyperventilating when...

Forgive us. We mean no harm. We want to help. But first let us in. Open yourself up to the possibilities.

I don't understand, I thought helplessly.

Open up. Open yourself up. Let us in.

I felt like Alice falling down the rabbit hole, caught in a mess of her own making.

Another glance over at Finn. He was chugging an orange sports drink, his Adam's apple bobbing as he sucked the whole thing down. Yeah. This guy really needed some tips when it came to teaching.

Focus.

Open myself up. Easy, right? I pushed deeper into myself, into the blackness inside me I'd always ignored, dismissed as something not worthwhile. Water sluiced over my skin as I fell, spiraling deeper and deeper. The soft whistling of the wind across the water and chirping of bugs grew more distant. It was almost hypnotic. Part of me realized I was sinking into my soul. That blackness was my soul.

And that was wrong.

It shouldn't be black.

But I couldn't quite grasp why.

I was caught up in the *sensation* of sinking. It was almost like falling asleep. Years ago, after weeks of training left me frazzled and exhausted, I'd taught myself to slowly relax my body inch by inch, moving from my feet up until I felt so numb and tranquil I would pass out. This felt like that, only deeper and much darker. I'd never known how suffocatingly dark it was inside myself—just how little light really came in. And I landed, feet sinking into smoke swirling in my mind.

That's it.

A beam of silver splintered the air in my periphery, the darkest part of my soul. I whipped to look but it was gone. A flash of gold flickered from my right side. Another flash of light I couldn't quite see. The inky black depths of *myself* felt less comforting and more threatening.

It's dark here because you've never let us in. You've never embraced what you are, what we are, what your magic means to you. The tinkling, glittering voices hummed happily around me, the words scrawling before me like captioning.

And what is my magic supposed to mean to me?

That's for you to decide.

Yesterday, the Kraken warned me the world was changing. I would see and experience things I'd never known existed. Things I would have to accept or deny. This felt like one of those moments. A beginning of my new life, a start of an endless chain that would define my very being.

Joy, I wrote, amazed when the word flowed gold and vibrant my hand. It hovered in the air for a moment, then faded. I reached out again. *I want magic to be good. I want it to be helpful. I want to do what's right. I want to figure this out. But I don't know how to embrace it. How to embrace...me.*

Can you show me? I asked.

Pools of pink and orange melted into view as I settled inside myself, standing in that smoky substance. In the distance, a white light burned so bright it hurt to look at. But it wasn't hot. Hues of blues and greens and golds flickered over my head, turning the dormant, dark space into a glittering world of light and color and promise. The warmth wrapped around my shoulders like a shawl. I touched what I was sure would be fabric, surprised to find a wrap of liquid instead.

Water. Me. My soul.

We would be honored, Zara. The laughter faded, the voices now serious. Goosebumps raced across my skin, sending tingles down my spine. *We will work* together *to shape the world. For that you have our promise.*

It is done. We spoke as one, joined as one. A God and her magic reunited once more. A seal solidified on my soul; a festering wound finally healed. I'd thought this moment would feel more radical, maybe something similar to being struck by lightning. But instead it felt like slipping into a spa. Warm and delicious and the very thing you needed without knowing it.

We can be electric, too, if you prefer. Don't ever doubt that. The laughter was back. Jets of water in a rainbow of colors arched over me, the water fizzing and foaming like champagne. *Time to send you back to the kelpie. Call for us when you need us.*

I blinked as water covered my head, filled my mouth. I started to panic when I realized I was back in the woods staring at the surface of a pool, my fingers fluttering in the chilled water. Liquid dripped from my hair, my skin, my clothes as if I'd been submerged.

Maybe I had been.

"Fascinating." Finn's lips were right next to my ear, his breath hot on my neck, but I felt too good to push him away. He really wasn't that much of a bother.

"Hmm?"

"After three generations of Gods I thought I'd seen it all. But you surprise me." He tugged me back from the edge of the pond. "Watching your magic accept you like that, how the water coated your skin like a shield, a clear shield. I've never seen that before." He looked out over the pond and the animals rustling in the distance.

I took that moment to relay what had happened, what *I'd* somehow accomplished, and he listened.

"I've never even heard of a God asking their magic to work with them," he finally said. "Even we fey *make* it do our bidding." He absently rubbed at one of his silver bracelets, one that was about an inch wide and covered with runes.

"It seemed to make sense. I don't know how it works. Who else can show me?"

"Yes. I suppose looking at it like that, it does seem pretty common sense."

Something else struck me about what he'd said. "*Three* generations? How old are you?"

He jerked a shoulder in response. "We fey live incredibly long lives. In fact, I'm still a baby in comparison to others like me."

"Other kelpies?"

"No."

The playfulness in his face was smothered. I immediately regretted the question. "What did I do differently?"

Finn folded himself gracefully on the ground next to me and trailed his fingertips through the water, idly watching the ripples cast on the smooth surface. I gave him time and laid down on the soft ground. My breathing turned deep and slow, the air crisp on my tongue. I also realized in that moment my impending migraine had faded, leaving my mind cool and clear, not unlike my element.

"Picture a pyramid, will you. At the very top are the Gods. The four elemental Gods. Some may argue there should be more, but it doesn't matter. Whether there should or shouldn't be, there aren't. There are four. Wind, Water, Fire, and Earth. Underneath the Gods are the fey. All of us—and we are plentiful and very adept at hiding. Below us are the priests and priestesses of the Order, then humans, followed by animals, insects, etcetera.

"The Gods are the strongest of all of us. That's why you're at the top. Our myths say the first Gods, the original elemental Gods, were immortal. Truly immortal. And they started off peacefully enough. They were fey and somehow became... more. Bigger. Larger than life. They delighted with their talents, the adoration from the fey over which they watched. They guarded the Earth and kept peace and harmony.

"That seems almost too good to be true," I said. The grass was soft under my palms and tickled the back of my neck.

"It is. They got bored. They demanded entertainment. And the once-peaceful Gods turned into cruel, senseless beings. They bickered constantly, fought amongst themselves, and encouraged war. They grew vengeful, resentful, and jealous. Eventually, they almost caused the end of the world. There was an apocalypse." Finn wet his lips and glanced at my enraptured expression. "That was right around the time the dinosaurs disappeared."

Holy stars. My ancestors had caused mass extinction?

And there were fey around back then?

They really weren't teaching us this stuff in school.

Finn waited until I gathered myself before continuing. "As punishment for nearly destroying the Earth and abusing their powers, the Gods were stripped of their immortality by the very people who worshiped them. It was punishment they accepted because, as the tales go, they felt remorse for their actions. When their immortality was stripped away, they were also cursed with much shorter life-spans.

"That eventually led to the first humans. Because some fey loyal to the Gods denounced their magic, they cast it away from themselves, never to be seen again. Without that magic sustaining their youthful lives, they grew old after several decades and died, joining their original Gods once more in the heavens. One positive for them: when they cast away magic, they somehow regained a startling ability to breed. Maybe it's like rabbits, the constant prey in a monster food chain."

He stood and brushed some dirt off his pants. Reluctantly, I followed his lead and handed over his backpack before shouldering my own. "Then how did the next Gods show up?" I asked.

"As we'd later discover, the Gods never fully vanished because their elemental powers are so unique, so necessary to the way of the world, that without them we would all shrivel. Rather than completely die out, they reincarnate when the world was most at need. Until their eventual, cyclical return, their magic was stored in their favorite pets, the Great Beasts, who were to call upon the Gods in times of need." Finn's hand brushed mine as we walked side-by-side. I recognized the many tall, narrow townhouses lining the street. The pool had been in some sort of community park.

"If that's the case, then why are the fey forced into hiding, like you were?" I asked, trying to puzzle through the story. "Just because the Gods go away doesn't mean magic disappears."

He smiled and waved at car that slowed as it passed. "Not necessarily. Without the Gods and their elemental magic, all magic suffers. As time passes, it dwindles and fades into a pale imitation of itself. While we still retain a little magic, we fey can't use much of it, so we're cursed to live like our sister humans after all." I stumbled over a crack in the sidewalk, but caught myself before I fell. Finn waited for me to steady myself and adjust my bag.

"I'm getting ahead of myself," he said, "because back then, the fey didn't know what was going to happen next. They didn't know where their magic had gone, but they didn't give up hope that it would return. Some chose to adapt and pretend to be mortal. Others retreated into deep hibernation. A few hundred years later, the Gods rose again.

"Understand this, they weren't the Original gods brought back from the dead. These were a whole new set of independent Gods. The world had fallen into famine, and they were needed to solve the problem. With the return of the Gods came the return of magic, and the fey were propelled back into their statuses of power. The problem was solved, things were good for a while, and then the Gods died out again."

Finn stopped at a street corner, uncaring of the police officer watching us closely from a cruiser. I followed him across the street, the hair on the back of my neck prickling with the intensity of the man's stare.

"That's kind of tragic," I said when the officer was finally out of view. "For the fey anyway. Forced to forever partially bear the consequences of actions that they weren't responsible for. That's awful."

Finn glanced over, the streetlight behind him casing his face into shadow. "It is. If they, if *I*, had a choice in the matter, I'd never give up magic. But there isn't a choice. And we must cope."

He scratched his head and turned down another street. As we'd walked, the homes had vanished, replaced by larger industrial buildings and businesses. A light shimmered from the window of a bakery and I wondered if the person inside was preparing dough for the next day.

"But it's been two-thousand years since the last Gods," I finally said. "Why haven't they reincarnated in all that time?"

"I don't know." He said. Then he sighed. "I've heard undercurrents that humans are getting better at handling their own problems. Issues that thousands of years ago would have spelled global destruction aren't happening as frequently. This stretch of time is, by far, the longest the Earth has gone without magic. But now you're back, I can feel magic stirring again. And it's incredible. It's like biting into fresh fruit when you've been marooned on a desert island." He fiddled with his lip ring. "Like seeing friends who passed away long ago."

His voice faded into nothing. Ahead, towering over everything around it, loomed a massive bell tower. He'd led us back to the hotel.

Something was still bothering me. "Earlier you said I was different. In my approach to magic, anyway. How is that?"

He crossed the road. "The Gods have always thrived by wrangling their given elements and extending total control over them, no questions asked. They are the top of the food chain. They are to be obeyed without question. And that extends to the elements.

"But you, you offered a relationship. You offered to work *with* the water." He peered at me as if I were an enigma. Starlight reflected in his gaze. "You could have made it bend to your will. I thought that's what you were going to do when you started out, but you didn't. You *introduced* yourself to it. You drew it to you with a promise. I've never seen anything like it."

He scrubbed a hand over his face, his five-o'clock shadow dark on his cheeks.

"I've never seen anything like it."

I tugged on his sleeve when we stopped outside the hotel. The chill of the summer air soaked through my clothing making me shiver. But there was another question I desperately needed to ask before I went inside.

"Finn, my history teacher told us the God of Air also died in the attacks on the temples." Finn's shoulders stiffened; the line of his spine straightened. "If I'm alive, could they also have survived?"

He stared into the glass doors leading inside, face unreadable. "Honestly, we don't even really know if Fire and Earth still exist. We know the temples were able to erect shields and the Order never publicly stated their deaths, but arguably we don't know anything about the other three Gods."

"You didn't answer my question."

Finn crossed his arms, shoulders slumped as he withdrew into himself. The stillness of the night settled around us like the folds of a blanket. Finally, he said, "It's possible. Yes, it's certainly possible."

"The Kraken says we must find them. How do we do that?" I leaned back, staring into the deep, starry abyss of the sky. It seemed endless, full of possibility.

"I don't know." Finn nudged me toward the door, his movements stiff. "But I promise I'll help figure it out."

9

Geoffrey

"You are an idiot."

My reflection in the bathroom mirror didn't respond, and I kept my eyes averted to the scratches on the backs of my hands. White peroxide bubbles burned in the dark grooves I'd dug with the ragged stubs of my fingernails. A disgusting habit from my childhood that I'd finally overcome nearly two decades ago. Now it was unmistakably back and worse than ever. Both the nail biting and the errant scratching.

I lowered myself to the toilet lid and resisted the urge to flex my hands. I'd scared her back there, the girl. It was obvious the grips of our shared consciousness had freaked her out. Hell, it freaked *me* out, and I'd known what was happening. Sort of. Mentally joining was simpler than I'd thought it would be. I'd fallen asleep with my hand pressed to the four brands, and *felt* for a part of me I'd thought was dead.

And it worked.

There she was.

In some strange hotel room.

Blind, bound, and more than a little panicked.

It was interesting that her magic had fought her.

My phone vibrated against the sink, and I glanced at the incoming text from my friend and commander of my military, before turning it off. Moving swiftly, I unrolled the bleached white sleeves of my dress shirt, buttoned the cuffs, and shrugged on the grey suit jacket I'd flung on a hook screwed to the back of the door. Under the sink, I found a box of multi-sized bandages and I slapped two on the backs of my hands—the large ones that are actually meant for scraped knees and such. As for my nails... well, those were a lost cause anyway.

I darted from the room and descended the stairs that connected my chambers to one of the tallest turrets in the tallest building on campus. It was an old structure, built shortly after the fall of the original Gods, and while it still maintained its original integrity, we'd added modifications over the years. Things like glass windows in the arrow slits, pipes for plumbing, and the all-important *electricity*. A yellow bulb flickered as I moved past. Two of the black-robed acolytes who were supposed to guard my room but were really only good for asking to grab a glass of water in the middle of the night attempted to follow me, but I brushed them away with an impatient wave.

In my eagerness to escape, I'd forgotten one critical thing. The brands that now glowed hot and fierce once more. Brands that had been dull and listless for the past seventeen years. Brands that shouldn't be anything *but* dull and listless now. Their eyes hooked on the beacons shining from my forehead and I could see their fear, taste their trepidation.

As the leader of the most powerful religion on Earth, I was used to fear.

But the power that came with being a *true* Hand of the Gods, that was something else.

It was a crawling sensation that burned in the throat like jealousy, that gnawed in the back of the mind like greed. An ugly sensation that had completely overtaken me the longer I'd been in the presence of that girl, the God of Water…

"Tell no one until I command you to," I ordered the pair. My normal guards had the night off, and while I recognized these men, I didn't trust them. They'd sworn oaths to the Order, but that didn't necessarily translate into oaths of loyalty to *me*. Word would get out soon enough. But there was something I needed to do first before the Council demanded answers—likely in the form of blood.

I kept my head bowed as if deep in thought as I descended the tower, slipped through a door concealed at its base, and entered the purple-hued dawn outside. It was early. Very early. That meant fewer people out and about. Which meant fewer people who could see the evidence of something being horribly, terribly wrong.

I'd meant to console Zara. I'd kept my distance, giving her space. I'd answered her questions and tried to coax her into answering mine. I had so very many, after all. The distinct lack of answers gnawed in my gut. But I'd hopefully have them soon. Soon enough, anyway.

The barracks that housed thousands upon thousands of our soldiers, a tiny portion of our standing army, loomed above. The fortress rose black against the dawn sky, complete with battlements along the edges and a spindly tower that housed the prisoners. The closer my long legs brought me to the fortress walls, the smaller I felt. The campus itself was an enormous, sprawling thing, and this was by far the largest of its buildings. The only one taller was the headquarters where I lived, and the ancient tower that loomed over everything. I slipped my hands into my pockets and focused on a small grey section of the wall slightly to my right where a door was cleverly concealed in the stones.

I'd never liked coming here. I'd never been particularly good at combat. It was why I was thankful for the position afforded to me by my birth, the power I held literally written across my very face.

A position of power I hadn't earned when I'd made my first rash decision.

A position of power I now clutched tight in an unyielding fist.

I refused to feel guilty over my command. I was seventeen and young, impressionable. I still believed the message sent to me by the Gods, but I'd handled it poorly, impulsively. Well, me and the dozen men and women who comprised our illustrious Council. They'd grown complacent in their positions of power; mortal power that gleaned hotter and sharper without the aid of magic and the Gods that ignited it. I hadn't realized the extent of their concerns about potentially *losing* that monumental power until our first meeting after I'd fully embraced my role as Hand.

After I'd glimpsed a dire future.

But when I'd claimed my rightful spot at the head of the sacred table, taken my seat in an ancient chair that reeked of furniture polish, I *had* scented their fear, their anxiety, their resentment. For seventeen years, they'd worried over their fates, waiting for me to assume power. And when I'd announced my intentions to decimate the very creatures that threatened their roles of global influence because of the threat the Gods themselves presented...

I'd realized their relief.

I'd relished in their blood-thirstiness.

I'd allowed them to carry me high on shoulders that gloried in the destruction I'd hewn.

I palmed my shaved head, quickening my pace as pink shafts of light split the barrier between night and day. So many foolish decisions. Such recklessness I'd spend my life repenting. I'd thought I'd rid myself of that feral emotion until I'd met *her*. Until I'd spent time in *her* presence, felt *her* magic stir in my veins.

Something in me had snapped.

I'd gone after her, hounded her like the dog I refused to be any longer.

I'd wanted her power.

It had scared her, but I'd gotten what I needed.

The stone wall was cool against my hand as I pushed a series of bricks inward, a sequence that opened yet another concealed door. This compound was full of them—secrets that is. Secrets that some hoped would die quiet deaths until none remained on Earth to speak of them.

Some of those secrets I knew.

But others I was still fettering out.

"I thought you might have forgotten the way, considering you avoid this place like the plague."

I closed the entrance as a lantern flared to life behind me, illuminating grey-washed walls and the numerous bookshelves and file cabinets lining them. When I turned, I smiled broadly at the man sprawled behind a wide desk across the room; piles of paper, torn post-it notes, and ball-point pens spilled across its surface in casual disarray. The wall behind him was laden with certificates of education and achievement.

"Toren, it's good to see you," I said as I strode across the room.

His gaze settled high on my face and he blinked once. His mouth split in a wide smile, exposing straight, white teeth. I unbuttoned my suit jacket and settled into a chair opposite him. I folded my hands in my lap, shifting to get comfortable.

"I only got back from Hong Kong last night. I was working on my report when I got your text." He waved a hand at the documents directly in front of him, his chicken-scratch handwriting scrawled across the top page. It was, by far, the neatest stack of paper on the table.

"How did it go?"

"Another uprising quietly put to rest. Just a small band of people calling for answers about the Gods and their lack of action. They wanted to know why they aren't able to solve the various problems of the world. We were able to locate their leaders without much fuss."

"Any deaths?"

"One. But we'll be able to bury that pretty easily." His thick, dark eyebrows drew together in a deep furrow. The base of his capped pen tapped on the middle of the page. "I've addressed the situation with my commanders. You won't need to worry about it happening again."

"I have the upmost faith in your abilities." My smile slipped away into something more serious. "If I doubted you, you'd be the first to know. But I wouldn't have put you here if I didn't think you'd be able to do your job well."

He nodded, but didn't look convinced as he stared over my shoulder, eyes unfocused and fixated on a table against the wall. I knew what was on its polished surface: a knife with colorful jewels encrusted in the handle, a gold brooch in the shape of a scarab beetle, and a polished brass lamp. Aside from his certificates, they were the only personal effects in the room.

His lack of conviction was understandable. Despite his many successes since taking the job as general of the Order's military three years ago, many on the Council still doubted his abilities. They did little to disguise their disdain.

I'd met Toren about five ago at some mixer. The Almasi family was well-known in many circles; it was an old name, an aristocratic one. They were derived from an ancient line of rulers who once held supreme power in the part of the world now called the Middle East. Over time, though, that power corroded; over the course of several centuries they lost land, people, and influence. It was a trifecta that almost always spelled doom, and they were eventually left with a modest estate.

But even hundreds of years later, the family still clung to the tatters of its pride and worked to revive some its once-honorable lineage. I was no stranger to his parents and the gleam of greed they couldn't quite conceal from their eyes whenever we spoke. They made a point of attending most Order events even though they couldn't always afford to do so. Over the years, and countless unpleasant encounters where they jockeyed for roles within the church, I'd learned to avoid them altogether.

Their son was an entirely different creature, though.

Toren stood and moved across the room to check the lock on the door. We couldn't risk anyone barging in on this conversation.

Five years ago, the Council hosted a showy, splashy dance that was publicly called a meeting of the world's richest minds, but was really a chance to glean information about those in power and find ways to use that information to extort them. Of course, the Almasi family attended. Lina served as an ambassador to some medium-sized country and weaseled her way into the event.

While trying to evade her manicured grasp, I'd ducked into a shadowy balcony and nearly collided with a young man holding a lit cigar. While I'd clearly caught him off-guard, he gave me a quizzical smile and merely moved over so I could lean against the marble railing. We'd stood in silence for several minutes, enjoying the cool evening air, when he'd reached out, offering me the cigar.

I'd taken a puff, relishing the delicious taste that danced across my tongue, and when I'd remarked on the brand, it was like the world lit up in his eyes. He'd launched into some diatribe about the nuances of flavor and quality, a conversation I could actually relate to, and we soon found ourselves discussing everything from smoking habits to international trade laws. I enjoyed his eagerness, his educated understanding of the world, and his ideas on how to make it better.

Toren finished toying with the knob, and I scrubbed the smooth wood of the chair as I and waited for him to settle in behind his desk once again. Bullet points dotted one of the crumpled papers on its surface. I couldn't quite tell what was written.

It wasn't until the end of the night, and Lina finally fettered out our hiding spot, that I'd learned his name. I probably should have been dismayed. But I didn't care. I soon sought him out whenever we found ourselves at the same events, our easy conversation helped me relax in ways I was unable to in every other aspect of my life.

When the Order's wizened general died peacefully in his sleep, it was a no-brainer for me to offer Toren his position. He was well-educated and insightful. In my eyes, his youth was something the Order desperately needed within its aging ranks. But to the other Council members, that youth was often considered a detracting factor.

"What did you need that was so urgent?" Toren's low voice pulled me back into the confines of his office. "Not that I don't enjoy our conversations, but I doubt this time you're looking for lively debate."

"No, not exactly." I sighed and picked up one of his many pens and toyed with it. "I'm in delicate situation right now."

He dropped his chin into the palm of his hand, elbow braced on the table. The flickering light from the lantern cast eerie shadows across his broad cheeks and dark eyes. Those eyes flicked to my forehead again, but he stayed silent. I appreciated it.

"I need this to stay between you and me."

"You're starting to worry me," Toren said.

"I need you to agree."

"On top of technically being my boss, you're my best friend. You know you never need to *ask* for my confidence. You already have it." He leaned back and started tapping the pen on the table again.

"The First of Four has risen."

"Given your face, that's kind of obvious, isn't it?" Now that I'd addressed the elephant in the room, he spoke more candidly. "We always knew it was a risk. It was always possible one of them might surface at some point. So which is it? Fire or Earth?"

"Water."

He rubbed his chin, thumb working circles against his jaw. He stared over my shoulder.

"How is that possible?"

"I don't know."

"You saw the child yourself."

"I did."

"You saw the *brand* yourself."

"I didn't lie."

"The temple was left in ruins." His line of questioning was as methodical as ever.

"Also true."

"Then how is she alive right now?"

"You're asking all the right questions," I said. "They're questions I've asked myself any number of times over the past twenty-four hours. I'm coming to you because I don't want to worry the Council yet. I know how they'll react, and I'd rather try to handle this without their interference first."

He stood, calf-skin boots clicking on the floor as he moved around the desk. He liked to move when he thought, he claimed it helped speed up his brainwaves. I turned in my seat. Rather than typical suits, he wore elegant vests and loose pants that allowed him to conceal weapons on his person.

"What are you thinking?" Toren asked.

"I want to bring her in. I want to hear from her about what happened."

"And what about your vision? They're going to bring our destruction. Wage war against the Earth."

"I still believe it."

"And you don't want her dead?"

The mistake that wouldn't stop coming.

I twisted my cuff-links. Despite my tumbling thoughts earlier, the path to me now seemed clear.

"Do I think there might be another way to stop the Gods? Yes."

"But…"

"If that doesn't work, I will still take her out."

He twisted on his heel, arms folded across his chest, broad shoulders tense. "What do you need from me then? You seem to have this figured out."

I dug into my pocket and tossed a note on top of his desk, right on top of the paperwork he had yet to complete. I'd recognized the bell tower image. I'd recognize the symbol of the Order anywhere. And that particular spire was distinct. Distinct in both its relationship and proximity to the Water Temple.

"Do whatever you must to bring her in."

10

Zara

It was late.

Incredibly late.

Kaz was going to kill me.

The elevator dinged overhead, that same cross between a doorbell and a dying cat from earlier, and the heavy doors slid open. It felt quiet. Way too quiet for a Friday night. Nervously, I checked my phone again. Plenty of battery life but no messages aside from the one I still refused to deal with from my mother saying we needed to talk. Why hadn't anyone reached out? Why hadn't Kaz? She normally hounded me whenever I wasn't immediately within reach. I nibbled a fingernail, wondering at the uneasy feeling that had sprouted in my stomach.

It was fine. Everyone must be out and about. The bars were still open at this hour. That's why I couldn't hear anything coming from behind the closed doors I passed.

Not even the dull murmur of a television.

I shifted my duffel bag from one shoulder to the other so I could reach my back pocket where I'd shoved my room key. I hesitated, holding it before me, looking anxiously between its shiny surface and the card reader fitted beneath the brass knob. The uneasy feeling in my gut spread, growing like a parasite. What was wrong with me? Kaz was pissed at me for being late. Maybe that's why she hadn't texted. She was mad. That was hardly enough for me to feel like I'd run from the scene of a crash.

But I couldn't hear the bright chatter of my teammates from the other side of the wooden surface. It was hardly late enough that everyone would have already passed out from a heavy night of partying after our big win.

I admonished myself and rolled my shoulders. I slid the key into the lock and turned, feeling the door heave as the deadbolt slid back.

The soft glow of the television bathed the room in bluish, fluorescent light. It was muted and an anchor from some national network silently delivered the latest update on the threat of an impending nuclear attack. Code red. The color flashed in the upper right side of the screen. A familiar color. A terrifying color. But not as terrifying as the scene in my room when I finally realized what I was looking at in the darkness: familiar faces—pale and stony in death.

My duffel smacked the ground, but I barely heard it as I moved inside the room. I couldn't feel my fingers. My arms and legs jerked in a strange disjointed manner as I edged toward the bed. A knot clogged my throat; I couldn't swallow past it no matter how hard I tried.

These were girls I'd competed with for years, celebrating wins and suffering through defeats, swimming through late nights, and sweating in early mornings.

My hands flew to my chest, pressing hard as I struggled to draw air. The edges of my vision sparkled as tears clung to my lashes.

Four people sprawled on the set of queen-size beds. My legs shook when I recognized Erin's curves and Diana's sleek black hair. Dorian's tattooed arm lay across Camila's stomach. Their eyes were closed as if asleep. The world seemed to move in slow motion as I reached out to Dorian, noticing a reddish froth staining the edges of her mouth. I touched her throat, checking for a pulse. Her skin was cold and dry, smooth like plastic. I pulled back, scrubbing my shaking hands against my shirt to get rid of the feeling, and nearly tripped over something on the floor.

My teeth clicked together, clipping the tip of my tongue, and blood filled my mouth. Twins Letty and Lola were crumpled, face down, arms locked tight around each other. Beside them, face-up, slumped Riley. The television flickered eerily on her wide and glassy eyes.

I stumbled back, gasping, and knocked into the body of an eighth girl collapsed on the dresser. I cringed as her body slipped down, landing on top of a hair-dryer on the floor. I vaguely remembered seeing her from one of the other teams. My chest felt tight; something wet landed on my hand. My numb brain realized I was crying. Tears slipped down my nose and chin as sobs shook my chest.

These girls, my friends, were all in various stages of getting ready. *Gods, they hadn't even gone out yet.* Whatever had happened, whatever struck them down, had come less than an hour after the meet. Fingers of horror slid icily across my chest. I could have been here. Had Finn not demanded my attention... I would have been here.

I would have come back with Kaz.

My breath caught in my chest, a scream tight behind the ball wadded in my throat. The bitter taste coating my tongue thickened, and I struggled to breathe. I needed to find Kaz. She had to be in here. We shared this room.

I paused by the bathroom door, my breath coming in gasps through my lips. It was closed. It wasn't like the entire team was here, but the ones we called friends were. There wasn't a chance in hell she would be anywhere else.

"Kaz?" Was that my voice? That high, shaky sound full of dread?

"You in there?" The silence settled like a physical weight between my shoulder blades. One of my hands pushed on the door while my other turned the knob and it slid open, catching a bit on the cotton towel one of the girls had laid down as a makeshift rug. The door swung wide and I dropped to my knees, tears streaking down my cheeks, dripping on the floor.

My best friend, my closest ally, my favorite person, was slumped in the fetal position, legs curled loosely to her chest. Her beautiful hair was wrapped in one towel and another was tucked around her chest. She'd been getting out of the shower when she'd fallen, impacted by the same thing that killed the other girls. A pool of blood surrounded her head, turning the towel bright red. She'd hit it on the edge of the sink when she'd gone down.

But it was her eyes, those once highly-expressive eyes full of warmth and kindness, that I knew would forever haunt me. They stared at the doorway, at the one hand extended toward the opening as if asking for help, looking at me. Accusatory. Disappointed.

I wasn't here when she needed me most.

If I'd been here, maybe there was something I could have done. Anything.

I was almost unaware of the high keening noise coming from the back of my throat, the banshee shriek of grief. Barely aware of the cold tile under my knees as I slumped forward, my hand straining toward her cold limp one.

My fault.

My fault.

The nonsensical words revolved in my head, a broken record spinning and spinning.

My fault.

My body jolted as I was pulled back against a warm, firm chest; a large hand folded over my mouth, finally closing off that awful noise.

"Shhh, Zara, shhh. Please for the sake of all that is holy, be quiet. We need to get out of here. Now." Finn. His hushed voice shattered my frozen state, ripping my shock to shreds.

I tore myself from his hold and twisted, smacking him square in the chest, the violence in my fists fueling my rage, my pain. He let me hit him twice more before throwing himself around me again, bracketing my arms to my sides as I flailed, struggling to get free. My breath came in hard and heavy now, large gulps of dizzying oxygen.

"Enough Zara. I need you to calm down." His voice was firm now, commanding. My body immediately stilled, responding to an authority figure. "You can freak out later, but we need to get out of here. Now. I don't know how much of the gas you've already breathed in."

Gas? I fell limp in his arms, and I think he sighed in relief as he hoisted me up in his arms and out of the bathroom. Kazandra's eyes still stared accusingly at me as we left.

My fault.

As I heaved in another breath, my brain finally recognized the wrongness of the taste coating the inside of my mouth. I tried to spit but couldn't draw enough moisture to my tongue. Now that the shock had been knocked from me, the incredibly real danger I was in hit like a tidal wave.

"Can you walk?" Finn asked. The blue-striped walls of the hallway stood out in stark relief. I couldn't recall him pushing through the door and setting me down. His hands now held me upright, my duffel slung over his shoulder. I shook my head and he swore, gaze darting up the hallway to the elevator before he hoisted me over his other shoulder. Long legs took us toward the emergency exit.

"Alarms," I heard myself say.

This didn't feel real.

It couldn't be real.

"No. I can control the fire exit alarms." He shouldered his way through, taking care to not knock my head on the frame, and sprinted down the flights of stairs. I remained silent, the rhythmic pounding of his feet jarring my body uncomfortably. His grip was firm as he adjusted me again to push the ground-level door open. Once outside, Finn set me down. "I know it hurts, but I need you to run. We need to get somewhere safe. I promise it's not very far, but I can't move as quickly if I'm carrying you. Not in this state, and I can't risk transforming right now."

I was still gasping, heaving for air. My mind felt detached from my body, and my stomach was roiling and churning, but I nodded all the same. His vibrant urgency pushed some primal instinct deep inside me. His face was pale, eyes intense as he searched mine, but his lips firmed and he gripped my chilled and shaking hand, tugging me through the streets.

I recognized some of the buildings but couldn't quite figure out where we were going. All I could do was press a hand to the soft back of Finn's t-shirt and trust him to guide the way. And I managed for a while. But after it felt like we'd been running for forever, I finally stumbled, tripping over feet that I'd stopped feeling ages ago. I couldn't focus. I couldn't see. A headache blazed through me, threatening to swamp me in a migraine. The strangled gagging that was my breathing sounded far away.

Finn dropped to his knees, cool hands cradling my too-hot cheeks, eyes tearing over my face. The sharp movement caused my head to swirl, a jagged motion that shot right to my trembling belly. Saliva finally filled my mouth and my throat clicked. I batted at Finn's hands, forcing them away and twisted to the side, collapsing on my palms as I heaved up what little I'd eaten the day before. My shoulders hunched again and my stomach rolled, expelling sea foam green bile. Finn rubbed my back in soothing motions and held my hair back from my face.

We stayed like that for Gods knows how long, my body fighting something that I couldn't quite understand, and the kelpie doing what little he could to comfort me.

Finally, I collapsed on my back, my throat burning angrily as my abdominal muscles quaked and quivered with exertion. I could see again. And I could kind of focus: a small miracle. Of course, the thing I focused on was a pair of eyes that burned jade on a face that was the color of the moon. Finn's hand gripped mine hard and I squeezed back, reassuring him I was okay.

Sort of.

"What's happening to me?" The rasp barely wormed past my worn-down vocal cords.

He shook his head, his mouth in a hard, grim line.

He said, "I hate to ask this of you, but we need to keep moving. It isn't safe here, but I have a place where we can go."

My muscles protested as I tried to move my arms. Yeah. Moving was literally the last thing I wanted to do. But Finn needed me to do this. And I needed *him* right now. "Only if you help me up."

Dark bangs fell across his face as he nodded and stood with a groan, pulling hard on my hand still clasped tight in his. Everything screamed at me. Literally everything. Muscles that I'd never known existed screamed, muscles inside my muscles screamed. But I stood nonetheless, forcing my coltish legs to cooperate. "Let's go."

He tugged my hand again and we raced toward a wooded area that smelled like the sea. The salty, briny scent only grew stronger as we surged toward the water's edge. I don't know how long we ran before the sea emerged, dark and ominous and frothing with anger.

"My home is nearby. It's my safe haven if you want to call it anything. Somewhere that I hibernate. We'll be okay there for a little bit. It's small, but no one else knows about it," Finn explained as we encroached upon a large mass of rocks. At the base, he paused and ran his hands up and down my arms as if reassuring himself I was still there.

"It's on a small chunk of land that juts into the sea. We need to get you near water. That's going to make you feel like a million bucks again." His attempt at humor fell flat.

He hadn't been wrong about anything yet so far, so he was probably right about this, too. But when I tried to move my legs again, nothing came. I was done. My poor body had nothing left to give. My knees locked, pitching me forward into the kelpie's body. He grabbed me as I slid to the ground. He tried to hoist me up, but stopped when I started trembling violently. Blind and deaf to the world, I let the waves of pain pull me under. Dry heaves wracked my struggling body, a body of which I was quickly losing all control.

Knives stabbed into my brain, spears shooting down my spine. A giant pulling on my arms, quartering my limbs. What was going on?

Somewhere I thought I heard Finn curse as he rolled me to my back, trying to cushion my head on his legs as my head knocked backward repeatedly. The motion sent shards of glass right into my sensitive nerves and down my body.

I was seizing.

Then I blissfully blacked out.

11

Geoffrey

"Explain."

Rage wasn't a hot enough word to explain the turmoil coiling greasily in my chest. I doubted a word existed for how I felt in this exact moment. The second Toren slunk into my offices, head bowed and hands clasped tight around his back, I'd *known*—known something had gone horribly wrong. On this, this was unacceptable.

"The girl escaped."

"So you said," I gritted. "How, for the love of the Gods, does that explain a room full of dead girls?"

His face was ashen, eyes downcast, everything about his body language read remorse. For once, he wasn't fidgeting with a pen or a button on his vest. The magnitude of the situation had shaken him.

Good.

My knuckles whitened as I clenched fists around the rounded arms of my seat.

"These were two of my best men in the region, you have to understand. I wouldn't have trusted anyone but the best with an assignment of this scale," he said and sat down. His fingers wrapped around a document in his lap. "They were disguised as police officers armed with an arrest warrant. It was something menial, assault, but enough to bring her in without raising any red flags."

"Alright," I muttered.

"Since you knew her first name and general appearance, it wasn't difficult to verify her identity and track her down. She was in the hotel where you said she would be. After they explained the situation to the manager, they released information about her room and my officers proceeded to the proper floor. Following protocol, they knocked on the door and one of the girls inside allowed them entry. That's when things get a little tricky." Toren's haunted eyes bored into mine as he implored me to hear him out, understand exactly what went wrong.

Through my teeth, I gritted, "Continue."

"She wasn't in the room. The girl who answered the door said they didn't know where she was and they hadn't seen her since a swim meet ended earlier that day. They showed the warrant, explained how serious the situation was, and asked the other girls in the room if that was indeed the case. The other girls seemed to agree with that assessment." He finally looked away from me and unfolded the paper in his lap. "I want to make sure I get this right, so I'm reading from their report."

"Go ahead," I said.

"My lead officer says when they turned to exit the room, the door swung open and the subject entered. While they recognized her from your description, they asked her to verify her identity to be sure. She answered that she was, in fact, Zara Ramone, and asked why they were there. When my lead officer presented her with the arrest warrant, she became agitated."

"It actually says 'agitated' in the report?" I asked. "If someone presented me with a fake arrest warrant I'd probably be more confused than anything."

The page crinkled as Toren peered down at it. His dark brows pulled together in a vee as he reread what was written. "Yes... it clearly says agitated."

I snorted but waved at him to continue.

"My second officer says when he reached for his handcuffs and asked her to turn around, she started backing toward the open door. She claimed there was a misunderstanding, and that she wouldn't come with them without speaking to her coach first. They told her that wasn't permitted—"

"I'm starting to see how this went so wrong," I interjected, fingers flying to my temples. They pressed against the pressure points. Hard.

Toren cleared his throat. "When they moved to approach her, she became violent. It says quote, 'her eyes began glowing and the walls rattled as if the pipes shook within them.'" Toren stopped and looked up, fear bleeding across his face.

"Geoffrey. No one has even *seen* a God in two-thousand years. They were trained, they knew what they were doing. But when presented with that kind of situation, you get stressed out and react." He spread his fingers wide in open defense of his officers.

My jaw clenched around my next words. "And that reaction was to release a canister of our most lethal gas? Does that not seem extreme to you?"

"They thought they were being attacked." Toren jumped to his feet, his report landing on my desk with a thud. "She has magic, she's one of the most powerful beings on the planet. Wouldn't you wonder if she was about to attack you? And if she attacks, you're probably going to end up being the dead one." His voice firmed with resolve. "I would think that. I wouldn't hesitate to react if it was me or them. Especially since they say she pulled a ball of what looked like water out of nowhere. She was clearly ready to do something."

The picture Toren painted wasn't irrational. I'd seen her myself when she was isolated, enslaved by her own magic. She'd lashed out verbally, fought back, argued. Someone with that little restraint over something so powerful could be very dangerous. Maybe she wasn't intending to attack the officers. No, that didn't seem to fit her personality if the paperwork about her past and my understanding of her from our short meeting was anything. But given the appearance of being threatening.

Hell.

I drummed my fingers on the desk, thinking. "Why did they even have Anisra?" The name of the gas was a play on the word for 'death' in an ancient fey language.

The gas was specially engineered to kill both human and fey creatures. Most fey couldn't get sick let alone feel the effects of poisonous gases. In most cases, the only thing that was truly toxic to them was the smoke from ash trees and those were in scarce supply. The Order took precautions tens of thousands of years ago and developed a gas that could wipe out the fey if necessary.

However, the gas had been stored away in the catacombs beneath the Order's headquarters when the Gods failed to rise again fifteen-hundred years ago. To my knowledge, it remained there, under lock and key. Few even knew it still existed. Few—save the Council and me.

"That was under my directive." Toren slapped a hand on the report and leaned in close. An undercurrent of fury tinged his voice. "I wanted them to have protection in case something were to happen. If she was clearly unstable and could possibly take out an entire block of people with her powers, for example, I wanted my officers to be armed in preparation for the worst."

I sighed and leaned back in my chair. The charged emotion slowly seeped out of me like air from a balloon. I scrubbed my hands over my face and brought them together directly under my chin, index and middle fingers pressed together. "What happened next?"

Toren stood straight, chest heaving as he collected his thoughts. He opened his mouth, then closed it and picked up a round, glass paperweight from my desk. He spun it around and around. I imagined he wanted to chuck it at someone. Maybe Zara. Maybe me.

"She bolted the second they dropped the canister. I doubt she knew what it was, but she probably knew it couldn't be anything good. I'm not sure. My officers pulled their masks over their faces just in time. But it was too late for the girls in the room. There is no antidote to the gas and they were hit with its full effects almost immediately." Toren's tone softened and he dropped the weight into my tray of outgoing mail.

"The officers exited and set up procedures to deal with the fall-out." He walked across the room, hands braced above his belt. The cream and black jacket of his uniform was unwrinkled, his medals aligned on his breast. His boots gleamed mirror-bright with polish. "These aren't just any girls, some of them are world champions. And they were all together. It wasn't like they could disappear without a trace."

I swore and stood to stare out the window. Puffy, grey clouds coated the skies like frosting, smooth and even. Beneath them, members of the Order walked with purpose or clustered in small groups to gossip. Everything was perfectly normal outside, a perfect contrast to how perfectly abnormal everything was in here.

"Do you know where she is now?"

"No, but I've got feelers out. If she emerges, which she will, we'll know about it." He faced the wall, a framed copy of the Order's directives in front of him.

"This is a complete and total cluster. Do you understand?" I snatched an orange stress ball filled with sand off my desk and squeezed it tight. "I'm already having a difficult enough time hiding away in my rooms to avoid being seen, and now with this…" I squeezed my eyes shut and leaned a shoulder against the glass to shield myself from the daylight.

"I can't hide from the Council much longer. I have meetings I can't cancel. This was supposed to be open and shut and instead…"

"I understand. I know I failed you. But I'll make it right. Give me another chance, please." He turned back to face me, arms sliding across his chest. A muscle in his jaw ticked. "I promise you I'll make it right. Don't tell the other Council members. You know how they feel about me and even though this is the first time I've messed up. They could try to use this to unseat me."

His earnestness was impossible to miss.

Stars, what a nightmare. But that's exactly what it was. A nightmare. It wasn't an end-all-be-all. This could be fixed. Everything that went wrong made sense in the most horrible kind of way. I just needed to figure out another way to get to her, find another way to bring her in. I wasn't ready to give up on her yet. Not over a misunderstanding.

I heaved a breath out and moved toward a bookcase laden with legal texts. "Where are the officers now?"

"I took care of them."

Dead then. It was a very "Order" way of dealing with things. Isolate the situation, kill everyone involved, protect yourself on the back end.

"Do they have family?"

"No. They were devoted to their work and little else," Toren said.

Another very "Order-ish" way of life. Complete and total dedication to the job.

I squeezed the stress ball again and slipped a hand into the pocket of my tailored blue slacks.

"I understand what went wrong. There were bad decisions made all-around."

Toren rubbed his mouth and nodded in a defeated kind of way. "I'll prepare my res—"

"I wasn't done talking," I interrupted. "You messed up. But you only messed up once. And as long as the situation involving the girls is contained, it will only be that. A screw-up. I will give you another chance to bring her in. But you better be more prepared than that. Use more force if you need to, and bring her in. But no Anisra."

Toren sighed and moved to a shelf where he toyed with the spine of one of the thicker legal texts I kept there. He was acting normal again. Whatever tension between us had dissipated.

"And Toren, I have to tell the Council what's going on. They won't find out about this particular incident. But they will learn that she is alive. You will need to act quickly because once that ball starts rolling…"

"It will roll right over everyone." Despite the threat hanging over both our heads, his shoulders dropped as the tension leached from them. "Thank you for giving me a second chance. I mean it. I won't let you down."

"I know." I walked over and squeezed his shoulder. When he moved toward the door, I offered one last piece of advice: "Make sure you pay the coroner well."

12

Zara

"All your fault."

"Your fault."

"If we hadn't met you, *you monster*, we wouldn't be dead right now."

"Monster."

"Traitor."

"Snake."

Whispers soft as feathers and sharp as razors permeated the air, barbed wire wrapping tight around my skin, pinching tight, and cutting deep. I wanted to push them away like some sort of physical being, but when I reached out I couldn't. I was bound.

"Beast. Demon. Monster."

A soft, red light flickered on, bathing the room in blood. My eyes bolted shut, but it was too late. I'd seen them. My friends, my teammates, girls that I'd laughed and cried with. All of them standing in a semicircle around my body where it hung, dangling from the ceiling by hemp wrapped around my wrists. The rope tore deep into my flesh, and blood trickled down my arms in warm streams. The bodies of my friends were contorted, cold. Their skin the glossy color of spoiled milk. More than two dozen glassy, dead eyes stared at me, accusations flaying me open more effectively than any whip.

Directly in front of me: Kazandra. Her lank hair spilled over her bare shoulders barely covering her breasts. Her skin was rotting away, her cheeks caving in as her head tipped at an odd angle as if someone had wrenched it that way and then left her like an abandoned Barbie Doll. Her smile was more of a grimace, complete with holes where teeth used to be. Unlike her peers, her eyes were bright red, her irises an unhealthy yellow.

They were far from unseeing.

They saw me for everything I was.

My true self.

They called me a God.

A lie.

I was a monster.

A cold hand slick with slime wrapped around my throat and I started to choke, eyes sliding shut to block the silent accusations. I wasn't sure why it was my fault they were dead, but it must be. It had to be. Somehow this was connected to what I was. Guilt settled firmly on my shoulders, a weight I'd never shake. They could kill me here. And that was ok. I deserved it. All of it. A lack of oxygen sent my mind into a dizzying tailspin.

I choked and water filled my mouth.

Water?

My eyes opened to reveal a wall of stone. I was submerged. Warm currents sluiced through my hair, sending it swirling. It tickled my cheeks and shoulders. The liquid surrounded me as I clutched my knees to my naked chest, my nose pressed to the bony valley created between them. I was suspended in this oddly peaceful realm where sounds were muted and images were dark and blurry. The nightmare of my dead friends a thing of the past. I exhaled softly, a waterfall of bubbles pouring from my nose.

You're back, the Kraken's voice penetrated my not-thoughts.

I think so.

Good. I need to see you soon.

Like that, Its presence was gone. I unfolded my limbs and reluctantly pushed off the floor of this little slice of heaven. Whatever was on the other side of the surface would be reality. Reality I wasn't quite sure I was willing to face.

All too soon, my head breached the surface; water flowed through my locks and over my eyes. I wiped some of it away and tread a little, slowly propelling myself toward the rocky ledge surrounding the pool. Everything felt a little out of focus, faintly skewed.

The last thing I remembered was Finn's worried face hovering above me as I seized. Speaking of the kelpie, where was he? I braced my arms on the ledge, noting a distinct lack of sharp rocks or edges, and looked around. I was in some sort of large pool set slightly off-center in what appeared to be a decked-out cave. Finn had mentioned some sort of sanctuary, and I believed it if the bed the size of four king beds shoved together was any indication of the luxuries within the cavern. There weren't any windows, but it wasn't dark thanks to glowing blue, pink, and yellow orbs that floated around the edges of the room. They were draped in silky moss hanging from the ceiling. A few trinkets, mostly shells and old cameras and dog-eared books, littered rocky ledges jutting from the walls.

I hoisted myself out of the pool and darted toward a clothing rack by the bed. My feet left small puddles on the ground. I tugged on a red polo that dwarfed me, and feebly tugged the white string around the waist of some grey sweatpants as tight as it would go. They still barely clung to the edges of my hipbones. It would have to do. It wasn't like I was going to actually see anyone.

Hopefully.

As I dressed, I took stock of my energy. The queasiness was gone, the rotting taste of death in my mouth vanished, the tiredness had retreated, my sore muscles healed. I felt invigorated. Finn had promised to get me somewhere safe. He'd promised the water would heal me.

He'd been right.

Now I needed to find the man himself.

The massive room opened up opposite the wall framing the bed. Through it, I could barely make out a slip of the clear, blue sky. Or maybe it was the sea. Hard to tell from this angle. My feet ghosted across the floor, naked without my signature high-top Converse, and I clutched my sweatpants tight with one hand. I didn't trust the string to hold.

I squinted into the sunlight, a hand shielding the worst of the rays. Turns out the strip of blue was the sky. The sea was actually a whirling, frothing, angry mess of grey. Sitting on a ledge hanging over the waves was Finn, his legs dangling over the edge as if teasing the waves to rear up and grab him. His shirt was crumpled in a ball next to him; the summer sun glittered off his golden skin and chiseled abs. As I approached, I noticed thin, white scars scratched across the muscles of his back, neck, and arms. Other, much larger scars, crossed lower toward his hips. It looked like something had taken chunks out of him and left holes behind. I wondered about the story behind them.

"It's rude to stare."

He didn't move as I padded over and sat down. Like him, I chose to dangle my legs over the ledge. The spray of the sea tickled my toes, and the frothy anger of the water below lightened, its intense fury diminishing.

"It started calming down a few hours ago. That's when I knew you were going to be ok. I'm glad. I'd be officially the worst guardian in the history of the Gods if you died within hours of officially being placed under my watch."

I chewed over that for a minute. "It isn't just me controlling the water, then? It responds to me and what's happening to me, too?" I swirled my fingers through a spray of saltwater, feeling it wrap tenderly around me in a light caress before sinking into my skin.

His eyes opened and that now-familiar gaze washed over me. I hadn't realized until now how much I'd needed to see that expression—a maddening combination of relief and exasperation. "Yes. Your element is an extension of you and your emotions, your abilities, your resolve, your resilience. It's both a weapon and a defender, a lover and a fighter. And remember, it's only as strong as you are." He pushed his weight off his wrists and brushed his knuckles together producing a soft swishing sound. His dozens of bracelets jangled. Then he leaned forward, elbows braced on his knees.

"How are you feeling?"

I rubbed the side of my neck, taking silent inventory. "Pretty incredible, actually. I felt like I was dying before, it hurt so much. I felt like I was slipping away into nothingness. It's much better now. Thank you." I gripped his biceps hard, and it swelled under my touch. "Whatever you did was a miracle."

"Not me, the Kraken." He shook his head, his hair ruffling a bit in the wind, refusing to look at me. "Water has natural healing qualities to it, and we were able to use it. Keep that in mind if you ever need to help a friend who's in a grave situation. Since you're the God of Water it works much better and faster, like turbocharging a battery. Given the graveness of your injuries, all that stuff on your skin, I figured it would be best to submerge you. The Kraken took over from me there."

"How long was I under?"

"Oh, I don't know. About a day, maybe more."

That was a long time. Gods knew how worried my parents and

coach were right now. I needed to call my mom at least, try to get a hold of her and tell her I was OK. She must be freaking out.

"Where's my phone?" I demanded, grabbing Finn's sleeve.

"Waterlogged. I tried to dry it out, but…" He plucked it off the rock next to him and handed it over. I clicked the side buttons and jabbed at the screen. Nothing happened.

"Why is it waterlogged?" I asked.

He shifted and pulled a leg up to his chest, fingers curling around his knee.

"How much do you remember?" The boy could seriously never answer a straight question.

"All of it."

"You're lying." He scrubbed his hands over his face, his pained expression causing my heart to twist in my chest. "What happened at the hotel was no accident. I think you were supposed to die."

He probably didn't mean them to be cruel, but his words echoed those from my nightmare.

My fault.

Despite the warmth of the sun's rays, I felt chilled. I drew my borrowed shirt tighter around my chest as if to fend it off. "Die?" My voice was dry, crackly like fall leaves.

He nodded and started brushing his knuckles together again.

Swish, swish. Swish, swish.

"Trust me when I say I know things because I've lived things. There are things I know I can't explain, things I don't want to explain," Finn said.

That didn't sound good.

"What killed your friends, what almost killed you, was a special kind of gas. I've never seen it in action myself, but I've heard of it. I'm familiar with it. All fey are because it's designed to kill them. I mean, it's designed to kill humans, too, but the point is that it can wipe out *everyone*. Kind of like a nuclear bomb, but more contained.

"It leaves behind a particular kind of residue. When it kicks in, it makes its victims froth at the mouth. That froth has an orangeish-reddish tint. I could see it on your friends." He swung his legs harder and did something unusual. He reached out and grabbed my hand, holding tight. "I think that gas was deployed hours before you showed up. It had started to disperse. You'd breathed in some, but the water pulled it out of you. That's the only reason why you're ok."

"Ok." I didn't know what else to say.

"That's not all."

Because of course, things could get worse.

When I thought I'd hit rock bottom, turned out there was a whole other basement level, some more dirt, and then more awfulness.

"Only one organization on Earth possesses Anisra. That's the Order."

The Order. The most powerful religion in the world. The religion that was supposed to guide me. The religion that... Geoffrey. He'd said he was my Hand. He said he was the leader of the Order. But he hadn't seemed malicious when I'd talked to him. Was that a ploy?

It hadn't felt like a ploy.

"Why would the Order try to kill me? It's supposed to protect me, right?"

He looked away from the water and squeezed my hand again. The lines in his skin hardened into mixed expressions of guilt and frustration. I didn't understand his inner turmoil. Didn't know if I really wanted to.

"I don't think so, Zara."

Nope. I didn't think I'd like what I was about to hear.

Geoffrey's green and grey eyes flashed before me. I recalled the primal expression on his face, the hunger for something, a desire I didn't understand. Until that moment when he'd launched himself at me, he'd seemed fine. Normal, considering the circumstances. A little intense, but who wouldn't be when you controlled an organization like the Order. But after what had happened, with what Finn was saying now, someone that powerful would know how to manipulate.

Wouldn't they?

"What do you think?" I asked Finn.

"I don't just think. I know. I know seventeen years ago the Air Temple fell from the sky and its ruins burned on the ground. I know seventeen years ago the Palace of Water slipped beneath the waves, everyone inside dead or dying." His jade eyes darkened to a shade that was almost black. Rage filled his voice and his jaw trembled with the emotion. "I know seventeen years ago it wasn't terrorists that attacked like you've probably read in your history books. I know the Order was behind the whole thing."

That couldn't be right.

The Order wouldn't do that.

Not to their Gods, not to their reason for existing.

I didn't want to believe it, couldn't believe it.

I took a shaky breath, scrubbing my hands on my forearms. "How do you know that? How do you, out of everyone on Earth, know that?"

His knuckles swished in silent contemplation. "I know the Order tried to kill you the first time. If they already tried to kill you once, they wouldn't hesitate to try and kill you again."

"Finn—"

He stood, not hearing my pleas. The boy who I'd felt a connection with beside that pond, the boy who'd pulled me from a room of death, slipped farther from my grasp than ever before.

"We need to get going."

"What aren't you telling me?" I stood with him, pushing into his personal space by putting my hands on his solid chest. "What's going

109

on?"

"That's a story for another day." He tried to smile, but failed miserably. "You need to trust me."

"I don't trust you." I countered. "I don't even know you."

"Then trust Lucy. We're going to see her now."

13

Zara

"I need to talk to my mom. I need a phone." I gripped Finn's arm, forcing him to feel my urgency. "Or my coach. If I can't talk to her, I'll talk to him. He can then call her for me. I've been missing for an entire day. They must be sick with worry."

"I understand." He nodded, face set in grim lines, and braced his hands on my shoulders. "I'll see what I can do in town. No promises because I'm not sure what I'll find at the hotel. But I'll do my best. Now you stay here and wait for Lucy."

He was leaving me. Actually leaving me on a beach in the middle of nowhere minutes after he'd admitted to keeping secrets from me. I threw my arms in the air but didn't try to follow. The pull of the ocean was too strong. And, though I wouldn't admit it to him, going back to the hotel scared me a little.

I flopped down on the ground. Thick grains of sand ground painfully into the backs of my legs. I didn't mind it. The pain meant I was still alive. I was still alive and my friends—and my *best* friend—weren't. I would never swim with them again. We'd never grab meals between intense training sessions, never find cute guys to flirt with.

They were gone. And I wasn't.

A breath shuddered out of me. It was all too much. I'd never seen a dead body before. I'd never even lost anyone particularly close to me. And now both had happened simultaneously.

A sharp chunk of shell jagged across my hand, and I realized I'd been clenching my fists too tightly. Blood welled around the cut. I examined the blood closely as it spread over the webs in my skin. Even my blood didn't look the same anymore. It was still red, but it had an odd gold, glittery sheen to it.

Someday you will be able to heal that yourself. It's one of the gifts with which the God of Water is blessed. The Kraken's voice was soft against my mind, like a paintbrush moving through watercolors. One of Its huge tentacles threaded delicately through the low tide and wrapped around my foot comfortingly. The cut healed as I watched. *But until you learn, Finn and I can help heal your physical wounds. The pain in your mind and heart though, that isn't so easily handled.*

Thank you, I responded and left it at that. If I thought too much about what I'd lost, I feared I would collapse in a puddle of guilt, unable to get back up again. The tentacle gripped my foot tighter for a moment, similar to how my mother would hold me close as a child, before slipping back under the swells of water.

I understand you aren't ready to talk. If it's alright, I'd like to work with you on your training.

I'll try, I replied. *But don't blame me if I find it difficult to focus.*

I have faith. Remember, this is only the beginning, The Kraken responded, Its easy patience grating on my tender nerves. *A lot is being thrown at you. You've experienced incredible loss. But you're strong. You'll get past this. As long as you focus. And focusing on your training is what's important right now.*

I threw my hands in the air and scooted away from the edge of the sea, my heart twisting painfully as I broke the easy bond between me and the Great Beast lurking beneath the waves. I shook out my ill-fitting sweatpants, turned around, and stopped. I couldn't act like this. I wasn't five anymore. I walked back into the shallows, the water lapping around my ankles and calves.

What would you have me do?

You've already established a connection with the water. In fact, it rocked the sea in its intensity. It's a strong bond, possibly the strongest I've ever felt. Now you need to see what you can do with it.

So, what? Make a wave? A hurricane? Create a new geyser? What?

Have some fun.

That froze whatever tirade was on the tip of my tongue. Have fun? I knelt in the water, my clothing immediately saturated.

Have fun? I repeated back to the Kraken.

It didn't answer.

Okay. I clenched and unclenched my fingers a few times, rolling the pads over the fabric covering my thighs. How to have fun? What would be fun? Everything felt so bleak. How could I even think about magic, about using it, especially for my own enjoyment, when my friends were all dead? When *Kaz* was dead?

Tentatively, I reached for the bond I'd created with my element. I sighed in relief when I found the fluid rope connecting us. I tugged the rope and felt my element eagerly respond to my request, tripping over itself to see what I wanted. Colorful light flashed, the liquid pooling and moving around me like a lava lamp.

Hey there.

We've been worried.

I know. But I'm here now. And I'm not going anywhere. The blue strands of whatever "we" were swirled around me in a mini-tornado touching my clothes, my skin, my hair, my *soul*, before settling down. I could still feel the electricity pulsing inside and out. I took that as a good sign.

I need something from you.

Anything. It, we, they, didn't hesitate.

I want to have some fun.

They giggled, a rich and tinkling sound similar to chimes. My spirit lifted and a smile touched my lips for the first time in what felt like weeks. It was such a freeing noise.

We are good at having fun.

My fingers flexed as an idea spun through my mind. My jaw popped as I exerted pressure on my molars, trying to figure out how to make what I wanted to happen, happen. Something hot and thick welled up in my veins. First, it flooded my feet, then my calves and upward, the dense, fluid substance spinning up inside me. Soon the heat filled my fingertips, and the chattering of my magic hit a fever-pitch, their excitement filling my chest with love and anxiety and nerves.

I lifted a hand. What I saw made my knees buckle. The world had shifted. It was like seeing it through a different lens, a new filter. Metallic bands of bluish-silver energy laced through the waves, darted under the surface of the water, threaded through the birds overhead, and the shellfish hiding under rock and sand. As the ripples of energy approached me, they grew hotter, whiter, until it pooled in a liquid puddle *inside of me.*

I was electric.

I was a blazing beacon awash in a sea of green and blue and white.

You're seeing the world as it truly is. It's called Iridescence. The Kraken's voice touched my mind. *All we are, all anything is, is energy and essence. As the God of Water, you are connected to all living things, for water flows through everything to survive. It's an incredible but a deadly ability, one you will learn to master in time.*

Curious, I searched for the thread connecting me to a seagull preparing to dive into the waves. It slid into my fingers like the line to a kite, and I tugged. The bird twitched, its balance thrown off enough to miss whatever it had been aiming for. Shocked, I released the thread, and the bird shot back into the blue skies overhead.

I had done that.

I had influenced its behavior.

You see. A truly dangerous ability it is. The other Gods will have similar influences. But your tie to living creatures is the strongest. You must always be aware of the consequences.

Even though I'd done something bad, I felt giddy. My thoughts were as light as campaign bubbles.

Now, show me what you were going to attempt, Zara.

The use of my name snapped me from my state of reverie, and I pulled the threads of energy back to my fists. I concentrated on the smooth surface of the water about twenty feet away and imagined movement, imagined the creature in the forefront of my mind. Energy trickled from my body; the water rose up in a small hump and immediately flopped over.

Not what I had in mind.

Try again, the many voices of the water chimed in my head. *Try again.*

Like with swimming, this wouldn't beat me either.

I grounded myself in the waves lapping around my thighs. The rhythmic movement helped stabilize my thoughts, and I plunged my hands into the clear, cool substance; my fingers dug deep into the sand, begging the water to give me all it had. The same warm, thick sensation bubbled up in my body, faster than before, and soon it sparked in my hands, flooding the backs of my eyes.

Once more I pictured movement, imagining a liquid hare skittering across the surface of the sea, and demanded it *happen.* The voices in my head cried out, and when I opened my eyes the water rose up and a creature formed: first a strong set of back legs, then a textured, fat body, two more legs, a wiggly tail, and a large set of ears later, and a hare perched on the water, sniffing and twitching.

Go, I called, and it rocketed forward.

Mind-blown, I rocked back on my heels as the hare skittered over the water, directing it back and forth, acutely feeling its connection to the water, to me, and to everything as if it were an extension of my own body.

Something heavy touched my shoulder, and I jerked like I'd brushed against a live power line.

My concentration shattered. The hare exploded in a firework of droplets.

As my concentration broke, part of *me* broke away with it. My mind, my being, my essence retreated behind something *else*. No, that wasn't right. Some*one* else rose from deep inside of me and *pushed* me back behind it. I felt my control over my body slip as something else took over. I could only watch helplessly, trapped behind my own eyes.

Whatever *It* was pulled my powers together, throwing up measures of self-defense I could barely comprehend. Water and energy soared toward me, rising in a massive wall of water between me and the attacker. *It* summoned an undertow, one so strong that even the most adept swimmer wouldn't stand a chance against it. Then *It* tugged at the water relentlessly, dragging at whoever or whatever was threatening me, *us*. A second, imposing wall of water rose at my back, arching high over my head, sucking in the massive amounts of water. A tsunami.

Someone was yelling.

The noise registered on some level, and I felt part of me shake free, pull away from whatever was holding me back. But as I gained the small foothold, I was shoved back. This time *It* landed on top of me, holding me down. Vivid purple eyes sparking with lightning and anger glared down at me, enraged at my feeble attempts to shake it off. Energy wrapped around my throat, choking me, and another tendril slid through my ears into my brain.

And I was gone.

I *was* It. And It was me.

We were one of the same.

Not human.

Beyond human.

God.

I embraced the feeling, the power, the energy. The rawness of it.

Whoever dared combat me would live to regret it.

More energy swirled and I embraced it. I loved the swirl and pull and twist, the burn of white and blue. They were going to pay.

Enough. The word rippled through me, a force of nature I couldn't ignore.

It robbed me of my abilities. One moment I'd fully embraced my element, and the next it was gone, leaving me gasping.

It retreated, pulling its tendrils of tempting, all-encompassing power back with it.

My body collapsed, caving in on itself, the stillness of the water a shock from the frothy anger and aggression that I'd fueled it with earlier.

I struggled to drag oxygen into my lungs, each movement burned. But it wasn't a good burn like earlier. This was the fight to survive. Salty water dripped down my face into my mouth, slack in open shock. Rivulets streamed down my lank hair and over my skin, sticking to my shirt and soaking into the sand as I braced myself on hands and knees. Raising my head felt like lifting a hundred-pound weight, but I made myself do it, made myself look at whatever had come at me earlier. Finn fought to his feet, my shock and awe reflected in his face as he stared at me. Had I hurt him?

"What was that?" Finn asked.

He was OK.

Thank the Gods.

14

Zara

"Are you ready to talk about it?" Finn asked.

I shook my head slowly. After reassuring me multiple times that he wasn't injured, Finn and I had returned to his cave in silence. He'd allowed me to brood with my back against one of the walls for a solid ten minutes before getting impatient with the whole ordeal.

"You lashed out at me using an incredible amount of power. Do you want to talk about that?" Finn asked. He sat on the bed, elbows braced on his thighs as he leaned forward.

"Not really."

I remembered the white-hot burn.

I remembered the unearthly high.

I remembered the tsunami and the satisfaction of seeing it rise for me.

And I remembered not knowing what in the stars was happening; I most certainly didn't want to talk about it. It was bad enough being a slave to my own body without reliving it. I motioned instead to a canvas bag Finn had dropped at my side. I tentatively touched the fabric.

"I'd rather talk about what's in the bag."

"Some clothing. Food. A few other odds and ends." Finn fanned his arms wide. "A phone."

"What?" I jolted, my arm already in motion as I ripped the bag open. My fingers floundered around the clothing and locked around a familiar-shaped box. I tugged the flip-phone out and opened it, stroking the raised keys reverently. "Why didn't you say something earlier?"

"There were more pressing issues," he drawled. "And then you decided to sulk, so I figured you needed a minute."

"Next time, get right to the good stuff, no matter how I'm feeling." I muttered, already keying in my mom's number. She'd forced me to memorize it among several other emergency numbers when my competitions first took me overseas. I paused. "This is equipped for international calling, right?"

Finn quirked a brow. "I may have been asleep for seventeen years, but I'm not a complete idiot."

Ignoring him, I pressed the little phone button on the keypad and thrust the speaker against my ear. It was silent for a few seconds, then started ringing. I was shaking, nerves rattling with apprehension. She had to answer. She had to—

"Hello?" Relief coursed through me, from my toes to the top of my head. "Who is this?"

"Mom?" I called, my voice high and small like I was a little girl again.

"Zara? Is that you? We heard from your coach…" A static burst interrupted the call. Then "…we've been so worried."

"I know, Mom. I know." I sighed shakily. "I promise I wanted to call sooner. I'm OK. I know what happened at the hotel. I know about the team and… Kaz. Everything has been crazy and I had to run, but I'm figuring it out." The words tumbled over one another in a rush to escape my mouth. "You won't believe what I've been through, what's been happening. I'm with someone who—"

"—hard time hearing you, honey." Something metallic clicked on the line. The tiny hairs on the back of my neck raised. "But I need to know if—" More static.

"What? Mom, what do you need to know?" My fingers gripped the plastic so hard I feared it might crack. Finn dropped down in front of me, brows lowered with concern. "Talk to me, Mom. I can't hear you."

"—come home. Be careful..."

The line went dead. My mouth dropped open and I jerked the phone away from my face to stare at the small, illuminated screen. I pressed the call button again and again, heart pounding harder and harder when only a busy signal came through the speaker each time.

"What's wrong?" Finn asked, tugging it from my limp hands. I'd thought I'd feel relieved having finally gotten a hold of my mom. But the complete opposite was true.

"We were having a difficult time hearing each other, lots of breaks in the connection," I said, staring down at the four bars indicating a strong signal. "Then she started talking about being careful and something about coming home. And the line went dead. Now it won't even connect."

He frowned down at the device and experimentally pressed the redial button. The screen read "calling" and then "number no longer in service."

"Did anything else sound strange to you?" he asked.

"Something clicked, but it sounded funny, like the line was interrupted for a moment. But it wasn't fuzzy or staticky. I don't know what that was. But otherwise—" I yelped when Finn smashed the phone on the ground. He scowled at the pieces and kicked them into the pool. "What was that?"

"I think someone was listening in."

I stared at him, comprehension dawning. "You don't think…"

"I think there are powerful organizations out there. And I think one in particular would be very interested to learn where you're going next." He cracked his knuckles, jaw locked. "I also think we need to get out of here sooner rather than later."

"Why do you keep insisting the Order has something to do with his?" I was back on my feet, fists clenched at my sides. "Why can't it be… I don't know. The CIA or whatever the British one is called. Why would my own religion come after me?"

"I know that Order agents were crawling all over that hotel." He glowered at the pond. I bit back whatever I'd been about to say. "I know those uniforms. And I know one woman there who says she works for them seems mighty upset your coach already went public saying you're missing."

My mouth went dry. I backed up until my knees hit the bed, and I sank into the soft mattress. Finn finally turned around and walked toward me, the zippers on his pants jangled with every step.

"The Order is now offering to help find you," he said. "They're looking for you right now. If you think about it, they have absolutely no reason to be interested in you unless they know exactly who you are. Otherwise you're just another swimmer. A famous swimmer. But just a swimmer." Finn shook his head. "I don't know how they found out, but they did. And I bet it has to do with the Hand."

My hands twisted in my lap. I couldn't keep what I knew from him any longer. "He came to me."

"Say what?" Finn's voice was deathly calm.

"Geoffrey. The Hand. He came to me. In a dream. He said we were connected, he knew about my magic. But he seemed crazy," I pleaded, trying to ease the shocked betrayal reflected in Finn's face. "He also said he didn't want to hurt me. He said he only wanted to find me, he wanted to talk, and then he did something or knew something and…"

"And then your teammates died. Apparently of carbon monoxide poisoning, if the coroner they paid off has anything to do with this." Finn's fist crashed into the wall. Several books fell from a shelf. "And you didn't think to tell me any of that until now."

My lip curled. "I'm not the only one keeping secrets," I fired back.

"Fine." He clutched his hair in twin fists and pulled so it stuck up in spikes. "Fine. You're right. I deserved that. But now, as your guardian, I'm saying we really need to get you out of here, away from them. Will you agree with me on that?"

I nodded. No matter what Geoffrey had said in the dream, the evidence looked pretty damning. "Do you have a plan?"

Finn let out a laugh that sounded more like a whinny. "Do I have a plan? Of course I have a plan. And it's genius." He tugged some papers out of his front pocket and dropped them on the bed next to me. My bag landed next to them a few seconds later. "Get changed. We're making you into a boy."

"You know this only works in movies, right?" I asked, spinning before a mirror Finn had drudged up from Gods know where. "And even then it's pretty iffy."

"Nonsense," said Finn, "you look great. This hoodie is the right amount of baggy."

I tugged the brim of my baseball cap lower on my head. After washing away the dried sand and salt and grime of the sea, I'd pulled it on along with the grey sweatshirt, baggy jeans, and black sneakers. But instead of looking like the 22-year-old dude on my fake passport, I actually looked more like a twelve-year-old kid. Green contacts concealed the unique color of my eyes, and I'd tried to contour my face using some of the makeup Finn had grabbed, but I'd given up after two attempts. I was useless with anything outside a mascara wand.

Metal rasped and I whirled, crossing my arms in an X in front of me. "I swear. If you try to cut my hair one more time..."

Finn muttered something I couldn't understand, but dropped the shears on one of the shelves without further protest. I'd pitched the nastiest of fits earlier, complete with flying fists, when he'd tried to cut my hair the first time. It seemed he wasn't quite ready to broach that subject again.

"What about you?" I asked, propping a hand on my hip.

"What about me?"

"Are you going to change?"

He tilted his head and zipped his backpack with a metallic zing. "You seem to forget I've spent the last few centuries finding ways to stay invisible. I'm already a nobody. *You* are a girl who won two gold medals. *You* are a girl who is now one of the most sought after missing people in the world."

I blinked and started rummaging through my bag. "But what about the security cameras? What if they picked up your face anywhere along the way? I mean, you were hanging out there for a bit, you know," I swallowed, forcing myself to not get sucked into that horrible night, "when everything happened."

"Excellent point. That's why I had some new paperwork drawn up for myself." Of course he had. A man as seemingly obsessed with details as he was wasn't going to let something like that slip. I shuffled my feet. "You are now looking at," he passed a hand over his face slowly, "your older brother!"

I sat upright with a jolt; he'd slightly altered his features as he'd passed his hand over his skin. The piercings remained, but his face was fuller now, less angelic, complete with alabaster skin, freckles, and red hair that curled over his ears. Finn flashed a dazzling Colgate-commercial smile, and shook out his body, preening under the attention. I watched in amazement as he shrunk a few inches, gained a few pounds around his waistline.

"That's incredible." The words slipped out as I got up to circle him like a prized pony. It really was all about the details. Finn looked like a completely new person.

"Babe, you ain't seen nothing yet."

"And what do I call *you* now?"

"Neil." He pulled his wallet out from his back pants pocket and flipped it open, showing me his driver's license. "Nathan and Neil. Aren't we just adorable?" I tugged one of his curls and watched it spring right back into place before slanting him a look.

"If you say so."

He gave me a mocking half-bow and moved to grab his bag, but I stepped in front of it. "And where exactly are we going, *dear brother*?"

"Hmmm. I really thought you would forget about that minor detail." He sat on the bed and patted the spot next to him. I crossed my arms over my chest and frowned. "We really need to disappear. I was thinking now would be a good time to hit the Caribbean. Lots of water around, plenty of opportunities to train, etcetera, etcetera."

"You promised to help me find the other Gods." My tone was dry.

His smile fell away. "Killjoy. In that case, there are a few things we can try."

I wrinkled my nose and motioned for him to continue.

"First." He patted the space next to him again. This time I sat. "First, I'd recommend trying to feel for the Gods with your mind. That seemed to work with your magic. Maybe it will work here."

I scratched my neck and folded my legs underneath me. The sooner we got this figured out, the sooner I could try calling my mom from somewhere else. Like before, I sank into myself, pleased to find that dark void gone and colorful hues in its place.

Hey magic, are you there?

Of course, what do you need?

Can you locate the other Gods?

A pregnant pause followed. A pink ribbon of magic swirled around my middle and I tugged at it, delighted when something buzzed against me. When I thought I might need to ask again, the voices returned. *A map.*

A map? I asked.

The kelpie. He has a map. Push your magic into it and use it to guide your way.

I blinked and found myself outside myself once again. Finn's bag was next to mine and I pulled it closer, rooting through the contents until I discovered a collapsible paper map in the front pocket. "What made you think to grab this?" I asked, unfolding it on the bed.

"Call it intuition."

"Interesting." I reached for my magic, a satisfied smile sneaking across my face when it pooled in my hand, ready for my command. Praying I was right, I pressed the blob to the middle of the map right over the Atlantic Ocean and waited, letting my essence fill the page. I focused on finding what was lost, trying to find a person I didn't know yet. I could feel my magic pooling and flexing and feeling for something when it popped.

A bluish glow burst from the United States.

I bounced on my knees and said out loud, "I need more."

Finn watched warily.

Trust yourself. Closing my eyes, I touched the paper again, this time with the tip of my finger, moving it across the page, waiting to feel something. Anything. A zing raced through my chest as I crossed the center of the nation. The Midwest. I tried moving up and down, tapping each state in turn, but that was the best I got. A regional awareness. I pulled back with a huff.

A cool hand pressed on my shoulder. "Hey, that was really good.

Considering neither of us really knows what's going on here, you narrowed down the possibilities a bunch," Finn murmured. Part of me took comfort in his words. Part of me still considered the lack of precision failure.

"But where do we start from there?"

Finn thought for a minute. "Well. I need to see a friend in Kansas City about a dog. Let's start there and see where it goes."

15

Geoffrey

"Y ou look like death warmed over."

A coffee mug filled with liquid that smelled enticingly like a vanilla-flavored latte was shoved underneath my nose.

"That's why I brought you your favorite morning treat." Toren settled into the seat beside me, a cup of his own black coffee cradled in his other hand. He took a sip and smacked his lips. He looked better this morning, healthier than the last time I'd seen him exiting my office.

"Have you made any progress?"

He sucked on his lips and bobbed his head in a so-so way. "Not really. But it's a waiting game at this point."

I nodded and folded my fingers inside the handle of the mug, twisting the cup first clockwise then counter-clockwise. It smelled delicious and looked even better, with the design of an opening rose artfully worked into the foam on top. But my stomach was in knots and the more I looked at the light brown drink, the steam rising from the rim, the more I wanted to hurl it across the room.

"I take it your meeting with the Council didn't go well."

"That's putting it lightly."

"What did they want from you?"

"Answers I don't have."

Toren sipped his coffee again and set it on the table in front of him, looking around the dining hall with vague disinterest. We were in the central part of the compound and I'd selected a table in the middle of the room where everyone could see me. I wasn't hiding my face any longer. If rumors were going to circulate, I wanted them to be because of my deliberate action. Not lack of it.

It was the middle of breakfast rush and it was packed, but despite the lack of chairs, there had been open seats to either side of me until Toren sat down anyway. Eyes lingered as soldiers and nurses and IT workers stuffed scrambled eggs and toast down their throats. I ignored them all. Toren ran a hand over his curly head of hair and eyed a soldier who looked more than a little helpless.

"Do you remember being that new?"

I didn't. I was practically born here, raised by people as bloodthirsty as they were manipulative. This dining hall was as familiar to me as a normal person's kitchen. But I shrugged to avoid talking about it. The soldier looked across the sea of bodies one last time before seeming to reach some sort of internal decision. The tray trembled in his hands as he crossed the room. He bee-lined toward us, gaze averted, and took the spot next to me. He leaned away, one butt cheek hanging over the edge of the chair in his effort to maintain distance, and I hid a smile.

"So what are they doing, then?" Toren asked.

"The Council? They heard me out. You're free to proceed as we originally planned. Bring her in." I rotated the cup in my hands. It was no longer steaming and the rose on top was starting to blur. "They'd rather she was dead, but they also want to know what happened, where she's been all this time. They want to know if she can drag the other two Gods out of hiding."

My gut clenched at the thought of Zara in the hands of the dozen members that made up the Council. Each member represented a specific region of the world; many had their own specialties as well—like trade negotiations or land acquisitions. Our governmental structure most closely mirrored that of a monarchy. Nearly everyone at the table was born into their position. The only odd ones out were Toren and the Council clerk. Both had assumed their positions only because their predecessors died heir-less and without extended family.

We had firm rules in place guarding against regicide. Those didn't protect just me, but everyone else on the Council, as well. They were to prevent members from killing one another and either seizing their power or using the lack of opposing power to their advantage. If one member killed another, they and the rest of their family, cousins and all, were to be put to death immediately.

The Order was big on bloodshed.

"You should drink that before it gets cold," Toren said, nodding at my mug.

I was thinking about the horrors that might await Zara now that the Council knew about her illicit existence, and I shook my head. I tapped the soldier who'd bravely bitten the bullet and pushed the mug toward his tray. His pale face turned ashen as he first looked at the mug, then at my forehead, then the mug again.

"Here, you can have my coffee as a special treat for joining our ranks. I'm not thirsty anyway."

Wide brown eyes blinked beneath bushy brows. I couldn't tell if he understood what I'd said or not. Surely, we didn't employ complete idiots, did we?

"But you always drink espresso to start your day," Toren said. "Are you sure you don't want that?" Toren reached for the mug and the soldier appeared more than happy to let him take it. I knocked my friend's hand away.

"No, I'm one-hundred percent positive I don't want to drink any coffee today. I'll puke it up if I do. I'm not feeling very good. I also insist that this good man here..." I trailed off, waiting for him to introduce himself.

Another slow blink before recognition kicked in. "Mateo. Mateo Lopez. Private, first-class."

"...Mateo, enjoy it with his breakfast instead."

Toren's gaze flicked from me as I stood, to the mug, then back to me. The muscles in his jaw flexed before his lips twisted in a brittle smile. "It's like I don't recognize you anymore."

I raised an eyebrow at Mateo, who obligingly lifted the cup to his lips and sipped, before smiling at Toren. "I think I'll take a nap," I said to Toren. "Then maybe I'll be able to focus later today. In the meantime, I expect that report on Ukraine on my desk when I wake up."

Toren took another sip of his coffee in silence.

16

Zara

Finn forced me to hike to some small town nearby. From there we grabbed an Uber outside one of the small 'mom and pop' diners and headed for the airport. I'd tuned him out about seven miles back when he started talking about magical signatures. I only checked back into his one-sided conversation when he called me out for not doing enough to contain my magic.

"You're like a beacon, noticeable as a lightning storm at midnight."

"How exactly was I supposed to know that?" I grumbled. "You've never mentioned it before. I don't know if I can turn it off."

Finn grabbed my wrist and ran a thumb over the soft skin on its underside. It felt nice. I almost forgot I couldn't stand him until he said, "But you can. You have to, or you'll draw every fey creature in a 50-mile radius right to us. And since we're going to an international airport, that's a lot of beings."

"If I'm such a draw, then why didn't more stumble across us at your *humble abode?*"

"I cloaked that area an incredibly long time ago." Of course it would be that simple. Why hadn't I thought of that? Oh yeah, because I was quickly learning that I didn't know anything about anything. "The shield somehow held up over the centuries. Besides, it's more difficult to sniff out a God when they are hidden than when they're mingling with tens of thousands of people."

"In that case, what should I do?"

"Think about it like wrapping a second skin around you, but this skin is like a black-out curtain. It keeps what's you inside and obscures it from those outside. Your magic will make it happen. You have to want it to. Give it a try, kind of like you did earlier. It may take a few times, but once you figure it out it'll become an instinct."

I tugged on the now-familiar threads of my magic and hummed as energy danced over my skin, sinking deep like lotion. My stunt by the sea helped me identify exactly where it was and how to draw it to me. I formed my query and set it loose, feeling the magic respond to my request eagerly. A thin, electric film danced around me and sank in. After a few tests, I didn't even feel like I was being strangled in plastic wrap.

Finn visibly relaxed next to me, his hand falling from my own to play with his own leather bracelet instead. "That's better."

"Why didn't you say anything before?"

"Everything's happened so quickly I haven't had a chance to." He said and nibbled on a nail. The lines around his eyes and mouth relaxed, nearly vanished. "It's like looking right at the sun. It's something incredibly intense and beautiful and even though it hurts, you don't want to look away. You're kind of addicting, like a candy I've craved for too long and finally found again." He snorted and I had a flashback to Geoffrey when he'd stared at me with a similar expression. "But now that you've cloaked, it's like you're just another powerful fey."

I wished I could wrap my fingers in my hair and pull it around my face like I used to do when I was younger and wanted to shut out the world. I didn't like feeling like a burden. I especially didn't like that I was a mystery to myself. Instead, I hummed in the back of my throat, clenched my fingers tightly together, and shut out everything around me, ignoring Finn's attempts at small-talk on the remainder of our trip to the airport.

I was feeling overwhelmed again and wished I could be alone for a few minutes.

I stayed quiet even after Finn paid our driver and hoisted our bags over his shoulder. I followed him through the automatic sliding doors, schooling my face to mask my inner fear. I was an imposter. So was he. This could go wrong in any number of ways.

At the ticket counter, Finn finagled his way through the complex series of stops we would need to take before actually getting to K.C. When he and the woman helping us seemed satisfied with whatever compromise they'd dreamed up, we grabbed our tickets and headed to the checkpoints. Despite my heart hammering hard enough I was sure the security guys could hear it, we made it through easily. My fake passport was glanced at and dismissed. I truly was a ghost.

A few minutes later we were sitting in the terminal, snacking on cheap burgers and chips with our bags haphazardly tossed on seats next to us.

Finn seemed to know I craved space and eyed the international news program playing on the screen above us with a skeptical eye. The United Nations Security Council was in a special meeting today; it was a closed-door meeting as they reassessed the threat coming from a group of three rogue nations banding together. Together they were equipped with a massive arsenal of nuclear weapons at their fingertips. These were countries that weren't even supposed to possess the knowledge to develop nuclear weapons, let alone be ready to launch them. But there they were, fingers over buttons demanding action from the rest of the world.

America had finally finished developing its missile shield, and the barrier now stretched in one large, light-blue dome encompassing the entire continental United States. Smaller shields were being erected over Hawaii and Alaska. The European Union was fuming over the whole thing, demanding access to the information so they could speed along their own defense programs, but the U.S. wasn't budging and slapped a big red confidential seal on the whole thing.

The whole point was moot anyway. If the nukes were launched, there wouldn't be much Earth left to even entertain the idea of sustaining a population. But I supposed everything was about appearances, and, well, it was an election year after all. The zippers on Finn's pants jingled as his knee bounced up and down while he listened to the report.

He was truly incapable of being quiet.

"What impact will the reemergence of magic have on this whole deal?" I asked, waving idly at the TV while slurping the last drop of Coke from between the remaining chunks of ice cubes in my to-go cup.

Finn's bouncing stopped, and he stretched his long legs out before him, crossing them at the ankles. He folded his hands behind his head and leaned back into the webbing with a sigh. It felt weird seeing him with red hair. He almost seemed approachable. "Hard to tell, really. Whenever magic rears its head, technology tends to fall to the back-burner. Call it the whole human versus fey complex. Whenever one rises to power, they tend to expound upon their natural abilities exponentially.

"What's unique about *this* situation is the sheer firepower we're talking about here. Weapons capable of destroying the planet in a few pushes of buttons haven't been around all that long, certainly not long enough to have to contend with the consequences of magic. Magic can be finicky. It's been known to completely shut down technology, sometimes it merely slows it down, sometimes there isn't any impact. Basically, we'll have to see."

I played with my straw, considering Finn's words. He gave me one long look and began flipping through a magazine he'd snagged at the checkout counter. Something about golf, I think. The terminal started to fill up as our departure time ticked closer, and I examined the faces of the people around us, surprised to see fey mingling with the humans. Startled, I looked around the room, but no one else seemed concerned.

I poked Finn in the side. He glanced up from his magazine. "What's going on?"

"What's going on where?"

"Why can I see the fey? And why isn't everyone freaking out?" I pulled on the bill of my cap.

Finn surveyed the terminal. He replied, "You're magical. You can see past their glamour for the most part." He returned to his magazine. I shoved my hands deep into the front pocket of my hoodie, trying to be inconspicuous as I peered down the aisle.

Across from me, a woman with flawless, dark chocolate skin and elongated, tipped ears tapped out texts on a cell phone. When she glanced up, I sucked in a breath at her lack of whites in her eyes and slits fanning out around her nose. Down a ways, a man twisted what I first thought was a dreadlock around his finger, but then realized it was really a long black snake, one of many spouting from his head. A small child peering out the monster-sized windows at the tarmac was actually a troll, and a winged creature the size of my big toe with purple-spiked hair was head-banging to a mini-iPod on the windowsill.

"How many Fey are there?"

He answered without looking up. "Well, it's hard to tell really. But I'd say it's about a 60-40 split in favor of humans."

I swear I saw stars for a minute. "You say that like it's nothing."

"Among us, yeah, I guess it is. That's why it's interesting to see what will happen with the shift swings back in favor of magic. Considering how long it's been since the last switch, humans are in for an incredibly rude awakening."

"Have any fully emerged yet?"

He wrinkled his nose and turned another page. A model posing in a gold bikini beckoned with one elegant finger. "Maybe in some smaller communities, sure. But most won't try yet. Magic is still really too fresh a concept for them to completely unmask.

"Most are waiting for a reason, call it a flash-bang moment, to come out of hiding. In many ways, it's easier to stay hidden, especially with how weak the magical field is right now, and how long it's been since people actually saw fey let alone still believed in them. Give it a few months and sure, more and more will start stepping from the folds."

Talk about revolutionary.

"What do they see when they look at me?" I thought about my cloaking spell and Finn saying they'd look at me and think I was any normal fey.

"You look human. But that's not a bad thing," he hastened to add at my expression of alarm. "Many fey look like humans. In all actuality, it isn't all that strange. Like elves," he coughed the word out like it tasted bad. "Being fey really only means 'possessing magic.'"

That shut me up and I spent the next half hour in a haze of thought. I barely noticed when we were called to board, didn't pay much attention as we found our seats, and only vaguely noted the wheels leaving the ground.

17

Zara

I huddled in my seat, face buried in my sweatshirt, biting back moans of agony.

I couldn't concentrate past the raging migraine that swallowed me whole. It had started about an hour into the flight and refused to let up. Finn nudged my side and I flinched before lifting my aching head. I tried to open my eyes, immediately snapping them shut when the overhead light cut a searing wave between my lids. Yeah, that wasn't going to happen.

"Hey, what's wrong?" Finn pressed his lips to my ear, speaking quietly.

"Migraine." I forced the word out between clenched teeth. I leaned against him and buried my face in his shoulder, trying to shove the pounding in my head away.

"That's weird," he murmured, rubbing my back in a comforting motion. "Being what you are, you shouldn't get sick. Or deal with human health issues for that matter, even things like migraines."

Hearing him, but neither comprehending nor caring, I groaned again. He slung his arms around me, pulling me close. It felt good. If we weren't careful, we almost stood a chance at becoming good friends. Maybe even great friends. Hell, this migraine had me all kinds of messed up. I tried to stop thinking. Maybe that would make the pain go away.

"Have you always had migraines? Headaches?" He said this in the tone of a man who'd had some major epiphany. "I've seen you rubbing your temples, but I figured it was a nervous habit."

With my face still pressed into his chest, I nodded weakly and brought my arms over my head to keep the light from sneaking through the crack. *Where was he going with this?*

If anything, Finn now sounded even more excited, and his voice got louder, only softening when I flinched against him in pain. "I need you to try something for me, Z. I know it really hurts right now, but I think this will make you feel better. No, I promise it will make you feel better." He moved against me, pushing me back into some sort of sitting position despite my pathetic protests.

"That's right, sit up. Open those eyes." I pursed my lips but didn't even think about doing that. Promise of no pain or not, I wasn't going to subject myself to that horror. "OK. Fine then. *Don't* open your eyes. But I do need you to reach out with your magic and find the glass of water on my tray. Find it, and then I need you to manipulate it somehow. Something small. Make it spin or slosh or rock or something."

I definitely didn't know where he was going with this, but I was able to muster up enough strength to send a strand of energy out around me like a force field, a radar searching for a target. The water blipped red on my metaphorical screen and I zoomed in. Carefully, oh so carefully, I caused it to form a funnel inside the glass, working up the sides but never breaching the rim.

"That's good, really good," Finn whispered. "Now, how are you feeling?"

That phrase, that one simple phrase stopped me cold.

The crippling migraine from before, similar to ones that kept me home from school for two straight days, was pulling back. The nausea receded. I risked slitting my eyes and breathed a sigh of relief when I didn't immediately feel like gouging out my eyeballs.

"How..."

"Your magic. It has to be your magic. Your entire life your magic has been calling to you, demanding attention from you, but you've never had an opportunity to release it until now." The more I spun the water around in the cup the better I felt. I balled my hands in my lap and fully sat up, looking around at the full plane for the first time, blinking soberly.

"Say that again?" My voice came out hoarse, and I reached for the glass after stopping the momentum to take a small sip.

"Think about it like this. You have a lot of magic, too much magic to control, and it's all building and building inside you because you didn't have an outlet. You bottled it all up and eventually, like anything that's become too much for its container, it exploded.

"Maybe the headache is a warning of that imminent explosion, maybe it was the explosion, I don't know. But what I do know is that you need to make sure you constantly use your magic in some way. It doesn't have to be anything major." He waved a hand at the glass I'd emptied. "But it needs to be something. You have to siphon off the extra stuff because you're a God. You're a literal repository for energy and magic. And since you're the First, you probably have even more energy than the others!"

"You're saying my migraines were always caused by my repressed magic, and now that I have an outlet, I'll finally be migraine free?" I asked stupidly. Seriously, why was this, of everything else that had been thrown my way, the hardest thing to grasp?

"Yes!" he exclaimed. "If you ever start to feel a headache coming on, remember that you need to burn off some of that extra magic you're carrying around."

I looked around the cabin and grunted, wishing I could tell what time it was, but the darkness made it impossible. I was suddenly ravenous and wondered when dinner would be served.

18

Zara

"Why are we here, again?" I grumbled. My hands were braced on my hips as I stared up at the sign boasting the words: *Dirty Deed.*

A nightclub.

Finn had roped me into coming to a freaking nightclub.

"I told you back at the hotel. There's a guy I need to talk to here. His name is Ryder. I used to know him a few years ago," he said, brushing hair out of his face. My eyes narrowed. A few years could mean anything from seventeen to four-hundred. "We need backup and he knows everyone in the industry. He'll be able to get us some security as we track down the Gods."

"Would he have answers about my parents?" I'd tried calling my mom at the airport when we'd landed using a phone at the help desk, but the number was still out of service. I'd tried calling my dad's phone, too, but he didn't pick up and Finn told me not to leave a voicemail. "Or about the Order?"

Finn stepped forward when the line moved, and smoothed his hands down his black, button-up shirt. "It's entirely possible."

"Does he know we're coming?" I asked, looking up at the sign again.

"Yes."

"Is this the same guy who gave you that package?"

"No."

Earlier today, after changing planes four times in about nineteen hours to finally get one that landed in Kansas City, I'd expected Finn to make us hunker down in a hotel and rest for the night. But he'd caught me by surprise when he instead opted to rent a car and drove us to some neighborhood an hour away from downtown, and then vanished inside a sketchy-looking house with broken windows and weed-ridden, uncut grass.

When I'd reached the limit of my sanity twenty minutes later, he'd emerged at the door, waved at a dark, shadowy figure inside, and strolled to the car clutching a package the size of a large Stephen King novel. He wouldn't even let me touch the stupid thing and tossed it in the back seat without as much as a word.

The kelpie was silent on the way back downtown where he rented a room with two beds using that crazy, never-ending reservoir of money he seemed to have. It was a good thing he was loaded because I'd lost my wallet somewhere back in Norway and couldn't even *think* about touching my bank accounts without alerting everyone to my presence.

At the hotel, I'd changed and removed my contacts because they burned my eyes. Then I'd tried watching television. Someone had already tuned it to national news coverage and the first image on the screen was my face. The story was a short one and similar to what Finn had told me. Eight world-class swimmers, all on fabulous career trajectories, died tragically when carbon monoxide filled the room at the hotel they were staying at. But one of the swimmers remained missing.

"Anyone familiar with the whereabouts of Zara Ramone is asked to call their local authorities immediately," the clip from the police chief's interview with media said. "At this point we don't believe her to be in any danger, but her parents are concerned about her well-being."

A quick montage followed, highlighting my achievements and those of my friends.

I'd gone a little numb again seeing the familiar faces. Thankfully I'd talked to Mom as soon as I could, because I couldn't even imagine how much this news would have worried her and my dad. But I couldn't figure out why she hadn't contacted my coach about it. Or called the authorities.

The television went black and Finn shielded it with his body, the remote clutched in one hand. "That's not helping anything."

"I was watching that," I had protested without any real heat.

"And I turned it off. Now go shower and change. We're going out. We're meeting with a guy I know."

I'd expected an office building or maybe a restaurant since it was getting late. But a nightclub hadn't occurred to me in the slightest. The beat rippled through my body, and for the first time all day I allowed the invisible weight of worry to fall from my shoulders. Maybe I needed this, a change in scenery. If we stayed at the hotel, I'd probably spend a sleepless night dwelling on everything that had gone wrong in my life.

We finally reached the front of the line and I presented my ID to the bouncer at the door. He didn't even so much as glance at the fake license and stamped a blue, double overlapping D on my hand. His fingers lingered over my skin after pressing the cold rubber to it, and I frowned as I pulled it back, giving Finn a glance. My counterpart winked and flashed his ID in response. The bouncer didn't linger over his face as he had over mine, and he ushered us through the door and into the darkened club with one last look that settled on my lips.

"Thank you for coming with me, Z." Finn mashed his lips to the shell of my ear. It seemed to be his favorite way of talking to me lately.

"Now let's go find Ryder and maybe get a drink."

Finn grabbed my hand, dragging me toward the bar. This might be a club complete with a stage for live musicians and dangling cages for dancers, but the bar was its centerpiece. It was raised off the ground. Five steps circled it completely, the fifth step butted right up under the ledge forcing customers to look up at the bartenders while ordering. It created a weird power structure and discouraged mingling. But that didn't seem to bother anyone, considering it was practically bursting with people all waving cash and hollering at the two bartenders, demanding their share of colorful beverages with inventive names. To their credit, the bartenders pushed out drinks about as quickly as they were shouted.

The mass of bodies didn't deter Finn. He pushed through the sweaty, hopping crowd and shoved me ahead of him when we reached the edge of the sticky bar top. His chest pressed against my back. The counter was high up, and only the top half of my chest cleared the surface. It was a peculiar feeling. The energy, the music, the beat of the room pressing against me made me lightheaded. A flash of green in the crowd snagged my attention, and while I was puzzling it out, I missed the gesture Finn flicked at the bartender, something that caught the man's attention faster and more effectively than any of the flirty women and the men waving twenties.

The man passed three glasses of beer to a guy standing behind a pair of tittering girls, and I took a moment to admire the flex of his biceps, the stretch of tattooed skin over his muscles, before he turned our way. All the breath in my body heaved out when those eyes met mine. If not for the bar top and Finn's arms, I would have fallen to the floor.

Amber eyes rimmed in shimmering gold bracketed an elegant nose. A lazy grin stretched across his face, a welcoming answer to my reaction. I was smiling. The feeling felt strange on my face, but I

145

couldn't stop. It felt *good*. From the razor's edge slashes of cheekbones to his strong jaw, even the dimple that popped in his left cheek, he was delicious as sin. He ran a hand through his midnight hair, cut in choppy two-inch lengths and styled in haphazard spikes, and crouched down, his long, rangy body briefly vanishing from view.

He looked like—and could very well be—the Prince of Hell. But I didn't care.

Tingles raced down my arms and I rocked my head back, heart rate sputtering back to life when I hit Finn's chest. I'd forgotten he was there. His answering rumble of laughter told me that he clearly *hadn't* forgotten. He briefly gripped my shoulder again, our water magics twining together like cats stretching before a warm window.

When the bartender reemerged, he clutched a clear bottle filled with liquid that looked like electric-green lightning loosely in one hand. He caught my eye again, then looked over my head at Finn. They appeared to have some sort of silent conversation that ended when the man nodded and motioned to the female bartender behind him. She scowled but moved to take orders across the whole bar, somehow moving faster if it were humanly possible.

This must be Ryder.

Stars above, Finn had left a lot of information out.

He set the bottle down with a loud thunk and three shot glasses appeared next to it in short order. The bottle sparkled as he tipped it up and poured three shots, his eyes never once leaving mine.

"Matches your eyes," he murmured. His voice was soft but rough, almost grating, like a lead singer in a rock band who just finished a two-hour concert.

One second.

Two.

I failed to respond. What was *wrong* with me? His eyes narrowed in good-humor, and he handed me a glass, making a point to touch my fingers in the process. I swear I saw white sparks fly, but maybe it was only inside me, the fireworks exploding in my chest anyway. But I thought he felt it, too. That immediate spark of chemistry, like a hammer hitting hot metal. In fact, his irises glowed white when we touched, the amber rims of those intoxicating eyes dilating. It only made sense that he was fey.

It would be sinful for any human to look that good and have that sheer amount of raw magnetism.

"What are you?" The words slipped past my lips. They were rude, but I didn't care as I embraced the wave of ecstasy his touch created. He didn't seem to care either as his lazy grin stretched wider, growing darker and more enticing. But he didn't answer.

"It's a pleasure to meet you, Majesty."

I blinked at the title and frowned.

Were Gods considered royalty? I'd never thought to ask Finn.

But he wasn't done yet. "To the return of the Gods," he said with a weighted look at me and threw his head back as he took the shot. I followed suit, gasping when pure euphoria flooded my veins. It wiped away the lingering darkness that marked the past few days. It tasted like it looked: raw and spicy and sharp. Part of me cried out, warning about dangers of the drink that I didn't know, but I batted it back, smiling lazily as the liquid numbed me. It was better, tastier, stronger than any liquor I'd ever consumed.

I wasn't even aware I'd closed my eyes until fingers brushed my face. The bartender's dark smile morphed again as he took in my expression, turning bright and light as the drink bouncing around my belly.

"Now it really matches," he murmured and leaned against the bar on his forearms, almost as if he were stopping himself from vaulting over it and grabbing me. Warmth spread through me. "Go have fun now. No need to stick around for what will, no doubt, be a very boring conversation for you and a mildly entertaining one for me."

Finn grumbled but stepped back. The music *was* enticing. Maybe that was the drink talking.

"Come see me again if you require any *other* assistance." I didn't miss the innuendo and a blush stained my cheeks. "Finn, your message was cryptic. Let's go back to my office."

I turned when a hand grabbed my elbow. "Don't go anywhere with anyone," Finn said, his face hovering close to mine when I looked back. "I'll find you once we figure some of these details out."

Later, stars knows how much later, I pulled away from the masses, desperately needing hydration. I hadn't intended to join in. I'd only meant to grab a glass of water and hover around the periphery until Finn reemerged. But the music was intoxicating. It pulled me in and before I knew it, I was lost.

My blood burned hot, my limbs loose, and I stank of sweat and beer, but I felt *wonderful*. Really good. I'd shed some of the stress dragging me down. I wiped rivers of sweat from my face and sauntered toward the bar. This time only a few dozen people lingered at the bottom of the steps, most already holding drinks as they stood around tall, round tables and talked loudly among one another.

But it seemed that most people had opted to hit the dance floor, alcohol long-forgotten. One of the girls dancing near me said something about tonight's DJ being someone "extra freaking special" but it all went over my head. All I knew was that old-school Linkin Park was blasting, the time change amped up a step, and I occasionally caught the vocals of a different artist, a different beat.

Stuff I knew nothing about.

But I liked it.

As I approached the bar, two rangy dudes with shaved heads and gauged ears stepped in front of me. My guard instantly went up. One of them put his hand on my bare arm to stop me.

"Hey there, beautiful," he told my chest. His eyes hadn't quite made the entire journey up to my face. "Whatt'ya say if we take this party somewhere else?" His friend ran his tongue over the lip of his beer bottle suggestively.

Ugh. He had yellow teeth, and they both stank of cigarette smoke. I pulled the one dude's hand off my arm and shoved it out of the way. They were so not going to kill this lovely buzz I had going. I said, "If I didn't know any better, I'd say your buddy here," I flipped a thumb at the dude with his lips now completely wrapped around the mouth of his bottle, "is the one interested in performing sexual favors."

It took a moment for them to get my meaning. But when it did, oh it was wonderful seeing the leering light die from their eyes and snarls form on their lips.

I couldn't resist. "Favors for *you*. In case that wasn't clear."

"You slut, wait till you see—"

"Yeah, I wouldn't finish that sentence if I were you, mate."

I knew that voice, the quivering mass off gooiness that was my stomach knew that voice, and I tried to brace against it, part of me wondering if it was already too late, the part of me that wasn't loving how he'd come to my aid unasked.

The two punks looked past me over my shoulder where I assumed Ryder lurked. The color drained from the face of the guy who'd grabbed me, and he took a half step back, reevaluating his entire night. His friend opened his mouth to probably spew some crappy, drunken retort when his pal smacked him in the back of the head.

"Dude, that's Ryder."

The guy with the bottle didn't seem to quite understand what that meant, because he looked back and forth between us, mouth wide open. Yep, he was definitely missing a few teeth, too. Ready to be

149

done with this whole thing, I took a step forward, hands balled in fists at my side, nails digging grooves into my palms, a threatening expression on my face. That seemed to jump-start whatever brain cells the booze hadn't burned away yet, because he, too, paled and smacked his friend's shoulder as they raced to the exit.

Bouncing on my heels, my fury replaced by triumph, I turned to Ryder only to find he'd stepped right behind me. The tip of my nose brushed his chest through his stretchy black t-shirt. Gods he was tall, towering over me in a mass of muscle and sinew and heat. His brow quirked and part of his mouth tipped in a musing smile.

"Whoa there," he said, gripping my shoulders as I tripped back a step. His hooded eyes searched mine as he lowered his head. His mouth stretched into that sexy half-grin that I might find more than a little irresistible. He didn't seem to be in any hurry to let me go if his fingers working small circles into my lower back had anything to say about it, but it was all good because I couldn't think of anywhere better to be right now.

Who was I and what happened to the person I used to be?

"I'm afraid we weren't quite properly introduced earlier, Majesty," he said in that same rough and tumble voice from earlier, a hint of gravel in his tone. "I'm Ryder. And this is my club." He lifted one of his hands from my shoulders and inserted it between our bodies.

A handshake.

I'd much rather he wrap that hand around my waist. I breathed in, his scent flooding my senses. It was like cinnamon and smoke. After a beat too long, I took his hand in my own much smaller hand, marveling at the contrast, and shook it firmly.

"You know exactly who I am." I responded.

"You did come up in conversation."

"And did you reach an agreement?" I stepped out of his grasp, sucking in a gulp of air now that I could breathe again. "Finn seemed adamant you could help."

Ryder tapped his chin with one manicured nail and lifted a shoulder. The sensuality in his face, though, drained away. "Finn and I don't exactly get along. We're friendly, but we aren't friends. Not anymore." His hand moved to his jawline and rubbed. "Unfortunately, while our discussion started off well enough, it derailed rather quickly. He's taking a breather right now. Maybe someday I'll tell you about our history. Maybe he will. But for now, it's a long story and the wrong time."

More secrets. I shuffled on my feet. Though the music pounded the walls, it seemed muted with my confused thoughts.

"Don't get me wrong, we'll figure things out." Ryder's feet moved into my lowered line of sight. "Until he returns, though, why don't you and I get better acquainted, since you are the reason why he's here anyway."

I got the feeling 'here' meant more than the nightclub. But since Ryder seemed unwilling to broach the topic, and I didn't really know him that well anyway, I'd ask Finn about it later.

"Alright." I said and scrubbed the thighs of my pants. "What do you want to know?"

"Let's get another drink first. I talk better with something in my hands." Ryder talked as he sauntered up the stairs to the bar, hopped the counter, and poured me a tall glass of ice water and another shot of the electric green liquor from before.

"Let's talk about me first. You asked what I was before." Teeth flashed wickedly before a shot of the green stuff tipped from a third glass between Ryder's lips, which he smacked with satisfaction. "How about you take a guess. You've seen how I look, how I act. You've been affected by my presence. No, don't scoff, I can tell. It isn't anything to be ashamed of. Take a guess. Think about it, I'm in no hurry. You'll get no judgment from me."

151

Ryder hopped the counter again and ambled over to a table where a pair of stools had magically appeared. A skill of his? Or did he have staff that anticipated his needs? Ryder held a can of IPA from a company I didn't recognize and took a seat, legs splayed wide as he braced a foot on one of the pegs. He motioned for me to take the second.

I cleared my mind, shaking the thoughts free, and truly pondered what I knew, what he said. After a few minutes of scrolling my mental dictionary, I said, "A succubus."

"Close. I'm impressed. Incubus. Male version of the succubus," he clarified. I took a huge gulp from my glass of water. "This is my club. My home. My feeding ground." He paused and peered at me curiously. I took another drink and re-crossed my legs on my own stool. The table was sticky. "Interesting. No reaction."

"Should I have one?"

"Not necessarily, but most do. It isn't a good one."

"I don't know enough about what I am let alone what you are to cast that kind of judgment."

His eyes narrowed with challenge. "What if I were a murderer? Most tales about my kind depict us as aggressive, sexually-frustrated, homicidal freaks."

"Are you?" I was enjoying this, the candid nature of this discussion.

"No," Ryder said slowly. "Maybe that was true several thousand years ago, but not anymore. I've learned to cope. It's why I built this club and many others like it before. I don't need to kill when sex is readily available all around us." He pinched his fingers and then opened his empty palm. "That isn't to say I don't divulge in the festivities myself every now and again."

I rolled my eyes and finished my glass of water. "Fair enough, but keep whatever you've got," I ran my eyes over his delicious frame suggestively, "away from me. I have too much going on in my life right now to not complicate it, even for one night." I slanted him a look and he laughed. It was easy talking to him. There was a distinct lack of pressure that I felt around Finn about the necessity to know everything about everything.

Speaking of the devil, er, kelpie, I spotted him shoving through the crowd, making his way toward us. Ryder followed the direction of my attention and lifted a hand in a wave.

"Finn, we were wondering where you'd wandered off to," he called.

"I've been searching for you everywhere," Finn gritted, ignoring the incubus entirely. "Where did you go?"

I shifted in my seat, confused. "I didn't go anywhere. I've been here. In the crowd. And then when I went to grab some water, Ryder found me." I tapped the table. "We only just sat down."

The kelpie glared at him. "Convenient," he finally said through his teeth. His hands folded around the edge of the table.

"You're being insulting," I snapped. "What's your problem? You're the one who wanted to come here. The least you can do is be civil."

"The lady has a point," Ryder drawled, swirling his beer around in the can. He didn't appear at all bothered by Finn's aggression, and instead beckoned to someone over my shoulder. A few seconds later, a girl carrying a third stool appeared and set it next to Finn who was making a visible effort to chill.

"There now," Ryder said. "Sit down and let's go over this again. Maybe having her here will help you keep your cool."

Finn dragged a hand through his hair and air hissed from between his teeth, but he sat nonetheless, body still and braced like a horse at the starting gates.

"Zara and I were getting to know each other. That's all. Now, before we get mired in the past again, since that clearly didn't go so well before, why don't you tell me why you're here." Ryder flicked a hand in the air. "I've ensured we won't be overheard."

"He can create sound-proof bubbles and obscure visible things," Finn explained, catching my confusion. "And if he says we won't be overheard, we won't be overheard."

I nodded and ran my finger around the rim of the shot glass as Finn started talking. As his words flowed, my heart rate picked up, my breathing came faster, as the weight of responsibility I'd shaken settled firmly back on my shoulders. We were on a mission and we needed help. We were only here because we had to be. I had to trust that Finn knew what he was doing. Everything he'd done through now had seemed to be in my best interest. I didn't think he'd deviate.

True to his word, Ryder set aside the dramatics and listened with rapt attention, though his eyes periodically drifted over the mass of bodies, keeping watch. He asked for clarifications about the Kraken and about my magic, his foot jiggling on the peg of his stool as he processed. But when Finn described the attack on my friends at the hotel, expounding on his suspicions, Ryder turned to me.

"Why would the Order try to kill you?" He leaned forward on the table, dark eyes sweeping across my pale face. "They're *your* protectors, *your* church. Why would they want you dead?"

Stunned at being addressed. I fumbled through my words. "Finn says they've tried to kill me before. That they were responsible for the attack on the temples two decades ago. And then I met the Hand—"

"You met the Hand? We're talking about the elusive, secretive leader of the Order who never leaves Rome." Ryder's wry tone dripped with condescension and he tapped his can on the table twice. "You stumbled across this guy in the middle of Norway on a whim. And, upon realizing his organization didn't kill you as intended," it was interesting that Ryder wasn't arguing that point, "he let you go and then decided to send his men to attack you later. Do I have that right?"

I leaned across the table, ignoring Finn's glower. "It was in a dream."

Ryder's golden eyes narrowed thoughtfully. A few beats later, his fingers spread wide. He and Finn shared a look.

"Yeah, seems that much is true," Finn muttered.

"Fascinating. I wonder if the other stories of the Gods are true, too, then." Ryder responded, his head tilted side to side, chin raised, and he folded his arms in front of him. "Interesting. Anyway, why do you suspect the Order of killing a group of girls?"

"Anisra." Finn said.

Ryder went still. "Come again?"

"Anisra. They used it."

The pulse in Ryder's neck throbbed. Wisps of smoky black uncurled from under his hands, and I tipped back on my stool when it spread across the table, reaching for me. The timbre of his voice deepened, turning soft as velvet, when he finally addressed Finn. "That's been locked away for centuries."

"I know. And I know you know better than anyone." Finn raised a hand helplessly. He glanced between us. "That's why I know it must be them."

Ryder cursed viciously and his head dropped; the searing intensity of his focus fell with it. My chest swelled as I began pulling in air once more. I hadn't realized I'd stopped breathing in the first place. Danger wafted from this man, this *stranger*, in waves. Like a Venus Fly Trap, he drew prey in with beauty and promises, but one snap and it was done for.

"I have a lot to consider," Ryder said. The smoke dissipated. The level of control he exerted was incredible. I'd watched Finn fly off the handle at craziest turn of emotion on more than one occasion. He wore emotions like clothing. But this guy, this guy was all about internalizing. I got the feeling we'd stunned him; I didn't think he'd meant to allow the smoke to slip.

"You're asking me to go against the Order. And we don't have a temple behind us." It felt like I was missing a very important conversation. Finn had mentioned it before, the Order and the temples being at odds, but Ryder's eerie comment made it seem like it was much more than that.

"There are many who don't appreciate the way the Order has treated them these past two centuries," Ryder continued. "But there's a difference between passive irritation and a willingness to actually go up against the establishment. Also, throw in a God and you've got yourself a very messy situation. If the Order does want her dead, there are fey who will make it happen, even at the cost of their magic. I can't trust just anyone."

I tugged the sleeves of my shirt over my knuckles. My body shrank in on itself as the weight grew even heavier. It seemed no matter where I turned, nothing got better. Nothing got easier. I risked a glance at Finn who appeared as defeated as me. His head hung on his shoulders.

"Fortunately, you picked a good place to find me. There are many here trying to hide from something." Ryder shifted his weight on the stool. His tone lightened. "Though some might recognize you, Zara, it's unlikely they'll report you. As far as nearly everyone outside of this table is concerned, you're a swimmer on hiatus. A teenager running from responsibility. Many here have much bigger problems than that." He flicked at hand at a woman with green hair talking rapidly on a cell phone. Two men wearing suits and scowls flanked her. A tattoo of an owl covered her entire arm, and the longer I watched the redder it glowed.

"She has secrets you don't want to know, for example. Like me." He smirked, all intensity from earlier having apparently faded—for now. Ryder pointed a finger at Finn. "I'll have an answer for you in the morning."

"Good," Finn said and stood. His back arched and he stretched. "We'll head back to the hotel." He rattled off the name of the establishment and our room number. "I'll plan on seeing you in the lobby first thing. Neither of us have phones."

"Fair enough." Ryder braced a hand on the table, then hesitated. "What's wrong?"

"I—" I didn't want to head back. Not yet. It was dark out and I didn't think I'd be able to sleep, even with Finn in the same room. I closed my eyes, shivering when Kaz's glassy gaze appeared against the reddish skin, and reopened them. I picked at my cuticles, not sure how to say what I needed to say without coming across like a scared little girl.

"I forgot, we were talking earlier, weren't we?" Ryder blustered. "And then you asked me about myself and, naturally, I monopolized your time talking about myself. Now you absolutely must stay and tell me all about you." My breathing hitched at the kindness and understanding I found in his face. Ryder sank back into his stool and held up another finger. Finn looked between us, jaw slack, as a young man dropped off another shot of the liquid lightning.

"You want to stay?" he asked.

"Would that be alright?" I smiled up at him. *Please don't make me go back*, I silently pleaded. *Please don't make me.*

"I don't know. It seems dangerous."

"Come now." Ryder interjected smoothly. "One more drink can't hurt. And I'll walk her back myself. I have a vested interest in her safety now, don't I?"

Oh, he was good.

Finn's tongue traced his lip ring in thought. Finally, he said, "One drink. Then you come straight back. No detours. No magic. Straight back. And Ryder leaves you at the door."

"Aye aye, captain." Ryder said, saluting the kelpie with a snappy gesture. Finn sighed, and I could tell he immediately regretted his decision. "Your charge is safe with me, sir, guardian, sir. I'll handcuff her to my own arm if I must."

"Nobody is handcuffing anybody," I said quickly. But I couldn't hold back a small smile at his gusto. "But I promise to stick to his side like glue."

"Are we talking Elmer's or Gorilla, here?" Ryder asked, propping his chin on one hand. "Because there's a vast difference in quality. And stickiness."

"I can tell you'll get along swimmingly," Finn cut in. "I'll leave you to it." He turned to go, but Ryder's hand snaked out and grabbed his arm, holding him back.

"Try to relax, Finn. Take some of the edge off, if you know what I mean."

Finn went pale and he tugged away from Ryder without comment.

"What was that about?" I asked, losing the kelpie in the crush of bodies.

"Don't worry about it." Ryder dismissed my question with a wave. "I'd much rather talk about you."

"What about me?"

He leaned in, hand coming up to cup my cheek as his face tipped toward mine. I did nothing to stop him as my heart tripped, uncaring of the sudden transition to intimacy. "Those eyes of yours are very intriguing, glowstick." He smoothed the crease that formed between my brows and his voice softened. "They make me want to know everything about you."

I leaned into his hand, playing along with his flirtation, then said, "Now that Finn is gone, what do you really think about having this problem dumped in your lap?"

His face twisted in an impossible expression. "Stranger things can happen. Have happened. The universe has a strange way of working, I've discovered. If you're here now it means something incredible is about to go down. I, frankly, find myself intrigued."

I shuddered, pulling away from his grasp. Yep, he'd gone a step too far. Too much. Too many feels. I didn't really know who he was, no matter who he was friends with, or how charming he could be. I needed to diffuse this before it grew into something that I really couldn't handle.

"Are you using your influence on me?" I teased, half-joking, half-serious.

"Nope. Trust me, you'd know if I were trying to influence you." He clicked his tongue against his teeth. "Then again, I'm not sure if I could even influence a God. I've never tried." He smirked as something occurred to him. "Maybe something to test out later if you're game..."

I couldn't help but laugh. It wasn't any laugh either, it was a full-bodied, deep from the belly laugh. The kind of laugh that sweeps you away as you lose yourself in the moment. He was too much. This whole night was too much.

When I finally looked at him again, I saw the grin stretched across my whole face reflected in his. I stopped him before he could say something else that would send me through a loop of lust, hope, and confusion. I snatched up my shot.

"Do shots technically qualify as drinks?"

Ryder's pupil's dilated. "Depends on how you look at it."

19

Zara

The chill of the night wrapped around me, nipping at my exposed skin, sneaking through the gaps in my clothing. Rather than wrapping my arms closer to my core, I welcomed the sensation, throwing my arms wide and spinning in a circle in the parking lot outside the club, unaware and uncaring of the wide-eyed glances cast my way. I drew in a deep gulp of air, marveling at the refreshing chill on my tongue, so completely opposite the heat and sweat inside the club.

Ryder's laugh boomed, loud and deep, at my unwarranted enthusiasm. The flat of his palm smacked the thigh of his jeans as he bent in two, equally uncaring of the few people around us. It probably looked like we were a pair of drunken fools.

We kind of were.

"You truly are something special," he hooted and reached out to catch one of my arms and pull me close. He was blazing hot, a mini-inferno right here on this brisk summer night. I welcomed it and pressed closer to his hard body, snuggling tight into his chest. He tensed in surprise, but after a moment his muscles relaxed, his arms tightening around my shoulders.

"What was the drink you gave me?" My words came out muffled and slurred because my face was smashed against his shirt, but Ryder had no trouble understanding.

"It's something we fey call *'Eliriah.'* It means 'light.' It's basically the essence of the elements boiled down into liquid form. Humans can drink it, but since they're so far removed from the natural state of the elements, it only tastes like a sweet, tangy beverage.

"For fey, like me and Finn, we have a purer elemental connection. It's like taking a shot of moonshine. It opens us up to the elements, too, making magic more easily accessible. Witches swear by it and will often drink it during rituals to open themselves up to the spiritual world when trying some particularly difficult task or spell.

"But you, you're a God." He pushed me away a little so he could look down on me. "You're the purest of us all. For you, there's no alcoholic comparison. You aren't drunk, you're something past that, and someday I want to know what you're capable of in this state. I'm sure it will be a wonder to see."

Awe trickled into his tone, and I swallowed hard, trying to imagine that kind of power. What exactly could I accomplish? Heck. What could I do *right now*? Suddenly, I had to know, I had to explore what I was, what I could be. I pulled away from Ryder and slipped inside my own mind, the links of my magic pulling taut like guitar strings. I played with the strands, the beat resonating deep inside me.

But it was something more. Was it only me? What was that shaking? Firm hands gripped my arms and shook them, but I couldn't figure out why. I brushed away the annoyance and looked around. No, the feeling wasn't something reverberating inside me. The ground was literally shaking. People around us were screaming, running from the club as the world swayed. Ryder's grip returned to my arms, hard and bruising. He was saying something to me, but I pushed him away again and knelt, pressing my hand to the rough asphalt in awe.

161

Using *Iridescence*, the world glowed silver and blue—long strands of life connected my body, my energy, to my element. From the leaves in the trees to the gasoline in the tanks of the few cars left in the lot to the man standing in front of me, I was part of it all. I wondered if this is how the trio of sisters in the Underworld felt as they carefully snipped the life from people, reeling their souls in for Judgment Day.

But that wasn't all. A river of blue flowed under my feet. A stream of water rushing beneath the city. It bubbled and frothed wildly, demanding my attention.

I wanted to touch it.

I had to touch it.

In its clamor for me, the water started reversing and rising, flowing from the gaping mouths of the gutters, spilling toward my outstretched arm.

Before it could reach me, something crouched in front of me.

No.

Some*one*.

A single, thin strand of bluish-silver tied me to it.

Him. Yes. Him.

His shadowy arm snaked out, fingers speared through my hair, and my mouth dropped open in what I think was protest. Before any sound could come out, a warm mouth fused with mine, soft lips firm against my own. My hands flew up, ready to push away the intrusion, but instead, they curled into the softness of fabric, pulling *him* closer. Silver sparked in my vision, silver that had nothing to do with my sight and everything to do with the shivers of bliss rolling through me. A low moan slipped out of my throat. A deep rumble reverberated in *his* chest, and I tipped my head back, dropping my internal walls, welcoming the invasion. He took advantage, tugging on my hair, pulling my head back our lips fused more tightly, tongues clashing in a sensual dance.

All thought of my connection to the world vanished as I drank him in, my body pressing against his as the ground stopped rocking. I was shaking, trembling, as his arms pulled me impossibly closer. I tasted wintermint and threaded my fingers through the short, fine hair at the back of his neck, whimpering softly as he sucked lightly on my tongue. It felt like he was pulling something from me, filling the void with a dark and demented pleasure.

I couldn't get enough.

Emotion crested high, but before it spilled over in a wave of ecstasy, *he* shoved me away. I tumbled to the road, the asphalt digging into my skin. The quaking in my body stopped. The sudden stillness foreign and strange.

I stared into Ryder's swirling amber and red eyes, the glow of his white irises, the look of shock that pulled his features tight. A few moments passed like that, us staring at one another before his face crumpled.

"Fuck!" He screamed, his fingers digging grooves in his hair. His face twisted in agony, bowing toward the street. "Fuck," he repeated, softer this time.

Drained and sober, I shifted to take some of the pressure off the cuts in my palms, wary again of the stranger in front of me, of the hints of danger I'd picked up on earlier. I scrubbed at my face, uncaring of the blood and grime. The movement caught Ryder's attention, and his head flew up again, dark eyes boring into mine.

Horrified.

Hopeful.

"Ryder," I started to say, the words soothing but wary, like someone trying to calm a rabid animal approaching with its hackles raised. The words barely passed my lips, and suddenly he was *there*, smashing me against the softness of his t-shirt and the hardness of his chest.

"I'm so sorry," he murmured into my hair, the heat of his breath fanning stray strands. "I'm so bloody sorry. I didn't know what else to do. You were going to break the water main. Everything was shaking. I thought someone was going to get hurt. I was screaming at you, shaking you, but you weren't responding. I didn't know what else to do."

Was that what I was doing?

Was that the river of blue?

I suddenly felt afraid of *myself*, my utter lack of awareness. The feeling of ecstasy was swamped by guilt. What if someone had gotten hurt? I didn't want that. I never wanted that.

"Well, I'd say your way of getting my attention was effective." My raspy voice cracked, ruining my attempt at lightheartedness. Gathering myself, I pushed past it and looked up through my lashes. "That was a pretty incredible kiss."

He shook his head and my expression faltered. "You don't understand. I could have hurt you." I pulled away. "I couldn't think of any other way to get through to you. I used my abilities to distract you, but I lost control. That shouldn't have happened."

"How exactly would you have hurt me?" I asked, pushing out of his lap, the rough asphalt of the parking lot grounding me once again.

"You need to understand how my abilities work," he began. "Incubi and succubi get energy from sex or at least energy derived from sex or sexual acts, like dancing. It's why I have the club. The incredible volume of raw, human energy takes away most of my hunger." He reached out to touch me, but stopped when I shook my head. His hand dropped.

"That sexual energy is more potent when it's actual, physical contact. It helps feed our deeper, greater desire: the desire to steal souls. Stealing a soul brings on an ultimate high for us, but leaves our victims like zombies." Ryder winced. "Now, there are ways to be physical without fully taking a soul. But even a little contact, even controlled, can chip away at that person's soul. It doesn't matter if they're human or fey. Everyone is affected. We can feed a little bit from someone, sure, but it leaves a mark. And if we aren't careful, we can take it all."

The night air didn't feel crisp and welcoming anymore. Out here, with him, with this conversation, everything felt more sinister. The steady throbbing coming from the club stopped as the DJ wrapped up his last song. The stillness increased my edginess.

"As if that weren't enough, the people whose souls we steal are damned to hell, cursed to spend their eternal lives among monsters. We are some of the few fey that are actually, technically demonic. We don't like to use that term, but it's true. That's why there's so much judgment about our kind."

"What kind of mark?"

"Your soul makes you who you are. When we take part of it, we are taking part of what makes you, *you*. In most cases, taking a little can take away some of your kindness, some of your light. We make good people bad, bad people worse."

I thought for a minute, taking inventory of my body. I didn't feel any darker. Maybe as a God, it took a little longer to kick in for me to feel different.

"Can you tell when you take part of someone? Is there a beacon or something? I mean, if there are more of you, shouldn't you be able to tell when someone has been touched by one of you? That way you know if you could take their soul or something?" I twisted my fingers in my lap, the words sounding foolish to my own ears.

"Of course." This time his fingers did brush my knee, the touch meant to be reassuring.

"How much of my soul did you take?"

Now he looked up at me, the darkness swirling in his eyes. His Adam's apple bobbed as he looked down my body, then back to my face, evaluating. "I'm not sure. I lost control pretty quickly there." He

165

fiddled with the hem of his shirt. "I don't know how long I actually tapped into you. But I can tell by the sheer volume of energy I pulled from you that it was a lot."

My lips trembled. I wanted to scream. "Could you check? I'm already not much of the person I used to be. I don't know how much more change I can handle."

"I'm so sorry," he muttered again. Shouldn't he be riding some sort of energy-high right now? I reluctantly put my hand in his outstretched palm, figuring it must help him gauge what remained of my soul. His eyes were closed, a little wrinkle on his brow between his brows, and then he opened them. I shivered at the red tint that clouded the darkness. The furrow deepened as he took in the signature of my energy.

"It isn't possible," Ryder muttered, cocking his head to the side a bit like a bird. He dropped my hand and then picked it up again. His head shook slowly. "There's no way."

Hope bloomed in my chest, replacing the doomed feeling that had settled in earlier.

"It's all there. Your soul. It's all there." His hand was chilly in mine but clamped tight like a vice. Good thing I had no desire to let go. "I don't understand."

"I don't feel any different," I muttered. Truth be told, I'm glad that his foray into the forbidden hadn't had any unintended consequences. Especially since it started with me losing control of my abilities yet again. I tried to not think about that other being who'd made me attack Finn the other day.

"This has never happened before. I swear on my life. I've never heard of an incubus or succubus walking away from an encounter like that without taking part of the other participant's soul." The rough pad of his thumb grazed the back of my hand. "I've been around for thousands of years and never, ever have I heard of this happening."

"You're telling me that every one of your kind is going to try to have sex with me now," I joked, trying to release some of the tension building between us.

Ryder's eyes flicked to mine, swirling and glowing that unnatural gold-red-white combination. A lethal combination I was learning didn't bode well. "What happened here needs to stay between us. No one else can know about this. I'm serious. If I can kiss you without repercussion, then there's no telling what effect your... uniqueness can have on others. And there are many, many others." That last part came out on a growl as he effortlessly slid to his feet, pulling me up with him. He glanced around the empty parking lot, the crumbling sidewalk. "It's getting late. Finn's probably going crazy with worry."

I brushed off the back of my jeans, wincing as pieces of dirt scraped my raw palms. Maybe the kelpie could help me heal them later. As we started heading back in the direction of my hotel, I glanced over at my somber buddy. "Shouldn't you be high as a kite right now?"

Ryder grunted. "That's the unbelievable part. Well. Part of it. I'm completely re-energized." I glanced back and saw him dragging his hands down the front of his shirt as if expecting sparks to fly from the cloth. "Hell, I'm overflowing with energy. I haven't felt this good in a decade at least." A smile quirked his lips, lightening his entire face, and I relaxed. "Which isn't really that long in the grand scheme of things. But probably seems like a lot to your poor mortal self."

I cuffed his shoulder, causing him to stumble and chuckle. "I'm not quite mortal anymore, you know. But I won't exactly live forever like you."

"Boils down to the same thing, doesn't it?" His full humor was back. "Anyway. Normally I feel drunk after consuming so much energy, but I feel happy. Lifted. Magical. I bet I could probably pull off some of my other skills right now if I wanted to."

Curiosity sparked again. "Will you show me?"

"All in good time, glowstick. All in good time."

"Why do you call me that?"

"You'll find out eventually."

"Patience isn't my strong suit."

"Find some."

We walked in companionable silence, the evening wrapping its tendrils around us as the clock ticked deeper into the night. It had to be almost 3 a.m., but I wasn't even the slightest bit tired. As the hotel appeared at the far end of the block, I broke the silence again. "You aren't commanded by Water. I'd be able to sense if you were like I can with Finn. In that case, which element are you?"

"No one commands me." His chest puffed dramatically. "You heard me before. *We* are demons, beings of the dark. Constantly waging war with the light."

"But that doesn't make sense. The Kraken told me all beings are dictated by one of the four elements, if not by several of them."

"Too bad for the Kraken. This will have to remain a mystery between us." Ryder held open the front door of the hotel, ushering me inside. I glanced at the desk, noting the absence of a clerk, and started to head toward the elevator. I fully intended to go to my room on the third floor, but musical notes caught my attention. Something dark and crooning that sang in my bones. Part of me registered Ryder calling my name, but I was already wandering down the hallway, searching for the source of the delicious sound.

Search for me deep
It won't be wrong.
Your soul I will keep
Down where it belongs.
Come on in, the water is cool.
You know you want to.

For who's to call you *the fool?*

Words laced with spiders and ghosts and hidden crevices and cliffs begging you to jump.

A sound, a poem, a voice I'd never heard before, but one I felt compelled to find. Of their own volition, my feet wound through hallways I didn't recognize before pausing in front of the clear wall of glass to the indoor pool. That's where I faltered, barely able to take in the scene before me.

A horse, big as a Clydesdale and dark as chocolate stout, stood in the shallow end. Seaweed and slime dripped from its luscious, shaggy coat. Its mane and tail hung in tatters, tangled with sticks and kelp and broken pieces of shell. Eyes burning bright as the sun glowed from deep inside its magnificent head as it faced the deep end of the pool where a young, blonde woman treaded water. Occasionally she'd slip beneath the surface, face strangely calm, as her strength waned. A trail of clothing similar to the hotel uniforms led from the door of the pool to the ladder.

The horse was the source of the music.

I sprinted for the door. I tugged and twisted the handle, but it wouldn't open. I slammed my shoulder against the glass, trying to smash it, anything that would get me inside that room. I couldn't see any ripples across the top of the water, no bubbles, no movement indicating a person's natural struggle to resurface. I fumbled for my magic but I couldn't think, couldn't grasp it, the strands slipping through my hold.

She was going to drown.

Someone was going to drown in front of me. Someone was going to die again, and this *thing* was responsible. And there wasn't anything I could do.

A scream, shrill and long and wrenching, ripped from deep in my soul, pulled from that void of blackness I'd thought I'd pushed back. A siren's scream, as Ryder would later inform me, a cousin to the mermaid that eagerly dragged sailors to the bottom of the sea and cut out their bloody, beating hearts. A shrill scream that, according to legend, shattered glass. And legend didn't fail me now. The windows surrounding three of four sides of the pool shattered at once, glass spraying in all directions.

Small shards dug into my hands as I pulled myself up, but I didn't notice the pain. I followed Ryder across the broken pieces. A stream of slick, red blood trailed from one of his ears. The horse's head turned from the water, fixing me in its unworldly stare. I barely registered the splash as Ryder dived in and hoisted the woman up.

"Whatever you are, you don't belong here," I told it, the words sounding broken to my ears. I raised my arm, drawing on what remained of my reserves, finally in control. Water swirled in the pool, reacting to my unspoken command, ready to blast the beast into the next realm. The horse blinked and reared on its hind legs, shifting right before my eyes.

"Probably not the best way to impress your charge, Finn," Ryder said blandly, the woman in his arms.

I stumbled back a step. The horse was a kelpie. My kelpie. A man I'd very nearly called my friend. A man who had tried to drown someone in front of me.

"Let me explain," Finn pleaded, now back to his human state. He fought the pull of the water to the edge of the pool. "I never expected you to show up. I never intended for you to see this."

Convinced I wasn't about to puke, I slowly rose.

My euphoric drunkenness from earlier was long gone.

"What exactly *did* you intend for me to see?" I cried. He flinched as if I'd struck him. I watched Ryder lay the woman on the side of the pool, relieved to see her chest rising and falling. "When were you going to tell me about this?"

"It's what I am. It's who I am. I need to… It's not… You can't…"

"I can't what?" My throat burned raw with emotion. This was the person in who I'd put my safety, my security. *I knew nothing about him.* "I can change the tides of this planet, I can feel connections with every living thing, but I can't comprehend why the hell you'd try to kill someone right in front of me? Try again. I'm done, so gods-damned done."

Ryder, soaked with chlorinated water, came to stand beside me. I knew he sympathized with Finn. I could feel it wafting off him in waves. He was guilty of crimes equally as bad, if not worse, than this. But I couldn't think about that right now. Days ago, I'd been normal, intense Zara, preparing for my next shot at the Olympics. Now I was a God, a brand spanking new God still figuring out that the fey were real, that everything I thought I knew was false. And the one person I'd counted on to help me navigate the maze was a killer.

"I can't believe you." I spat. And I stormed from the room, barely feeling the shards of glass that cut through the soles of my shoes and stabbed into my feet. Gripping Ryder's hand like a lifeline, I stepped onto the elevator and pressed the glowing button for my floor, relieved when no one stepped on with us despite the late hour.

Ryder twitched, and I looked at him sharply.

"He's a kelpie. Same as I'm an incubus. It's not like he can turn it off."

"Shut up. Shut up right now or you can join him downstairs cleaning up the mess."

He shut his mouth and made a show of zipping it as the elevator door dinged and opened, displaying the purple carpet of my floor. I stomped down the hallway toward my door, but stopped short of opening it, key card gripped in my hand. *De ja vu* swamped me. Another time, another place, I'd opened a door that looked very much like this one. And what I found inside haunted my dreams.

Ryder took the card from my limp fingers and opened the door. This time, thankfully, the room was blissfully empty.

"Are you ok?"

I shook my head at Ryder's concern, dismissing it. I was running on autopilot.

"I need to clean up. Wait here a minute, please."

Before he could respond, I slipped into the bathroom and locked it behind me. I dragged my fingers through the massive tangle that was my hair, ignoring the greasy feel of sweat on my skin. What was happening to me? One minute I was me and the next I wasn't. One minute I was a driven athlete and the next a giant octopus was telling me I was supposed to save the world.

I couldn't do this.

I couldn't breathe.

Cold porcelain bit into my arms as I fell on the sink. I looked into the mirror, expecting to find a face of fear framed by a wave of lank hair. Instead, I met my own eyes, realizing now why Ryder called me "glowstick." My aquamarine eyes literally radiated light. No matter how much I blinked it wouldn't go away.

It was too much.

Too much evidence of how very inhuman I was.

Too much evidence of how much I'd lost in such a short time.

The heel of my palm hit the glass, sending a crack shooting up the middle of my face. That was how I felt right now. Fractured. Broken. My knuckles made second contact, splintering my face. One more punch and the mirror shattered.

I shattered.

Ugly, harsh sobs ripped from my chest, and I collapsed.

The scrape of jeans against my face was familiar, welcoming, and I wrapped my arms around myself, struggling to hold myself together.

I didn't hear wood crack as Ryder kicked in the door.

I barely registered his arms close around me, pulling me close, the cold, hard tile of the bathroom floor hard but incredibly real in this moment.

I only knew my own pain.

20

Geoffrey

The desk rattled as my phone buzzed, the ringtone silenced. For the first time in hours, I looked up from my computer, engrossed in endless amounts of paperwork, and glanced at the screen. Toren's name stood out against the yellow background, signaling an incoming call.

I reached for the phone, then hesitated. My eyes flew to the five television screens that hung side by side across the wall opposite my desk. Each was tuned to a different news channel from different regions of the world. The tension in my neck didn't ease as I scoured the captions. None so much as hinted at the reemergence of the Gods.

Before the phone clicked over to voicemail, I slid the green button to the right and brought it to my ear.

"We found her."

I pressed the back of my hand to my mouth. It trembled. Conflicting feelings of relief and trepidation rushed through my veins.

"Where?"

"Kansas City."

Gods. She'd made it across the ocean. Someone must be helping her. The girl was intelligent. I'd figured that much out for myself as

I poured over her grades, her accomplishments, the unique history that made up her being. She followed a straight and narrow line right to the top—of athletics. However, all those documents didn't hint at someone well-versed in espionage.

"You have the situation contained?" I asked.

"We know where she is. My regional commander is briefing the mayor now."

I'd discussed any number of battle-plans with Toren before, but never had I heard this level of resolve in his voice. The pounding in the back of my head lessened. I set the phone on the desk and turned on the speaker. I scrawled my signature on the page I'd printed out and set it in my outgoing mailbox. Another fresh report awaited my review beneath it.

"What, exactly, are you telling the mayor?" I asked.

"She's aware we're operating on official Order business, that my commander has orders right from the top. She's aware of Zara's existence and understands the potential threat to her city if she's not contained. I'm assured we will have permission to move a unit into the area with limited potential for causalities."

With a city of that size, it would be difficult to keep the news from getting out altogether. Fortunately, the Order had offered its support in finding her from the beginning. But given we hadn't released her true magical identity to the public, we could hit a bit of a snag. I glanced up at an American cable news network and calculated the time difference. "Did you consider grabbing her in her sleep?"

Toren blew out a long breath. It sounded like static over the wireless connection. "Considered it, nixed it. The windows of the hotel don't open. We'd have to cut through the glass and her room faces a busy street. But that isn't really the issue. There's a complication."

"What kind of complication?"

"Someone is with her," Toren said. "You'll have the report in your inbox shortly. Basically, we tried snagging her at a club, but a different subject intervened. My sources tell me this particular subject is highly volatile and very dangerous. He followed her back to the hotel and, from all accounts, hasn't reemerged."

Before I asked, I knew the answer. "Am I to assume by dangerous you mean fey?"

A pause. "Yes."

It only made sense. I could feel magic stirring all around me. It made me antsy and twitchy. Other mythical creatures would feel it, too, and they would start emerging from the folds if we couldn't bring Zara to heel.

"We've dealt with fey before," I began.

"Fey with shackles on their abilities, sure. But now that magic is awakening…" Toren trailed off, the words hovering unspoken between us. It was obvious. We couldn't anticipate what to expect. Not anymore. The rules of the game were changing—quickly.

"How do we know this fey is allied with her?"

He coughed. "My agents, uh, *saw* them together."

That didn't necessarily mean anything, but it was better to err on the side of caution.

"You see, this guy. He isn't like most fey. He's not just a peon in the cogs of the system trying to get by. He's a major player in all this. He's been around for a long time, he has connections—I'm looking through his file now. Despite the lack of magic, he's hardly stood idle over the centuries."

The backs of my hands burned. Looking down, I realized I was scratching them again. The healing cuts oozed from the fresh damage. I'd forgotten to replace the bandages this morning. This whole situation was going from bad to worse.

"Do you have a name for this guy?" I asked.

"Does the Harkon family ring a bell?"

Of course it did. I leaned back, teeth clenched, and the chair squeaked.

Fey royalty. *Powerful* fey royalty.

"I thought so," Toren said when I didn't respond. "And this one is the youngest. Goes by Ryder. He's a bit of a black sheep of the family, so to speak. Which works in our favor, because at last check, his family disowned him. And that family has remained staunchly loyal to the Order over the centuries."

"So you're thinking they won't come running to his aid if they get wind he's in danger?" I asked, peering up at the television screens again. Nothing had changed.

"Not in the least. Getting into dangerous situations seems to be right up his alley."

"Fine," I said. "But do you think that someone with that amount of power is going to be ok with a unit of fifty or so troops showing up and just *taking* someone that you say he's shown an interest in?"

"He's not stupid. When forced to face even a tiny fraction of the Order, especially within the confines of a densely populated city—even with safety measures in place—we expect him to see reason." Toren's tone had turned clipped and brittle.

"If you think you can get her to surrender peacefully, I believe you. But Toren—"

"Yes?"

"You're walking an incredibly fine line."

"You got it, boss."

The line went dead.

I had to trust his instincts. Toren knew his people, he had a strong grasp on strategy. He knew what was at stake here. If he said he could contain the situation, then he could. He'd done it dozens of times before.

With less harrowing stakes, a tiny voice whispered.

I smoothed the sheet of paper in front of me, eyes skimming the words without really seeing them until something snagged my attention. A name. Mateo. Mateo Lopez. I frowned, eyes moving to the top of the report again. It was from the medical examiner explaining the soldier had recently died of heart failure. It had apparently gone unnoticed and undiagnosed.

Strange, though. When I'd met him, he'd exhibited no outward signs of distress, aside from the stress of sitting next to me. And new soldiers got physicals on day one. It should have been caught then.

I peeled a sticky note from the stack on my desk and scribbled instructions for my secretary to pull his medical files.

Then I set the report aside and sighed at the endless river of black text that awaited.

21

Zara

I woke slowly after a blissfully dream-free night.

As consciousness rolled in, I realized I ached all over—starting with the hard tile grinding into the edge of my hip. My cheek leaned on something soft, something with a steady heartbeat. Breath tickled my ear as the being holding me close dozed. My adrenaline ratcheted up a notch until I remembered Ryder kicking in the door and pulling me into his arms.

Sure enough, when I opened my swollen, salt-crusted eyes, I saw broken bits of door and mirror littered the floor. He'd pulled me against him, acting like I was less of a stranger he'd recently met and more of a friend, whispering nothings into my hair as I cried. We'd fallen asleep like that, surrounded by shards of debris, the harsh florescent light beating down.

I took a moment to savor the sense of security his arms brought me, to breathe in the unique smoky-cinnamon scent that was Ryder, before I pulled away, scrubbing my scabbed hands over my face. The movement woke Ryder who peered at me through slitted eyes, a question reflected in them: *Are you OK?*

Was I OK?

Could I ever be OK again?

I shook my head. His lips thinned but he didn't speak.

I nudged him from the bathroom so I could clean up, grimacing when I saw the full extent of damage we'd caused last night. It would cost a fortune to fix. The sweltering heat of the shower only made me feel mildly better. Standing hurt. The bottoms of my feet were tender where the shards of glass had sliced through the thick skin. Finn would have to help heal them and my hands later.

Ryder must have dropped off the fresh clothes I discovered on the sink, and I pulled them on without thought. After kicking aside pieces of the bathroom to make a trail to the door, I waved at the incubus from the opening, offering use of the facilities.

He'd looked irresistible in the dark last night, all six-foot-six of lean muscle and unabashed swagger. But the tendrils of daylight reaching through the curtains somehow made him more devastatingly handsome. A fallen angel. The light teased highlights of purple and orange in his midnight hair, and further emphasized the slashes of cheekbone riding high on his face. The single dimple I'd spotted in the club was tucked away. He glanced over at my invitation, uncurling his rangy body from where he sat on the edge of the bed, and patted the comforter next to him. I sat, leaving about a foot of space between our hips, not quite sure where things stood with us.

"Come now, we're well past that." His large hand hooked around my hip, and he tugged me closer, his thumb rubbing small circles over my dark-washed jeans. "I assume it's back to work today? Hunting down the other Gods?"

A corner of my lips twitched. "You got it."

"And how are you feeling about Finn? Last night got pretty intense."

I plucked at the comforter. "I don't know. I mean, I do know. I hate what he was going to do, I hate that is a part of him. But I guess I also understand that he can't help his instincts. I can't imagine what it's like having an internal drive like that. I saw how you got when your instincts took over." My arms curled around my body.

"That's incredibly mature of you." Ryder's tone was carefully neutral. "So, you feel OK working with him?"

"I think so. I kind of have to. He's really the only other person who knows what's going on. And he's operated in my best interests for the most part." I hesitated. "But I still don't trust him."

"I don't think that's a bad thing," Ryder said. The tightness in my chest relaxed. "The only thing you truly have at the end of the day are your instincts. Follow them."

Silence filled the room.

Then Ryder spoke again. "I didn't think Water ever woke first."

I tipped my head up to scrutinize his dark gaze. Finn had filled me in on the plane, pulling out bits and pieces of religious history lessons I'd long forgotten. The First of Four to wake was always the strongest and typically regarded as the leader of the bunch. Most of the time Fire claimed that position of power. Air would also take the reins from time to time. Earth had only come First twice. Water never.

"I suppose there's a first time for everything." I shrugged. Even the Kraken hadn't understood why I'd woken First this time, but It's pleasure at the discovery was a palpable thing.

"I'd say we're in for a particularly turbulent time." Goosebumps raced across my skin. That sounded foreboding. "If the healer is needed first, something is going to go incredibly, horribly wrong."

My brow furrowed. Historically, Fire possessed the most destructive abilities while Water was the most serene, regarded as a supreme healer in a number of cultures. I hadn't thought to examine the situation like Ryder was, and I wondered if the idea had crossed Finn's mind at all.

"OK. I'm in." Ryder's bright shift in tone caused me to jerk, my hand clenching on the comforter.

"What?"

"I'm in," he said. "I'm coming with you. "

"But you... the bar—your job. Your home?" Words sputtered through my lips like a faulty sprinkler.

"It's all replaceable," he said as if it were truly nothing. Maybe it was. "I've been around for thousands of years. Things have gotten stagnant here. Predictable. Boring. My blood burns for adventure. And pretty little you stumbling through the doors of my club was obviously the sign I was looking for. You're stuck with me now."

"But we were only coming to you for help finding extra security. We weren't asking you to—"

"And I don't trust anyone else with your security, I've decided. You're simply too important and far too interesting." Ryder slapped my thigh and tingles that had nothing to do with pain raced through my muscles. He stood. "I'm going to shower since stars knows when I'll be able to again, and I'll meet you downstairs in a jiffy. Get going. Use those weird superpowers of yours to figure out where we're heading next."

Ryder disappeared into the bathroom. The hiss of water through the shower head told me how sincere he was about all of this.

Given Finn's feelings toward the incubus last night, he was probably going to be *pissed*.

With that, I shrugged and headed for the door. Images from last night flickered before my eyes: the monstrous horse, the trail of clothing, water sputtering from a woman's lips as she convulsed next to the pool. To hell with Finn. Maybe that's who he was. Maybe he could have moments of weakness, too. But if he could have moments like that, so could I. And Ryder was becoming a weakness. If he wanted to join, far be it for me to stop him.

I opened the door and there was Finn, sitting on the floor, leaning against the frame. He'd probably stayed the night there. My heart tripped at his thoughtfulness, of not coming into the room even though it was his, too. I nudged his thigh with my foot and he blinked into wakefulness. A watchful guard he was not.

"You have fifteen minutes to get ready. Ryder's in there now." I stuck my thumb out at the door. "If you're still in this, meet me in the lobby."

He stared up at me with bloodshot eyes, a myriad of emotions crossing his face. And he nodded.

Then I headed downstairs.

Paper crinkled as I smoothed the deep creases. My head bent so low over the map my nose practically touched it. My hair fell in a curtain around me as I studied the crisscrossing blue and red lines. I pressed my palm to the page and thrust my magic into it like I had before. A point north of here pulsed silver and I circled it with a felt pen.

I wasn't sure why it worked this time. Maybe proximity played a role.

The hotel manager hadn't given me a second look when I'd requested a copy of one of the maps tucked back in a cubby behind the front lobby desk. She'd been distracted by the phone pressed to one ear as she babbled about talking to the police about vandals and the cost of window replacements. After hearing her end of the conversation, I found it difficult to look her in the eye and accepted the colorful document with mumbled thanks.

I wished I still had my phone. Just holding the slim, rectangular box would have provided me a level of comfort. Now, though, I picked up a box of cards from the table tucked in the corner of the lobby and spun it around in my hands. It was an old habit. The box wasn't quite as long as my phone, and the edges felt strange against the pads of my fingers, but it would do for now.

At least I knew where we were going. I slapped the page triumphantly and leaned back. A woman at the table next to me glanced over and wrinkled her nose over her to-go cup of coffee. I bared my teeth in a feral smile, and she looked away.

"Keep that up and your face will freeze like that," a voice warm as molten chocolate murmured beside the sofa. I scooted over, allowing Ryder space to share the small sofa with me. He scrutinized my face again. "Much better. Any luck?" He pointed at the map in front of me.

I snorted. "Take a look."

As Ryder hunched over the page, the woman looked over at me again and this time I cast her a mild smile. I couldn't risk my face freezing after all. She frowned and turned her attention back to the newspaper in her lap. The headline written in broad letters across the top caught my attention: *Evacuations in South Korea as nuclear crisis from North spreads.* The subhead said something about the United States sending a navy fleet to help millions of evacuees flee the island nation, and goosebumps pimpled my skin. Nuclear war was looking less like a hypothesis and more like an eventuality.

"So will you help us, or not?" Finn's steely words scattered my thoughts. "We need to move."

Ryder cocked an eyebrow and tipped his head to the side, some of his still-damp hair flipped into his eyes. This time highlights of green and gold glittered in his locks. I clutched my hands together in my lap to resist touching its softness. The incubus stretched his long legs and slung his arms over the back of the couch, cupping my shoulder possessively. Secretly delighted, I shook off his hand, but not before Finn noticed. His eyes narrowed dangerously.

"Something I need to know about, here?" Finn sputtered, his color rising. He tugged on a hoop pierced in the top of his ear. "Why exactly *did* you stay the night, Ryder? That wasn't part of our agreement."

"You're out of line," I snarled, the rawness of his emotions only succeeded in igniting mine. "He was going to walk me to the door and leave as planned, but then we stumbled across you and your midnight snack." I took a deep breath. "Since I was upset, he chose to stay to make sure I was OK. This," I spun my finger in a circle around the table, "could all arguably be *your* fault. You should be glad he convinced me that you can't help who you are." Finn's jaw ticked and I leaned back. Ryder's chest rumbled underneath my shoulder as he tried to contain his laughter. I elbowed him in the side but it only made the shaking worse.

Men.

"You might have a point," Finn ground out, sounding a lot like admitting that was the equivalent of pulling out his fingernails. "But now that it's daylight, and you're safe and sound, I need an answer about what we discussed last night." His right eye twitched, trying to silently communicate something. I glared and wondered where the woman had gotten her coffee. Maybe I could use some after all.

"I'll be tagging along," Ryder muttered mildly.

"No. No way in hell are you joining us," Finn growled.

"Well. I am the best. And I'm the most powerful of everyone I know, with one small exception." His shoulder butted mine playfully. "And since you are in a dire situation dealing with the Order and all, I think it's best I throw my weight into the ring. This could be fun."

Fun? Dealing with the Order was *fun*? Nothing about any of this was fun.

My fist balled in my lap. One minute he made me feel all relaxed and tingly, and the next I was the most violent version of myself I'd ever seen. *What was up with that?* I caught Ryder watching me from the corner of his eye and his body shifted subtly in anticipation of the slug. Reluctantly, I un-balled my hand. The smile that spread sensuously on his lips indicated that he knew exactly what was going through my head.

"I may not have seen you for a few hundred years, but you broke the pact first," Ryder continued, talking to Finn. "And you dumped a huge problem in my lap. I feel it necessary to handle this personally. Especially since she's involved. Deal with it and move on."

Finn's gaze darted between the two of us. *Hundreds* of years? These guys hadn't talked in *hundreds* of years? At a complete loss for words, the kelpie scoured the map in front of me. He knew he was caught between one hard place and another, but we had an agenda that couldn't be put off while he tried to work out a better argument. "Where are we going?"

I cleared my throat and leaned over the map again, brushing strands of hair out of my eyes. "Wisconsin." I jabbed the circle I'd drawn before. Right in the middle of the northern part of the state, right in the center of the Wakee Indian Reservation. My finger tingled when I tapped the location again.

Finn regarded the map, one finger pressed to his lips. "You know, since you're coming with us Ryder, you could prove yourself useful in a really big way."

"Not gonna happen," Ryder drawled.

"But you can teleport."

"You can teleport?" I gasped, spinning to face the incubus. "That's a thing?"

"Oh it's a thing." Ryder scratched his elbow. "But it's not something I can do right now."

"Why not," cried Finn. "You used to do it all the time—"

"Because I'm nowhere near full strength." He patted his shirt, then his pants, and withdrew a stick of gum. "Because I haven't used magic in two-thousand years. Because regardless of magic returning, it's nowhere near where it needs to be for that kind of thing. Because if I were to try it right now, even after you supercharging me, Zara," he chewed for a second, "I risk splicing us into tiny pieces. Some where we're going and some left there."

That sounded disgusting. I shifted in my seat and I caught the woman staring at me again. Why did she keep looking over here? And why did I get the feeling she was listening to everything we were saying?

Finn was leaning so far forward in his chair he was practically falling off, but noticed my shift in focus. Lazily, he leaned forward and twisted his body one way and then the other as he stretched. As he did, he shot a look at the corner behind him. When he faced front again his expression told me he'd seen her and had gotten a similar vibe.

"Ok. If teleporting is out. It's really time to go," I said and patted Ryder's thigh, wincing at the false cheer in my tone. Ryder eyed me in that way he had where I could see the gears grinding away in his brain but didn't object when I stood up. Thank the gods the man could pick up on nuance. But as I grabbed my bag, the woman who'd been watching me lifted a cell phone to her ear.

Her lips formed an unmistakable word: "Now."

The world stood still for a moment.

Then it sped up. Ryder swung her way. He must have heard her and had lifted a hand to do... what, I'll never know. Because the piercing shriek of a siren pierced the air.

Beyond the woman, through the wide, plate glass doors that formed the front of the hotel, the street lit up, awash in blue and red flashing lights. My mind whirled with confusion, my breath freezing in my lungs. A dozen police cars blocked the road in front of the hotel, holding gawkers back, as people wearing black, uniformed armor and clutching military-style guns marched to the front of the hotel. There were maybe fifty of them, faces all obscured by helmets outfitted with shiny black visors. Their shoulders were emblazoned with red and gold patches, the symbol on them was an O with a forward slash through them.

Everyone knew those symbols.

Everyone knew those uniforms.

The Order.

Finn had been right about everything.

I'd unconsciously moved to the automatic doors at the front of the hotel. In that moment, staring at the face of an establishment I'd never truly considered in my life, seeing exactly what I was up against, I felt incredibly small. I was one girl against an unrivaled military.

A loudspeaker clicked on with an unmistakable squeal followed by: "Zara Ramone, come out now. Keep your hands raised where we can see them."

I'd never felt so cold in my life. It radiated from my bones, from my soul. They knew exactly who I was. And they'd come for me.

A handful of people clustered in the lobby. The manager stood frozen, eyes fixed out the window, her painted mouth hanging wide. The woman who'd obviously issued some sort of command was on her feet, one hand braced on the butt of a gun hanging from her belt. She was fixated on me as if *I* were the threat. *What could I possibly have done to deserve this?*

"Zara, we know you're in there," speaker guy called again. "Come out of the building with your hands raised. You are surrounded. There is no way out. If you surrender peacefully, we can guarantee your safety, by the command of the Order."

The soldiers stood in five long rows, hands clutching their weapons diagonally across their chests. A helicopter droned overhead, dipping into view long enough for me to notice a lack of news station logos. A long gun jutted out from a wide door thrown open along the side. I could feel the eyes on me, people in the lobby slowly realizing I was the object of the Order's attention. Innocent people, even a few fey, all waiting to see what I would do.

I didn't want them to get hurt.

The person on the loudspeaker issued the command again.

I took a step toward the door and Finn was there, gripping my arm.

"Don't you dare go out there. We can figure this out." His eyes pleaded with me to listen to him, begged me to stop and think for a minute. But I'd made up my mind. If they wanted me this badly, badly enough to hint at violence to even more people, they could have me.

I'd accept whatever consequences came with that.

My magic already buzzed right beneath my skin, drawn there by my heightened anxiety and threat to my safety. When I lifted a hand to gently brush Finn away, I found it coated in ice.

"You don't have to come with me," I said, the words hollow in my ears.

I stepped away from him toward the doors, incapable of stopping the ice dripping from my fingers forming icicles. I was so cold. So incredibly cold. When the doors slid open, I heard Ryder scream, "Zara, get down!"

I whirled, dropping low on instinct as three *somethings* whizzed over me, where my head had been. A second later, I realized that loud popping was a gun firing, the woman in the corner approaching with a look of absolute intensity fixed on her face. I threw myself to the side as two more bullets soared by, one grazed the outside of my arm.

Ryder was a blur of shadow.

One second the woman was moving, finger already pulling back on the trigger, the next she was across the room. Her back hit the wall with enough force to dent it, her head snapping back at an angle. Something cracked and her body went limp, a trail of blood dripping from a corner of her mouth. Ryder stood over her, hands tipped with black claws clenched. He snarled as he snatched up the gun and broke it in two.

He turned to me, beautiful golden eyes now bright, radiant red.

Smoke curled around his shoulders. The skin on his face had thinned, if such a thing were possible, as if a beast hid beneath, trying to get out.

Behind me, where the bullets had flown, someone screamed for help. I scrambled to my feet, turning to see a man hunched over the body of the manager. His hands were folded across her chest, pumping rhythmically, as a bright red stain spread across her clothing and pooled on the ground. He called for help again, before pressing his mouth to hers and breathing into it.

Even I knew, by the amount of blood alone, she was already gone.

I wanted to scream. I wanted to yell and holler and lash out. This wasn't fair. That poor woman wasn't a part of this. She should still be standing there, behind the counter, ready to help the next customer. Instead she wouldn't be going home. Ever again. Whoever was waiting for her at home would never see her smile, never hear her voice, never hold her close.

The chapters had ended in her book.

And it was all because of the Order.

22

Zara

The ice that had melted from my hands and puddled on the ground froze over as a surreal, deadly calm washed over me. A wave of clarity flooded my mind, grasping me by the core, and shaking me. The Order couldn't be allowed to operate like this, to take lives at will, to threaten the innocent and the weak.

I swung to the door, face set and blank. The loudspeaker blared again, the person behind it repeating the same promise of no violence. Lies. Ryder moved to my side in three steps. His clawed hand was surprisingly gentle as it gripped my shoulder. The lack of give in his skin, now morphed black as ink, was evident. Juts of bone that resembled horns curled from his temples as the hazy smoke that was his magic spilled from his pores.

I didn't even feel the pain from my arm where the bullet grazed it.

I flexed my fingers, and the ice from the floor flew upward, wrapping around my hands in a strange version of clear armor. Finn stepped to my other side, his face firm with resolve as his shoulders hunched forward.

"I'm not surrendering."

I was done hiding.

Claws dug into my shoulder, a grip of support.

"If they want me, they have to go through me first."

Glass crunched under my feet. One of the windows had shattered when a bullet hit it. As I walked through the front door, I spared a glance back. The humans in the room peered out at me from behind furniture. The man who'd tried to help the woman had stopped, hands stained red, mouth fixed in a grim line.

It was the fey, though, on whom I focused. A handful of them flexed their magic, eyeing my icy fingers and the black brand swooshing across Finn's neck. I shrugged off my light jacket, revealing the crest that pulsated with power and light, knowing what I was asking. Knowing they understood. Two of them flashed feral grins, magic already in motion as they moved forward.

The loudspeaker called again. "Zara Ramone. You have two minutes to come out peacefully or we will be forced to take action."

I pointed at the door.

"That's me. I'm Zara, and I'm the true God of Water. I'm a seventeen-year-old girl who wants to swim, and I didn't want to be dragged into this mess. But you saw for yourself. You saw that woman, that person working for the Order—" I pointed at the badge now visible inside her jacket where it was flung open across her body, "—come after me. This isn't the first time, and it certainly won't be the last. This needs to stop and it won't until I do something about it."

Enough hiding.

Time for the world to know that everything was changing again.

Time for them to discover the Gods weren't quite so dead after all.

Ready to play, I called out to my element, feeling it stir in my belly.

So soon? Energy eagerly snaked up my arms and down my legs, blue sparked out my fingertips, wrapping around my body in a mini-typhoon of power.

Time to kick some serious ass.

192

Let's do this.

It was like a geyser opened, Old Faithful bursting forth from the ground. I choked in a strangled breath as electric power pumped into every last cell. It flooded my eyes, my mouth with a tangy taste, demanding release.

Soon, I called to it.

It relented enough to let me breathe, and I strode through the doors like a gods-damned reawakening.

For the first time, I truly embraced what I was, what I had become. I was the God of Water.

And I was pissed.

The man on the loudspeaker stopped mid-sentence. It cut out with a squeal as I gazed at the wall of soldiers. They shifted as one, the barrel of each weapon aimed directly at me. The police officers had moved back, pushing the bystanders with them about two blocks away. The helicopter remained a dull drone overhead, and I breathed in deep.

"I'm the person you're after. My name is Zara Ramone and I am your long-lost God of Water. You think to try to kill me. You think to threaten violence to bring me in. You kill my friends. You kill my allies. And you kill people I'll never know.

"I'm giving you one chance, one chance as *my* Order, as soldiers in *my* army, as people who are supposedly devoted to *me* to stand down. I will not ask again."

Nothing.

Not a twitch, not a sneeze. No reaction. Even the wind didn't dare blow. The wall of dark visors remained fixed, fingers steady on their triggers.

Then came that irritating bullhorn. "Put your hands up. We don't wish to shoot."

"Too late for that."

Twin balls of electric blue ice tumbled into my hands. Ryder and Finn darted forward, Finn shifting into full horse form as he moved. He threw his head back, red eyes glowing hot as embers, and whinnied, the sound shrill and piercing.

Three soldiers knelt, fingers falling to the triggers of their weapons. Behind them, a modernized cannon hummed, a glowing green light spinning up from its dark depths.

Yeah, I'd call that first move.

The three of us moved as one. Ryder flung out thick, dense smoke that acted like mist before throwing one of the soldiers to the ground. Finn charged right into the foray, head down, razor-sharp hooves crushing feet as he knocked soldiers off-kilter.

I went for the cannon, flinging one of the balls of ice at it as hard as I could. When it hit the exterior, I unclenched my fist, long jagged spikes of icicles shooting outward, gouging deep holes into the metal exterior. Its long gun snapped off when one particularly sharp edge sheared through the barrel. Not waiting to see what would happen next, I fell to the ground as a barrage of bullets flew, pressing my palms to the ground, calling the massive amounts of water beneath the streets at once.

Gunfire spattered as the cement cracked open, a tower of water towering twenty feet tall roared out and slammed into the wall of men blocking me from escape. The armored soldiers scattered, some washed away by the fury of the frothing waves.

Someone screamed behind me and when I turned, a soldier was ripped backward, helmet flying off, and he vanished into the darkness. Ryder emerged.

"Don't lose control again," he warned. "But if you do, know that I'm not afraid to bring you back." Laughter laced his voice as he jumped into a flurry of motion, roundhouse kicking one of the first men who dared broach the fine mists. Another man got an elbow to the gullet, and I winced in sympathy before moving forward to find my own battles.

A dark horse blurred in the fog, monstrous in size, rearing up on its hind legs, backwards-facing hooves lashing out as it whinnied, the sound like bones scraping in a graveyard. When the kelpie came back down, it trampled a few men in front of it, blood spraying and bones snapping. Before I could call out to him, Finn darted back into the fog searching for more prey.

Bullets peppered the ground at my feet, and I hissed when something sharp bit into my side. I touched it briefly, gasping when my fingers came back red. Three men charged, guns blazing, finding strength in numbers. Tingles numbed my fingers and toes as I pulled on the ankle-deep water still gushing from the broken mains. Three towers of water spun up in front of me like snakes and lashed out, hitting the men in their faces, the water forcing its way down their throats.

They drowned where they stood.

I backed away, not hearing the thumps of their bodies hitting the pavement.

Three deaths. Three deaths at my hands.

I was officially a killer.

I didn't have time to think about it now.

A green laser shot through the haze as I searched for a new target. A creature with clawed hands and butterfly wings yanked me back, but not quickly enough as the beam bit deep into my biceps, driving me to my knees. The fey crouched, scanning the dark, and I noticed horns curling around its temples. A booted foot emerged and the fey leaped up, claws sinking through the soldier's plated chest. Blood spurted and he died.

An eagle the size of a Saint Bernard bolted from the fog. Its wings flapping, talons dark with blood, as it headed in the direction the laser had come from.

Strong arms seized me. I struggled against the person's hold, but it wasn't any use. They were much bigger than me, and I hadn't been paying enough attention. The cold, metal barrel of one of those guns kissed my temple, and I ceased my flailing, fairly confident a bullet to the brain would actually kill me.

"Orders were to kill you on sight, girl. But now that I've seen you, I don't know if I want to follow through," a male voice hissed. Hot, garlicky breath wafted over my shoulders. "I kinda want to have some fun first." He pressed his teeth to my neck and bit down. Panic white-washed my mind of all thought as I kicked back, trying to connect with something, anything.

You're never defenseless, my friends screamed, breaking through the barrier I'd thrown up in my head. Power flooded my body in a torrent. I flicked an arm to the side, my best attempt at a cross-body punch and shockingly, an arm of water shot out behind me, smacking my attacker right in the head, sending him reeling to the street and into the water. Enraged, I pulled the water tight around him, a cocoon wrapping tighter and tighter.

He screamed as the vice crushed his bones.

I turned away before he died, blood pouring from eyes, nose, and mouth.

Four.

Something dark and scaly raced in front of me, an extra set of arms extended as it ripped out the throat of a soldier I'd missed in the darkness. The thing tipped back its head in a howl, blue eyes blazing. It spared me a glance before streaking off in search of more victims.

I tore through the fog. Fog that I'd initially been thankful for now obscured my view of the fight. Every now and then I saw soldiers firing weapons. Once, a pair of gremlin-like creatures darted out, ears flapping wildly as they charged down a soldier who'd popped up behind me. Purple magic flashed and sticky webs flew, cutting off the man's yell for help.

A bright green laser flashed through the swirling smoke, barely missing my leg.

I needed to see.

I crouched and dipped my hands in the pool of water, encouraging it to swirl underneath me. It knew what I wanted to do and worked itself in a waterspout capable of holding my weight. When I was comfortable with the feel of water swirling around my knees and feet, I ordered it up, way up, above the smoke and haze that I assumed meant Ryder was OK.

From above, I could see the true extent of the chaos. Flashing blue and red lights surrounded the black cloud spanning about half a block in front of the hotel. First responders curved along the sidelines, guns in hands but clearly unsure about what was happening. Finn was charging at one cannon as another shot beams that merely bounced off his scraggly hair. Without missing a beat, he morphed into a black tiger with grey stripes and swiped at the cannon, knocking it on its side and smashing the barrel.

I hadn't known he could do that.

At his back, a fey with spiked hair that still appeared remarkably human batted a few remaining soldiers away with blasts of golden magic that shot from her hands. A pouch at her side glowed with each blow. One of the soldiers managed to get a shot off before he fell and she crumpled with a whimper.

Ryder darted into the sunlight at one point, one of the soldier's guns in his hands, firing into the haze at members of the Order trapped inside. Red light glowed at his wrists, but I couldn't tell what it was.

People were starting to notice me on my waterspout, hovering high above the action. Fingers pointed and cell phone cameras flashed as I tried to think. I couldn't tell how many members of the Order remained, making it difficult to tell what I could do on the ground.

But something nagged at me.

I was forgetting something.

A chatter of gunfire sounded from my right and I spun the waterspout around, dancing a bit as the water sucked at me, barely holding me in place. The helicopter. I'd forgotten about the freaking helicopter. Ice coated my skin as I faced the angry black military buzzard. I smashed my hands together and webbed my fingers, ejected the stream water out from my body toward the machinery. My body bowing at the effort it took to direct and magnify the power.

The chopper jerked hard to the right, the gunner never letting up. Water sprayed as bullets hit my spinning tower. Thinking fast, I threw up a wall of water. Somehow it worked as enough of a buffer, stopping the bullets before they hit me. It fell away as the helicopter buzzed past and I swiveled around, calling the water to me again, forming two hands reaching from the dark mists below, watery extensions of my own body.

I swung one of the arms at the body of the chopper, satisfied when it rocked on impact. Not enough force, yet. I swung out again, trying to make the water flow faster so it felt harder. The chopper rocked to the side but it was heading toward me once again

An idea came.

A stupid idea. But I was out of other ones.

It might work.

My element swirled close to me, a bodysuit of water drenching my clothes and my hair, forming a protective curtain of liquid and energy. I crouched on one knee, Iron Man style, unflinching as the gun swung around once again. I needed to wait for the right moment. Bullets spattered the tower of water beneath me, coming dangerously close to shredding blood and bone.

A little closer.

My breathing slowed to nothing as the open side of the chopper passed. Something punched my stomach, but I was already in motion, the water propelling me into the body of the helicopter. I skittered over the metal floor and slammed into the opposite wall, barely keeping myself from flying back out the opposite side. My actions caught the men by surprise. The one not manning the gun or flying the contraption scrambled to bring his weapon up in time.

But it was too late.

I saw my eyes, bright as the inside of a flame, reflected in his visor.

They glowed hotter.

And I exploded.

The water that wrapped me in a warm, wet cocoon became a living grenade, shooting needles of water punching through the chopper. The mechanism that caused the blades to whirl exploded, sending the chopper swirling in a tight, fast tailspin.

I was the only one left alive on board, the needles of water having punctured literally every other surface. And I realized we were going down. Hard.

I jumped.

Arms flung wide, air whistling past my body as I fell from sixty stories up.

The water would catch me.

It had to catch me.

From my periphery a fireball exploded as the helicopter slammed into a nearby high rise, sending glass and steel raining down on people below.

I couldn't protect them.

Faster and faster I fell, the hard surface of the street approaching at an impossible speed.

I could feel my energy burning in my belly, trying to pull a in wave to cushion the fall.

But it wasn't going to get there fast enough.

I didn't know what I was doing.

All the doubts I'd had about myself hit me at once.

I was going to fail before I even started trying.

The wind whipped moisture from my eyes, hazing my view of the ground.

Three stories.

Two stories.

A crush of fresh water barreled down the sidewalk, rushing to meet me, but it would be too late.

I closed my eyes.

And slammed into something hard that cushioned my fall.

Golden eyes regarded me warmly before a crushing wave of water sent us tumbling several blocks down the street. I clutched Ryder's hand until we came to a stop, sputtering and spitting out water.

"We really need to work on your landings." His voice was like a blanket on my shattered nerves. "Execution started off beautifully. What a swan dive. Pure poetry." He kissed his fingers. "The exploding helicopter was a nice touch. But the landing... not your best attempt. I might not be there to block your fall next time." He dragged his hands through his sopping hair, sending it shooting up in haphazard spikes, before finally looking at me, his smile faltering.

I felt... weak.

Confused, I ran my hands down the front of my shirt, maybe to get some of the water off, and was surprised to find the fabric ripped around my stomach. It felt sticky. I looked down, mouth going dry as I watched blood seep from the bullet hole that stupid gunner had punched in me.

This was bad.

This was really freaking bad.

"Hey guys, we need to get a move-on. They're subdued for now. That fog of yours has everyone confused, nice one with that, Ryder, but we need to get outta here... Holy shit." Finn's mile-a-minute mouth stilled when I assumed he saw the reason I was lying on the ground. My hands had fallen away from the injury, exhaustion setting in. Ryder was at my side, applying pressure to the ugly, red wound, struggling to stop the bleeding.

A finger touched my chin and tipped it up as my head lolled. Finn's face was speckled with blood and gore, his expression frenzied, lips tight with concern and fury. Ryder spoke to him in a harsh language I didn't understand and kept the pressure on my wound. Finn nodded.

"I'm going to be brutally honest with you. Is that OK?" Finn asked. I drew in a deep breath, suddenly afraid at the amount of effort it took, and blinked, not trusting myself to speak. "This isn't great. The good thing is that you are a God. You might not be immortal, but even injuries like this that would kill the average human in a matter of minutes, can be fixed. We have time. *You* have time. But we need to get moving."

He broke eye contact and spoke to Ryder in that weird language again. Dark strands of hair blew across his pale forehead, catching on streaks of someone else's blood. I vaguely wondered if he had gotten hurt. Then those grassy eyes were then back on mine, evaluating, as his tongue flicked his lip ring.

"This is going to hurt like hell, but I need you to stay with me. OK?" I nodded slowly, wondering how much more painful things could get. My head had barely stopped moving when he ducked down, sliding his arms around my body and lifted up. The staunch pressure Ryder had applied vanished and pain racked my body in violent waves.

I opened my mouth to scream but choked on blood instead.

Turns out it could get worse.

I drove my nails into my palm. Finn said I would get through this. I needed to get through this. My body bounced in his grip, the scenery moving before my eyes as Finn jogged down the street, ducking around cars and trashcans tucked in back alleyways. Ryder led the way, searching for something as his head twisted first in one direction, then another.

Behind us I could still hear the wail of sirens, the occasional burst of gunfire.

"They fey?" I whispered.

"They're fine, mostly," Finn muttered. "They're holding off the Order so we can get you out of here. There weren't many soldiers left, anyway. They'll escape if things get too bad."

Ryder's frenzied searching stilled and he launched himself at a black hatchback SUV tucked into a corner. He whisked a thin, flat piece of metal out of his jacket pocket, followed quickly by smaller pieces. Ryder's fingers twitched and flicked and moved like snakes, fiddling with the lock on the driver's side door until it clicked. He yanked it open and went to work.

"I need a few minutes to get her ready to drive," Ryder muttered, almost to himself, as he tucked his lean body under the console. "You get our girl situated in the meantime. I don't want to stick around any longer than necessary in case those goons followed us."

Finn grunted in response, but was already tugging the back door open as carefully as he could to avoid jostling me around much. Slim chance of that though. My hands were clenched so tight they were probably going to have to pry my nails from my palms with pliers. Every little movement felt like an earthquake.

He took his time setting me down on the leather seats, laying me out comfortably. He even stuffed an old sweatshirt from the backseat behind my head and cotton t-shirts over my arms to warm me up. He frowned as he appraised me, then reached out and started tugging my shirt up.

"While I will accept a good old-fashioned ass kicking as a solid substitute for a movie—" enough blood had cleared my throat to talk, and I slicked my tongue over cracked lips. "—I really must insist on dinner before we do this."

Ryder cackled from somewhere in the front seat, cursing when he cracked his head on the underside of the steering wheel where he pulled at wires. Those wicked eyes flashed back at me over the center console, humor glittering in their depths, before he shook his head and returned to his work. Even Finn cracked a small smile of relief.

"No time for that, Z. I already told you you're not my type." He held out a bottle of water that he must have found in the back. "I do need you to bear with me as I pour this on your injury. I can't submerge you yet—I need that to really help—but it should slow the bleeding."

"Weak-sauce. You owe me whiskey later, then."

"Let's get past this hurdle first," he said, "and I'll buy you a whole bottle of the good stuff."

"Got it! Hot damn, I still know the tricks." Ryder's sudden burst of enthusiasm, along with the roar of a motor, caused both of us to jump. Finn's lower lip was back between his teeth as poured the water over my skin and swiped at it with one of the shirts. I barely felt it. Ryder tucked himself into the driver's seat as Finn pulled my legs across his.

"Let's go."

Ryder didn't need to be told twice. He floored it onto one of the main roads. Finn fixated himself on my injury once again. My shirt was bunched over my ribs and his fingers lightly probed the broken skin. He upturned a second bottle and it tingled, but my magic wasn't catching on the water and healing my body like it had earlier.

Should the pain be receding this quickly?

Should I be feeling quite this light-headed?

Why couldn't I feel that connection?

For the first time since he'd appeared out of nowhere to get us to safety, I noticed the toll battle had taken on Finn. Blood and gore didn't splatter only his face, it was over his whole body. He had scrubbed his hands clean with some of the water, but the rest of the skin on his arms, neck, and clothing was coated in the stuff. His grey polo was soaked with sweat, and he'd removed his jacket at one point. He caught me watching him and gave me another reassuring smile that didn't meet his eyes.

A rasp of breath escaped my lips, and I settled back onto the hoodie, trying to get comfortable. I must have closed my eyes and nodded off at one point because the next thing I heard when I regained consciousness was Finn arguing with Ryder.

"...need to stop and get her underwater."

"We don't have time for that right now, we need to get out of here."

"You don't even know where we're going."

"She drew it on a map, kelpie. We're going north."

"What makes you think they won't follow us there, *Inkie*."

"Cut that shit out right now." Ryder's knuckles were white as they clenched tight around the wheel of the Subaru Outback. "The last I heard from you was four centuries ago. We hardly know each other anymore."

Finn scoffed. "Nobody made you tag along on this field trip of ours."

"You called me up."

"I needed your help. Not your personal attention."

"Whatever. I'm not leaving. You know how my soul craves adventure."

"Correction, your soul, or lack thereof, craves danger. There *is* a difference."

"Maybe I'm here because it's blatantly obvious that you need someone around to help fend off the forces of evil following you around."

"Doesn't that go against everything you stand for? Doing something good for the sake of it being good?"

Silence filled the car, heavy as gravity. I peered through my lashes again to look past the edge of the seat at Ryder whose jaw was clenching and unclenching furiously. "You aren't the only one who wishes they could be more than what they're meant to be." Raw emotion bled into his voice, and my heart clenched.

The emotion was lost on Finn.

"Oh please. You've always loved being a playboy, a Sucker of Souls, the Epitome of Sin. You're still a legend in our old circles. Hell, even circles that you aren't a part of, you're legend." Finn's voice came out bitter as hops. "There's no party too big to grace your presence, no man or woman too beautiful or powerful to escape your enchantments. Don't tell me that now you're a wall flower."

That didn't sound like the Ryder that had held me in his arms in the parking lot, or the Ryder that broke down a door because I was hysterical. That wasn't the man that had followed me through glass doors to face almost certain death because of my recklessness. But the way Finn talked, the earnestness in his voice, I couldn't help but reconsider.

"Habits change, Finn. Circumstances change." I shouldn't be eavesdropping like this. It wasn't my place.

"Circumstances like meeting a God."

"Circumstances that you know absolutely nothing about," Ryder hissed through clenched teeth, sadness lost in an undertone of steel. "And you know as much as I do that there's something about her. Something special. Something that I've never seen or felt or dreamed before. She's a game-changer, man. And I want to be there when she forces the world to spin around her finger."

Yeah, definitely time to make myself known.

The car hit a bump in the road, jostling me in the backseat so the moan that slipped past me was incredibly real. Finn's face was above mine a millisecond later, the piercing in his eyebrow twinkled in the soft light. "Z, you're sweating really bad. I don't like how you look at all."

"I really don't feel very good."

"It's going to be OK. We're going to stop in a minute and get some help."

I was shaking, my vision blurring.

Where was my magic?

"No," the word shot out of me from nowhere. "We don't have time to stop."

What was going on? These weren't my words, my thoughts.

Finn looked as surprised as I felt.

Let me in, a female voice whispered. The same female voice that I'd felt when I'd lost control at the beach all those days ago. *Let me in, or you'll die.*

Who are you?

That's unimportant right now. You've lost too much blood. You exerted too much power. You're drained. You need me to help.

You don't sound like the Kraken, I said.

I'm not the Kraken. But It helped me once before, too.

Who are you? My resolve was weakening. If the Kraken had helped her before, she couldn't be that bad. Whoever she was.

Let me in, now. You need me to fix this mess. Let me in NOW.

The word boomed and my grip on control slipped. I floundered, lost in my own body, reality blurred in my own eyes as someone new took the reins. Someone I wasn't sure I should trust.

"We're pulling over at the next exit. We need to submerge you in water to fix the damage to your body. We can't wait much longer."

"No. We can't. That's the first intelligent thing you've said yet. If we don't deal with this now, I'm going to die." My voice sounded foreign to my ears, harsh as the ocean during a storm and equally angry. Finn drew back, but my hand shot out and grabbed him by the shirt, tugging him close. "You're going to fix me, kelpie. Deal with it."

His eyes darted between mine and his skin went sallow. Even Ryder risked a glance to the backseat to see what was going on. His face hardened as he looked at me, something cool and calculating taking over his features.

"Do what she says, Finley."

Finn glanced at the back of the headrest, then back to my injury. "I don't know how to help you. I don't know what to do."

"That water bottle you found? Pour it right over the wound, again. Do you know if the bullet went through or if it's still embedded inside me?"

"Went clean through and through."

"Good. That makes it easier. Now pour, like that, the water is going to act as a catalyst as *you* help me heal. I'll guide you." His eyes flickered over mine and flashed away as if it were painful to look at me for long. "As a water elemental we are tied together. You get your energy from me. I tapped mine earlier, but you have plenty still running through your veins. I need it." My voice was clipped and sharp as a winter wind whistling through the Rockies. "Lay your hands on the injury."

"I don't want to hurt you."

"I'll hurt a lot more if I die."

He pressed on the wound. Hard. The being in possession of my body didn't flinch, but my spirit felt every touch, crying out in agony. Her, no *my*, hands gripped his, pressing down even harder, pushing what remained of the tatters of my power out and connecting with his. Our combined hands glittered dark blue. Abstract shapes and patterns and swirls rose from my skin. My insides burned. I wanted to scream, but the sound was locked deep inside. Finn flinched as if sensing my agony, but kept his hands still as she wrenched his power from him and used it as if it were her own.

Wildfire ripped through me, and I tugged on it, the pain of it bringing me to the surface for a moment. I gripped harder, pleading with him for help. He glanced up and seemed to realize I was myself again before I was shoved backward by the *Other* presence, slammed into a corner.

Stay back there where you belong, she hissed.

It's my *body. It's* my *power you're controlling.*

And you'll thank me when all this over. Now shut up.

I did. Silently holding in screams as fire burned and bristled and roared.

And then it was gone.

Her grasp on Finn's hands loosened and he pulled back, his face gray and his breathing harsh. But he managed a low whistle as he examined the skin. He was shaking. Ryder glanced back again, eyes skittering over my face, and gave a single nod at seeing my flesh healed and whole again. He spared another look out the front windshield and turned back, a wry twist to his lips.

"Nice work. Now tell us who in the name of the Gods you are."

Not-me stilled, a small smirk sneaking over her features. "I'm Zara."

"All three of us know *that's* false. Now talk."

"How did you figure it out?" Her voice was confident, catty even.

"It was pretty obvious, really," Ryder's voice was disgusted, and he was peering through the rear-view mirror at something. Finn? "And since you aren't going to tell us who you are, we don't really need to know any more. We want Zara back."

She, we, didn't see Finn's fist.

23

Geoffrey

"That was a gods-forsaken nightmare."

The plaques hanging on the wall rattled as the door slammed shut behind me. Toren raised a dark eyebrow.

"On the contrary, I think it went quite well."

I paced behind my desk and pointed over his head at the array of monitors. Three of them showed footage of a girl who was clearly Zara standing on a waterspout in the middle of the city. A fourth broadcasted a roundtable of so-called experts discussing the very same footage playing on the monitor in the background. And the fifth zeroed in on a massive crowd of protestors swarming the streets of London. Many held signs demanding answers from the Order.

Every major news network, and most of the smaller ones, had fixated on this single story, replaying footage of the Order gathering all the way to the helicopter exploding, discussing the implications of the return of the Gods.

"No. Nothing about this is going well." My voice was soft, an indicator of how hot the rage in my stomach was burning. "You assured me this situation would be contained. This, right here, is hardly *contained*." I tapped in my phone's passcode and flung it across the desk at Toren. He looked down. Hundreds of missed calls, dozens of voicemails, and too many notifications to count stared up at him. Our PR team was working overtime trying to contain the closest thing we'd experienced to disaster since the attacks on the temples.

Toren scanned the desk, then lifted the front page of the main newspaper of Rome. Zara's defiant stare-down of the helicopter, *our* helicopter, dominated the display above the fold. *Are they back?* was blasted in big black letters over its propellers.

He poked a finger at the picture. "Every single person saw that she attacked *us* first. They saw her unleash her powers, and the powers of other malicious fey, on the innocent people of Kansas City. We look like the good guys here."

I clenched my jaw and tugged the paper from his hold. I flipped it open, revealing more photos, primarily one of Zara standing before an assembled group of Order soldiers, looking very much like a warrior princess than a mere seventeen-year-old girl. And she was clearly outnumbered.

"And everyone is also talking about this. A team of our soldiers surrounding a downtown hotel in the middle of the morning, demanding a *girl* come outside. They saw a teenage girl staring down the barrels of fifty weapons, demanding they move away, or else she would be forced to take action."

"And we look like heroes," Toren cried, shoving the paper away. "When our soldiers stepped up to take her into custody—"

"Soldiers with guns pointed at her head."

"—she lashed out. That girl is clearly unhinged. And the Order knew it! We look like we were trying to control a highly volatile situation. Which we were! She's a danger to society and needs to be brought in. If anything, this increases the pressure on her to turn herself in. This can't be held against us."

"But it can. And it is. I didn't want..." I slammed my hands on the desk and stood up. I moved to the window and stared out at the endless blue sky. "I didn't want to make a spectacle of this. I didn't want her to feel threatened even more. Especially after what happened back in Norway."

"And why is that?" Toren fired back, already on his feet. He braced his fists on his hips, right above the daggers that dangled at his sides. He hadn't shaved in several days and looked older for it. "Why are you so determined to treat her like a saint? To give her the benefit of the doubt? She is a threat to our very existence, and you're acting like you yourself didn't spout those very words."

His breath came out hard, black eyes flashing with temper.

Because part of me doesn't want the vision to be true.

I pinched my nose and leaned a forearm on the windowpane rather than voice my thoughts on the matter. The brands on my head throbbed, a constant reminder of what I was and what I believed. I stood there, breathing, watching the clouds hover low on this sweltering day, until my blood-pressure calmed.

"Why did she say it was 'too late?'" I asked.

"What?" Toren fell into his chair, legs crossed at the ankles.

"Outside the hotel. They ordered her to stand down or no one would be hurt. And she said it was quote 'too late.' What did that mean?"

"She's probably delusional, seeing danger around every corner," Toren said. "Or maybe she was talking about Norway. Maybe she's fixated on that. I don't know. You're asking me to get into the mind of a girl who either doesn't know enough about anything or knows far too much about everything. I can't play those kinds of mind games." He threw his hands in the air before snatching a pen out of the holder. "I don't particularly want to."

"Her arm was injured."

"What?"

I hadn't meant to say the words out loud. The footage our team had shot on the ground of her exiting the hotel came to mind. Every inch of her was filled with determination, her eyes alight with fire and fury. Why would she look that way? And why was blood dripping down her arm from a long cut right above her elbow?

"Nothing. Never mind."

He tapped the pen on the desk.

"What would you have me do next?" he asked. He was staring down at Zara's face on the newspaper cover again. "You heard the Council. They want her brought in, dead or alive. What do you suggest?"

"I'll handle this personally."

Shock flashed across his broad cheekbones, the natural furrow over his nose deepening. "You can't be serious. What happened out there, what happened in Kansas City, that wasn't my fault. There was nothing I could do to stop that from happening. Everything was thought out." Words were flying from his mouth, getting louder and louder until he was practically shouting.

"I consulted with you. I ran through every scenario with my best tacticians. No one thought she would flip out like that. No one. Those fey friends of hers, sure. But not her. You can't take me off this. Not now. The Council barely has faith in me already. My age, my family—they doubt the title enough as it is. If you remove me… Geoffrey, don't do that to me. You'll make me look weak. You'll make *us* look weak."

I sighed and shook my head. He didn't understand that we already looked weak.

I pushed away from the window and moved behind the desk once again. I scooped up my phone and slipped it into the jacket pocket of my suit. Another glance up at the television screens hardened my resolve. I made sure I was completely calm, one-hundred percent committed to my plan, before speaking.

212

"There will come a day when, as a leader, you'll know when it's time for you to personally step in and handle whatever is happening. Today marks that moment for me. You did admirably, and I'm sorry if I haven't given you enough benefit of the doubt." I wetted my lips. "But this burden is mine to bear. I created this mess, now it's time for me to solve it. I'm sure, in the meantime, there are other problems that likely need your immediate attention."

Something ugly flashed across his face, an expression of pure disgust and resentment. He'd never before looked at me that way, like he looked at his parents, and it tugged at something in my chest. But the second appeared, it was gone. In its place was a tight, understanding smile. I wondered if I'd even seen the expression at all.

"Let me know if you need my assistance," he said stiffly.

"Always."

As soon as he turned and left, I pulled my phone from my pocket and started making calls.

24

Zara

I wondered about dying.

How exactly was one supposed to feel in the midst of death's grasp?

Was there some seven-step acceptance program involved?

Were visions normally associated with the afterlife?

If so, sign me up, because I could really get used to this place.

"Would you like another drink, miss?"

I leaned back in the pastel pink patio chair and up into the face of the handsome gentleman who kept my teensy cup filled with shots of hot tea. I'd been here for hours, watching clusters of people in a wide range of genders and ethnicities pass on the street, caught up in the minutia of their own lives, and the sun had yet to move even a smidgen across the gorgeous, eggshell blue skies. A small, white umbrella with scalloped frills shaded me from its glare.

I cradled the dainty china and smiled up at the server. "Surprise me."

"Right away, miss."

The drink coated my tongue, a heady blend of sweet and floral that was what my body craved. I groaned into the bottom of the cup.

I'd never seen this place before in my life, yet everything about it delighted me.

If this was dying, I didn't mind one bit.

"I see you've found my favorite spot."

I stilled, senses drastically heightened, afraid to move a single muscle. I knew that voice. I'd never forget that deep accent that sounded so very elegant while speaking nothing but lies.

Geoffrey took my lack of response as an invitation and tugged a chair that matched mine in every way but color away from the table. Its surface was so small that when he sat, our knees brushed. It took everything in me to not punch him in the face.

I admired the stoniness of my hands as I set the empty cup back on the surface without so much as a rattle or a tremble. He flicked the button of his smart blue blazer open and twisted the silver cuff-links at his wrists. The motion revealed tattoos that wrapped around his wrists in an array of twisted flames, cool waves, and lightning bolts.

"What are you doing here?"

His bi-colored eyes revealed nothing as they flickered across my face. "That's an odd question."

"Does the underworld make you face your fears before it accepts you into its dark depths," I pondered aloud. That actually made a fair bit of sense if I thought about it hard enough.

Geoffrey's brows raised, wrinkling his forehead and smooshing the symbols. "Are you dying?"

"I thought I was."

"Why would you be dying?"

This was starting to feel less like a dream and more like that place from before. That reality disguised inside a dream. When he'd first found me and sicced his dogs on my friends. The simple beauty of this place felt sinister all of a sudden, and I tugged the capped sleeves of my lacy, white dress tight against my skin.

"Where am I?"

"Where did you think you were?"

"Stop answering my questions with questions."

The intensity of his gaze never weakened. "Tell me what I want to know."

I shot to my feet, icy resolve crumbling. His careful tone, a blend of strength and concern, reminded me so much of my mother in that moment that I craved her; I wanted to sink into her arms, and hold her close. Let her shut out some of the world, if only for a little bit. I scoured the pavement for my purse before remembering this was a dream that wasn't a dream, and despite how fancy it looked I didn't have a purse. My chair fell backward as I shoved away from the table, the café, and *him*.

"Please don't go, Zara."

I paused, one hand braced on the chair, the other clenched at my side.

"It's taken so much to get you here. Please, don't run off. I'm horrible at this. I truly am." Geoffrey almost sounded like he *cared*. "Please sit back down. This is my favorite café in all of Rome. Hear me out. At least for a little longer." The waiter was back in his spiffy black and white outfit, a rotund cup in one hand and a small plate in the other. "Frederick even brought you something. Please *sit* and I promise to keep you no longer than one cup."

I stared, my mind a twisting knot of questions, then turned and fumbled my chair upright once more. I sat slowly as Frederick placed the items on the table before us. I gazed down at the rich, brown depths of the latte, and the careful swirls of white foam on top of the milky espresso.

"You have one drink," I said.

I wrapped my hands around the wide base of the cup and brought it to my face. Stream uncurled on my skin as I breathed in its heady aroma. Vanilla. So basic, yet so completely perfect. Geoffrey had stopped fiddling with his sleeves, and his green and grey gaze was fixed on the cup as I took a sip from the top of the foam. His nostrils flared when the scent carried on the wind, and he appeared almost... dazed.

"You know you can order one of these yourself, right? It is your dream."

A sheen a sweat gleaned across his brow, and I didn't think it had anything to do with the midday heat and humidity. Though that damn sun still had yet to budge even the slightest.

"I need you to stop running from me."

I crossed my legs at the knee. "I'm here, aren't I?"

"Not here in the dream. In real life. You need to stop hiding and come to Rome."

My lips uncurled in a sardonic smile. "Why would I do that?"

"The Council of the Order wants to talk to you. *I* want to talk to you."

"What about?"

"Your motives. Where you've been hiding all these years. What you intend to do now that magic has been unleashed on this planet." He scooped up the buttery scone Frederick had deposited before him and took a bite. Crumbs tumbled down the front of his mossy-colored dress shirt.

I took a deeper, longer gulp of my latte, the scent no longer an enticement but a challenge. "And you think I actually have answers for you about that?"

"Yes."

"You have much more faith in my abilities than me, I'm afraid." I brushed off my hands. "Why can't I just talk to you here? Right now?"

"After what happened in Kansas City, that's not an option. You're growing considerably more dangerous, Zara, reckless even. You're lucky you didn't kill anyone with that stunt you pulled." He sounded exactly like my father. Admonishing me for something that wasn't even my fault, trying to reduce me to nothing even when I'd done nothing to deserve it.

My laugh was hollow, ugly.

"That's really rich coming from you."

His frown deepened.

"You aren't leaving me with many options here," he said. "You either come in or I can't guarantee your safety before the Council. And trust me when I tell you that you'll need all the help you can get when you come head to head with their finest."

Coffee sloshed over the rim of my cup as I slammed it to the table.

"And you left me *no* choice," I gritted through my teeth. "You and your minions hunted me down, surrounded me, sent that woman to shoot me when I was about to surrender. You're hypocrites. All of you. I can't stand how little regard you have for innocent life." I smacked my hands to my upper chest, my cheeks burning, eyes stinging with outrage. "I even offered you a *second* chance to let me go, to protect the people that you claim to want to save from *my* recklessness. But you *still* came after me. AND THEN YOU NEARLY KILLED ME!"

My hand slid down the front of my dress and pressed against my stomach, exactly where Ryder and Finn had desperately applied pressure some time ago.

"You nearly killed me," I repeated.

Geoffrey's deep tan had turned ashen, eyes wide and haunted on his face. The X's of scars carved into his cheeks stood out sharply against the bone. A single hand shook where it rested on the table before he clutched it tight.

"What woman?"

"The woman in the lobby."

"She shot you?"

My hand drifted to my arm where I remember the burn of the bullet. The pain had been lost in the typhoon of emotion and adrenaline that flooded me in the following moments. His eyes tracked the movement, lingering on the bluish threads I tried to push down again. "She tried to."

He cleared his throat and re-crossed his legs, a hint of long white socks flashing between the hem of his pants and the tops of his scuffed loafers.

"We didn't have a woman inside the hotel."

"I call bull."

"All of our people remained outside the building. They only needed you to come outside. You would have been allowed to surrender. No harm, no foul. Straight and simple." His voice was thin, strained. He reached for a napkin, and when he didn't find one, he snatched one thrown atop a nearby table. The starchy fabric blotted the sweat evident on his forehead, and the symbols of the Gods pulsed black and white.

That slightly manic expression was back.

I took three massive gulps of the latte, wishing I'd never made that promise.

"I don't know what to tell you," I said. "But I watched as she made a call to someone. My friend and I heard her tell them to go. And the second after she said that, *your* people started screaming at me to come outside. When I tried to do that, because I didn't want anyone getting hurt, she pulled a gun and started firing." The café faded as my words took me back. "When that manager died you left me no choice, Geoffrey. You—"

"You're wrong."

What was happening? Something dark and hungry now twisted his features as he lashed out at me, feet swinging to the ground as he pushed himself up. Just like last time, he'd pulled a Jeckyl and Hyde.

The rational leader of a global organization swamped by this rabid creature.

"That lobby was cleared. Our surveillance showed only you and those two fey with you in the lobby at the time. The manager was hit by stray gunfire when she entered at the wrong time." He stood abruptly, chair falling aside in his rush. I scrambled backward, the hem of my dress catching on the edge of the table. Magic pulsed under my skin as fear speared its icy fingers through my veins.

This wasn't the same person.

This couldn't be the same person.

"I read the reports. I watched it all happen." I shivered at the words. *Why wasn't he listening to me?* "You charged outside. You attacked my soldiers. You used magic and influenced other fey to do the same. You destroyed my helicopter and killed my people. You're the reason you almost died."

"That's not true," I cried, air coming in gulps as my legs knocked against furniture. The comforting waves of people had long since vanished into the depths of his dreamscape. Frederick was a figment of imagination, incapable of coming to my rescue. My hand landed in cake as I stumbled back again, barely evading Geoffrey's careful stalking.

"Come with me, Zara, and put this all to rest."

"Never," I yelled and brought up my hands to ward him off as he closed in.

And then he stopped, twisted features smoothing as his mouth dropped open. We both looked down at the icicle protruding from his chest, right where his heart would be. It dripped brownish liquid onto his otherwise clean shirt. The latte. I'd used it to save my life.

My hands flew to my mouth in horror. A trickle of blood ran from the corner of his mouth as he looked up, the madness still evident in his smirk.

"You're going to regret doing that."

I blinked.

In that half second, the café vanished and I reappeared in an entirely different world. This one was shrouded in darkness. Stars glimmered overhead, their soft light reflecting from the smooth pool of water before me.

At least Geoffrey, and the bloody hole in his chest, was gone.

But I really, really wanted to wake up.

Brace yourself, a whispery female voice warned. I'd heard that voice somewhere before. *The fates have summoned you. Remember, you're stronger than you know.*

"You've answered our call, God of Water." Three new voices, speaking in harmony, circled me. When I turned to look, six pinpoints of yellow light reflected from the shadows of a surrounding wood. "Now it is time to embrace who you were always meant to be. The world has waited long enough."

These were the most convoluted dreams in the history of dreams.

How could I have answered a call I didn't remember getting?

I led you here. Have faith. Your future is already set in motion.

I pressed my hands to the sides of my head, unsure where to look or where to turn.

"Do you believe you can walk on water?" The trio droned.

Did I what?

Yes.

A fist gripped my intestines and twisted. The word spilled from my mouth: "Yes."

Wait. What? Whose voice was that? Was that my voice?

When was I going to wake up?

It had to be a dream.

"Let the Trial begin."

I scrubbed my arms. I was shuddering, shivering, suddenly

nauseous. What was I supposed to do? Walk on the water? The lake in front of me? I mean, that should be pretty easy. I could *breathe* underwater and stand on a twister of the stuff, so, theoretically, walking on top of it should be cake.

Right?

I tried to draw on my magic but it was like blocked it. I tried pushing it out of the way, but nothing happened.

"Not magic. Belief."

Oook. That's how this was going to go down. I *only* had to walk on water.

Because I wanted to.

Brilliant.

Sure, no problem over here. I eyed the water, wondering if some malevolent beast lurked beneath the surface. Not a ripple. Nothing. Even the crickets were quiet. I breathed deep and swung my arms out to loosen my shoulders. Wispy strands of hair tickled my neck, and I swiftly braided them back. Luckily, I still had my orange hair tie.

Here goes nothing.

One bare foot stepped out on the surface and met solid resistance.

No one was more surprised than me.

The surface trembled but held.

One step.

Two.

And a few more for good measure.

You found out you have magic and now you think you can do the impossible?

I was, wasn't I?

I wanted to pull on my magic, clutch it tight for reassurance. But I didn't dare.

I scanned the horizon, only now realizing I was standing in the middle of the lake.

I'd done it.

I'd walked on water.

But did you?

As I pressed my fingers to my face in amazed shock, something cracked. An ominous, horrifying sound that echoed through the trees and bounced off the glass on which I stood. Afraid, I stepped back... into nothing.

My back crashed into the water first. It dragged me under, surrounding my head. Instincts barely gave me enough time to gasp in a last, saving breath. I sank hard and fast. I clawed out, hands swirling, legs kicking, reaching for the murky surface. But it was like hands pulling me down, down, down. I couldn't breathe. The gills weren't coming. My magic wasn't flowing. My lungs burned red as I struggled to keep what little air I had left inside of me.

There was no saving me now.

And I realized now this was no dream.

I'd read somewhere the brain couldn't comprehend its own death, that's why it would always wake it's subject up from a dream right before dying. Well, judging by the diminishing stream of bubbles pouring from my mouth, I was getting pretty up close and personal with death right now. Physics demanded my lungs expand, attempting to pull in oxygen. But it only found water.

Just water.

Water flowing into my lungs.

A feeling much, much worse than getting stabbed and shot.

Worse than Anisra.

Worse than seeing Kaz. And that manager.

Death had me tight in her grip.

This was truly the end.

A soft, white light glowed faintly in front of my face. I couldn't quite make it out, but I felt It's powerful, hungry energy.

"We find you unworthy. A trial failed is a sentence to die."

Words that meant nothing to me.

My muscles were already going lax as I floated there, suspended in the element I loved so much.

Wait.

I knew that voice. The world stilled. The Kraken? A rough tentacle wrapped around my middle and towed me to the surface, tossing me to the grassy shores. I coughed buckets of water from my lungs, my throat burning hot with the effort as I dragged in searing breaths of oxygen. I'd never tasted anything more beautiful in my life.

That's right. I was alive.

For now.

Heaving in gulping breaths, I squinted out at the lake. A glowing human-shaped figure hovered on the surface, facing off with a trio of small, dark bumps.

She was tricked. She wasn't ready for the Trial. Spare her this time. Definitely the Kraken. I'd recognize that too-patient tone anywhere. What was It arguing with?

"You know the rules of the Trial."

I also know there's no room for trickery here.

Trickery?

"She attempted, she failed. She will die. It is the way."

I dispute the findings.

The lumpy bumps straightened to their full heights, now towering over the Kraken. From where I was laying, collapsed as my body tried to recover from yet more brutal abuse, I could make out the glint of those six golden eyes from before.

The Kraken's words seemed to have some sort of effect on them. What was It doing?

"Are you evoking the Challenge?"

I am, the Kraken murmured.

"You realize the consequences of tying your life-force to hers." The Bumps seemed to be in some sort of disbelief.

I do.

"The Gods are no longer immortal. When she's gone..."

I know what I'm agreeing to. The Kraken cut off the trio of melodic voices.

"If she fails again?"

She won't. She will learn. I have more faith in her than any of the Gods before her.

"So be it. One life for another. Your Challenge is accepted." I could scarcely lift my head and watch as a golden glow surrounded the trio standing on the water. One was tall and lanky, the middle one shorter and robust, and the third stood as tall as a child. All wore beautiful cloaks spun of starlight and webs that pooled at their feet. But their faces were feral, twisted with scars and hooked noses, their hair hanging lank and snarled down their backs.

Golden light glittered from the Kraken's chest, expanding and filling the air around It in a cloud of mist. It was beautiful. And then it was gone, sucked into the haze.

I blinked slowly. Where the trio had stood—nothing.

The Kraken let out a long gasp, bending in two as if in pain. And as It bent, a horrifying, gut-wrenching agony filled me, ripping at my tattered emotions and raking sharp claws over the broken shards of my soul. And then it stopped.

My head flopped to the ground. I stared as the Kraken straightened and floated over to me. It touched my cheeks with a glowing, human-like hand, and stroked my cheek. Magic bloomed, warm and familiar, connecting with me once again. The Kraken bent close and I could make out Its sexless face and colorless eyes.

"What did you do?"

You'll understand one day, Zara. It didn't appear to have a mouth so the words must be flowing between our minds. I'd thought It sounded tired before. Now It was world-weary.

"Why would you sacrifice immortality for me?"

Oh it's much more than immortality. It said. *But I can feel the hope rising once more, I can feel the energy and excitement echoing in the core of the earth. You will usher in a grand period of change.* It stood and scanned the darkness. *Change that only comes but once in a million years.*

"What?"

It pressed a finger that buzzed with electricity to my lips. *No time for questions. Your protector comes. It's time for me to go.*

The Kraken's hand melted from mine, and I heard someone calling my name even as the glow of the mythical beast faded.

"Zara! Where are you?" Ryder sounded more amused than concerned. "If we'd known you were going to disappear, we would have shackled you down."

His low chuckle filled the grove, and I closed my eyes against the swell of emotion rising in my chest. I was back. At least, it felt like I was back.

Rather than respond, I wrapped my arms around my knees and leaned my cheek on pants I now recognized as flannel. The Kraken must have dried them for me because my magic was back. It twisted and twined under my skin, danced in my chest. My relief was palpable.

But whose clothes were these? The last thing I remembered was bleeding out in the back of a car. Lovely memories and such, considering I'd ripped Finn's magic from him in a morbid form of elemental rape.

Leaves crunched and the warmth that followed Ryder everywhere enveloped me. He touched the top of my head, sifting his fingers through my hair. My rough braid had come undone at some point, but I was past caring. I preened, leaning into the soft feel of his fingers, a low hum sounding in the back of my throat.

"Found you."

"Was I lost?" I murmured.

If he wanted to ignore what had happened before, I was more than willing to go along with it.

"In a fashion. Finn seemed to think so anyway." He tugged some knots out of my hair and folded to the ground behind me. He separated my hair into familiar ropes and twisting them into some sort of complicated, twisty braid I couldn't begin to comprehend. I relaxed into his touch, enjoying the languid feel of my body as the pain of nearly drowning slowly fell away.

I didn't even want to think about that twisted conversation with Geoffrey.

If anything, it solidified my distrust of the Order and its motives.

"You've been out for two days," he murmured wryly. "It's good to have you back in the land of the living again."

"Days?"

"Yep. We pulled over shortly after that... whatever happened in the car. We've been at some stupid crummy, run-of-the-mill motel in Iowa since then. This pond thing, I think it might be something farmers use, isn't that far away. It stands to reason that you of all people would somehow stumble across it." His voice was teasing, and a hand slipped over my shoulder, beckoning for one of the other spare hair bands I wrapped around my wrist. I tugged one off to hand it over, but he snagged my wrist instead and tugged me around to get a look at my face. His gaze swept over me sensually, and I drank in his darkness, the comfort it brought. His amber eyes finally stopped on mine.

"There you are." He sounded awed.

I bit my lip and twisted back around. Warmth soaked my cheeks uncomfortably. I didn't understand how he made me feel, this sensation of belonging and understanding. It felt more intimate than the kiss we'd shared, and I pressed my lips together at the memory. I imagined he was smirking when he tied off the braid and tugged on my shoulders in an unspoken cue to get moving.

"Why did you say that... like that?" I asked when he pulled me upright.

"We kinda lost you for a bit back there, in the car. But you're back now. We'll figure this out."

"How did you know?"

"I'd know those eyes of yours anywhere, glowstick," he said. "That *thing* back in the car wasn't you. I don't know who that purple-eyed bitch was, but I sure as hell don't ever want to see her again." He shivered for effect, but I had a feeling he would actually be more than willing to go toe-to-toe with it if it meant helping me. "Oh, and all that ordering us around like we were your minions wasn't really your style."

I spotted the glow of the motel sign straight ahead. I truly hadn't wandered all that far. A few minutes later, Ryder opened the dingy door to a truly shabby room. I only had a second to see the drab, floral comforter on one of the twin beds when I was tackled in an ironclad hug. Relief overwhelmed me as I breathed in the scent that was wholly Finn, a mix of sea and cotton, and wrapped my arms around him tightly. Unbidden, my magic spilled out and twined around his, liquid warmth settled between us.

I realized I didn't hate him.

I never had.

Not even when he was in full-blown kelpie mode.

No, this man was digging a hole deep into my heart and stars help anyone who came between us. Even my magic embraced him like a friend; the water magic languished in the feel of other water magic. He felt familiar.

He felt like *family*.

Speaking of family, odds were they'd seen the debacle that was Kansas City. There was no way my face wasn't out there, no way the media hadn't made the connection. Not since the Order had everyone looking for me. I needed to get home and see my mom, check on my dad.

I dug my nose into the softness of his shirt and pulled Finn even tighter.

"Don't you dare vanish on me like that ever again," he breathed into my neck after a few minutes. It tickled and I squirmed in his hold. "We're partners in this. You hear me? Wherever you go, I go. Don't think otherwise."

It was hard to believe that a few days ago I hadn't even liked this guy, and now... we were Partners. With a capital P.

I drew in a deep breath and tried to pull away, but he kept his hands firmly wrapped around my shoulders as he stared at my face. First, I saw relief and then something darker as he zeroed in on the braid slung over my left shoulder. He shot a look at Ryder leaning on the wall to the bathroom and spun me around to take a better look. I could feel him tracing the looping, swirling patterns of my hair, careful to not pull hard.

I looked from Finn to Ryder and back to Finn, confused.

"We'll be talking about this later," he said in a low whisper to Ryder. I tugged away, a hand protectively folding over the artwork, and I caught the expression in Ryder's eyes—something longing and pained and beautiful.

I was missing something.

But now wasn't the time.

I turned back to Finn as guilt crept over me.

"Finn, I am so sorry for before..."

"Don't think anything of it. Gods know you'd suffered yet more trauma."

He thought I was talking about running away.

He couldn't be more wrong.

"No, I need to apologize. For before." He turned to me now, arms tensing at the words that tasted like ash in my mouth. "I had no right to do that to you."

"What happened before—" The hostility rolling off him in waves subsided. "It wasn't you. I don't know who it was, but it wasn't you. OK? And we'll figure it out, we'll figure out what is going on inside you. Whatever it takes." I reluctantly nodded and took a seat on the edge of the bed, arms wrapped around myself once more. When he held up two fingers, I felt a little better.

"Second, I would do anything to protect you. Anything. Even die for you." He knelt in front of me and pulled my arms away from my body. He shifted and tucked my hands between his. The dark slashes of my symbol glared like a beacon on his skin. "I've sworn an oath to Water. I've sworn my life to protect *yours*. If my magic is the only thing that can save your life, I want you to promise that you'll never hesitate to take it. Take all of it. Promise me."

Unable to pull back, I forced myself to meet his eyes and I nodded. "I promise."

I promise to do whatever I can to save you, even if it costs me my life.

"Well. Let's hope it doesn't come to that again," I murmured, smiling to lighten the atmosphere. "I'll do a better job at, you know, not getting shot, and you keep your magic to yourself."

"Now that we've got all this sorted out—" Ryder snorted and pushed off the wall he was propping up, "—we really should get going. It'll be dawn in a few hours, and I'd like to get to the reservation before nightfall."

And there was that wonderful smack of reality.

"Where are we anyway?" I asked, looking around for my bag.

Finn dropped it unceremoniously in front of me along with a change of clothing. I didn't recognize any of it and absently wondered about my clothing from the fight. They'd probably burned it or something.

"Off I-35, about 30 miles south of Des Moines. Right on the way to Wisconsin," Ryder said, pulling the last of his stuff into a black duffel. Since when did he have stuff?

I frowned and scratched at my scalp through the braid, stopping when Ryder leveled a look at me.

There was a change of plans.

"I don't want to go to Wisconsin yet."

25

Geoffrey

The casing of the phone cracked when it hit the vinyl side of the plane.

My head dropped, cradled in my hands as I scrubbed my eyes.

It was the magic. Her magic. It was making me insane. Every time I got close to her, even mentally, it was like part of me snapped away. I became an entirely different version of myself. An ugly version I wanted to lock away because it reminded me too much of that boy I'd left behind long ago.

Now the magic buzzed inside me: hot, wild, and fierce.

I raised my head, flexing my hands reflexively to shake away the edginess that burned in my blood, seared my skin. Two deep breaths later and I regained some feeble control. The rising tide of helplessness receded.

If only Toren would answer his phone.

Things weren't adding up. Not the photos, not the stories.

Zara had been earnest when she'd lashed out about how we'd tried to kill her. Part of me wanted to believe her, wanted to believe that she wasn't lying. That she wasn't plotting something malicious at this very moment.

She'd looked so shocked, those aquamarine eyes wide and horrified when I'd accused her of firing the first shot. She was either a hell of an actress or...

I wanted to pace, but the private jet I'd selected from the Order's fleet was too small to allow the movement I required. Instead, I wrung my hands in a poor attempt to keep from scratching them.

Toren had no reason to lie.

None.

And he'd stood before the world, proud and tall at my side, explaining away the events of what had happened in Kansas City. His words were sure, his reports sound, his conviction unshakable. It also didn't make sense that he'd want to take her out.

He had nothing to gain.

I needed to talk to him, for reassurance if nothing else.

He was one of my only allies in the entire world. If I couldn't put faith in that, like I couldn't put faith in the actions of the Gods, then I was truly nothing.

My subconscious twinged, a detail struggling to rise.

Something about that dream wasn't quite right.

Aside from the obvious.

The pilot's voice came through and overhead speaker. "We're estimated to land at 6:04 p.m. local time, sir."

I squeezed my hands in my lap and peered out at the choppy grey waves beneath the belly of the plane. It was a risk, a calculated one. But if I were seventeen and on the likely verge of a traumatic breakdown, there was only one place I'd want to go.

My fingers burned.

When I looked down, smoke curled from my fingertips.

That sense of helplessness swirled uneasily.

"Make sure my car is waiting."

26

Zara

Finn slipped the straps of a backpack over his shoulders. "And where, exactly, *do* you want to go?"

"Home."

"Nebraska? Why?"

"I want to see my parents." I shrugged. "I've only talked to my mom once. They've probably seen me on TV back here in the States. They need to know what's going on. And I need answers, answers that only they'll be able to give."

Ryder cursed and dropped to the bed. "That's a waste of time. And I bet the Order is anticipating you'll head there next."

I spun a finger at both boys in a universal gesture to turn around so I could change out of my grimy pajamas.

"Good thing it's not your call," I quipped.

Ryder bristled. I could tell by the tension in his shoulders. "It is her right, Finley?"

Finn swiveled on his heel as I tugged on the sleeves of my jacket. I opened my eyes wide so he could see the color of my irises. He flipped me off. "Unfortunately, yes."

Finn opened the motel room door, gesturing us outside with a frown. He dropped the sarcasm. "Whatever that thing was before isn't listening right now, are they?"

I hesitated right outside the door, my foot hovering above the ground. Good question.

"No," I drew out the vowel as I mentally spiraled inside myself, probing corners of my powers for a hidden entity. Granted, I wasn't quite sure where she was or if I could even really tell if she was listening or not. Or if she was even there anymore. "No."

Ryder's stiff shoulders relaxed marginally. "Good. She doesn't need to know what we're up to."

"I've never known a subject's eyes to change like that during a possession," mused Finn as we ambled up to a car I assumed was ours. "I know people can look disjointed when a witch has them in their control, but I've never heard of the possessor having such a distinct, external look before."

Ryder offered a one-shoulder shrug in response.

"Purple eyes aren't all that common either..."

"You and I both know of two beings with eyes that color." Ryder slanted his eyes at Finn. The kelpie scratched his head, ruffling his dark hair, and ran a finger over his teeth before bouncing his head in an undecided, agreement sort of way. He tugged the door open and slipped inside.

"Could you get a read on whoever it was inside of you?" Ryder asked. "You'd have the closest access to them."

I settled into my seat and buckled in as we pulled out of the lot. "Female. Powerful. Very powerful. Knowledgeable about my abilities, the extent of my powers. She's kicked me out of my own control twice now," I said. "She's fierce, arrogant, demanding. And she likes to have control."

The vehicle slowed and Ryder pulled into a gas station near the interstate.

"We desperately need gas if we're going to hit up Nebraska... or anywhere." From my spot in the backseat I could see the gauge dipping beneath the E. His tone lightened and he patted his belly in an adorable kind of way. "Also, time to grab some munchies. I'm starving."

"One sec," I said. "Before we all leave, I want to throw out the option of teleporting one more time. That sounded totally awesome before."

"I really wish you hadn't said anything," Ryder grumbled at Finn. "I can't teleport. I just can't. I'm getting stronger every day. But it's not there yet. You could kiss me silly right now," my jaw dropped, "which I would be completely on board with by the way, and I still wouldn't have enough energy."

"Worth a shot," Finn mused.

I smacked Ryder's shoulder and hopped out, reaching for the black credit card he offered for snacks. It was one of many I'd noticed in his wallet. Rather than letting go like a normal person, he shifted his grip and wrapped his fingers around mine. My stomach trembled as his eyes drifted over my face, back to the braid, then again to my eyes. I winked and he smirked, shoving me toward the door of the convenience store.

"I demand chocolate. Lots of it. M&M's, Snickers, Twix." I walked away as he rattled off more names. I found the selection easily enough, murmuring something to Finn about needing sandwiches or something with substance, and blindly snatched up a dozen bags of treats.

As I passed by the large front windows leading to the register, I glanced outside. I'd expected to see Ryder squeegeeing the windows or checking for trash in the back seat, anything to burn some of the massive amounts of energy he always radiated. What I hadn't expected to see was the fierce intensity on his face, the bent-at-the-knees stance that was somehow predatory as he stared at a brunette fiddling with one of the pumps next to ours. His hands were curled into fists on the hood of our car. The woman turned toward her vehicle, and he visibly forced himself to relax, to turn away from her. I wondered at the restraint it probably took to hold his hunger back and at the weird tightness in my chest as I watched.

My focus on the window shifted, and I caught sight of myself staring back, at the intricate braid I could now finally see over my shoulder. I shifted the bags in my arms around so I could touch the intricate knots, admiring the beauty of the silvery strands I normally tied back without a care.

These knots meant something.

Finn had hinted at it earlier, and now I knew why.

I turned from the window and practically knocked into Finn. His arms were as laden as mine, but he only had eyes for my face, my dazed expression. A subtle shake of his head had me swallowing back the question I dearly wanted to ask, and it took some real effort to act casual as we paid for our cache.

Finn snatched the cheap plastic bags in one hand and exited the building. The bell dinged as he rushed away from me and my questions. But I lingered. A newspaper on the wire stand leaning heavily against the wall by the door blared a headline I couldn't ignore. I picked up the top copy, opening it to its full, front page glory. I skipped past the color-coded nuclear threat warning topping the page and ran my thumb over the pixilated grey-and-white square boxing in my face just above the fold.

"*Missing Omaha swimmer not among dead teammates in Norway,*" The Register boldly proclaimed. "*Current whereabouts unknown as officials search for attacker.*"

Concern for my parents spiked, and my resolve to head home hardened.

It physically hurt to fold the newspaper back up and set it back on the stand. Over the stack of newspapers, a muted television played live coverage from one of the national cable networks. Closed captioning scrolling in black and white along the bottom.

But above it was me.

Me hovering over Kansas City on a twisting rope of water, twin balls of bluish water writhing around my clenched fists. The camera zoomed in on my face as the helicopter approached for the second pass, my expression stony, eyes blazing that unnatural crystal aquamarine Ryder was so fond of.

I pressed the knuckles of my hand to my mouth as I stared up, reading scrolling copy.

"No fatalities," I was relieved to read.

"Mass destruction," was less comforting.

"Cat's outta the bag, I see." Ryder said, munching on a Kit Kat.

I didn't respond, couldn't speak because my heart was in my throat as I watched myself jump from the towering spiral of water onto the helicopter. The ropy mass collapsed and moments later blue energy exploded out of the chopper. Long, porcupine spikes punctured the armor. The cameraman lost me as I jumped from the spiraling death-mobile. Then the black fog swallowed me whole.

"Incredible. Reckless. But incredible," he muttered, his lips close to my ear to keep the clerk from hearing. Something like pride shimmered in his voice. He bit into the candy with a crunch. "For someone who learned they're the all-knowing master of water a few days ago, you showed considerable awareness and restraint."

I turned, hope brimming.

He brushed a stray strand of hair from my cheek. "For most of us it takes decades, centuries to learn total control of our abilities. Gods have less time, by default, but even for them, it typically takes years of practice and training to harness the level of power you possess.

"It's why most of the Gods remain in their temples, raised by a plethora of priests and priestesses. You are the first to have ever been torn away from that regimen. I wonder if all that swimming you've done, the training you've gone through for the Olympics, has worked as a substitute. It's not like the element is a stranger to you." A horn blared from the parking lot and he sighed heavily. "Time to go, our child is getting impatient."

I took one last look at the television screen now showing a live look of the destruction spanning a full block of downtown K.C. The newscaster had several pundits around the table, and even more on video conferencing, all speculating about the possibility of *the* God of Water actually existing and what that meant for the state of global affairs.

Finn opted to drive this time, his handling of the car much smoother than Ryder's aggressive swerving and jerking around the most minor traffic irritants. Rather than go shotgun, Ryder sat right in the middle of the back seat.

"No one likes that spot," I commented.

"No one clearly has had a chance to sit next to you."

"You're being ridiculous." But I allowed him to draw me out of my funk with mindless car games. He'd even pulled a deck of "UNO" cards out of some hidden compartment in the vehicle. Our conversation was purposefully kept light and relaxed.

Before long we were crossing the bridge over the Missouri River, passing a billboard showcasing a pair of giraffes craning their long necks to look down on passing traffic. Nerves jangled and I straightened to better look out the window. I ignored Ryder poking my thigh when I missed my turn in the game. Finn followed my directions without comment.

Grey clouds with bellies full of water finally burst, showering our car as we drove onto my street. The sound of droplets pinging on the roof was hard and metallic. My dad's rusty, Ford Explorer was parked outside and I heaved a sigh of relief. It was a Thursday. Mom worked accounting at some big firm and would be home by now, but my father was a college calculus professor and often got lost in his work for hours on end.

Nervously, I tugged at the ropes of my braid, but with a single, slanted look from Ryder stopped me from doing any real damage to his intricate work.

As we got out of the car, cool droplets of rain coated my skin and soaked my jeans and jacket. They clung to me as if drawing energy from my body, or perhaps passing energy on. It tingled pleasantly.

Finn insisted we grab our bags *just in case* and walked beside me as we hopped up the four steps to the front door of the yellow house. My hand automatically went to my back pocket for my keys before I remembered I'd lost them. I hadn't been home in forever, but it still felt awkward pressing the doorbell.

A rustle came from inside, the quick clips of heels clattering on tiled floor, and the lock rattled as it turned. Our door didn't have a peephole. It was something my father had always meant to rectify, but we got so few visitors that it hardly seemed to matter. My mother pulled the front door inward and stumbled back, hands flying to her mouth.

"Zara?" she whispered. "We've been so worried. Ever since Norway. And your phone call." She was still dressed for work: snappy black paint suit with red pumps, her dark hair pulled back in a severe bun. I offered a weak smile and reached for the screen door since she seemed incapable of movement. Ryder and Finn followed me inside.

"Who is it, Laura?" my father called from somewhere inside the house. I imagined he was tucked away in the den with the TV turned to the Cubs game. "If it's the FBI again, show them in. It's not like they'll find anything they didn't find before."

Tears trailed from Mom's eyes and caught on the edges of her fingers that bracketed her nose and covered her mouth. We'd never been the type of family that touched or hugged—especially as I'd grown out of adolescence—and with company present I wasn't sure how to move or act for that matter. I glanced back at Finn and Ryder who, despite the walk in the rain, appeared as dry and styled as magazine models. Ryder passed a hand through his hair, trying to smooth it down, but it kept springing up in a flurry of spikes. He quirked a grin and shrugged.

"Laura?" My father's voice sounded closer.

Mom seemed to snap out of her shock, and swiped at the wetness on her face. Her skin was splotchy beneath the makeup. The swelling in my chest burst and I moved those last few steps, right into her embrace. My face smashed against her shoulder, and I clung to her, arms digging deep into her slender waist, pulling every ounce of comfort from her hug as I could get. She let out a watery gasp, holding me close, her hand pressing against the back of my head. I didn't care what she did to Ryder's art, so long as she held me as tight as she could.

She pulled back, eyes burning with love and happiness and... despair. They darted between my own, red-rimmed eyes with concern I found alarming.

She spoke first, "Honey, there's something I need to –"

"Laura."

We both froze. Her eyes darted from my face to over my shoulder, back at the kitchen at the other end of the long, dark hallway. Her lips went white with tension and she drew back, pulling me to her side. A lumberjack of a man stood there, his back to the light. But there was no mistaking my father. He was a big bear of a man with beefy arms and a black beard cut close to his face.

He stood there for a moment, shoulders rising and falling with his breathing.

Then: "You're here."

My father had always been a matter-of-fact kind of guy. I'd always considered it an oddity of his supreme cerebral approach to life. But even that was par for the course for him. He sounded like he barely knew me, like I was an irritating neighbor who always stopped by at the most inconvenient of moments. Not like the daughter he'd adopted as a baby and raised within in his four walls.

The tenuous control I'd regained over my emotions trembled.

"I'm home. I promise I tried to call, but neither of your phones are working," I said in the smallest voice I'd ever used in my life. I felt like I was four inches tall and made of mud. My mother edged ever so slightly closer to me as Ryder's overwhelming body heat soaked into my back. Finn had also moved, gripping my arm in silent support. I cleared my throat, thankful for it. "I hope you don't mind I brought some guests with me."

Another beat passed before he turned sideways, the light finally found his face and the severe frown cut into his lips. "Well, come on in. Laura, check the curtains."

A chill settled on my skin as she peered down at the now empty opening to the hall, before turning on her ice pick heels to the front sitting room. Finn gave me a strange look, clearly picking up on the vibes everyone was sending out.

"I need to keep watch," Ryder said and flicked a thumb at the room that darkened as metal rings slid across the rod, curtains drawing tight against the murky evening light. "I'll be listening, though. If you need me, you won't even need to ask."

Then he was gone.

Rattled and more than a little confused, I grabbed Finn's hand and guided us into the kitchen. I peered around. It looked *different* than I'd left it during Christmas break last year. Foreign somehow. The bright yellow walls and white crown molding were the same, but the pictures that used to hang on the walls and the decorations of daisies of which my mother was so fond were gone. The mixer and toaster—even the coffee maker, all vanished from the counter tops. Even the circular table lacked its traditional blue-pattered place mats. The stainless-steel appliances and granite counter tops gave it an impersonal and sterile edge.

"Are you moving?" The words sort of fell from my mouth. I'd expected divorce, but were they selling the house, too? "What happened to your phones?"

My father, now perched on a stool at the island with his arms crossed over his bulky chest, eyed Finn's hand clasped tight in my own. He still had yet to smile, even offer the vaguest hint of relief that I was here. His lips pursed as he looked past me and at the French doors through which I could now hear my mother's heels approaching.

As she flipped off the dining room light, she said to me, "We need to talk."

"...sure." I was drenched in cold sweat, eyes darting back and forth between the people I loved, the people who now felt a little like strangers. I blinked and more words tripped out of my mouth, a torrent of language I'd been dying to spit out all coming to me at once. "I mean, there's loads I need to tell you. I'm sure you've been wondering where I've been, what's been happening to me." I'd dropped Finn's hand, and my own now moved in animated flapping gestures. "You won't believe—"

"Zara, we know." My father's deep voice cut through my near-hysteria.

"You know what?" asked Finn. "You know the Order is after your daughter? You know that she's a God? What do you know?" His hand gripped mine again, his body leaning in front of me protectively.

My father's voice was cutting. "We know everything."

Someone could have shot me again and I wouldn't have been more surprised than I was in that very moment, at the arctic air that was my father's voice. Finn looked between my parents, and drew me over to a stool tucked underneath a built-in desk, and lowered me to it. His body remained positioned between me and them.

"Steve—"

"No. Enough," Dad said. "We've played this charade long enough. Seventeen years we've waited and now it's almost too late." He turned to peer through the sliding glass back doors into the yard. The dusk light cast long shadows across the peeling paint of the deck.

I couldn't have heard that right.

My mouth opened and closed, but sound wouldn't come out. I swiped a clammy palm across the front of my forest green jacket and shivered.

My father turned back around, pinning me with a stare I'd never seen before on his face. But it was a stare I'd seen on the faces of my competitors at the Olympics. A stare so fixated, so determined, that what came next couldn't be anything except the truth, their perfect truth.

"We aren't who you think we are."

As far as truths came, that was pretty foreboding.

I tried to swallow but the spit had dried in my mouth.

"We took you in, fed you, we clothed you, we gave you an education. But we aren't your parents. We aren't even married. We are two people following the orders of a dead man."

And truths didn't hit much harder than that.

"So who are you, then?" Finn asked, voicing what I was thinking.

I couldn't look away from my father. Or whatever he was.

Goosebumps raised every last hair on my skin.

"We are two of the last operatives of the Air Temple."

27

Zara

Finn bent over my father's sleeve of tattoos, examining the symbol hidden among the swirling patterns. A swirling current of air with an arrow underneath. He brushed his fingers over the much larger brand engraved on his own neck, then turned to me with sad eyes.

"It's real. So is hers."

My mother's Air tattoo was hidden behind her ear, tucked cleverly into her hair.

So obvious.

So glaringly obvious.

And I couldn't be more oblivious.

I'd shrugged off my jacket and now scrubbed at my own brand. It was growing darker, but still several shades more grey than black. A glass of water had appeared on the counter beside me at some point, and I sipped from it.

"I think you should start from the top." How I could sound so calm, so put together, when my insides were a gnarled mess of uncertainty and anger, was beyond me. Maybe I was growing used to feeling the extremes.

Mom and Dad—I couldn't quite bring myself to refer to them by their real names, *if* those were their real names—exchanged a glance. "Laura, go get her box. I'll keep it brief."

She nodded and pushed off the counter. Her heels lay haphazardly on the floor, a spill of blood on its clean surface. Before exiting the room and heading to what I could only assume was upstairs, she stopped in front of me and cupped my cheeks.

"Honey, no matter what, know it wasn't always a mission for me. I love you. I've always loved you, ever since you were dropped in my arms as a tiny thing and stared up at me with those big, beautiful eyes. You deserve to be angry with us for our deceit, but know it came from a good place. For me anyway." She kissed the tip of my nose and vanished into the hall.

My father—*Steve*—leaned against the counter and sighed deeply. "We were only supposed to be here for a few months. Zara, we're partners, Laura and I, nothing more than that. We were paired up as teenagers in school, trained in the temple together, learned how to spy. We were good at it. That's why we were sent here." He shrugged in a dismissive kind of way. "Details of our initial orders aren't important. What is important is that we arrived here the day before the attack on the temples.

"We'd gotten word through inner channels about movement within the Order. A sudden call of secrecy. Blackout meetings, sketchy stuff. No one had quite pieced everything together until it was too late. The Air Temple collapsed first. As I've pieced together in the years following the attack, the Order seemed to approach under the guise of a routine inspection. Once they were within the borders, and inside the shields, they attacked. The city burned."

I knew all this. Sort of. A warped version of it anyway.

The propaganda version the Order apparently wanted everyone to believe.

"The Water Temple fell next. That was quickly confirmed. Earth and Fire…well, they remain mysteries even to this day. Things were chaotic, to say the least, in the days that followed. Many of our friends vanished. Lines of communication, both open and buried, went black. No one knew what was going on, who was responsible, only that our worst nightmare had finally come true." He smoothed an eyebrow and propped his foot on the rung of the stool.

"I now know the Order was cleaning house. How it came to learn about the immense underground networks established by each of the Elements, I'll never know. But its methods were effective. Laura and I were only saved by the fact that we'd only visited our church once. And that was late at night through a back door. We'd arrived early on accident. If the Order knew about us, they likely assumed we'd gotten sidetracked along the way. There was no record of us being here."

"I'd heard of operatives like this, but never encountered one," Finn said. "I'm sure we used them at the Palace of Oceans, but that was above my pay-grade."

"I guarantee it," Dad agreed. He picked up a pen and tapped it on the counter. "Three nights following the attack, we were here, in this very house, plotting our next moves. We were scared, worried, and at our wits end. We couldn't be sure if moving was the right option, but we didn't have many of those."

"And then someone knocked on the door." Mom reemerged, silent without her signature heels. She now clutched a polished, wooden box the length of an average candlestick, maybe four inches wide and an inch deep.

"Despite every instinct screaming at us to not answer the door, we did. The priest from the temple was there. In his arms, he held a baby wrapped in a light blue blanket. That's you." Her brown eyes pinned me to my seat.

Finn walked over to the glass back door, one hand covered his neck across the brand. He paused, then turned back. He asked, "What happened next?"

"He told us who you were and how imperative it was that your identity be kept secret. He told us the world believed you to be dead, that the Order and it's new Hand believed that to be a truth. He also told us that we were one of the last options available. We were operatives of Air, and you're clearly the leader of Water, but who could possibly imagine that you would end up hidden by us?"

Ryder sneezed in the front living room and I heard a drawer open and close.

"Those who were protecting you were running out of places to turn," Mom said. "More and more operatives and priests and priestesses were turning up dead, their churches ransacked. You'd been passed from church to church, person to person, shuttled along an underground railroad, deep into the heart of the United States. He said he was in danger, he said it didn't matter as long as he knew he'd kept you safe. And we agreed. As a last testament to a dying religion."

Mom pulled up a stool next to me and pushed the box into my hands. "Aside from the blanket, this is all you had."

"It's beautiful," I said and slid my nails along the seam, but didn't open it. The symbol of water was painted in gold across the top. In cardinal directions around the symbol were more runes drawn in silver I didn't know.

"We took you in," my father said. "We promised to keep you safe, we promised to protect your future. He left that night and was killed the next day. Zara." For the first time I felt a hint of warmth in his voice. "We never told you who you were, because we never wanted to risk your safety. That meant we couldn't risk you potentially risking your safety by accidentally letting something slip. We gave you the gift of water in the only way we could. We sent you off to that school so you could master something you were meant to own in the only way we ever thought you'd be able to do. We sent you away to protect you."

"Exactly like the Water Temple did following the attack," Finn said. He leaned against the wall, one boot braced on top of the other. "That makes sense."

All these years I'd thought he wanted me out of his hair.

I'd thought my father resented Mom's decision to tell me I was adopted because that might reveal an emotion I wasn't ready for. I'd doubted his love on more than one occasion.

But I could see now he was afraid. Afraid for me, afraid for Laura, afraid for himself. Afraid that me knowing even that small piece of my past might set the wrong things into motion. But I didn't know how to tell him I understood, so I remained quiet.

"I'm only thankful you found your magic, that the Order found you, when you were old enough to handle the hard reality that the world has teeth and it's not afraid to use them."

I opened my mouth, almost spoke, then closed it again. I took another small sip of water, then tried again. "So Finn was right? You know everything?"

My dad nodded grimly. "We may not be actively playing the game, but we haven't lost our connections *to* it. And we know the Order was listening when you called."

"I—"

"We've got incoming." I jerked at Ryder's voice, dropping to my feet. Finn appeared at my side a moment later, head tilted as he listened to something. The incubus darted into the kitchen, amber eyes dark and hooded. "A lot of them. We need to get out. Now."

"But—"

"There's no time." The whirring of helicopter blades beat against the windows even as Ryder grabbed my hand and pulled me to the back door. Night had folded her robes around us. Finn was already pulling back the sliding doors. "If we don't leave now, we never will."

"I don't want to leave you." I called, tugging hopelessly against Ryder's grip. "There's so much I need to know, so much I need to ask."

Dad's eyes were somber as he looked back at the front of the house, at the pounding on the door. "We swore to protect you. Let us fulfill that promise."

"I love you, Zara. Never forget." Tears streamed down my mother's face as she pulled the door closed behind us. I pulled the box close as Finn scooped me up and half-ducked, half-sprinted to where Ryder hid in the shadow of the house, along the side yard.

No. Forgetting was something I refused to do.

28

Geoffrey

I knew that helicopter.

I screamed as the sleek, black shadow streaked across the sky. I recognized the artillery sticking from its nose and sides; I could visualize the specially-engineered two-pronged propeller that added increased dexterity and speed, the reinforced steel plating that made it virtually impenetrable, the hidden chambers stored beneath the seats.

I'd drawn the creation up myself.

Only one other person had ever seen it.

"Stop the car," I yelled. My hand was already yanking on the handle, my body falling out of the vehicle at a sprint even before it fully stopped moving. Not even ten yards later, the house became visible at the top of the hill, and a dozen or so big, black vans soared past me, red and yellow lights flashing on their hoods and roofs.

I knew those lights, too.

And those vans and the shape of the armor framing the bodies of those spilling from their guts.

My body was one with the wind as I pushed myself to move faster, eyes fixated on the whirring shadow circling overhead. *Why was it here? How was it here?* No one knew where I was going. I'd kept my mission confidential, only the pilot knew of my plans.

If I could just get close enough.

If I could just move fast enough.

I could stop...

A siren blared three sharp blasts.

The helicopter changed course, swerving with single-minded focus as hidden compartment doors sealed in its underbelly swung open. I raised a hand, a useless, pathetic hand, as greenish liquid slipped out, drenching the outside of the house as it passed overhead.

Another blast of the siren...

And the house exploded.

Chunks of brick and siding soared past me, nearly spearing me through as I fell to the ground. Something heavy smacked my shoulder and I rolled, trying to find cover underneath one of the cars parked in the road. Overhead, massive flames licked the sky, fiery shingles drifted to the ground. The leg of a table smashed the asphalt in front of my face, sending rock and debris flying.

My body shook.

This shouldn't have happened.

I'd never ordered this. I'd never wanted this.

These soldiers should never have been here to begin with.

As the thwack of heavy things hitting roofs and cars and earth subsided, I rolled out from the safety of the vehicle. I was only three houses down from the devastation, now joining several dozen people spilling from homes and cars to stare in horror at their neighbor's grave misfortune. Flames—flames coming from me, fueled by my rage— licked up my arms, burning the sleeves of my dress shirt and jacket. Smoke and steam spilled from my pores, the smoky flavor of ash coating my tongue.

When I got close enough, I grabbed the nearest soldier by the front of his vest, ripping him right off his feet. He started to yell in protest, but caught sight of my face, of the symbols I knew to be blazing bright as daylight, and the gun he touted fell from his hands with a clatter.

"What the hell are you doing here?" I yelled, spit flying.

"Sir, I don't—"

"Who gave you the gods-damn orders to be here?" Over his shoulder more soldiers turned to stare at the spectacle. Most started backing up the moment they saw my fiery hands. The inferno that used to be a home roared in my ears as the explosive liquid—another Order specialty—drove the flames to burn ever hotter, ever higher.

"Sir, orders came right from the top."

Fire melted the armor I clutched in my fist. "Come again?"

"The general, sir," he yelled. "General Almasi. He hand-picked us all. Top-secret clearance only. We were instructed to destroy the home the God of Water grew up in and everyone living inside. We had it on good authority she'd be here. And sir, we spotted her. She was definitely in that house when it went up." I wanted to close my eyes but couldn't.

She couldn't be dead.

Not after surviving all that—she couldn't.

In my periphery, a dark cluster of shadows shifted in the alcove cut between two of the suburban-looking houses. Shadows that were too dark to be only shadows. I turned my head a little, keeping it just in sight.

A shape slunk around the edge of the house. Something that looked exactly like the incubus who'd been with Zara at the hotel. I shook the rattled soldier in my hands, if nothing else but to buy him time, to buy *me* time to see...

The other fey follow at his beckon, a smaller person wrapped in his arms.

Greenish-blue eyes blazed.

I dropped the soldier. He started ripping at his armor, trying to pull the melted Kevlar off. But it was no use. It would have to be cut from his very skin. A few of the soldiers tried to help, but quickly realized what I already knew.

I knew how I looked.

A man on fire, standing with Order soldiers before a flaming house. A man who'd very nearly killed one of his own men in front of dozens of witnesses. A man who kept showing up at the absolute worst moments.

I knew what that girl must be thinking of me right now.

The dozen or so remaining members of the unit jumped out of my way as I advanced on the house. I knew she must hate me. I knew she must think I'd orchestrated this whole thing. I knew she'd believe the absolute worst of me. And I didn't blame her. Not one bit.

But there was one thing I could do, aside from helping her make yet another escape.

If she was here, then that must mean her parents were, too. Or I could only assume anyway.

The helicopter landed on the street and two people, a man and a woman, jumped out. The woman wore a badge pinned on her shoulder in the shape of a snarling tiger. She was in charge of this operation, one of Toren's regional second in commands. Confusion flickered in her eyes, but she raised a gloved hand in a quick salute, heels snapping together with a click.

"Sir, I wasn't expecting you here."

"I'm fully aware of that, captain. I have new orders for you."

"Anything within my capabilities is yours, sir."

"Are you aware of the location of my general right now?"

"Yes, sir."

"I need you to take me to him immediately in that helicopter, after I take care of some unexpected business."

"Sir?"

"Wait here."

I didn't say anything more, only turned on my heel and advanced on the house. My arms ignited as I approached, my flames burning hot enough to melt sand into glass.

29

Zara

My shock only lasted another block before I shoved myself out of Finn's rib-cracking hold. As I regained my footing, I tried to figure out what to do with the box I'd been given. But in our haste to escape the house, we'd forgotten all the stuff we'd lugged inside, so I gripped it tighter and pumped my arms faster.

Ryder was a blur of shadow darting from one corner to the next. When he solidified, he was crouched low to the ground, head swiveling and tilting as he scouted for danger. Finn remained behind me, pushing me faster despite the lack of anything indicating pursuit.

Geoffrey had seen us.

I watched his head swivel, eyes falling on the shadows where we hid.

Yet he hadn't drawn attention to us.

Maybe he got off on cat and mouse games, because that's exactly what this was.

And he was one big, fat cat brimming with magic to boot, if his flaming arms had anything to say about it. The very fact that he was there, that he was with the Order, that he was on one side of the sidewalk and we were on the other stuck with me.

There was no trusting him.

My body moved mechanically, legs whirling and lungs pumping, while my mind scattered in the wind. At one point, I switched to my secondary vision, the metallic strands of blue somehow wildly comforting. Even better, in this mode my companions looked like flares with blurry arms and legs. I couldn't stand to see the concern and pity etched on their faces a minute longer.

And suddenly we stopped.

My body jerked backward as Finn grabbed me around the waist, stopping my forward momentum in one heavy jerk. I flipped back to my normal vision as Ryder circled a red, souped-up Monte Carlo parked in front of a house. He'd clearly been trying to tell me something.

Okay, apparently, I couldn't hear people as much as I couldn't see them. Good to know.

I needed to get that fixed ASAP.

Ryder finally stopped circling the car, satisfied with his find. A slender piece of metal appeared between his hands, and he slid it between the window and the body of the car, nodding when the lock popped. He caught me staring quizzically and flashed a toothy smile.

"It pays to be ready for anything," he said. "Why use magic you don't have to?"

He yanked the door open and shoved the front seat as far back as he could, wedging his body between the cushion and the console in a move that felt like *déjà vu*. It only took him a few minutes to link the wires that brought the engine roaring to life, but it felt like hours. My paranoia kept me spinning around on the cracked pavement, peering at windows for prying eyes.

The distant thrumming of a helicopter had stopped.

Finn pushed me into the back seat and slid in next to me. Ryder was glued to the wheel. He pulled away from the house, and I noted the address, pushing it somewhere back in the recesses of my mind. Someday I would make this right. Someday, when homicidal freaks weren't actively trying to kill me, I'd do something to pay these people back.

"Well I'll be. A full tank of gas. We're really cooking now," Ryder hooted, winding the car through the neighborhoods before spilling us onto a main thoroughfare. "Wisconsin here we come."

I stayed silent as the boys bickered over the radio settings. Numbness wrapped tight around me, the sensation suffocating like plastic wrap. It frightened me how little I felt, but I welcomed it all the same. My gaze darted out the window into the blackness that was the sky, half-convinced a massive helicopter would swoop down and suck our vehicle into its belly.

Instead, the reds and greens of traffic lights blurred as we passed beneath; the headlights of fellow vehicles shone like beacons through the window. How could the outside world appear normal when it was so completely not? The people around us were probably heading out to dinner or meeting up with friends and family, maybe getting some shopping in before the stores closed for the evening.

In one car, I caught a flash of green skin and black, almond-shaped eyes.

Even the fey were going about their business.

Every muscle in my body tightened as we pulled onto the interstate. My skin felt too small, too hot. It was devastatingly uncomfortable. My breathing was tight and controlled, a narrow point of focus holding me together. As our car passed beneath the green, metal signs loudly proclaiming upcoming exits, I became unnervingly aware of the hollow silence that filled the small space.

The boys had never settled on a station.

A pair of eyes watched me now, Finn braced against the center console as if resisting the urge to reach out and touch me. I blinked blankly, my body swaying with the motion of the Monte as Ryder picked up speed.

I didn't speak, barely breathed, grateful for those green, green eyes centering me.

An insane sensation of falling overcame me. The silence a physical thing pulling me down, down, down into a dark abyss.

I broke when we crossed into Iowa.

To my ears it was incredibly loud. The sharp snap of something vital, something important cracking clean in two. A trickle of foreboding silence followed by a crisp rumble, cold as ice, one that didn't stop, one that only grew louder and louder, an avalanche of emotion shaking against the barrier of numb I'd erected, groaning until it pushed through. And then it became a roar. Grief and anger and pain cascading over me with like sharp rocks.

The sound of a soul collapsing.

Ugly sobs ripped from my chest. My arms banded around my legs like steel as if that was the only thing keeping me from blowing apart. I flinched when a hand brushed the back of my knuckles.

"Leave me alone."

It felt like I was screaming but I came out as a whisper.

"Just leave me alone."

I slumped to the side, pushing myself into the corner between the back of the seat and the door, my face hidden as I lost my damn mind.

"Not on your life, Z." And suddenly Finn was there, his strong arms easily wrapping around me, knees and all, hugging me to him. He pressed his lips to the top of my head, murmuring sounds and words I didn't understand for who knows how long. Slowly, I turned to him, folding myself into the warmth of his body, welcoming his unyielding strength. The show of selfless support permeated the too-clear bite of grief, and I pressed my nose deeper into the soft fleece covering his chest.

Inhale.

Exhale.

Repeat.

He smelled of brine and sea and sage.

The combination melted into my skin, lulling me into a false sense of complacency.

Tears still streaked down my cheeks, but they'd slowed.

Sobs still wracked my body, but the tremors were less intense.

Finn had left his hand braced on my leg and I fiddled with the dozen or so leather bracelets wrapped around his wrist. Maybe I wasn't going to break completely. Maybe my body wouldn't turn to dust. Maybe I didn't have to be the only one holding myself together.

I sank into those thoughts, the comfort surrounding me in a cocoon. Time lost all meaning. I focused instead on Finn's scent, the smell of a home I'd never known, and the hands circling me, holding me tight. I may have dozed, but it was difficult to differentiate from the black behind my eyelids and the black of blissfully dreamless sleep.

"We need to stop for the night." Finn's soft voice brought me back to the surface again. "Even a few hours. She needs to re-hydrate, maybe get some real sleep. She's in no state right now to do much of anything, let alone find a God."

Ryder rumbled something in response, and I turned back to the window, shutting them out.

30

Zara

I don't know what woke me.

Only that it was sudden and intense.

One moment I was asleep.

And the next, I was very much awake, staring up at a white-washed ceiling.

My eyes perused the room I didn't recognize. Though I knew plenty about low-key hotel rooms, and their beige paint and generic paintings, to know that's what this hovel was. More importantly, I was nestled between two furnaces, the heat of Ryder at my front and Finn at my back.

In such a short period of time, these two beings had come to mean so much to me.

I lay there, letting the moment sink in. Ryder had fallen asleep with his back propped against the headboard, face angled down toward me. It was relaxed, the lines of laughter and tension smoothed over in sleep. If he were anyone other than a kick-ass incubus, I would have said he looked almost vulnerable. Finn's breathing came low and slow as he clutched me to his chest, his arm draped over my stomach.

My grief was still there, a dark and potent thing, but it had taken a step back, hovering in the recesses of my mind. I couldn't ignore it, but it wasn't overwhelming. I took stock of my body and its many aching muscles. My eyes were puffy and swollen, but everything felt intact. And that was a blessing.

I swear I didn't move, but I must have done something because Ryder's eyelids lifted, those gold coins of eyes glittering as they locked with mine. Concern and wariness dug fresh grooves around his lips and corners of his eyes. I offered a weak half-smile and some of the fear in his face faded. He smiled back, his hands reaching out to tangle with mine.

"Morning." His low voice woke Finn. The kelpie's arm tightened around me for moment before pulling away. "You're looking a little better."

I cleared my throat, for the first time feeling the grating ache from overuse. "I feel better," I replied honestly.

He looked past me at the window and the purple haze of dawn filtering into the room. He ran a hand through his hair mussing it more and scrubbed at his eyes. His black, rock band shirt was remarkably unwrinkled. I shifted as Finn moved behind me and pulled me upright with him. His tongue worried the hoop in his lip, but his gaze was cool and clinical as he looked me over, searching for signs of injury. He seemed to be satisfied with what he saw because he nodded and stood up.

"I could use a shower right now." He groaned as he bent, vertebrae cracking as he worked out the kinks in his back. "But you should probably go first." The boys were avoiding talking about yesterday. And I was OK with that. I went to run my hands through my hair and winced when I felt the tangled mess that had been my beautiful braid.

"Probably a good idea." I said.

A little soap and a lot of scalding water helped push the grief even farther back. However, it and I still circled one another like boxers in a ring, knowing sooner or later we could have to come to blows. It was a relief to shuck my torn and dirty clothing and tug on a new pair of dark washed boot cut jeans, black t-shirt, and salmon-colored jacket.

More clothing I didn't recognize.

More clothing that fit me perfectly.

Another bag filled with odds and ends like rolls of tape, toenail clippers, and a matchbook.

Ryder relaxed when I emerged from the bathroom and saw me looking more or less normal. He fluttered his fingers and shut the door to take a shower of his own.

"Do you want to talk?" Despite his question, Finn was screaming signals to the contrary: crossed arms, crossed legs, lowered eyes, hunched back. Whatever guilt it was that he carried everywhere was more obvious than ever.

"Not really," I said. "Are you OK?"

He hesitated. "I'm holding together."

I sat on the bed to tug on some black boots and started lacing them up. A terse silence hung between us. Ryder finally emerged from the shower, dressed in creased clothing snatched off some shelf at a big-box retailer, and rolled his eyes at the two of us. Finn ignored him and slipped into the bathroom.

We high-fived when he let out a long string of expletives about cold water and inconsiderate roommates. Needless to say, he was in an out pretty quick. His glower only deepened as he pushed us from the room and into the grungy parking lot. The kelpie was still grumbling as he stomped up to a bulky Yukon parked outside and slid into the driver's seat.

I stared.

"We have to be careful. That means switching cars whenever we can," Ryder said, and hip-checked me. When I moved toward the back, he easily redirected me to the passenger seat so he could sprawl across the middle-row of seats.

Finn's black mood lifted as we hit the road, the large tires of the SUV easily eating up the miles and spitting them out behind us. I rifled through my bag searching for a bottle or can or *something*. As I pushed aside a bottle of vitamins—*seriously, what were they thinking here?*—my fingers closed around a long, wooden object.

The box.

I slowly pulled it out and reverently rubbed its glossy surface. I vaguely remembered dropping it on the floor when we spilled into the Monte last night.

"I found it on the seat when we were swapping out the cars," Finn said beside me. "I didn't look inside."

I smoothed my hands over the polished wood, nerves high in my throat. Whatever was inside could potentially change everything. A sign advertising dollar sandwiches at some fast food joint blurred by the window. I ran a thumbnail across the crease where the base and lid met, tension tight in my shoulders.

"What's in the box?" Ryder squawked from the back seat. "What's in the box?"

"It's too small to be a head," I joked, understanding his reference. His uncanny ability to bring levity to this dark universe was deeply appreciated. But even that glimmer of humor faded when it popped open with a snap, and the lid lifted easily.

My breath caught as I examined the contents. Notched in velvet at the base rested two gorgeous silver rings. The metal was polished, the loops unbroken. Both were twisted into cresting waves of water, the tips of the waves jutting out in such a way that I wondered if they were meant to lock together.

The remaining item was wrapped in plain, oiled leather, my crest stamped in the tanned surface. What it contained was both magnificent and mysterious: a dagger with a black leather-wrapped handle stamped with a cresting wave and a shimmering turquoise blade longer than my hand. It was roughly as wide as the span of my middle and index fingers, with an edge so sharp it split one of my hairs. I knew because I tried it. The design of the blade, though, was peculiar not only for the color but for the physical design. It jutted outward in the middle of the blade at a slight angle. The outside edges were straight, but tapered at the top at a sharp forty-five degree angle.

Why this—why a weapon—had been left for me was beyond comprehension. I turned the box around in the dawn light, scouring it for writing on the wood. I ran my fingertips over the lacquer and poked at the fabric for hidden compartments, searching for anything that might help explain this mystery.

Nothing emerged.

"What is it?" Finn asked, closely watching the expressions cross my face.

"Rings and a knife," I muttered, the simple words a disservice to the masterpieces I'm sure I held in my hands. I turned the box, giving him a look. A tiny furrow knit between his brows, but he didn't look any more enlightened by the contents. I offered it to him as he drove one-handed, but he pushed the box back into my chest lightly.

"I think it's probably best if I don't touch those. Whatever they are, they're meant for you. Until you figure out what they're for, I don't know how they'll react to anyone else touching them," he explained. "Magical talismans have a history of volatility."

Ryder snorted and he badly tried to cover it with a cough. "That's the understatement of the millennia."

"Could you for *once* keep your fat mouth shut?" Finn twisted and smacked Ryder's shoulder, exasperation etched on every feature. "Deal with the problem at hand?"

"It's a little hard to forget about that mistake with that one staff that brought the fall of Andromeda." The name rang a bell. Andromeda had been an ancient and thriving civilization in what would later become the Nordic region that simply vanished off the face of the Earth one day. Nothing but a large scorch mark remained.

"...or how about when those twins fought over that weird skeleton necklace — *remember that* — while out wandering the oceans and bam!" Ryder smacked his hands together loudly for emphasis. "The Bermuda Triangle was born?"

Wait. That was a real thing?

"Are you done yet?" The wry mutter from Finn.

"Oh far from it. It's hard to forget that one time when... oh what was it... that *Rethroki* prince. Jarrthra? Jemmiha? Whatever. When he went messing around with the cursed crown jewels and summoned that giant with the club who carved out the Grand Canyon. Remember that? It took all *day* to send him back to his own dimension." He thrust a hand sharply through his hair, sending it into spiky disarray as if he had actually been one of those called in to banish such a beast.

Maybe he had.

Before he could truly get on a roll, I interrupted. "So what do you recommend I do with these things, then?"

"I think it's pretty obvious they're yours. I wouldn't risk losing them. Keep everything on your person," Ryder responded and turned to look out the window again.

I wasn't quite sure what to do with the dagger so I tore a strip from a spare shirt I found in the bag and tied it around my leg beneath my jeans. I slipped the twin silver wave rings on my middle fingers. After a few tests I figured out I was right: they did lock together when I twisted the backs of my fingers together, knuckles aligning. My magic refused to stir no matter how I fiddled with the jewelry.

Part of me was afraid of pushing my magic into it, though. Especially in a moving car.

266

A hard and sharp object jabbed me in the shoulder. I reached out and snagged it without thinking. "Finn picked up something else for you," Ryder said when I met his eyes in the rear view mirror. I pulled the object into my lap and stared down at an elaborate metal case.

Ornate silver scripting was engraved in the top.

"It says: *The Word*. But that's all I know. Cross my heart," Finn said, focus fixed on the road.

I gulped, my mouth suddenly dry.

The story of my origin, my history. The teachings of the Order. The rules that dictated my religion. It all was here, right here in my hands. The answers to so many questions. I peeled back the heavy lid to reveal the artistically decorated cover of the book itself, the four elements painted on the corners. I flipped through a few pages, the paper thick and textured under my fingers. It was like one of those ancient books written by hand by solitary, dedicated monks, complete with embellished letters and hand-painted stories adorning the edges. The edges of the pages were dusted in gold.

It was easily the most gorgeous thing I'd ever seen.

A piece of history.

A true artifact, like the items left by my temple.

"More than just any copy of *The Word*," Finn said, pulling me from my reverie. I dropped the hand I hadn't even known I was pressing to my mouth in wonder. "An *original* copy of *The Word*. What you're holding right there, it's priceless. Maybe only a dozen copies still exist. And most of those are incomplete or damaged in some way. In fact, the Order headquarters may be the only other place on Earth where something this pristine still exists."

"Where..."

"These were copies only given to High Priestesses and Priests of the temples," Finn continued. "Original copies. Copies outlining the *true* history of what happened between the Gods and humans, the true treaties forged between the two races, the true reasons for why humans stripped the Gods of their powers and why the Gods permitted them to do it.

"These books are church secrets, only forged when the original Gods were still alive. After they passed, the Order designed new books and squirreled these ones away, forever tucked into long-forgotten alcoves, away from prying eyes and hands with torches. What you have there, Zara," he tapped the cover with one long finger, "that's the truth. It's very important and very valuable."

The weight of his words was impossible to ignore. I looked down and smoothed my fingers over the pages once again.

The truth.

It was right here in front of me.

In a language I couldn't speak.

A language I couldn't read.

Yet.

"Where did you get this?" My words were barely a whisper.

"If I told you, I'd have to kill you."

The package.

The package we'd driven to the outskirts of Kansas City to acquire. But *how* he'd even known about it...

He dipped his head as if he could read my thoughts.

"But I can't read it."

"I know. But someday you will." Finn fist-bumped my arm, a vow of confidence.

"Until then," said Ryder, "I picked this up at your house. It was tucked under the glass plating of your coffee table." He passed me a second copy, this one as boring as anything that rolled out of any mass-market publishing house. Nothing original or unique about it.

"You need to read it. It might not be exactly what's written in the *real* version, but it should have many similarities. You need to know your past because you need to know what the rest of the world knows and believes. You can't be ignorant about yourself any longer. I took it to help you. They would have wanted you to have this."

I shook my head, chest quaking a bit as I breathed deep.

Inhale.

Exhale.

Repeat.

"You knew they were going to die."

Silence echoed loudly in the confines of the car. Then Ryder said, "Yes. And they knew it, too. But they needed to talk to you first. That's the only reason they stayed. Zara, I'm so sorry. I know that doesn't fix it or change anything but—" I waved a hand to silence him.

This had been a book my parents owned.

The only possession of theirs left.

The only thing that remained of my home.

My fingers matched up with the worn spots on the pages exactly. I imagined my mother reading this book night after night, looking for answers after I'd arrived at their doorstep. I imagined my father paging through it, searching for hope and inspiration.

My parents were sworn members of one of the temples.

And I'd never known.

They'd encouraged my ignorance to protect me.

That all ended now.

I turned the first page, greedily eating up the words, devouring stories of old as Finn and Ryder bickered over everything and anything: which route to take, the appropriate speed to go without getting pulled over, even something about grilled cheese and which cheeses melted the best versus cheeses that tasted the best.

I pulled the book closer to my face, the 8 a.m. sun bright on the pages.

Something about the text seemed eerily familiar yet completely foreign, like hearing a song from your childhood on a badly tuned radio; I knew the words but couldn't quite call them forth. It was easy to get lost in the tales of the First Four. How Ash of Fire and Lyre of Air had created a tornado of fire and light to fight off an oppressive dictatorship. How Davarius's command over soil had shaken nutrients to the top of the soil, changing landscapes so farming was more feasible. And how Kaleal had used her Trident to carve waterways into dry and barren lands otherwise deemed useless for generations.

Together they'd cured a horrifying famine.

They'd also changed Earth forever.

The descriptions of the Gods felt like coming home. From Ash's fiery hair to Davaris' charcoal skin, I instantly knew what each of them felt like, looked like. Even Kaleal's violet eyes felt more like fact than fiction. She was my history and these were my past friends, my allies.

I wondered what my new allies would look like and where I would uncover all of them.

Questions rose as I paged through the book.

"What happened to the talismans?"

"The what?" Finn twisted the dial controlling the volume of some station they'd finally settled on. Ryder had wanted metal. Finn wanted country. Pop it was. Go figure.

"You know. The talismans. Kaleal's trident and the cursed sword. Where are they now?"

"The Order keeps track of them and protects them until the next generation of Gods is born. I imagine they're being held at their headquarters in Rome. They'd want to keep them in the most secure place possible. You don't get much more secure than that."

"What do they do?"

"That's a bit of a mystery, really."

"How do I get them back?"

"You'll need to go to the Order to do that."

"Let's do that."

"Ok, glowstick." Ryder smirked. "Tell ya' what. When we finally get to Wisconsin and find whichever of the Gods you say we're going to uncover there, and escape safely at that, *then* we will head to Rome and find some way to beat the best security in the entire world to get your stuff back. But *only* then."

I narrowed my eyes. He extended a pinkie. Hard to break a pinkie swear. I notched my finger around it, trying hard to not remember the last such promise I'd sworn.

And hadn't kept.

31

Geoffrey

Twin mountain peaks encompassing the width and length of the outside wall, framing a large door propped open with a wedge of rubber, boldly proclaimed this particular church's affiliation. The fist in my gut clenched as I passed through the entrance. The guards who'd followed me from the helicopter remained outside, taking up spots on either side of the door, guns drawn.

I knew he was here.

Toren had always favored Earth, even though he tried to disguise his disdain for the theatrical side of the Order. This was exactly the type of place he'd settle into.

He'd appreciate the irony most of all.

My eyes swept across the narrow, clear windows that ran the length of the church on both sides. One window for every row of pews. I forced myself to keep my gun holstered under my jacket as I marched up the worn, red carpet carefully running the length of the center aisle. A skylight carved into the roof cast rainbows on the pulpit. I'd attended any number of masses, been recognized at any number of churches.

Yet this, right here, felt oddly foreboding.

I clenched a fist as flames flared in my chest.

Midway up the aisle, I paused. A young man wearing a white Henley and cargo pants lay across one of the pews. Long hair fanned over his slack face, eyes closed in anxious slumber. Every so often he'd twitch. The movement tugged on the rope that shackled his arms behind his back. More white rope twisted around his ankles.

"I see you've met our guest of honor."

At front of the church, a large, wooden Earth symbol hung from the ceiling. I knew the man that stood beneath it was the man I'd formerly considered my best friend. But now I only saw a monster. My eyes flickered back to the person I'd never seen before. He moaned.

"What have you done?"

It was a rhetorical question. An empty one at that.

"The better question is: what *haven't* I done?" Toren hooked his hands around the edges of the pulpit and leaned forward, a wicked grin split his face in two. "When did you finally figure it out? Was it when you saw the helicopter that you'd never wanted to engineer? Was it the explosion that crippled a neighborhood? Or was it my soldiers so eagerly following *my* directions. Hmm?"

I'd already figured most of it out.

But hearing the truth in his voice... it cracked my heart wide open.

I turned from the sleeping boy, making a mental note to return for him. "What was the point of it all?"

"Ah, ah, ah." Toren waggled a finger. "Now that's jumping ahead. This begins with a story. A story of a young man who made a foolish decision that cost him everything. Please, take a seat. This will take a few minutes." I sank into the pew at the front of the room, the seat hard and unyielding, hands pressed to the wood at my sides.

My weapon pressed against my chest, it's weight comforting in its closeness.

Patience.

"I know you're aware of my family's legacy and our subsequent fall from grace," Toren said. "What you don't know is the reason for our failures. And that all lies with one, stupid decision. A grandfather of mine with more greats than I can remember was on an expedition, you see, when he stumbled upon a lamp. He collected antiques and he recognized it being worth far more than the sale price. He purchased it from the vendor on the spot and returned home.

"Once home, he discovered why it was such a cheap buy. It contained a *djinn*. Having recognized the scent of a new master, this *djinn* spilled forth and offered its services. Three wishes, only a few spare limitations. The world was his oyster."

The brass lamp on his table.

An ancient artifact lying in plain sight.

Toren twisted so his weight shifted on the pulpit. One of his forearms leaned heavily on one side as he stared up at the skylight. "My ancestor, though, was an intelligent man. He knew of the *djinn's* cursed nature. He knew that once he'd used his three wishes and failed to free the *djinn* from its eternal life of servitude, that *djinn* was free to take his soul."

"Sure," I said. I was familiar with the myth. The wise avoided the fey like the plague and the stupid fell victim to their charms. I shifted in my seat, forcing myself to keep my head straight and not look back at the door. Five minutes I'd told the guards. If I didn't emerge in five minutes, they were to come inside and await further instruction. I estimated two minutes remained.

"The temptation was too great to give up the lamp. So, he made two wishes for material things. And the third he used to free the *djinn*." Toren's face twisted into a snarl. "That decision cursed our family. That man was the last of us to know true wealth and supreme power. He waged a number of wars and subsequently lost them. When he died, his son assumed the throne and quickly lost it. What little wealth remained was soon gambled away, lost to the sand and the winds. And so, our cursed luck continued through the generations, despite every attempt to the contrary."

I blinked. Surely five minutes had passed by now. Where were those guards? I tried to stand but my legs only twitched in response. My body felt heavy, my arms not strong enough to heft the weight.

"And that's where you come in, Geoffrey. You were a prodigy, a leader who was going to change the world. Everyone thought it when you were born, and they *knew* it when you took control. You smashed the ancient teachings to pieces, understanding the meaning of *true* power and how it belongs to those *in* power. Not to teenagers with a crisis of the ego."

The guards weren't coming.

That was obvious.

And Toren had it all wrong. I'd never ordered the deaths of the Gods to keep power for myself, for the Order. I'd done it to save the world. It was a rash and stupid decision. I'd never meant to cause as much pain as I had.

The weight of the gun, once so comforting, now tugged on my jacket like an anchor. I wanted to grab it, pull it from its holster and fire it. But I couldn't make my arms move. Couldn't lift them off the seat. I was paralyzed and couldn't figure out how or why.

"Most of your peers thought you were an impenetrable fortress." Toren's voice tightened and he rounded the podium to stand on the top step. "You kept few people in your confidence, handled decisions with ease, you reshaped the landscape of the Order and its role here on Earth for the better. But my parents weren't counted among your peers. They were *less than*. And when you are *less than* those around you, you learn to scent out the weakness. And, Geoffrey," he laughed, cold and animistic, "you have an incredibly soft underbelly."

My mind felt foggy. I wanted to defend myself, wanted to contradict him. But the words weren't coming. *Why couldn't I move? Why couldn't I think?*

"You're the first Hand in two-thousand years, a man with everything to gain and nothing to lose. And yet, you fall victim to the wants and desires of very single human being on this planet: companionship. You crave it so much, you don't question it when you find a complete stranger who dares to laugh at your jokes and challenge your opinions." He threw his arms wide, embracing the heavens. "My parents recognized the trait and realized our family would find its salvation in *you.*

"You are nothing but a doll to which we attached strings. Slowly gaining your confidence, then your loyalty. And it's truly tragic, because you're the opposite of whiskey which only gets better and stronger with time. You're more like fruit, soft and mushy as it spoils. You started to loosen your grip on that power you used to hold so firm. Age turned you compassionate rather than cunning."

Only a miracle kept my face blank, even as my world swayed on its axis.

"When you came to me and made it clear you wanted mercy for those deplorable Gods, I saw my opportunity. My chance to bring you down and raise myself up. Every move you've made, I've been one step ahead. That's how a true leader works. The Council never wanted the Gods to return. It's content with its power. It's sickened by your insistence on second chances. All I had to do was take advantage of that lack of faith."

"You've undermined me this entire time." My mind focused enough to force the words out. Everything inside me bled, my sense numb.

"You got it!" He held a finger high, a priest preparing to direct his flock. "I've discredited every one of your decisions, driven wedges between those whom you trust. Every move I've made has been a mark in the favor of the Council and its true desires—desires that used to be yours, you know—and exemplified how inept you are as the head of the Order.

"I even got that poor girl to hate you with every fiber of her being." He smirked. "She'll never know how much you tried to save her life."

Tried…

"You know she's still alive?" My head felt foggy.

"Of course I know she's alive. My commander saw her scuttle away just as you did. You see, it's all part of the plan. And she's my final act."

I couldn't think about Zara. Not when my tongue felt like fuzz in my mouth.

"What I still don't get," I took a deep breath, each word felt like climbing a mountain, "is how this gains you any power. I can't be voted down. And you can't kill me. Not without dying yourself…" I frowned, slumping on my elbow as he approached.

"You missed something, Geoffrey. A key part of my story. Remember those two wishes my grandfather made?" My vision grew hazy around the edges. My body had never felt so heavy, but I forced my head upright on my shoulders. "One of them is incredibly important to your narrative. You see, he wished for a poison so undetectable it was as if the person infected with it had died of natural causes. A poison cursed to kill the victim, but never anyone in my family, with my blood. That poison has been passed down from generation to generation until…me."

He held up the jeweled knife, pride shining bright in his eyes as he unscrewed two of the jewels, each revealing hidden vials of clear liquid.

My head hit the pew with a thud.

I was so foolish.

So incredibly foolish.

My demise was right there in front of me.

And I'd missed it all.

"I've already tried to poison you once. I wanted to end this game before it went too far. But just far enough that I'd gained enough traction within the Council. But you passed on that opportunity, and some poor young man died in your place."

Mateo.

I'd known something was wrong with that report.

"How..."

"How did I finally poison you?" He finally left the pulpit and descended the stairs of the altar. Grimly, he pointed at the pew and held the stones out for me to see. "Poison doesn't have to be ingested. I used the emerald one in your coffee. The ruby, though, that only requires contact with the skin."

My palms on the seat.

I'd never even considered the possibility. I'd thought he'd try to shoot or take me prisoner. But not this.

The world blurred in my eyes.

"You don't think they'll find it suspicious when I turn up dead?"

A corner of his mouth pulled back in a smirk. How I'd never noticed his deceit I'd never know. It was vibrantly obvious to me now. "The Council wants you dead. And the Gods, too. If they get what they want, do you really think they'll pour many resources into answering the whys and hows?"

No. Not the Council I knew.

The Order was all about blood.

"All that matters is that neither I nor my men, are seen anywhere near here when your heart finally stops beating. You see, Geoffrey, you really should have taken better care of yourself. Your obsession with finding that God led you to make foolish decisions. A lack of self-care. Had you treated those scratches on your hands, the ones you insist on giving yourself, maybe you wouldn't have gotten that infection. And maybe sepsis wouldn't have set in.

"And maybe you wouldn't have been alone in abandoned church searching for her when you went into shock."

He shrugged.

"Either way, you still have maybe two or three hours left in you. It will be a slow and agonizing death. The poison, you see, doesn't cause sepsis or its symptoms, or the symptoms of any disease really. That all happens after the fact. I can't really explain how it works. All I can tell you is that I will be far away from here—killing two annoying little Gods when you finally breathe your last."

Either I couldn't open my eyes any longer, or the poison had made me blind.

Two Gods?

"I pity you, Geoffrey. You could have been someone truly great."

His feet shuffled down the aisle toward the exit.

The man in the pew.

Could he be Air?

"Grab the God and let's get out of here." Toren called to some guards I hadn't noticed. "They did well hiding the brat of Air, but not good enough. Especially when he takes matters into his own hands. I want that broadcast up and running as soon as possible. I want to be at Lake Wakonahe with plenty of time to set up."

Toren's voice drifted away like dandelion seeds in the breeze.

I could barely feel my body let alone my magic.

Odds were I was going to die here.

Odds were Zara and that boy would, too.

The only thing I had left in my arsenal was one antiquated idea I'd once considered foolish.

I prayed.

32

Zara

"Welcome to Wisconsin," Ryder called cheerfully, pointing at the sign beside the building. "I need to stretch my legs, and we have to gas up. Finn, be a doll and fill her up while I peruse the offerings of this fine establishment."

Ryder flicked a credit card and popped his door open.

"Think he'd notice if we ditched him?" Finn asked rhetorically and turned the card over in his fingers before flipping his own black card out of his wallet. Existing for thousands of years must give you plenty of time to establish a solid credit score, I supposed.

He groaned as he stretched his long legs for the first time in hours. Despite the long drive, the kelpie still looked fresh in his light blue polo and factory-worn jeans. I, however, looked a mess. I peered at myself through the rear view mirror, and attempted to untangle some of the hair framing my face. No dice. I reluctantly popped the lock and stepped outside. Finn was meticulously cleaning the windows with dirty gas station water, a squeegee, and a spare paper towel.

A bell dinged overhead as I pulled open the door to the convenience store. A sticker pasted to the metal siding showing the height of everyone that walked in was peeling at the edges. The scent of day-old coffee and lukewarm pizza teased my nose. Definitely a gas station. The female attendant glanced up, her eyes darting from me to the peeling sticker, then returned to flipping the glossy pages of her magazine.

Good to know that even with my hood up I didn't appear to pose much of a threat.

I snagged some toothpaste and a brush before high-tailing it to the restrooms in the back-left corner of the store where I immediately attacked my hair. Large knots caught in the bristles, but eventually it smoothed enough for me to tug it back in a tight braid. I ran the toothbrush over my teeth and tongue, then attempted a smile in the mirror and grimaced. Yeah. I definitely did not look like a girl without a care in the world.

Better to go with the resting bitch face.

I pushed through the door, intending to pay for the items I'd grabbed, when my shirt snagged. I twisted, thinking it had caught on a shelf, and found Ryder. My feet moved of their own volition, carrying me back toward him. He dropped my shirt and his fingers curled into my hair instead, pulling my head back as his face dipped closer. My lips parted in anticipation as we moved, stopping until our faces were about an inch apart. Those eyes were intoxicating, drunken, easy to get lost in. Mine fluttered closed as he shifted closer and whispered against my skin, "Where are you going so fast?"

My eyes opened half-mast, lost in the sensation of his body against mine. His lips brushed my cheek, enough to send tingles dancing delightfully across my skin. "I picked something up for you." He pressed a t-shirt with a screen-printed moose and a clever phrase about Wisconsin into my hands. "It reminded me of you."

I nodded mutely. I felt drunk, my head light, and my body pliant. Everything about him felt good, from the muscles smashed under my hands to the way he hungrily held me close. I fumbled for the handle to the door only to find he'd already opened it. Ryder pushed me back into the small room and locked the door with a click of the button, his eyes hot and wild.

I was all about what was happening here.

I shrugged out of my jacket and hung it on a hook reserved for purses next to the sink, not once breaking eye contact. His Adam's apple bobbed as I reached for the hem of my old shirt, and I saw his hands clench as he stepped back to lean against the wall, not once looking away. Hell, he was barely blinking. Slowly I worked the shirt over my head, breathless as the crumpled fabric dangled from my fingertips.

It should have felt awkward, standing there under Ryder's intense scrutiny as he leaned back against the wall. But I felt empowered standing there before him in my plain black bra and jeans. His eyes melted, his breath audibly catching in his chest.

His throat worked.

"Gods you're beautiful." The words were honey dripping from his lips. They were spoken so softly I wondered if I was even meant to hear them. "You don't know how beautiful you are. You can't possibly understand."

He took a step toward me, then two more until our chests were flush once again. His eyes were dilated, the blackness pulsing outward so the gold was but a sliver around the rim. Fingers brushed my bare sides, over the jut of my hips. Lightning raced in my blood.

A corner of his mouth quirked as if he could feel its zing before his face dipped low. His breath teased my cheeks in a subtle warning before his lips captured mine in one breathless move. I sank into that kiss and wrapped my arms around him, feeling him pull me impossibly closer as his tongue touched my lips, asking entrance. I opened to him, feeling my magic sing as it intertwined with his.

Somewhere behind us, a faucet gushed. I was eons past caring. All I could feel was heat and fire and energy as he pulled me tight, his tongue probing my mouth, sparks flying around us. Our magic collided, at first resisting in a fury of cool water and intense darkness, and then accepting, swirling and clinging and morphing into something deeply sensual. Something so deep it rattled my soul. I embraced it, diving my fingers deep into hair now tinted with sparks of orange and purple, shuddering at his groan.

No. That wasn't my soul rattling.

The hinges of the stall to my left were shaking, everything was quaking, and someone was banging on the door. Ryder pulled back, his hands cradling my face carefully, like I was something delicate and breakable.

Something other than what I really was.

His breathing was harsh, uncontrolled, his chest heaving as he forced himself back.

"I've existed for thousands of years. I've wooed queens and tasted emperors. I've been besotted with fair maidens and danced with young men. I've sucked the souls from the pure and laid waste to the weak. And somehow, some way, I've always been waiting for you." He pressed another soft kiss to my lips, gold swirling in his eyes, mixing tenderly with the deep blackness. "What are you doing to me?"

"That's my line."

The room stilled around us.

The rushing water stopped.

The maddening knocking on the door finally ceased.

"You should put on your shirt."

Reluctantly, carefully, I extracted myself from his arms, and I tugged my old shirt over my head. No way was I wearing that moose. The jacket quickly followed. I brushed his chest, not quite sure what we were to each other, what this moment meant. Ryder didn't seem to know what to say either.

I was OK with that.

With one last look back, I pushed the door open again and all the warm and mushy feelings flooding my body vanished. My body went rigid as I stared at the television screen and the anchor talking over a photograph of young man police called armed and dangerous. A young man finally in custody, a suspect in a number of terror plots, a man to be wary of.

I knew that man.

I'd never met him before in my life.

I'd never seen his face until now.

I'd never known his name.

But I knew in that moment, that heart-stopping moment, that Joseph Windrunner was the God I was looking for. The God I was desperate to find.

The God of Air was no longer hidden.

And the Order wanted me to come out of hiding.

33

Zara

"Calm down and start over. Chronological order this time."

Finn's large hands squeezed my shoulders. I'd sprinted from the gas station the second the news report had ended. Shaking, trembling hands had thrown open the passenger door, reaching past the wide-eyed kelpie, scrambling for the creased red and blue streaked map.

Panicked when I couldn't find it.

I had to find Lake Wakonahe.

Finn slipped out from the passenger seat, hands flipped up, palms flat in a universal gesture for surrender. I'd spotted the map tucked haphazardly in his back jeans pocket and had gone crazy, streaks of red and spots of black dancing across my vision. My panic so all-encompassing that I completely forgot to reach for my abilities.

Forgot that I could fling him halfway across the parking lot with a thought.

Luckily for the stupid kelpie, Ryder had snuck up from behind, wrapping me in his arms and a blanket of some sort of magic. Magic that made my nose itch and eyes water. Magic that danced and swirled and tickled the back of my throat. Magic I hadn't known he possessed.

But he was an incubus after all. It only made sense that he'd have gifts to draw people in, entice them, even calm them.

It was that logic that punched through my panic.

I went limp, cheeks burning as I realized how insane I probably looked to everyone around us. Sure enough, people were moving to and from the convenience store, sneaking glances out of the corners of their eyes, lips tight in disapproval.

"They have him. The God of Air. They have him. And they're going to hurt him. Hurt him. They want me. Will have me." Sentence fragments, fragments of fragments, dripped from my lips as I struggled to make sense of everything. Finn dipped his head to my level, hands still gripping my shoulders, and he looked me in the eye. Ryder shoved more of his rich, chocolaty magic into the air, into me, and I shuddered.

"You're not going batshit crazy on us, hear me?" Finn took a deep, calming breath. "We aren't going to let you. But we do need you to start making sense before you even think we're letting you back inside that car. Now. From the beginning."

I sucked in a breath, then another, clenching and unclenching my fists as the haze cleared from my eyes, evaporated from my thoughts. I stood straighter, swaying against Ryder's grip. His answering growl rumbled against my back. Yeah, didn't think I would get away quite that easy.

"OK. OK. I'm good. But something snapped. Like part of me broke away, seeing and knowing that he was in danger." Finn cocked an eyebrow and opened his mouth to say something but I interrupted. "Joseph Windrunner. He's the God of Air. Don't ask me how I know that, don't ask me how I can be certain. I just know. I know it like I know the color of my eyes.

"His face was on the news, his picture on the TV. The anchor was calling him a suspect, an accomplice in the Kansas City tragedy, the chaos that I caused, and a suspect in additional terror plots. He said that Joseph was being held in a secure location by the Order, and that the Order was still searching for the true pretender, the real perpetrator. Me.

"They showed the footage of me blowing up that helicopter and the haze of blackness on the ground that was you, Ryder, that you created. They called it smoke and mirrors. They called me a Godly pretender. That there's no way the Gods have returned. They said it was treason to pretend to be one of the Gods, that I'd broken one of the cardinal, holy rules, and I need to pay for my crimes."

My blood pressure was spiking and I drew in a trembling breath, squeezing Finn's fingers so tight they appeared bloodless.

"A map came up next. A map showing the reservation and other areas where Joseph allegedly committed crimes. But I didn't see that. It was like the map was made for me. All I could see was Lake Wakonahe. It was lit up like an emergency room in the dead of night. Impossible to miss, impossible to look away.

"Text that I know wasn't there, text that I shouldn't have seen but it was meant for me rolled across the screen. The Order told me to show up there or else they'd start cutting him apart, piece by piece. I have an hour. An hour to get there."

Panic clawed up my throat but I shoved it back down.

Ryder released me and I sagged against the car, mentally exhausted and physically drained. I feebly rubbed my eyes with the backs of my fingers and blinked grit from my lashes.

"You didn't see any of that," Finn said, eyeing Ryder.

"I saw the guy's photo but that's it. I might have seen the start of that footage from K.C. roll, but honestly I can't remember. Her magic started fizzling and made it a little difficult to concentrate." Finn rolled his eyes and Ryder stepped forward, fists clenched. "You think I'm kidding, but it's like nothing I've ever felt before. Like being jolted by a live wire and you can't pull away. You don't want to. But you know you have to."

What was he talking about?

"Anyway, let's find this lake. If we only have an hour, we should hurry it up."

Finn was already unfolding the paper, laying it flat on the hood of the car. He pinned it down with his thumbs on the corners to keep it from blowing in the breeze. He jerked his head, giving me space to look. I leaned across it, examining the surface, waiting for the lake to stand out as clearly as it had on the television screen.

Nothing happened.

My brow wrinkled and I folded my bottom lip between my teeth, worrying the cracked and dry flesh. I touched the paper, finding the small town we were stopped in on the edge of the border, but where was the lake?

Also, why would they want me to come to a lake knowing I was the God of Water?

Was it poisoned?

"It's not here. I don't know what's wrong, but I'm not finding it. I can't even feel him like I could earlier." I pressed on my stomach.

Finn rubbed between my shoulder blades and pushed me lightly to the side, before also shaking his head. He also couldn't find the mystery lake.

I felt Ryder's hard gaze prickling the back of my neck and turned. Gold swirled with black as he contemplated my words. A few beats passed and his lips curled in a wicked smirk.

"OK. It's not on a map. It's probably called something else, then. I'll figure out what the locals have to say. Give me a minute."

And he strode back to the gas station, arrogance in every cocky step.

The second the door closed behind him, Finn pounded. "Really, Z. Him? An incubus?"

Yeah. I'd totally expected to have this conversation today.

Right now.

Because we didn't have enough going on. Emotions already on edge, my anger stoked hot and burning bright. I turned from the building where I could see Ryder through the glass, leaning on the counter shamelessly flirting with the clerk, and crossed my arms across my chest. "And this is your business...how again?"

Heat flooded his cheeks. "You don't know what you're getting into."

"I'm perfectly aware of what I am and what he is. I know that he doesn't have a gold star past, but I also know that he isn't that person anymore. And I'm good with that. I managed to somehow get past you almost killing someone in front of me, didn't I? Someone who wasn't actively trying to kill one of us, anyway." I dragged a tip of my boot on the asphalt, rubbing some loose gravel under the worn rubber. I missed my Converse. My temper sharpened again. "Also you're one to pry into my life, my secrets. You've hardly been forthcoming."

Finn's eyes flared hot, and he spiked his hands angrily through his dark hair, turning from me. A second later he spun back, eyes wide and hot with guilt and frustration and fear. "Fine. You really want to know why the Kraken picked me as your guide? You really want to know? It's because I need to atone for my sins. I want, no, I *need* forgiveness. *Your* forgiveness."

I tripped in my haste to back away from his outburst of emotion, heart clenching in my chest.

"You already know I've sworn my vows to the Temple of Water. But what you don't know is I was a member of the inner circle. I was part of the elite, part of those who protected the secrets of Water no matter what, sworn to save *my* God no matter what the consequences."

I pulled my arms tight around me at his harsh tone, the venom in his voice.

"It's a tradition of kelpies, part of our heritage, to bind ourselves to the Gods of Water. And we're always met with favor, always let in without hesitation. We're hated by just about everyone for what we are, for what we have, for that connection. But we are devout. It's all we have."

He looked at me now, eyes bright and pleading. "I was in the control room that morning, the morning the boats came. It was a beautiful day—bright and blue and perfect. I was joking around with a few of the other guys about stupid plans we had later, and then we spotted the Order's boats on the horizon. They didn't have the flags or markings like they typically do. It was odd, but I'd seen the Order's ships often enough to know what they looked like.

"We stopped them at the border and I recognized the captain of the lead ship. I'll never forget his name or his face. Not as long as I live. I asked him why he was there. I was in charge of the control room, in charge of security, and I hadn't gotten any instructions, any notes about the Order stopping by." His hands smacked his chest as I sank to a crouch, my back pressed against the car.

"He told me that a meeting was scheduled with the High Priestess. The Hand had some critical information he wanted to address. He sounded so sincere that I let him by. I let all of them by. Ship after ship after ship. I should have known."

Finn choked, fingers shaking as he brushed at a tear slipping down his cheek. I felt my body growing cold, the numbness I'd carefully tucked away before was now spearing its icy fingers through my chest.

I didn't want to hear this.

Any of this.

"I let them right by. Right by the border where the bubble started. The bubble that was supposed to encase the entire compound in the instance of an attack, sending us cascading deep into the sea. We would have been untouchable there. But instead I let them through. Our immaculate defense system immediately compromised." His voice hitched and he met my eyes again, gaze boring into mine. Searching, pleading.

"After the last ship passed the border, they drew out the guns and the bombs and the balls of fire. I *knew* I'd messed up the second I felt that first fireball hit the temple, destroying the infirmary before anyone even saw what was coming.

"When I was messing around with my comrades I'd missed an incoming communication from Air. It was right there in front of me, bright as day on the console. A warning. The Order was already laying siege there. They knew there was nothing they could do to stop them but they tried to warn us. They fucking *tried to warn us* and I missed the comm by twenty minutes. Twenty." He slammed his hands down on the hood of the car, denting it. Dark hair sprouted from the backs of his hands, the start of his shift, but he shoved it back with a shriek.

His pain was palpable.

I was in no position to soothe it.

"I fired off our own warning to Earth and Fire, telling them what was coming. Telling them that it was also too late for us. I hoped they saw it, hoped that their commanders weren't as stupid as I was, that getting not one but *two* alerts would keep them sharp. But I needed to do more. I had to do more, so I turned on our beacon.

"The beacon sent a bright beam of light into the sky pulsing out a warning. We only ever planned to use it as a last defense because it tells everyone exactly where you are and what's going on. But all the temples had one and were trained to look to the skies, to see the signs that a beacon had been activated at any of the three other camps. I knew they'd see it. I also knew that the second I activated it that whatever the Order had come to do would only be that much worse. They wouldn't want any of us escaping alive." I was freezing, the pain leeching far into my bones. I wasn't sure it would ever fully fade.

Finn's face was bloodless, eyes hazy as he recalled that horrifying day. "I'd already sent the rest of my team out to join the battle. Most of them were boys. Human teenagers with so much life ahead of them. Teenagers who sacrificed their lives that day in bravery I'll never know. Because I looked out there and knew I would die. I saw the chaos, the blood and the destruction and the tragedy and knew this was the end of the line.

"I'm one of about a dozen kelpies left on Earth, Zara." His voice cracked. "We've been hunted to the brink of extinction. I couldn't die, couldn't lose it all, not without doing my part to carry on our lineage," his voice was unsteady, skin ashen. "And I couldn't face that reality. I couldn't accept that was the end, that that was how I was going to go.

"Instead, I ran. I could have gone up to the highest towers, I could have helped sneak the High Priestess out. I could have done more that day to help protect you, to protect our home. But I didn't." My knees buckled and I barely kept myself from sinking to the ground, a bullet through my heart. He couldn't look me in the face. "I ran. I fled like the coward I never knew I was. And I hid. I went into hibernation in my secret space and I hid from everything until the Kraken woke me."

His face snapped to the side when I slapped him. I wasn't even aware I'd moved until my palm met this cheek, an explosion of magic and suffering colliding in a potent punch. His face was twisted, fallen, disgusted with himself as he slowly swiveled his head again to look at me.

We were two strangers after all.

He'd betrayed his people.

He'd betrayed *me*.

But as I opened my mouth to speak, words dripping with acid on the tip of my tongue, a searing pain lanced through my right eye, cutting a deep groove across my brain. Sparks of red flashed across my vision, and I bent in two.

"Zara…hear me. Run. Go. The God of Air…dead. Toren… be next."
Like a badly tuned radio, Geoffrey's voice filtered through my head.
A threat and a promise.

Geoffrey had said all those days ago that we were connected. He,
me, all the other Gods. His connection to the First was the strongest.

I don't know when he got there, but Ryder's hands suddenly gripped
mine and pulled me to my feet. Cuts filled with grit and sand burned
from where I'd cut them as I'd fallen.

"He's threatening Joseph."

"You aren't making any sense," Ryder said.

"Geoffrey. He's in my head. I could hear him, like in my dreams, only
more disjointed." I tugged on my hair helplessly. "He was threatening
Joseph. Or saying he was dead. I'm not sure. But we have to find him.
If we don't…"

Finn cursed.

Ryder cleared his throat. "It's a good thing I'm pretty sure I can
teleport now, isn't it? And that I know where we're going."

My head whipped around and I thought I heard something crack in
my neck. "Are you sure?"

He rocked back and forth on his heels. "About eighty percent sure."

"That… that doesn't sound—" Finn started before his mouth
snapped shut at my glare.

I gripped Ryder's shoulders, getting right in his face. "Yes or no?
This is entirely your call. You know your limits. But we're in a pretty
desperate situation right now. And I don't know what we'll do if you
don't think you can do it."

He grimaced. "I can do it. Being around you in general has helped.
You're always throwing off magic. Add in the kiss and the impossibility
of this situation… I have enough. I can do it."

"That's good enough for me."

"Shouldn't we form some sort of plan before we go teleporting into the middle of nowhere?" Finn asked, stepping between Ryder and me. "Maybe strategize a little?"

"Strategize for what?" I fired back, heart pounding a hot and fast tempo. "We don't know what to expect. I got a straight threat from the Order a few random words from a guy who hates me to work with here. And time is running out." My voice cut off on a whine.

"He's got a point though," said Ryder. He shoved his hands in his pockets and pulled out an ever-present stick of gum. "We might just be facing your Hand and a handful of his biggest goons. Or we could be going up against an entire army. And I can't guarantee I'll be much help after teleporting. I think we plan to combat an army and downgrade from there."

I took a steadying breath. That made sense. We couldn't afford to be stupid about this.

"Alright. Fine." I nibbled on a nail, sorting through my thoughts. "Finn, do I remember correctly when you in Norway that there are fey everywhere?"

34

Geoffrey

ot yet.

A web of bluish-white encased my heart, pulsated around my lungs.

I'm not done with you yet.

Limp muscles flexed and locked.

I think I blinked.

Your story is only beginning.

Awareness trickled through my abused brain as the vibrant taste of *life* swept across my tongue. I didn't know that sweet, feminine voice. But it was my salvation.

"Who are you?" I asked, words I shouldn't have been able to speak.

Muscles in my arms flexed.

My legs braced.

Don't let me down.

"What?"

A panel of stained wood and a patch of dirty red carpet appeared as I blinked. My cheek pressed against the surface of the hard pew. I was alive. The hand that had gone limp at my side twitched, blue sparks spitting from the skin as magic took hold, burning the poison from my veins. A haziness still floated in the back of my mind as I struggled to grasp... something.

When you feel the jolt, pull with all you have, Geoffrey.

"What?"

Pull.

35

Zara

"It's like a pull," Ryder explained for the umpteenth time. "That's how it will feel."

"Somehow I doubt that," I said, but moved between with boys obligingly with my arms outstretched. The thought of touching Finn right now made my skin crawl, but holding hands was apparently part of how this whole thing worked.

Ryder smiled again with a confidence I wasn't quite getting myself, and accepted my offer. His rough thumb stroked the back of my hand. Finn's face was full of questions as he looked from my eyes to my hand and back again, but reluctantly he reached out and loosely clasped it in his sweaty grip.

Yep. Skin definitely crawling right now.

"Alright, let's go," Ryder gasped. His grip turned ironclad.

The little hairs on my arms stood on end, little amber-colored sparks flicking off the ends in tiny fireworks. Static charged my hair and clothes. A weird whooshing filled my ears and I could barely feel my feet. With extreme effort I turned to look at Ryder, his face twisted with intense concentration, hair flapping in an invisible wind. His eyes glowed red from the slit between his lids and his features grew sharper, thinner, meaner.

I could understand why incubi were considered demons in many cultures.

A jolt rocked my arm where it was clenched tight in Ryder's fist. His palms glowed gold, the light seeping and reaching and engulfing the three of us, and as it spread its evil tendrils all I could feel was pain, mind-numbing pain. I could feel us shaking like lids of metal trash cans in a hurricane, the sound filling my ears an aggressive, never-ending roar. Light blazed and then...

It was quiet.

Completely still.

I cracked an eyelid I didn't remember closing, then immediately wished I hadn't.

Directly across from us, maybe fifty yards away, stood three-hundred or so odd soldiers. They assembled in long, neat rows and wore familiar black armor and grey face-masks. Each person also clutched a big, lethal-looking gun. A dozen or so cannons, similar to the ones that shot green lasers at us in Kansas City, perched at the outer edges of the small army.

It was a small wonder we hadn't teleported right in the middle of that nasty little mess.

Something heavy thudded to the ground. Ryder. His normally dark tan took on a grey pallor. His eyes were open but exhausted, lifeless. No wonder teleportation wasn't something he could do on a whim. Even with my magic filling him to overcapacity, it had taken everything he had to get us here.

"Here" apparently being a small, isolated desert.

I frowned as I surveyed the cracked, sunken earth.

I understood now why the Order brought me here. We were in the middle of a massive lake bed that had run dry some time ago. What had once contained cool, crystalline water was now a crater in the ground. An outer wall rose high at our backs, dipping maybe fifty feet. We stood in a part that was maybe one hundred feet deep, and when I scanned the horizon, I couldn't see the other end. The earth itself was dry and dusty, void of vegetation.

No wonder the lake wasn't on any map. It technically didn't exist anymore.

"Well look who finally showed up."

I... had never heard that voice before.

I stepped away from Finn and Ryder, moving closer to the too-still army. I did recognized the patches symbolizing the Order soldiers, but I didn't recognize the man who stood slightly forward, apart from them. His face was blank, his eyes dark as he surveyed me, then looked past me at my companions. He dressed simply: bare arms bulged from the holes of his dark vest, and a long sword hung from his hip. It rested against his dark pants that tapered at the ankle, ending in black shoes.

At his feet knelt the boy from the photograph on the television. Joseph's hands and legs were bound in white rope. Someone had stuffed a gag in his mouth.

The God of Air looked remarkably unfazed. If anything, he was bored, maybe even a little annoyed. Wind fluttered across his face, blowing his long, shoulder-length hair around his neck. Glasses with plastic, black frames had slipped to the tip of his nose. He was maybe three or four years older than me.

Unbidden, my magic sprang forward. It arced painfully, ribbons spurting from my body like flares from the sun. It reached for him, wanting him, demanding to awaken the power that burned in his core. Power he was born to wield.

I resisted its will and pushed my magic down, trying to ignore the fervent chanting in my head.

The man in front watched me watch Joseph.

"Who are you?" I said.

Dark eyes narrowed beneath thick brows that nearly met in the middle of his face. "I'm Toren Almasi, general of the Order, second to the Hand."

"So Geoffrey sent you."

"Of sorts."

What did that mean?

"Why am I here?"

"Isn't that obvious?"

I glanced at Joseph who twisted his torso unhelpfully.

"And if it's not?"

"Then you're stupid, like he said."

Whoa now. My hands went to my hips. "So what does that make you since I was able to escape back in Kansas City? That should have been a pretty open, shut situation, right?"

"Maybe I wanted you to escape."

That didn't make any sense.

"I—"

"Have you heard of this place? Do you understand its significance?"

A gust of wind flicked my braid over my shoulder. I scuffed a boot on the ground. "No." This time I deliberately sent my magic out, and felt an answering ring. The fey had answered my call.

"Thousands of years ago, this part of the continent was struck with a peculiar catastrophe. The Great Lakes were drained over a span of mere months. I'd go into the details but it's entirely too messy."

Oh, so the general liked to talk did he? Lovely.

He does like to hear himself talk, that's for sure.

My eyes zinged to those of the man kneeling on the ground. His head tipped to the side. Given he was gagged and tied, his mobility was pretty limited.

Got a plan?

You can talk to me?

You sound like this is the strangest thing that's happened to you all day.
My lips trembled. The pull on my mind strengthened.

The general continued, "A densely populated area soon found itself without any source of water. What were they to do, but to call in the Gods to save them? Fortunately for all involved, while they'd aged considerably, the Gods were still around. Earth and Water responded to the request and banded together to solve this particular crisis."

Is this the strangest thing to happen to you all day?

I mean, I was kidnapped. But on the stress-o-meter, that probably ranks about a seven, he replied. I could tell I was going to get along with this guy just swimmingly.

"But their solution had unintended consequences. Like most things surrounding the Gods," the general said. My eyebrows winged up. Someone held a grudge. "By refilling the lakes, they were forced to draw water from other surrounding bodies of water. Where we're standing used to be a massive lake surrounded by trees and wildlife. Their actions sucked it dry and killed everything in the area. It's one of four lakes that suffered greatly."

I sensed a metaphor here.

But I also sensed something else.

Something more substantial.

Something that...

"You have no powers here, Zara. Your magic is useless in this barren wasteland. I called you here so you could witness both the destructive nature of the Gods, and the destruction of one of your own."

Oh. So that was the metaphor he was going for.

"Oh," I said. Behind me, Finn rustled. I hoped he was fulfilling his part of our plan and communicating with the fey.

I'd hate to see what ranks a ten on that scale.

I'm pretty sure we're about to see it in a few minutes. His head bobbed on his shoulders in a so-so kind of way, and the general cuffed him on the ear.

Joseph appeared unfazed. *So, what's the plan.*

Pretty sure you'll see it in a few seconds.

You might want to say something now, because...

"Are you two communicating somehow?" Oh, that was why. The general jerked Joseph to his feet and held him against his chest. A jeweled knife I hadn't noticed before was now clutched to his throat. My magic trembled in my hands but couldn't find anywhere to go. Behind the general, the assembled soldiers shifted, the barrels of two-hundred guns pointed right at me.

It was *de ja vu* all over again.

And I knew how this particular story ended.

"I hope you're both paying attention now," Toren called, teeth clenched as the knife kissed Joseph's neck. "Because Joseph Windrunner, God of Air, as the general of the Order, commander of its many armies, I sentence you to die."

The knife moved as I did, my feet sending me lurching forward just as...

...an arrow sprouted from the general's shoulder.

No, that wasn't right. The arrow had flown right past me, hitting its target with precision. Behind me, someone let out a whooping holler as the clatter of dozens of guns firing at once filled my ears. I tasted blood in my mouth. The knife clattered to the ground as the general yelled, face contorted with surprise and pain. His hand shot to the shaft of the arrow as he tried to jerk it out. Joseph collapsed to his knees, shoulders and abdominal muscles working furiously as he tried to both free himself and wiggle away at the same time.

I skidded on the ground, sending gravel flying across its cracked and thirsty surface, falling by Joseph's side. My fingers blindly groped for the knife as I dragged the God of Air several feet away from his self-proclaimed executioner. The sharp edges of its jeweled handle pricked my skin. I yelled in triumph, seeing Joseph's eyes ignite with understanding, and together we rolled him onto his stomach where I slashed the ropes binding his arms and legs together.

Only then did I look back at the dozens of fey sprinting toward us, weapons and magic at the ready. Many clutched translucent shields in a variety of colors and sizes, shields that deflected the bullets being sprayed in their direction. My jaw dropped with my body as I pushed myself lower to the ground, army crawling away from the Order soldiers.

I'd known they were coming. But I hadn't expected so many.

I recognized Finn's horrific horse form. Smoke curled from his nostrils and eyes blazed red as coals as he charged forward, tossing his head in irritation as bullets hit his hide. Large, hairy wings sprouted from his back and flapped errantly as he propelled himself forward. Many of the other fey resembled creatures I'd only read about in history and picture books. From green-skinned pixies with translucent wings to shifters with feline forms and claw-like hands. Above them, creatures the size of my hand fluttered on butterfly wings, trailing streams of smoke and powder behind them.

Some of them shot arrows from wicked-looking bows while others fired bolts and balls of colorful magic from their hands and eyes. There were dozens of them, maybe even hundreds, an army unlike anything I'd ever witnessed. And they'd come for me.

Joseph snatched up a gun one of the soldiers had dropped and popped to his feet. He lifted the sight to his face and fired, his motions practiced and easy. Blood sprayed from a soldier's neck and down he went. Joseph reached for me. Sparks danced between our joined hands, magic singing loud in my ears, the connection necessary to awaken his magic barely starting to form.

And a blue orb shattered the ground, ripping our hands apart, and sending us flying before I could fully trigger it. Coughing, I pressed my sleeve to my face, trying to breathe through the smoke, searching for the God, but not finding him. He'd gotten lost in the fray.

A roar sounded behind me, and when I turned back, I found the general, mouth twisted as he dropped the barbed and bloodied arrowhead to the dirt. His attention fixed on me as he started forward, uncaring of both bullets and magic alike.

I still clutched the jeweled knife and it cut the underside of my palm as I scrambled backward.

He might not be worried about getting shot, but I certainly was.

A shadow fell over me, and something imposing dropped to the ground. The general looked over my head, his eyes tipping up and up and up. My blood froze as my head tipped back. Towering over me, skin hard as rock and black as night, towered a creature with swirling red eyes and twisting horns that curled over his ears. Clawed hands reached for me, gnashing teeth bared.

But for some reason I wasn't afraid.

Even before the scent of cinnamon and smoke washed over me as he scooped me off the ground.

Ryder had come.

A giant winged horse charged past him, hooves flashing as he kicked an Order soldier in the head. The man fell to the ground in a spray of blood. He didn't move.

"Hang on," Ryder yelled over the screams of battle. The fey had hit the Order forces with everything they had. The world around me slipped into a tiny vortex as he transported us to the outer edge of the battle. He dropped me to my feet when we landed, and I felt him sway against me.

"You shouldn't have—"

"Be mad at me later. Though you're hot when you're angry." He tweaked my nose, then turned to the battlefield. "There's Anisra in those cannons. I can tell. You need to shut them off."

304

"But I—"

Firm lips pressed hard against mine, fingers still sharp with talons gripped the back of my head, smashing my face tight against his. And I kissed him back. Kissed him for all I was worth, knowing that there was a real possibility this might be our last.

And then he was gone.

A cluster of soldiers stood between me and several death-machines. That's why the soldiers all wore masks. So they'd survive, while we died.

And Ryder had left before I'd had a chance to tell him my magic wasn't exactly working.

I gulped and jumped to the side as a large bolt of yellow light zipped past me. The fey who'd thrown it fell to the ground with a watery shriek. A soldier shot her in the head. Tingles of bluish-silver threads shot to my fingertips, but when I tried to send them out, nothing happened.

Desperation twisted in my chest.

But I had to try. I'd hate myself if I didn't.

While the terrain itself was relatively flat, it was littered with boulders big enough to hide someone as small as me. I used those to my advantage, darting and running toward the action—and those cannons—until I was able to scoop up a gun some soldier had dropped. As I rounded the curve of the last boulder standing between me and one of the cannons, a soldier popped up. The barrel of her gun rose with her, but I moved without thinking, lashing out with the butt of my weapon, cracking her in the face.

The distraction cost me, though.

The barrel of the cannon burned white-hot.

And it was pointed at –

"Finn!" I screamed, stupidly pushing through fighting humans and fey alike. My voice was lost in the sounds of battle. The cannon fired.

A beam of light that blurred at the edges fired from its mouth—*not Anisra*—and a sharp whinny split the air like a siren. A gigantic hoof the size of a couch smashed down beside me. Finn flew backward as he stumbled and droplets of red rained down. A second hoof crashed down as he let out another ear-shattering scream. Both front legs lifted, scraping the skies, before the horse tipped back, wings beating frantically, and he collapsed on his side.

The ground shook like a small earthquake.

Those caught under his falling body didn't emerge again.

I'd thrown my hands over my face, peering up through the open webs of my fingers as he fell, staring in shocked horror.

"Finn!" I screamed again, jumping over bodies, magic blazing hot and useless whenever someone stepped in my path. I had to get to him, had to save him. I barely noticed the soldier at my right collapse, but the boy wielding the gun who killed him was impossible to ignore.

"Follow me," Joseph yelled, thrusting his gun in the direction of my fallen friend. "I'll clear the way."

My back slammed against his as I gripped my gun, firing it at people who came up behind us. Sometimes I hit them, other times magic knocked them out. I yelped when Joseph nearly ripped my arm from my socket and dropped me by the kelpie's head lying heavily on the ground. Joseph's hand lingering on my elbow, drawn to the painful pull of magic between us. It wanted to ignite. A few seconds more.

Gunfire chattered and my shoulder exploded in agony. A bullet punched through the muscle. Joseph's eyes blazed hot and he turned around, already firing at the man who'd shot me. I returned to Finn as the God of Air stood guard.

The kelpie was wheezing, painfully drawing air into his lungs. His slimy, seaweed infested hair was drenched with sweat. One great, red eye rolled toward me as I called out his name again, softer this time. Steam from his nostrils curled around me as I placed a hand on his nose, and he shuddered.

"It's ok, pal. Let's get this sorted out," was the warning I gave him before sending a blast of magic through him. I prayed it would work. The Kraken said I needed either It's or Finn's direction and I had neither. So I was shocked when it worked, the healing part of my abilities blasting past those requiring the presence of water. The bluish thread connecting Finn with me pulled tight; his body wanted to heal, it knew what it needed to do.

The beam had sliced clean through his chest, leaving a gaping, sucking hole in its wake. Everything in my body revolted against the agony he was feeling. Blood gushed from the injury, staining everything around us bright red. I slammed my eyes closed as I shoved my magic harder into him, working with this will, praying for the wound to heal. It rushed in torrents of energy, flowing from me like water from the mouth of a waterfall, uncontrollable in its intensity.

If the Healer is needed first, something is going to go incredibly, horribly wrong. Ryder's words from what felt like forever ago burned in my ears. I couldn't lose Finn. Wouldn't lose Finn. I was a *healer.* I could *do this.*

My concentration split as my magic branched out, a roaring inferno tearing through his veins, and all at once, the tide changed. I knew I'd won. His own magic rode the wave, taking over for my abilities and releasing me from its hold.

I pulled out, drained from the effort.

"You hang in there," I said, gasping, leaning on his nose. "I can't do anything else right now, but Gods help me if you die. I'll come to the second life and kill you again with my own hands. Understand?" I hoped my expression was as hard as I envisioned it to be, but the soft whinny he gave in response told me I probably wasn't successful. "I need to find those cannons and shut them down."

Forcing myself to leave his side without a backwards look, I started moving forward again. Joseph had left me at some point, and I wondered if he was anywhere nearby. The cannon that had fired at Finn lay in pieces on the ground. Another fey must have gotten to it. Beyond it, though, I saw another cannon. This one had a different nozzle.

Anisra.

A few soldiers hunkered down around the machinery, helmets and gloves on the ground next to them as they tinkered with the mechanics. Smoke billowed from a hole toward the back. Someone had hit it, but obviously it wasn't enough to bring it down completely. A circle of guards surrounded it, effectively shooting and killing anything that came anywhere near.

Weariness dragged on my body, but I pushed forward, using the gun as a baseball bat.

I didn't know how I didn't get shot.

I barely made it half the distance before I ran square into a mass of bodies, including five masked soldiers. Three of them toted guns and swung them my way, fingers squeezing the triggers hard.

A shout to my left was all the warning I got before a half-naked man whose bottom half was all deer scooped me up and jerked me to his side. The gunfire hit the dirt around his hooves. A herd of the beasts bearing crossbows spouting arrows poured around us as I scrambled onto the fey's back, laying low to avoid getting shot.

"I need to get to the cannon!" I shrieked in his ear, leaning as far forward as I dared, clutching him as hard as I could. "I have to stop them from unleashing Anisra."

His antlered head lowered, and he charged forward in a full-strength gallop as he loaded another arrow into his crossbow. A pull of the trigger and another masked figure crumpled.

"Sometimes the best way forward is sideways," he said. A thick, ropy scar snaked across the left side of his face and stopped at the corner of his mouth.

A female version of whatever these guys were cantered up on our right and snarled, her black hair flying over a tanned face and glittery green eyes. She didn't carry a crossbow, but instead clutched a curved blade in one bloodied hand. She didn't stop looking for danger and shot to the side, sinking the weapon into the stomach of someone else who was shooting at us.

"The pixies were able to circle around to the right of the cannon," my savior explained, a rumble shaking his chest again as I adjusted my grip. "They're taking out the defenses as we speak."

Sure enough, I could see that we were circling the cannon from behind, approaching from the opposite side. The pixies glowed a brilliant emerald in my second sight, the misty, swirly magic of theirs glowing a similar color as they cut down wave after wave of Order soldiers. One of the smaller pixies that seemed to be leading the charge turned toward us as we approached, her ink-filled eyes taking me in steadily.

The deer-guy came to a halt on the edge of the action and I slipped from his back, jarring my knees as I landed hard. He was much taller than I'd anticipated.

"Had you waited but a moment more, I would have helped you down."

"No need." I was already moving toward the cannon. Over my shoulder I tossed, "Thanks for the ride, though."

"Anytime."

The pixie leader grabbed my arm and dragged me forward. I tried not to focus on how her long green fingers had not one but *two* extra knuckles. She thrust me through the mass of warring bodies. Her other hand bore claws that she sunk right into the chest of a human and twisted out his heart. The bright, metallic scent of fresh blood filled the air and saliva coated my mouth as my stomach roiled.

She wrenched me forward again, this time a whip of thorns lashing out and strangling someone rushing at us, before pushing me roughly in front of her, pointing right at the Anisra cannon. My path forward was clear, the rest of the human defense distracted by an onslaught of fey bodies that resembled gophers.

"Take it out." Her lips brushed the shell of my ear as she spoke in the most musical voice I'd ever heard. It was like vocalized honey. "I'd hoped to meet you under friendlier circumstances."

And then she was gone with a flash of that whip.

I wasted no time. The machine was easily three times taller than me. They must have finally gotten it working again because someone had equipped the damn thing before they'd been attacked. Red blood dripping from the console and deep scratches in the metal body of the device told of their likely fate. It was on some sort of timer.

A timer that had less than three minutes remaining.

A timer that just finished *syncing*.

A timer I had a really bad feeling was connected to *all* of the cannons.

I stabbed uselessly at the controls, not sure what I was doing but hoping, somehow, I would punch the off-button. Hell. I wasn't going to be able to stop the timer. I'd have to destroy it some other way. I darted around the front of the machine, looking up and up at the long nozzle that would start spraying the killer gas in to the air.

I was out of ideas.

I was out of magic.

...or was I?

The general had said former Gods of Water and Earth worked in conjunction to pull the water from this area to another—forcing the climate to drastically change in this spot. And this spot alone. But if a God were able to draw that kind of reaction from the Earth, then surely a God could do the opposite.

The timer beeped, its beat matching that of my heart.

What if the fates or whatever it was that had asked me to walk on water before hadn't literally meant it? What if...

The world around me faded as my hands ghosted toward my face.

Magic hummed and twisted and buzzed beneath my veins.

What if they were only asking me to do the impossible: perform a miracle.

The laws of my kind stated I needed my element nearby in order to manipulate it. I couldn't create it with my own two hands. Earth didn't work like that. Mass was mass, and volume was volume. They were set in finite amounts.

But my entire life I'd grown up not knowing the rules.

My fingers curled into fists.

Why should I start living by them now?

My body pulsed hot, white light blinding me to the world as I called on my energy, as I begged my magic to do what I desperately needed it to do. My magic, the *friends* who helped guide it, strained as they rushed to comply with my demands, not knowing or realizing or caring that I was asking the literal impossible.

A crack shattered the air.

My ears cleared as the sound of screams and gunfire died.

My body straightened as the first tremor shook the ground.

The fey knew what was happening. I could see it in the way they rushed from battle, abandoning their counterparts in the belly of the lake bed, sprinting and flying and ghosting toward the great walls.

Another tremor, this one louder and longer rattled the earth at my feet.

The crack in the ground from a mile away raced toward us, raced toward me, splitting the bottom of the lake in two.

A geyser of water shot high in the sky.

No, the lake wouldn't slowly refill.

This would be as violent as the impact of a meteor.

Spray from the geysers soaked my feet, streamed from my hair.

And then it happened.

Euphoria rocked my insides, shook me so hard I thought I might rattle apart.

Shards of sunshine splintered the clouds, beams landing on my upturned face, engulfing me in a spotlight. I gasped at the heat full of energy and vigor, my arms spread wide over my head in astonished delight.

I was an element.

One with the Earth.

One of four most powerful beings to ever breathe.

I was the God of Water.

And I was the First. And I would awaken the others.

You are worthy of water.

An inferno of raw power burst from my body, sending the world rocking on its axis. So much magic, too much for me to ever hold, to ever use, consumed me whole, the feeling both the most painful and most pleasurable sensation I'd ever felt. My connection to the world ran deep. Part of me still connected to the universe beyond my newfound abilities registered trees on the outskirts of the lake bowing outward, the ripple effects spanning farther and farther.

In that moment, the world changed again.

Just as it had hundreds of times before.

Magic was back.

Something shadowy snatched me up, pulling me tight against its chest, and I opened my eyes, unafraid of what I might find. Warm, gold eyes blinked back at me. Of course he'd have wings.

"You're glowing again."

"I may never stop."

Below us, the earth spewed violently, water gushing in immense waterfalls and spouts and geysers. The world once broken, was now right again. A whirlpool churned angrily in the middle of the not-so-dead lake, sucking in soldiers still screaming, arms flailing, unable to slip from the unrelenting current. At the bottom of the massive pool were heavy cannons filled with poison.

We'd won.

We'd actually won.

36

Geoffrey

I'd done as the voice had asked.

I'd pulled when I'd felt the jolt.

Things had gotten incredibly uncomfortable for a few seconds. Then when I'd opened my eyes… she'd emerged.

Zara.

She was alone for once, lacking both her fey shadows. Her back was angled toward me as she sat on the ground, chin perched on the top of her knees as her arms held her legs to her chest. Her silvery hair fell in a tangled waterfall down her spine as she stared out over an immense body of rippling water. The sun was at that perfect angle where its beams hit just right, sending sprays of blue and green and yellow arcing across the horizon.

It hit her in such a way that she appeared to be glowing.

My heart thrummed in my chest at the simple beauty of the moment.

Fey creatures milled around off to her left. Some sprawled on the ground, others stood in small clusters. Most were wounded, but most were in various stages of repair. They hadn't noticed me yet, for whatever reason, and while they seemed to keep the girl within their lines of sight, none seemed willing to approach her.

Something had happened here.

Something big.

Something I'd clearly missed.

But I didn't miss him or the jeweled knife that glinted in his hand.

He kept it down by his side, carefully angled away from the fey creatures as he slunk forward on silent feet. He wasn't dressed like an Order soldier, but he still looked very out of place in his own semblance of a dark uniform. For all his subtlety, Toren was acting pretty brash.

And he was aiming for the girl I'd tried so hard to protect.

My body twitched and it was as if I suddenly… found my body again.

I was moving, my throat working as I sprinted across the grass. I couldn't spit her name out, couldn't warn her of the impending danger. I could only run, sparks of magic already igniting in my hands as I tried to find some way to make it work. I was drawing attention, but the wrong kind of attention. The kind of attention that drew attention *from* the thing they needed to see.

Why weren't my damn vocal cords working?

Someone rushed toward me, yelling at me to stop. Someone who was clearly stupid if they didn't see what was about to happen. Zara lifted her head as the shadow fell across her. And she jerked forward when she caught the edge of the knife in her periphery. But it was too little, too late.

Toren was already in mid-movement, knife moving, aiming for her heart.

My magic burst forth like a wildfire, blasting from my hands…

As someone tackled me.

The God of Air. The boy from the church. His brown eyes were wild. The feeling of his restrained magic so close causing my already tenuous control to slip.

315

Then came the screams.

First male and guttural – fading quickly.

The God of Air whipped around, dropping me as he shifted toward the sound.

Now female and shrill.

The fire. I'd lost control. *He'd* made me lose control.

And she'd paid the price.

37

Zara

I'd seen the shadow and the knife.

The glitter of those damned jewels told me that at least one key member of the Order had escaped my wrath-filled flood. I'd already started drawing on my magic to stop him, to fling the general to the side and drown him where he fell.

Then something hit me.

Bright and white and red.

I remember thinking it looked like a ball of fire. But it was too hot to be fire. Too bright to be natural. Flames surrounded me as the general fell away. My magic leaped to my defense, but it was so much, too much. My skin sizzled and popped, my bones cracked, my hair and clothes burned to ash around my body. I'd never felt this much pain. Never imagined that this kind of pain was possible.

I was past thinking, past reacting. Whispers of magic twisted and swirled inside me, desperate but trapped as I couldn't find the energy to use it. I was dying.

Help. I shouted, flinging out my thoughts as far and wide as I could. But nothing.

I couldn't even tell if I was on fire any more. My nerves had gone with my skin.

I was little more than a husk and a thought.

A breath away from death's door.

And then I saw him.

How, I don't know. Because my eyes shouldn't still work.

But I saw. I saw the slender, scarred face. The deep scars. The bi-colored eyes.

I saw him reaching for me, flames licking up his arms as he stared first his hands, then at me in horror and disgust.

He'd done this.

He was going to kill me.

And if I went—I was taking him with me.

I flung out the last ribbons of my magic, closing my eyes as he went soaring toward the lake. Barely believing when the last dying flickers of the comforting blue of my magic died.

This was it.

Death by fire.

Geoffrey had won after all.

Gods I hurt, every inch of skin burned, seared raw. My lungs scorched. My nerve endings raw.

But I wasn't done yet. I dragged in a harsh breath, the effort taking everything I had left in me.

Something flickered in my veins. Something completely unlike the gentle currents of my water magic. This was foreign and unwanted. More smoke and flame on top of the remains of my torn and blistered body. I wanted to rally against it, pitch it against my water. But I lacked the strength and instead allowed the ash to coat my veins like a fiery poison.

I didn't understand.

I barely felt the double sets of knees touch down on my right and left, barely felt Ryder drop his jacket on top of me. Vaguely realized that someone was pushing their magic into me, forcing the healing process to begin as our abilities melded.

I closed my eyes.

Only for a moment, I told myself. Sinking a bit deeper into my body, shying away from my searing nerves, the desert-dry touch of my skin. I needed a few minutes where it didn't hurt so much.

Somewhere far away I thought I heard something say...

You are worthy of fire.

But that couldn't be possible.

Water and fire didn't mix.

38

Zara

"…come back, Z. Please come back."

"…go away."

"What did she say?"

Hell. My skin felt wrong. Dry and papery. My lungs whistled as air moved through them.

That could only mean I'd survived.

"How bad is it?" I drawled, my tongue a heavy weight in my mouth.

I opened my eyes, squinting up at the green-skinned face of the female pixie-leader that helped me get to the Anisra cannon in the first place. Her ink-black eyes regarded me seriously. She smelled faintly like roses, and she lowered herself close enough to kiss.

"You know, we weren't really all that well acquainted before, and I'm sorry if I gave you any impressions that I was into women. But I'm not. In fact, let's say I'm not into either gender until this whole saving-the-world thing is behind me," I muttered dryly, wincing as the skin pulled around my lips.

She full out grinned now, like, face-splitting, white teeth flashing grinned. It was blinding. And a little horrifying. Each tooth was pointed and when she opened her mouth to talk, I realized they were arranged in double rows. Like sharks. I couldn't even quite comprehend how that worked. I slicked my tongue around the backs of my teeth in response.

"If I went for women you would certainly be high on my list. Well, maybe not in your current condition, but regardless," she said in that same beautiful, lilting voice as before. "Alas, that's not the case. I'm merely one of the better-trained healers in my clan. I did what I could to help your cohort here. The kelpie." She fluttered a hand full of fingers with extra digits.

"I assume you're saying it didn't work."

"Just hang in there a little longer," Finn muttered from somewhere over my shoulder. I vaguely registered the steady lapping of water beneath me. "If you could tell your magic to stop fighting me, it would help." The piercings on his face shimmered in the sunlight as he finally moved into a position where I could see him. Green eyes bulged against his paper-white skin.

Memories sputtered through me. The battle. Finn falling, bleeding everywhere. Water filling the lake. Ryder flying me to safety before being called over to help with something. The shadow that fell over me. The knife.

Geoffrey.

I reached up and grabbed Finn's arm. Or tried to anyway. I was too weak to do much but brush the hairs on his skin. A large bandage wrapped around his chest, and I could tell he was holding one of his arms awkwardly, but he looked otherwise ok. "You're ok?"

"Sort of." He shrugged and pulled away, his hands leaving my ribcage. I missed their warmth immediately. He toyed with his lip ring and swished his knuckles in that nervous manner of his. "Just like you probably feel: 'sort of ok.'"

"What were you saying about my magic?"

A look I couldn't decipher crossed his face. "Get it to quit fighting me. It burns. It's weird."

I remembered the sensation of ash and fire rubbing against cool and water.

Had that been real?

Had Geoffrey been real?

The words stuck in my chest. I didn't want to speak them out loud. Didn't want to believe them.

"I don't know what to do," I admitted. "I don't know how to heal myself." I winced as pins and needles raced across the muscles and tendons and skin of my legs.

"Finn thinks we need the Kraken." Ryder said, finally appearing in my line of sight.

My throat worked as real fear spiked in my gut. I didn't know where it was right now.

Right here. The Kraken called. A tentacle slipped through the grass and a few people let out shocked gasps when it wrapped around me, strong and slimy. *We'll have you right as rain in no time, Zara. Forgive me for taking so long. It took longer than I thought to get here. Lost lakes aren't necessarily the easiest to pinpoint. Take a deep breath.*

I complied even though I was already moving.

"What the hell? Lucy, when did you get here?" exclaimed Finn from somewhere behind me before I plunged into the ice-cold water of the lake. In that moment, I felt better, every ache and every open sore — basically my entire body — instantly soothed. Like slathering buckets of aloe vera on a sunburn, but one-hundred times better.

I'm going to speed up the process considerably, little one. But I need you to tell your magic that everything is ok. It's doing its damnest to keep you safe, so it's locking everything else out. That's why they weren't able to heal you completely. That's why you can't heal yourself. I've never felt it before, but then again, no one has ever embraced two elements before. It needs to relax or you'll never heal.

Two elements?

I barely heard it, only registering enough to reach inside myself and find my magic. Yes, the Kraken was right. It coated my skin with a second wall, protecting me from additional external damage.

Two kinds of magic.

One I knew and one I didn't.

One a woven canvas of blue and other a flickering banner of red.

My heart clenched as I examined the shield, coaxing my magic—or was it plural now?—to loosen its ironclad grip. It argued, pleaded and pouted, but ultimately relaxed enough to let the Kraken in. Something cool and refreshing wrapped around my bones.

There we go.

The magic felt different than it had before. It had always felt smooth as alabaster, fluid in my gasp. But now it was pricklier.

As my body healed—or what I assumed was healing, it was really one giant itch—I took stock of what I'd always taken for granted. Ten fingers, ten toes. Two arms. Two legs. A head. Some other stuff in-between. My eye was finally working. My rings were still there, somehow. Probably hooked around my bones when I'd burned alive. My knife was gone but I figured Finn or Ryder would have enough presence of mind to grab it if it did indeed still exist.

I slowly tilted myself upright, already feeling immensely better. I looked down at myself, at the swiftly healing burns and bruises. He really had done his damndest to kill me if these injuries were any sign. I lifted my arm so I could see the brands. My water brand remained, loud and proud, and black as fear. Just like the symbol on Finn's neck. Underneath it, and just as dark, was a new brand. This one a burning flame.

The symbol of Fire.

Don't fret about that right now, little one. Focus on healing.
But what does it mean?

You passed the Trial by Fire.

And...

Never before has one of the Gods passed two different trials.

This means what? I asked.

I'm not sure.

But you're ancient.

It's rude to call someone old.

Can't help what you are.

I'll stop healing you if you don't stop acting like a child.

All too soon the Kraken released my body, depositing it on the shores of the beautiful Wisconsin lake I'd brought back to life. I still couldn't quite wrap my mind around that. About how I'd accomplished the impossible. I brushed the silken, sea green dress the Kraken had gifted me, wondering at the way breezed around my body. My hair had even grown back and I quickly looped it into a semblance of a braid as I looked around at the bare terrain, trying to not feel the dozens of eyes fixed on me.

A shadow crossed in front of me and I flinched before looking up into Ryder's golden eyes. They weren't swirling now. He must be as drained as everyone else. He pursed his lips looking me up and down and ghosted a hand over the symbols on my arm, eyebrows raising marginally as he considered what it meant.

"If you ever do anything like that again, I will kill you myself."

"Dare you."

Specks of amber danced in his irises. "I'm glad you're back."

Finn was angled off to the side. The thick bandage wrapped around his chest seemed stark and clinical against his olive skin. The pixie from earlier with the manic smile was cross-legged on the ground, elbows braced on her knees and middle fingers and thumbs connecting in a meditative stance. She was solemn now in her group of a dozen or so other pixies, and I wondered what she was thinking.

Behind her stood a small herd of those half-deer people. In the center of the mass: the man who'd helped get me to the cannon in time. He caught me looking and a bright smile flashed across his face. He waved, then returned to some arrows he seemed to be repairing.

A few others I didn't recognize stood awkwardly. I made eye contact with each one, subtly nodding my head in thanks. In response, each did something odd: touched their left index and middle fingers to their lips, before pulling them away in a slow swoosh that looked a little like a 'u.'

Some of them turned and left after my acknowledgement.

But the pixies and deer-creatures remained.

I nibbled on my bottom lip and rubbed my chest. A question burned there. I couldn't ignore it anymore. "Was it the general who attacked me?"

"Yes." Joseph walked up, hands stuck in his pockets. "He's dead."

"Was it the fire?"

"Yes. I stopped your Hand. He arrived out of nowhere. It was weird. But he was fixated on you. He saw the general going for you when no one else did." His jaw worked and he brushed some hair back from his eyes. Ryder was a silent shadow next to him, eyes shielded in self-loathing. "He was running toward you, trying to do something. I don't know. Either warn you, or stop him. Maybe attack you himself. It was really confusing... and I tackled him as he..."

"Launched a ball of fire, like a dragon." Ryder finished the sentence Joseph couldn't quite bring himself to spit out.

"It's unclear if he was aiming at one or both of you."

I shuffled my feet, the questions hung in the air like flies caught in spiderwebs.

"Did I kill him?"

Finn had moved closer but still kept his distance. Now that I was healed it was as if he didn't know how to communicate with me. I was grateful, because I certainly didn't know how to interact with him. Ryder's hand brushed the backs of mine, refocusing his attention.

"You pulled a giant rope of water from the lake and wrapped it around him. That flung him into the lake and I... I didn't see him resurface. One of the other fey even searched for him, but they came back emptyhanded."

Pain sputtered through me.

I'd never know his motivations. And if Geoffrey had tried to help me...

I tried to look anywhere except at the scorched grass beside the lake. So many questions I had and so many answers I lacked. His actions had never made sense. One second, he seemed friendly and curious, the next, the Order was trying to gun me down.

I mentally reached for that connection Geoffrey had threaded between our conscious states.

Nothing but static.

Maybe he was dead.

I brushed the back of my hand over my mouth and turned to Joseph. A curious creature had landed behind him, an eagle the size of a barn with flat eyes that bored into me. Joseph stood under Its impressive breast, idly stroking Its white and black-speckled feathers. Golden claws splayed out on the ground, large grooves under them where It periodically flexed. It looked like a creature carved from wood, with hard angles and too-smooth feathers, as if It had gained life from the top of a totem pole and decided to take flight.

I approached the oddity, not an ounce of fear in my step.

Joseph smiled and lifted his eyebrows, moving aside so I could maneuver under its beak. This must be the Great Beast of Air. The eagle clicked its beak a few times and bowed, low enough for me to touch the feathers on its face while looking it straight in the eye. Its flat gaze was weirdly unnerving, so unlike the complexity of emotion that I always saw swirling in the Kraken's gaze.

A jolt of electricity raced up my arm, lighting up my brands.

What are you?

A Thunderbird. It fluffed its feathers proudly.

You came for Joseph?

And to see you.

Why?

Its massive, curved beak clicked. *I can bring tears to your eyes; resurrect the dead, make you smile and reverse time. I form in an instant but last a lifetime.*

Was that an answer?

"It talks in riddles." Joseph tilted his head in a shrug.

"I assume you answer riddles?"

"I eat them for breakfast."

I rolled my eyes. "Do you know what It's saying then?"

"The answer is memory. I imagine you somehow remind it of a memory."

I turned back to the bird. *That didn't answer my question.*

Not all questions were meant to be answered.

Must Great Beasts always speak in riddles?

Ask me what you really want to ask me.

I'd never thought to pose my question to the Kraken. Maybe I'd been waiting for this. Joseph seemed intrigued as he waited for me to speak.

What happened to the God of Air?

He died.

Then how is Joseph here?

It cocked Its head at me, entirely bird-like in manner. *How are any of us here?*

The heels of my palms smashed to my eyes in frustration.

Magic doesn't die, the Thunderbird intoned, bland as ever. *Magic is incomprehensible in its complexity. It's constantly flexing and warping and twisting and reimagining itself. What happened then was...unspeakable. But magic has a way of persisting. As evidenced by you standing here before me despite your turbulent history—and for Joseph, chosen for who he will become.*

Beware what you don't know, God of Water. And know that what you do know might not be so.

The open line I'd tapped between us snapped. The Thunderbird fluttered Its wings but was clearly done with the conversation on that wonderfully foreboding line.

"Good luck with that," I said to Joseph, flipping my thumb at the bird. It preened.

"I told you, I like riddles. We'll get along just grand." He sifted so he was in front of me again, that blinding smile back in place. "Do you have a plan yet? Or are you still playing this game by ear? Because I really don't have a clue what's supposed to happen here."

I returned his smile. "Getting impatient?"

"I've only waited my whole life for this. Who wouldn't?" He shoved the sleeve of his shirt up, revealing the birthmark branding him as the God of Air — a single gust of wind with an arrow underneath. It pulsed red-hot under my scrutiny, and my magic stirred to life as my own marks burned on my arm. I still had so many questions, so many concerns about what the past would reveal and what the future would bring, but for now...

"Do you trust me?" I said.

"No."

I smiled again at his honesty as I extended my hand. Ripples of blue and red energy raced through my veins, looping around my skin. "Good. I don't trust you either."

Then I grabbed his hand, our bond snapping into place like two perfect puzzle pieces.

Welcome back, God of Air.

Blinding light of all shades and colors flared from our hands, absorbing both of us in a ball of light and mist. Thunder roared overhead and lightning shot from the skies, striking both of us in a blazing electrical jolt. I struggled to maintain my grip, stepping closer to wrap an arm around him as he stood, a beacon of sun-white energy, head thrown back as he pulled from me and the sky. As the light flared even brighter, I knew our journey had just begun.

Epilogue

Geoffrey

They'd pulled me from the water, the few soldiers still alive. The few still somehow loyal to me.

They'd rushed us away from that awful lake, toward helicopters waiting to return to headquarters.

They thought they'd saved me.

But I was more broken than they knew.

Heat surged through my head.

I didn't move.

Three elements activated.

I didn't feel the pain.

It was nothing compared to the void in my chest.

Betrayed by my best friend.

Attacked by the one I'd tried to help.

And bombarded by magic that I didn't want.

And it didn't want me.

You want to fight to the death, God of Water?

You found it.

If you enjoyed part one of The Elemental Gods, I kindly ask that you leave a review.
Reviews are the lifeblood of every author's career and every star and sentence counts.

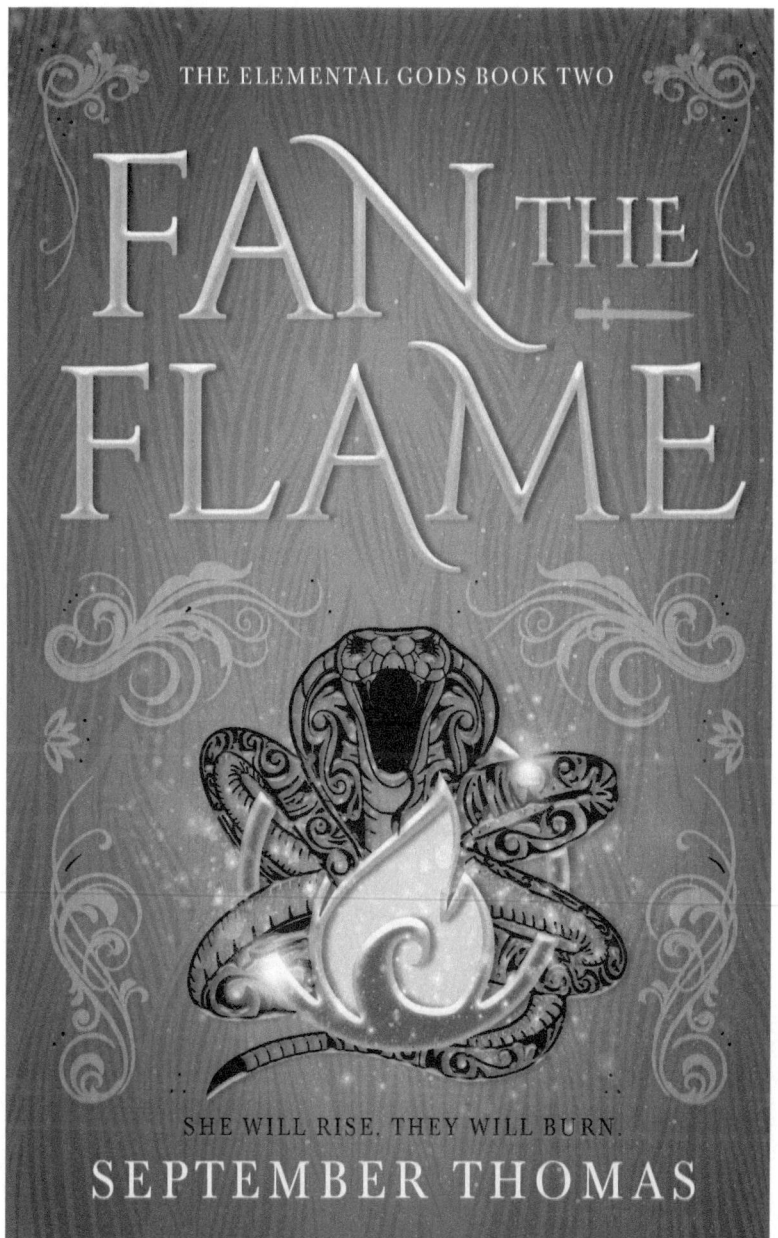

To pick up your copy on Amazon now, click here:
https://bit.ly/ElementalGods2

To stay up-to-date with the latest release information, sign up for my monthly newsletter. There, you'll also find free and other exclusive content related to both The Elemental Gods series and my other work (including a free prequel novella told from Finn's POV!)

For more information, head to www.septemberthomas.com.

Acknowledgement

Writing this series has been an incredibly humbling experience.

I've always found writing to be a very solitary task... but publishing isn't. And I've come to adore and appreciate everyone that's helped make this dream a reality.

Seriously, you're the best.

To begin - mom and dad. Without you teaching me to read, encouraging me to pursue a career in journalism, and pushing me to write whatever I wanted to write, I wouldn't be here today. Your unwavering support mean so, incredibly much to me. Thank you for never saying no to things that truly mattered to me, and for always telling me to pursue what I love.

Fiona - I couldn't ask for a better editor. You saw this book for what it was, in that "looks-like-carbon-but-will-be-a-diamond" sort of way, and pushed me to make it that much better. Thank you for calling me out on things that didn't work, while building up the things that did. The final product is the best debut anyone could ask for.

All great books need a fantastic cover, and Natasha you took this book and ran with it! Not only did you capture the true essence of the series, but you displayed it in such a beautiful and mysterious way. Even writing this I've got a copy of the cover up on the screen. I may be obsessed, and I'm truly excited to see what else you'll come up with for the remainder of the series.

David, thank you for bearing through extensive email chains, and enduring revisions upon revisions upon revisions for the website.

Your quiet support through this whole process has helped keep me sane.

To my first-ever beta, Amsley. For reading this book about five versions before the final print and not launching it across the room in horror. To Josh, for enduring my constant jabbering about a complicated mental universe that only seemed to keep getting more complex.

And to Sydney, for providing that moral support only a best furry friend can do.

About the Author

September Thomas is the author of the Elemental Gods series. She lives in Nebraska with her boyfriend and rescued Australian Cattle Dog. She also boasts a large collection of (decorative) owls that some consider amusingly ridiculous.

You can connect with me on:

- https://www.septemberthomas.com
- https://twitter.com/SeptemberAuthor
- https://www.facebook.com/SeptemberThomasAuthor
- https://www.instagram.com/september.thomas

Subscribe to my newsletter:

- https://www.septemberthomas.com